MY DIGITAL SOUL

About the Author

Mike was born and raised in Kalgoorlie, in the goldfields of Western Australia before moving to Perth to complete a degree in Electronic Engineering. With a good science fiction book in hand and a life-long passion for innovation, Mike has always imagined a future where technologies that are improbable today may be inevitable tomorrow. When not writing, Mike runs a software development company (www.cyinnovations.com), loves 1970's heavy rock music, fishing in the Australian never-never, and cheers on his beloved West Coast Eagles AFL team. Together with his wife, Mike lives in an empty nest with their black Labrador, Louie.

You can connect with me on:

https://mcgintywriter.com

https://www.amazon.com/Michael-McGinty/e/B0BBGD7WD8/

https://x.com/mcgintywriter

https://www.facebook.com/mcgintywriter

Scan a QR code.

Mcgintywriter

Amazon Author

Facebook Author

Twitter

Also by Michael McGinty

NOVELS

Entropy: A Post-Apocalyptic Novel of the End of Humanity

SHORT FICTION

Starfarers: The Last Marine
Starfarers: Starvation

Themes: science fiction, AI, technology, mythological horror

Rating: adult concepts, strong language, drug use, sexual
references, mild violence, and gore

MY DIGITAL SOUL

A Novel by Michael McGinty

First published in 2025
Copyright © 2025 CYI Publishing

First Edition

ISBN: 978-0-6454814-7-1 (Trade Paperback)
ISBN: 978-0-6454814-9-5 (Hardcover)
ISBN: 978-0-6454814-8-8 (Trade Large Print Edition)
ISBN: 978-0-6454814-6-4 (eBook)

Editing by Edwina Harvey (IPed)
Cover design and image composition by Adam Hay Studio, UK
Stock images: Shutterstock/Adobe

Always for Mara

Especially for Jenny

In loving memory of our brother Barry who fought the MND beast like a true champion. We miss your jokes and cheeky laugh.

Please support the fight against the Beast that is motor neurone disease (MND) at https://fightmnd.org.au

Chapter 1

Susan

"YOU CAN'T TRUST any of them," the gelada hisses.

With her forefinger hovering inches above the keyboard, Susan eyes the screen with deep distrust. She looks and feels hideous.

"I'm … I'm not sure," she says.

"Don't overthink it," the gelada insists.

"But there might be another way," she replies. "Maybe they just need some—"

"They say they're your friend," it growls. "Then you turn your back and—BAM! They've got you." It leans closer, its warm breath in her ear as it whispers, "Just do it, and all your problems will disappear."

Like a sudden, transient shock, the gelada's words jolt her back to clarity. She whips her head around at the voice. "Don't tell me what to do!" she shrieks. Turning back to the keyboard, her face spasms into a pitiless scowl as her finger pounds the DELETE key.

***

At five o'clock on a Friday afternoon, two years earlier, Dr. Susan Parker sat before an enormous mahogany desk in a cavernous office, marveling at the surrounding opulence. From the coffered ceiling and wood-paneled walls to the gilded fittings and fixtures, the room reeked of wealth. Across from her, a plush leather chair sat empty, while on the wall behind it hung the imposing portrait of an elderly gentleman. To her left, an expansive window offered a drizzly autumn view of the East River across to Roosevelt.

She'd been impulsive and had already admitted as much to herself. Rarely, if ever, would she agree to take an ad hoc chance like this. Like responding to clickbait, it was a guaranteed shortcut to fools' remorse.

The rules of life were simple. Every objective needed a plan. The plan must be grounded in facts and supported by logic, which gives certainty to the outcome. And that outcome demanded your full commitment. Rolling the dice and hoping your numbers come up was never a good idea, as far as she was concerned. As a seasoned engineer, she had that same dogged mindset etched into her DNA.

So why on earth had she agreed to be here?

When her cell phone rang late the night before, she had assumed it was a hoax and hung up. After the person called again, though, they assured her it was indeed *the* Brice Woodlands of Woodlands & Woodlands & Company renown.

"I have a proposition I'd like to discuss with you," he'd said.

The call was brief and, despite his reluctance to provide any details, she surprisingly agreed to meet at his Upper East Side office before he hung up. It was a once-in-a-lifetime opportunity, he'd said, and that caught her attention.

Later that night, as she tossed and turned in bed, her mind kept circling back to Brice Woodlands. While the lateness of his call and the lack of specifics were irritating, his promise of an unprecedented opportunity was utterly intriguing. After staring at the ceiling for what seemed like hours, she finally got up, made a cup of hot cocoa, and headed to the study.

Skimming through an online search revealed that W&W & Co. was a Fortune 500 powerhouse, 51% owned by Brice Woodlands and his younger brother, Bryan, with the remaining stock held by several large investment firms and pension funds. They were real estate moguls whose fingerprints appeared on almost every major property deal in New York City over the past fifteen years. The 'two *B*s from the two *W*s,' as one cheeky business reporter once quipped.

What any of that had to do with her, she had no idea. She did software.

A tall, middle-aged woman in a smart navy suit appeared at the half-opened doorway.

"I'm sorry, Dr. Parker. Mr. Woodlands has been delayed a few more minutes. Would you like something to drink? Tea or coffee?"

"No, thank you, Jean," Susan replied, then felt a flicker of panic that she'd remembered the woman's name correctly from the name-plate on the reception desk on her way in.

With a polite nod, Jean shut the door.

Susan turned her attention to the portrait of the elderly gentleman on the wall. A polished silver plaque along the bottom read: '*In loving memory of Barry Woodlands*'.

Their late father, she presumed: the harsh wrinkled face; the white handlebar mustache stretching from ear to ear; and a permanent sneer that sent a slight shiver down her spine. His dark, brooding eyes seemed to scrutinize the room as if—even from beyond the grave—he still kept watch over his onetime business empire.

"I certainly would not like to meet *you* at the wrong end of a boardroom table," she muttered, giving him a wry smile.

Again, she questioned her presence here. She tried to connect the disparate dots: property, money, software, Woodlands, and herself. There had to be a common denominator. Perhaps they required a new app to manage their vast property portfolio or some other software-related task. However, she was manifestly overqualified for that. It would be like taking a sledgehammer—i.e., her—to crack a walnut—i.e., the … whatever.

Scanning her surroundings again, something appeared odd. Aside from the retro-looking telephone handset on the desk, there was no other tech in the room, anywhere. No laptops or screens. An office without modern devices in this day and age? *Luddite* was her immediate thought. Glancing at the door, she wondered how long you could keep a person waiting before it was okay for them to get up and leave. She was about to grab her bag when the door burst open and a hulking man, as large as a bison, stormed into the room. He paused inside the doorway, standing with his feet apart and hands on his hips, glaring at her.

Susan stood up, smiled, and extended her hand.

"Mr. Wood—"

"Parker," he barked. "I want *you* to create God in the Machine. You have two years."

Without taking her hand, he swept past her, rounded the desk, and dropped into his chair, motioning impatiently for her to sit. Then, ratcheting a lever at the side of his seat, he jacked himself higher until he was peering noticeably down at her. With a rigid jawline and pinched mouth, he was either smiling or grimacing—she couldn't tell which.

Susan balked. She wasn't easily rattled. As a team leader with considerable experience, she'd handled her fair share of problematic people, but his entrance had been nothing short of formidable.

"God?" she said, steadying herself. "In two years?"

"Money's no issue," he replied. "Whatever you need. And you can have the whole damn downstairs basement for yourself. Fill it with your computers and whatever wibbely goobely things you need."

Words suddenly failing her, Susan's mind snapped into design mode as she tried to grasp the enormity of building an esoteric deity that represented all the known faith traditions. There would be contradictions everywhere, ethical and moral. Surely someone, somewhere, would take offense at the notion of a software 'God', regardless of any precautions taken.

"You can't be serious," she finally said, raising a questioning brow. "You want me to create the same God who created the universe in only six days?"

"It's easy," he replied. "You hop on your little typewriter, punch some keys, and presto: God."

With his hands raised, palms cupped and facing the ceiling, he reminded her of the risen Christ, his smug expression suggesting the success of such a monumental, technological undertaking was a fait accompli; the impossible made possible with just a snap of her fingers.

"I'm sorry, Mr. Woodlands. I don't think it's that simple. There are too many variables. And what makes you think I can replicate God in software?"

"You won that award, didn't you?" he said. Then he leaned forward, eyeballing her while, on the wall behind him, the carping eyes of Barry Woodlands fell upon her too. "The one the newspapers and TV reported. The youngest and first woman of color. Beat every other square-headed nerd in the country, didn't you?"

Susan straightened. "The Teo award? I don't see the relevance."

He pulled a yellow manila file from a side drawer and set it on the desktop. After retrieving a pair of spectacles from his breast pocket, he wiped them with fastidious attention before placing them on the end of his nose.

"Dr. Susan Ronelle Parker," he began, reading the file. He paused, peering whimsically at her over the rim of his glasses .

"Forty-five years old. Female. A Ph.D. in computer science and software engineering by age twenty-five. A postdoc in artificial intelligence and machine learning from MIT at twenty-nine. Specializes in cognitive neuro-software engineering. Winner of the Dr. Charlie Teo Award—named after the famous Australian neurosurgeon who pioneered brain mapping in the early two-thousands. Recruited by

Neuro-Labs shortly thereafter."

For the next three minutes, he gave a detailed account of her education and employment history, awards, citations, and even personal information—religious affiliation (Baptist, lapsed), hobbies, and social footprint. Apart from a few minor inconsistencies, the rest was accurate. And disturbingly invasive.

"You've certainly done your homework," she said, forcing a tight smile once he'd finished.

Susan still worked at Neuro-Labs, where she led a team of eight accomplished software developers and scientists. They were attempting to replicate rodent memory structures by mapping the neuro-electrical activity in rats.

"We train them to perform simple tasks, stimulate those memories, then extract the resulting metadata from the hippocampus region of their limbic system, beneath the cerebral cortex," she would explain whenever someone asked what she did for a living. "We're basically making digital recordings of their memories," she'd add when their eyes glazed over. Although still in its infancy, the technology was mindbogglingly brilliant, and they were doing fascinating stuff. Still, she couldn't see what any of it had to do with creating a software version of God.

"So, Parker," he said, drumming his fingers on the desk. "See you first thing Monday?"

Monday? Not only was he rude, but presumptuous as well. She'd had dealings with his kind before—powerful people who always got their way by steamrolling the meek and defenseless.

She remained silent, motionless, eyes fixed on him.

"Come on, Parker. Imagine the fame. They'll erect a huge statue of you right in the middle of Silicon Valley."

She shook her head in refusal. "I can't just walk out on Neuro-Labs. I have a team of professionals who rely on me for direction and continuity. I can't just leave on a whim."

"A whim?" He feigned mild offense before throwing his head

back, roaring with laughter. "I've already spoken to them. They're amenable to letting you go—at the right price. They balked at twenty million, so we'll offer fifty. Heck, a hundred million if they want to play hardball. That's a goddamn lot of research funding."

"You've spoken to *who*? About *what*?" Susan's insides suddenly plummeted. Her life plan was unraveling. Things were spiraling out of her control. After thirteen years of devoted service, Neuro-Labs was about to sell her off.

He grinned unapologetically, giving her a half-hearted shrug. "What are they paying you, Parker?"

Dismayed, she glanced at Barry Woodlands, then at the expansive window, the door, and back at him.

"Well, I ... err ..."

"Don't be shy. Give me a number."

"A number?" Susan's mind stalled. This wasn't like her. She was always decisive, logical, and structured. On technical matters, at least. But now? "I ... err ... ninety thousand—"

"Too low," he grumbled. "Double it. Triple it. Heck, give me something that starts with eight zeros."

She hesitated. "Two hundred—"

"Done! Four hundred million a year with benefits. Plus a car. A damn Tesla. One of those fancy new flying models, if you want."

Susan gasped aloud. Shaking her head in disbelief, she tried to make sense of what had just happened. Within thirty chaotic seconds, she had quit her job, accepted an obscene pay packet—which included four hundred million dollars a year plus a damn Tesla—and agreed to build God.

This was nothing short of insanity.

With the news of her betrayal by Neuro-Labs still sinking in, the office door eased open. From the corridor, a wiry, bespectacled man wearing a gray pinstripe suit, a white face mask, and yellow rubber gloves peered in. This had to be the elusive younger brother, Bryan, she guessed. Either that or a well-dressed janitor. During her online search the night before, she'd discovered that he was a recluse, rarely seen in public, and no one had been lucky enough to capture a clear photo of him during the past 20 years. A decent gust of wind might blow him clean off his feet, she supposed, meeting his intense gaze.

"Is this her?" the man asked in a muffled, high-pitched voice. When Woodlands turned to him and nodded, the man furrowed his brow, studying her with interest.

"And she's agreed?"

Another nod.

"Good," the man said and shut the door.

Before Susan could ask about him, Woodlands turned back to her and said, "Remember, Parker, you've got two years. And I want real people in the Machine as well. They'll pay good money to meet God. We'll make it an experience. A tourist attraction. Okay? Good. See you bright-eyed and bushy-tailed Monday morning."

With a flick of his fingers, he waved her away.

Susan's head was spinning. She wanted to protest, to retract her consent and demand her old job back. Darn it! She started to say as much, but Woodlands only grunted. Then, humming a deep-throated melody, he picked up a newspaper and began to read. Above him, the sneer on Barry Woodlands' brushed face now resembled a triumphant smile while sheeting rain streaked across the expansive window, the sky reduced to a somber gray as the late afternoon faded into evening.

Perhaps this was how life unfolded for most people. They find themselves buffeted along from one day to the next by the unknowns it throws at them. Their hopes and plans dashed at any instant. Yet, they seem to carry on, without resistance, without complaint, forced to accept their lot.

With his irritating tune still swimming in her head, she got up and headed slowly for the door. The air in the room turned unexpectedly heavy and unbreathable. As she reached for the door handle, the humming stopped.

"Parker," she heard from behind her.

She turned. He still had his head down, reading.

"God could only create the earth, sun, and moon in six days," he said, still with his head down. "The rest of that universe stuff out there? It took him a whole lot longer." He glanced up and flashed an irreverent smirk. "So, you'll be fine."

After leaving the W&W offices, Susan headed along East 60th toward the subway entrance on Lexington, lost in thought. The traffic snarled and honked, pressed bumper to bumper. Raindrops drummed on her umbrella as people brushed past without a word or care.

At the top of the subway stairs, she paused. Looking down into the abyss, she shook her head at the absurdity of it all. As a skilled and resourceful engineer, she always took pride in maintaining her composure in times of crisis. Yet here she was. In one rash moment, she had somehow tossed her future into the lap of the gods of chance.

This wasn't like her at all.

Chapter 2

Roxy

AT 9:34 P.M. ON THE TUESDAY before last, Roxy Rodriguez was descending the front steps of her upper Manhattan apartment when the heel of her right stiletto caught on the edge of a tread and her ankle buckled. Lurching forward, she reeled in shock as her long-haired Pomchi, Paris, spilled from her hands and hit the sidewalk below with a tiny yelp. Had she not reflexively reached out and grabbed the handrail, there was a high probability she'd have tumbled down the stairs and broken her neck.

"Holy shit!" she cried, followed by a prolonged guttural noise that some might think belied her petite appearance. But Roxy didn't care what other people thought or said. She just righted herself, thanked her lucky stars, and gave the offending tread a swift and well-deserved kick. "Fucking useless step," she told it.

At the foot of the stairs, she knelt to scoop her poor little dog off the pavement. "That naughty step," she said, planting a kiss on the dog's cute little snout. She stood again, tested her ankle, and then headed off along East 79th toward the river.

When the job pinged on her Executive Sleepovers app twenty

minutes earlier, it caught her off guard, and she almost spilled her strawberry daiquiri. Tuesday was the one day off in her busy schedule, and she'd forgotten to mute her cell phone notifications. The client was a regular *john*, quite wealthy, and had requested her services at his apartment within the hour, while the accompanying footnote—ON THE DOT!—suggested urgency.

After a quick shower and beautification, she donned her knee-length Astrakhan coat and strapped on her black suede Jimmy Choos that had cost her a bomb. She tied a pink ribbon around Paris's pointy-eared head and grabbed her carry bag. A quick snort of nose candy—one line shot up each nostril to sharpen her senses—and Roxy was raring to go.

The pavement passed swiftly beneath her feet as she hurried down East 79th, just as the last ten years had done the same. The familiar bumps and cracks of a path she'd traipsed countless evenings before. She marveled at how far she'd come in life. A little ol' girl from Tompkins County finding her way in the big ol' city. Loads of money in the bank. Oodles of bling. A two-bedroom apartment in NYC, with a glimpse of Central Park—if you looked hard enough—and paid for in full. All at twenty-seven years young, no less, and achieved through her own volition.

Well, hers and her bestie, Paris, that is.

Janice. That was her real name. Janice Bottoms. Just the sound of it made her cringe. It wasn't a name that would cut it in her profession. She needed a moniker with a dash of class plus a smash of street cred. A name that would stick fast in a client's head, like an earworm that drove them nuts while seducing them with its promise of escape from their mundane lives.

Roxy R was her trademark. Each time a client whispered it in her ear, it gave her a sense of triumph. She had the feeling of ultimate control she always craved. But it was all based on a lie. Hell, she wasn't even Hispanic. She had a complexion just enough 'off-white' to pull it off. And with her curly auburn hair straightened and dyed

Puerto Rican black, nobody bothered to question her ethnicity. She was a professional, and her assumed persona had to justify the asking price.

Without looking, she started across the intersection at Lexington. No sooner had she stepped from the curb than she glimpsed a sudden flash of yellow as a taxicab screeched to a halt within inches of her, the fright knocking her clean off her feet.

"Jaysus fucking Christ!" she cried as she lay sprawled on the road.

The cab driver wound his window down and gesticulated furiously to the adjacent pole where the pedestrian signal still flashed a *'Don't cross now, you idiot'* orange. "Watch where you're going, goddammit," he yelled.

Roxy sprang to her feet. Rushing to the cab, she pounded her petite fist on the hood. "Why don't *you* watch where you're fucking going?" she yelled back. She was about to round the vehicle and confront the driver, eyeball to eyeball, when a gentle hand landed on her shoulder.

"Are you alright, dear?"

She swung around.

A man with a grandfatherly smile took her arm and ushered her back to the sidewalk. He wore a black shirt with a white clerical collar, a black jacket and pants, and had Paris tucked under his arm. The plastic name tag pinned to the front of his jacket read: *'Rev. Maxwell Smith'*, and underneath that: *'Helping others by the hand of God'*. A small gold crucifix on his lapel glinted under the streetlight.

Cripes! Clergy! Her past had come back to haunt her.

She jerked away from him.

When they were fifteen, Roxy and her best friend, Cathy Moore, had been the center of attention for a short time. They even appeared in the local newspaper. As devout, God-fearing people, their parents had sent them to the local Catholic school, where Fr. Joe Blow was the head of pastoral care. Many of their classmates said he was a kind and gentle man, but a few swore he was 'handsy'. He sometimes looked at them funny-like, they said. Cathy always claimed he was fucked-up weird.

"And who would name their kid Joe Blow, anyway?" she used to say.

It all started out as a bit of fun, really. During one slow day, with little to do, she and Cathy hatched a plan to lure Fr. Joe into the girls' locker room. If he entered and tried anything funny, that would prove his guilt beyond doubt. More importantly, they would be the epicenter of attention, talked about by the other kids for their bravery and determination to expose the predator in their midst. They assured each other they'd be heroes.

When Cathy called him into the locker room, Fr. Joe at first declined. But when she became overexcited and started to choke and scream as if she were seriously injured and on the verge of fucking death, he rushed in without a second thought. Somehow, he saw through what they were up to. Waving a damning finger in their faces, he said it was a mortal sin. Against the ninth commandment. "Thou shalt not bear false witness against thy neighbor," he'd told them in a sanctimonious voice. Then he insisted they attend reconciliation. "To confess your failing before God and repent before an appropriate penance can be meted out to complete your absolution," he'd said. And, under the Safe Schools protocols, Headmistress Bryant would need to be apprised of the situation.

That's when it all got out of hand. It wasn't her fault that they panicked. He'd molested them, they claimed. And once the local newspaper reported the incident, they had no option but to stick to their story.

Nobody knew what happened to Fr. Joe afterward. Some kids said he was sent away to Perth, Australia, pensioned off to a life of luxury in the sun and cocktails by the sea. Others said they'd seen him wearing a big, fat, gold Rolex and sitting behind the wheel of an expensive Volvo as he cruised out of town. Cathy worried they were both going to hell for what they did. Although Roxy wasn't so sure that she believed in hell. She supposed it was a place made up by adults to exploit their kids' naivety. The yin to heaven's yang, she supposed. Whatever the truth, she was sure Fr. Joe was sunning it somewhere in the land of comfort, because they always look after their own.

When they reached the sidewalk, she snatched little Paris from the pastor and shoved him away. "Take your fucking hands off me, you pedo!" she cried. Then, again without looking, she stepped back onto the road, cursing under her breath as she scurried across the intersection.

Further along the street, she spotted the largest ruby-red apple she'd ever seen. It was right on top of a pile, on the sidewalk in front of the local bodega. She'd done it before without detection, but this time, when she plucked it from the pile and ran, the owner noticed. He yelled at her and shook his fist. But she only giggled as her lanky legs carried her off down the street, wobbling in her heels under the weight of her Astrakhan coat. It wasn't her fault that the apple looked so delicious.

After taking a large bite, she tossed the rest away.

The day she left home was a complete disaster. Unhappy memories of a loveless childhood still upset her a decade later.

"You won't ever amount to nothing," her father had yelled, loud enough for the whole fucking hood to hear, while her mother sat sobbing at the kitchen table and refused to say goodbye. So, she grabbed a bag containing her meager possessions and headed to the bus station, alone.

She resented them both. "Keep holy the Sabbath," they pestered her. However, she soon realized that the Sabbath was the busiest day of the week to make money. And money was all she needed in this life and the next. It wasn't her fault that they were just Bible-bashing country hicks who were forever stuck in Smallsville, USA. They never had the gumption to leave the fucking place or think beyond the narrow views of their tiny world.

They didn't love her enough.

They called a few times and left messages. But she wasn't the least bit interested in the ins and outs of their dowdy lives. After swinging left into East End, she passed the entrance to Schurz Park at East 84th.

The foot traffic was unusually light for a weeknight. Further ahead, she noticed a tall, elegant figure approaching at an unfaltering pace, its spindly legs disappearing into a half-length coat.

Fucking Darleen.

Darleen was a high-end operator who exclusively serviced clients from the Forbes Top 500 executives list in New York. She was one of only ten girls with a genuine 'Best Sleeper' award plastered over her Executive Sleepovers landing page.

What the fuck was she doing on Roxy's turf?

"Darling," Darleen meowed, smiling a tight smile as she neared.

"Darling," Roxy meowed, smiling a tight smile back.

As they air-kissed and embraced, Roxy couldn't help but rest her head on Darleen's fur coat. *One, two …* She wondered whether it was real mink. … *five, six …* She'd always wanted a mink coat. … *seven, eight …* At that moment, she wanted Darleen's coat more than anything. She squeezed it tighter, wishing with all her heart that the coat was hers until Darleen began to choke. … *ten.*

Fucking bitch.

Darleen pulled free from Roxy's crushing grip and stood back in shock. Grimacing, she straightened her coat and checked her hair. "Ciao, honey," she said, gritting her teeth. Then she turned and scurried away.

"Ciao, honey," Roxy yelled after her, while Paris growled.

When she arrived at the client's building at the appointed time, she pressed the call button for his apartment.

"Hello?" came a voice after a brief delay.

"Hi there, Jacob," she teased. "This is your *appointment* calling. Are you ready to be a bad, bad boy?"

"Hello? Who is this?" the voice asked.

Roxy froze. It was a woman's voice.

"Jacob?"

"No," the woman said. "Who the hell are you?"

This time, she detected venom.

"Umm … housekeeping?"

Through the speaker, the voice rang out, "Jacob! You bastard! Is this what you do every time I go away?"

Another voice, a man's this time, came through the speaker. "Honey, I can explain. I just—"

"You lying, cheating bastard."

There was more shouting, followed by the crash of something made of glass. Then a door slammed before Roxy heard silence.

"You stupid bitch! Why are you here now? I specifically made the booking for ten o'clock *tomorrow* night."

She released the intercom button and slumped backward against the wall. Snickering to herself, she reached into her carry bag for her cell phone. She brought up the job details on the Sleepovers app. Yep. That's what it said, all right: 10 p.m. on Wednesday, and tonight was *definitely* not Wednesday.

"Fuck!" she said, clapping a hand over her mouth.

She didn't feel sorry for Jacob. It wasn't her fault he was a jerk. She was sorrier for herself. She'd just lost a night's wage. Probably more, because he was repeat business. He was cash flow. And, if he left any negative feedback on 'Executive Sleepovers' about her poor customer service, it would impact her overall rating, which would be totally unfair.

The evening had turned to shit.

Cursing her rotten luck, she decided to take the long way home. She needed some fresh air and time to calm down. With Paris under her arm, she headed uptown along York. Halting at the lights on 90th, she looked down at Paris.

"This is the start of Cortney's turf. We can't go there." When Paris's little ears pricked up, Roxy gave her a furtive grin. "Well, since we're no longer on the job, we're fucking tourists. Aren't we, girl?"

After continuing along York, she then swung left onto 93rd. A few blocks later, she glanced up at the numbers above the entrance of a four-story brownstone building. She'd seen the address before but couldn't recall where or when. Taking out her cell phone again, she scrolled through her contacts list.

There. Bradley Brown. He'd sent her a text message out of the blue three years ago. She hadn't bothered to reply, but saved his details anyway.

Bradley was her old flame from Ithaca High. They'd dated seriously from sophomore to senior and were crowned the king and queen at their prom. After high school, brainbox Bradley flitted off to Harvard to study medicine, while she packed up her few belongings, stormed out of her parents' house, and came to New York City to study … men.

She pressed the doorbell for Apartment 305 and waited.

Good old Bradley, she thought. Fervent memories of them writhing around in the back seat of Bradley's dad's white Mercedes came flooding back, and she felt a sudden longing in her loins. She glanced down at Paris.

"Maybe it won't be such a shit night after all," she said, pressing the doorbell again, much harder this time, and for longer.

"Hello?"

"Hi, Bradley," she purred.

"Who is this?"

"What? You don't remember me?" She tried to sound offended. "Have you already forgotten about what we did on prom night? The fun we had making out afterward?"

"Janice? Is that you?"

"Yes, it's me, Bradley. Can I come in?"

"Wow, this is a surprise. I texted you once, but never heard back.

I didn't think I'd ever see you again. Thought you might've gone west. Become an actress in LA or something. Are you visiting? Come on up. I'm on the third. Wow, this is unexpected."

With a loud *clunk*, the security lock on the front door released. When the elevator doors parted on the third floor, she alighted and hurried along the dimly lit corridor toward his apartment. At the door, she set little Paris on the floor and pressed the buzzer. Then she stood back, unbuttoned her Astrakhan coat, slowly drawing it apart, and thrust one unending leg forward to reveal her tanned, naked torso and the pertness of her left breast.

The door swung open, and Bradley's beaming face appeared.

"Janice!" he said. Then his expression morphed into horror as he beheld her. "Janice? Oh my God." He slammed the door shut. "No, Janice," he pleaded. "I'm married now. My wife is out tonight with her girlfriends. She'll be back in the morning. We can't—"

But Roxy didn't flinch. In the drawn-out silence that followed, she sensed weakness. Never mind coveting thy neighbor's fucking *wife*; right now, she was about to comprehensively covet her neighbor's goddamn *husband*.

"Please open the door, Bradley."

"No, I can't, Janice."

"Please, Bradley," she begged.

"No, it's not right. My wife—"

Pouting, she gave the door a hateful glare. Bradley's wife be damned: she would find a way into his apartment. She issued a loud, heartfelt sob and thumped the door with her fists while Paris whimpered at her feet.

"But I need your help," she mewled. "You can't send me away because they're chasing me. They'll find me, and who knows what they'll do to me." Forcing tears to well in her eyes, she stepped back from the door and waited.

There was a prolonged, tantalizing pause.

"Who is after you?"

Roxy couldn't help but smile at the concern in his voice. Still the same old Bradley. During their earlier years together, she only needed to shed an unloved tear to get what she wanted. It wasn't her fault that he was putty in her hands.

"*They* are," she lied.

The door inched open, and when his face reappeared, she barged her way into his apartment with Paris skittering in at her heels.

"Please, Janice!" he cried as she flung her Astrakhan coat to the floor.

Chapter 3

Ahmad

In the summer of '21, at 12:43 on a mid-August afternoon, Ahmad Husseini dashed through the dusty alleys of the local bazaar in Kabul. Around him, others were running too. All had fear etched on their stricken faces. The wares of the street vendors were still there, piled high on foldaway tables and strung across the fronts of taut tarpaulins, while the vendors themselves had mostly fled.

Ahmad breathed hard as he ran in the heat, his calf muscles straining under the midday sun.

Without warning, a small child darted across his path. He tried to swerve, but they collided, both falling heavily to the ground. Dazed, the child sat up, staring open-mouthed at him. Then it bawled. From a nearby courtyard, a muhajjabah (veiled) woman rushed out. With a disapproving glare, she grabbed the child's arm and whisked it off the street, disappearing behind a closing door.

Ahmad picked himself up, dusted himself off, and ran again.

Ten minutes later, he threw open the front door of his house and stood between the jambs, heaving for air. On catching his breath, he shouted in Hazaragi (Persian Dari dialect), "The government has fallen. The Americans are leaving. The Taliban are coming."

His wife, cradling their infant daughter, glanced up from her toshak (floor cushion), her eyes wide in alarm. "Husband," she said, "what should we do?"

He regarded her with grim resolve. "We must leave," he replied. "We must hurry. There is no time to waste."

Ahmad never understood the mujahideen's (Taliban fighters) intense hatred toward him. With his high cheekbones and monolid eyes, he was at first proud as a boy to learn of his descent from the great Genghis Khan eight centuries earlier. However, once he grew old enough, he came to know the real affliction of the Hazara. He was considered rāfidī (rejectors of the caliphate). They called him qalfak chapat (flat nose) and Shi'a kāfir (infidel). Although, their hatred seemed to be driven more by a loathing of his genetics than his beliefs. He often wondered back then whether a horse might hate a donkey for just being a donkey.

He and his wife had simple upbringings. Under the protection of the Americans at the nearby Bagram Airfield, they had led peaceful childhoods in a rural district of Parwan Province. With their towering frames, impressive battle dress, and enormous weapons draped over their massive shoulders, the Americans appeared to Ahmad—as a child—like gods. But when he told his mother this, she rebuked him, saying that he must never think such things, let alone say them aloud.

"Tell me what you hear," he once pestered a U.S. Marine. He was pointing to the stereo headphones dangling around the soldier's neck, from which a high-pitched, metallic sound could be heard.

Every Monday afternoon, the Marine would stand outside the main gate to the air base, doling out chocolate bars to the swarming children. He called himself Brick, but young Ahmad knew from the writing on his shirt that his real name was 'SAUNDERS'. Considering his compact stature, the nickname seemed appropriate to little Ahmad.

"It's Saxon, man," Brick had replied. He removed his headphones and handed them to Ahmad. "Gods of heavy metal," he added, smiling.

When Ahmad slipped the headphones over his ears, he was at once startled by the deafening racket. Amplified musical instruments with thunderous, growling melodies reverberated throughout his skull while the pounding percussion hammered upon both his senses and imagination. He could not stop himself from laughing. His eyes and mind were wide with excitement at the wondrous new sensations that churned his insides.

"I think I like Saxonman," he yelled at the top of his lungs. "Gods of heavy metal," he had said, returning the headphones to Brick once the song ended.

"What of your brother?" Ahmad's wife asked him. "Khanomash (his wife) and their children?"

Aside from his older brother, he had no other relatives living in Kabul. The two families had moved to the city a few years earlier in search of new opportunities under the U.S. occupation. Both had two children, each a boy and a girl of similar ages.

"We must warn them," she said, the fear in her voice escalating as she spoke.

"I have just come from his house," he replied. "They are leaving also. The Americans have retreated to the airport. There are planes, many planes, to take us to America."

"Then I must pack," his wife said. She placed the infant down carefully on the chobi (floor rug). "We need clothing. The children will need food. And we must take—"

"No," he told her. "Inshallah (God willing), we cannot draw attention to ourselves. We must go with whatever valuables we can conceal. Money, some jewelry, and only the clothes on our backs. We will buy food along the way. Nobody can know we are leaving."

Ahmad's wife looked at him, her concern not waning. "But our friends. Should we not say goodbye to them?"

"No one must know we are leaving," he repeated. Although his heart was pounding, he placed his hands on her shoulders and squeezed them hard to calm her. "Take off the jeans and T-shirt," he said softly. "Wear the black abaya (whole-body robe) with the niqāb (face veil) and hand gloves."

Ahmad paused as he stepped out of the front door of his house to look back one last time. Although they had only lived there for a few short years, it was a place of memories; both of the children were born there. Glancing at the gravel street and the surrounding mud-brick houses, he tried to commit every insignificant detail to memory.

He had a duffel bag in which he had placed his swaddled daughter on top of three bottles of chilled water. Leaving a small opening for the girl to breathe, he zipped the duffel bag while his wife took the hand of their four-year-old son.

"If anyone stops us," he said, "we will tell them we are out for shopping." After closing the door, he hoisted the duffel bag, and they set off for the airport.

"Husband, do you have airline tickets?" his wife asked as they hurried along the street a few minutes later. "Did you bring our identification papers? Did you extinguish the chulha (stove)? Did you lock the front door?"

"Āre (yes)," he replied in a soft, uncomplaining voice to each of her questions.

Apart from the occasional person brushing past them from behind, they moved unimpeded through the streets of Kabul toward the airport. When they turned a corner about halfway there, they encountered a group of ten or twelve people. Leading the group, two men with hunting rifles were yelling and waving their weapons menacingly above their heads. He raised a hand, signaling his wife to halt.

"We should go this way," he said before directing her and the boy into a side street.

The nearer they got to the airport, the congestion grew. Cars and taxis, overloaded with passengers and belongings, jammed the streets.

People panicked. They cursed and wailed as they fought each other through the crush. Some excited children clambered over an abandoned Humvee nearby. The American flag was missing from the pole at the rear, while, on the turret, a small boy, manning the M2 Browning, pretended to shoot at the passersby. Across the street, an angry young man was waving the white flag of the Taliban. The young man yelled something at Ahmad, but he pretended not to hear; his gut muscles clenching with fear as they hurried past.

After deciding to find a safer way forward, they detoured into another less crowded side street. When a door ahead of them suddenly swung open and an elderly man crawled onto the street on his hands and knees, they froze. Then, three men appeared behind him. They were carrying low-caliber rifles, one of them brandishing a large hunting knife. The man with the knife directed the long blade at the elderly man, who was cowering on the ground.

"Are you one of them? An American sympathizer?" the knife-wielding man spat. He glanced up and saw Ahmad and his family. "What have we here? More sympathizers?"

Seizing his wife's arm, Ahmad tugged her behind him. "No, not us," he replied, shaking his head vehemently. "We are out … shopping."

"Shopping?" the man said, his gap-toothed grin widening as he turned to his two accomplices. "Shopping, he says."

Ahmad nodded, trying to smile. "Yes, shopping."

The man thrust his blade at the duffel bag. "What's in the bag, qalfak chapat (flat nose)? Loot?"

"No, it is just—"

Before Ahmad could react, the man snatched the bag from his grasp and threw open the zipper. When his infant daughter wailed with fright, the man dropped the bag in surprise and stepped away.

"Huh, shopping," he sneered, then waved them on with his blade.

With one hand clasped around the handle of the duffel bag and his wife in tow, Ahmad fought his way through the crowd, through the mayhem, through the awful sights that would remain with him forever. Until at last, at 4:16 on that mid-August afternoon, Ahmad and his family arrived at the madness that was Hamid Karzi International Airport.

For the remainder of the day and well into the next, they huddled together outside a chain-link fence. Beyond the wire, the lucky ones queued in long, orderly lines, waiting to board the enormous aircraft. Ahmad could hardly breathe. The stifling heat and crush of bodies around them were unbearable. One bottle of water was almost finished. He hadn't taken more than a sip since they arrived, preferring instead to slake the thirst of his wife and children first. Using some wooden offcuts and a piece of tattered canvas they found, he erected a small shelter to help keep the blistering sun off the little ones' heads.

As he squatted there, gazing through the fence, he wondered how they might survive such dire circumstances. And he prayed his most powerful appeal to Allah, the one true God, for refuge.

Throughout the following day, they watched in desperation as the American planes lifted into the sky, one after the other. Big metal beasts of salvation, each crammed with hundreds of fortunate souls.

"We're only taking U.S. and allies first," an impassive Marine informed him after he had shoved his papers through the wire.

"But I—" was all he could say before the Marine returned his papers, about-faced, and ambled away.

During the fourth day, he managed to purchase a bottle of water, enough for a few more days if they were careful, and scavenge a little food so they might each have a morsel.

That night, while he cradled his daughter and stroked his son's head, Ahmad prayed again. If Allah would care for them, if they made it safely out of Kabul, he would devote his life to sharing the

Prophet's message with all.

"Allāhu akbar," he whispered, hoping God would favor him and the Messenger, peace be upon him, was still pleased with his efforts.

"Have you spoken to your brother?" his wife asked a few days later. "Or his wife? I tried to call them again, but my battery is finished. They must be here somewhere."

Locking eyes with her, he maintained a somber expression.

"No, I have heard nothing," he said with a despondent shrug. "Perhaps they were able to get on a plane. Maybe they have departed already."

"Inshallah, I hope we see them soon," she replied. "When we are all together again in America."

Ahmad only nodded and looked away.

Ten days in, the crowd outside the fence had swelled to overwhelming numbers. Ahmad could not believe his eyes. Never in his life had he witnessed such appalling despair. People were clambering over each other, yelling and crying, desperate to escape Kabul. There were reports of some being crushed to death against the fence at another checkpoint. The Taliban had posted sentries around the airport; for their protection, the Taliban informed them. There were whispers that ISKP (Islamic State) had infiltrated the crowd.

Ahmad's wife suggested they return home for a few days to wash and rest, but he convinced her it was much too dangerous.

Food and water were difficult to come by, and the sanitary conditions were deplorable and degrading further. The awful smells around them revolted him, and all their modesty was forgotten.

"Do not worry," he assured his wife once again. "Have faith. Allah will provide for us, and the Prophet, peace be with him, will be pleased with our sabr (patience). The Americans will help us. We will soon be on a plane and on our way to America."

Twelve days after arriving at the airport, Ahmad was a broken man. His wife was consumed by worry, while the little ones cried inconsolably. They were all sunburned, hungry, and thirsty, and he worried whether Allah no longer favored him. They had slept little, kept awake by the constant whine of engines as U.S. aircraft arrived and departed minutes apart, day and night, while the noxious fumes from the aviation fuel burned their throats and made those around them retch. Nobody would listen to him. Whenever he offered his papers to any Marine who passed close enough to the fence, they would take them from him, and, after a brief inspection, return them, saying, "Soon," before moving on.

In the late afternoon, around five o'clock, they heard a loud explosion in the distance. A pall of thick black smoke billowed above the buildings on the far side of the airport. Later that night, somebody informed him that a man wearing an explosive vest had detonated it at another checkpoint. Many believers were dead. There were whispers that some U.S. Marines had died as well. Ahmad immediately thought of Brick handing out chocolate bars to the children. He was saddened by their deaths and the loved ones they leave behind.

"خداوند روحشان را می گیرد تا بهشت را بدهد" (God takes their souls to give them paradise)," he whispered, and wept for them all.

Around midnight, he decided to return to the city to find food. When he informed his wife, she tried to stop him. She reminded him of the dangers and told him she feared for his safety.

"But there is no more food to be found at the airport," he replied. "And it will be safer to move around under the cover of darkness."

Before dawn, he returned with a solitary can of beans, which he handed to his wife. While she heated them over a small fire, she turned to him and said, "Husband, you look troubled. Are you feeling unwell?"

Ahmad only shook his head. For the first time since their arrival at the airport, he allowed himself a feeble smile. "Do not worry, wife," he said. "Alhamdulillah (praise be to God), everything will be okay, for Allah has bestowed *rizq* (sustenance) on us." Taking the hot beans from the fire, he praised his good fortune and shared them mostly between his wife and the boy.

Surrounded by razor wire and concrete walls, Ahmad stood before the battered sheet-metal gate of the evacuation checkpoint. His heart and mind were empty. The fourteen days of waiting and hoping had been insufferable. Around the checkpoint, discarded clothing, children's toys, and plastic bottles littered the ground.

Again, he peered beyond the gate in a daze. Again, he handed his tattered papers to the closest Marine. Again, he lowered his head while the Marine read. Another minute passed.

"How many?" the Marine asked, looking up from the papers.

Jerking his head upward, Ahmad blinked sharply. "Pardon?" he replied in English.

"People? How many people do you have?"

His heart almost burst from his chest. He wiped his grimy hands down the sides of his tunic, then across his face, hoping to improve his appearance. "Four. There are only four of us," he stammered, trying to get the words out before the Marine could move on. He spread his arms wide to introduce his family, who were on the ground close by, sitting in filth. "And the little ones take up no room at all. We have identification papers and visas, as you can see. I helped U.S. God bless America." His hands trembled while the Marine examined the papers a second time. "Saxonman," he said, smiling expectantly. "Gods of heavy metal."

After raising his eyes from the papers, the Marine gave him a careful, expressionless once-over.

"Interpreter?" he asked.

"Yes. Yes. Interpreter," Ahmad straightaway replied. "Very much information I gave to U.S. Marines. I helped very much."

The Marine swiveled an abrupt one-eighty before disappearing with the papers. When he returned a few minutes later, he was accompanied by a woman dressed in civilian clothes and wearing a Kevlar helmet, a flak jacket, and dark sunglasses.

The Marine signaled to Ahmad. "This one," he said.

The woman inspected Ahmad's face, followed by his papers. She then pointed to his wife and children.

"Come," she said, smiling as she waved them through the gate.

Ahmad studied the plastic identification bracelet that they had fastened to his wrist. He fumbled with the small box of earplugs they had given him, turning it endlessly in his hand.

After they had passed through the outside checkpoint, the smiling woman, whom he learned was a consular officer, had escorted them to the terminal closest to the East Gate. Following a brief medical check, they were given clean COVID masks, some food, and water, which they accepted bā sepās (with thanks). Now they sat waiting with others in muted anticipation.

From the noise and confusion outside the building, Ahmad was sure the only world he knew would soon be gone. Kabul was falling. He heard loud explosions, sporadic gunfire, and many people yelling and screaming. Children were crying. The Marines patrolling the inside terminal appeared edgy, with stern expressions and trigger fingers poised and twitching.

Long after nightfall, they were herded downstairs with the others to another checkpoint where Ahmad presented his ID'd wrist to a Marine at a makeshift desk. In his other hand, he still held the duffel bag containing his infant daughter. After passing the red light from a barcode reader over his bracelet, the Marine consulted the passenger manifest on a laptop on the desk and nodded. When he opened the duffel bag, they scanned his infant daughter also.

As they crossed the tarmac together, the chaos outside the wire continued. Before them, a C-17 transporter loomed large in the darkness, the air around them thick with insurgency and desperation.

The tears welled in his eyes as he recalled himself just hours ago, pushed up against the fence, envying the lucky ones. And he felt ashamed of his good fortune.

At the rear of the aircraft, he paused at the foot of the ramp. Fleetingly, he thought about turning around and running back to Kabul to beg forgiveness for what he had done. For what he had done. Lowering his eyes to the duffel bag, he gazed lovingly at his infant daughter and stroked his son's head with heartfelt affection.

"For my family," he whispered.

Then, taking his wife's hand in his, he led them up the ramp and into the belly of the beast. The ziba (beautiful) beast that would take them to freedom.

At 11:59 on the night of August 30th, in the summer of '21, Ahmad squatted in the cargo hold of the C-17 with his wife and children at his side. As the wheels lifted from the runway, he removed an ear-plug and lowered his face mask. He turned to his wife and, with an awkward smile, said, "خدا واقعا بزرگه, Fattanah."

His wife looked at him in astonishment. "Yes … Ahmad," she replied in English. "God is truly great." With a gentle tug, she pulled the boy away from him and returned her gaze to the floor.

Chapter 4

Roxy

At forty-three minutes past midnight, Roxy cast off the sweat-soaked bedsheets. Bleary-eyed and naked, she glanced across at Bradley lying motionless beside her. Not only had they finished almost a bottle of tequila between them, but she had exhausted him with her … adroitness. Unlike in their younger days when they would fumble around, awkward and clueless, this time had been different. Now, they were experienced. Each knew the other's endgame and how to get there by way of the most adventurous path.

Little Paris was nowhere to be seen.

She lay for a while, admiring his strapping body and listening to his slow rhythmic breathing. After kissing his forehead, she got up and staggered to the bathroom. Once she'd finished there, she set off in search of her Astrakhan coat.

In the living room, she stopped to leer at a ginormous TV screen on the wall, wincing as her sluggish brain tried to unscramble the flickering images. Some loudmouthed drama queen reporter going on about who-the-fuck-cares. In clumsy increments, she scanned the room, slowly taking in the expensive-looking oil paintings hanging on the walls and the oh-my-god ornaments propped on fancy pedestals. When she entered the apartment, it hadn't seemed this fucking big, over twice the size of hers.

"Huh. My Bradley must be rich," she mumbled, squinting through the slit of one bloodshot eye at a long wooden table, which was surrounded by eight shiny brass chairs with black velvet seats.

In another life, this could all have been hers. No! It *should* have been hers!

Her coat was still lying in a crumpled heap where she'd left it by the entry door. From the inside pocket, she removed a palm-sized zip-pouch and from that, she took out a metal spoon, a length of rubber strap, a disposable cigarette lighter, and a plastic syringe. From another pocket, she produced a small bag of white powder. Their ticket to Neverland.

She'd done it plenty of times before. It was an expected perk of the sleepover service. The client asks, and the client gets. She flicked the cigarette lighter, but it didn't spark. "Do you have a lighter?" she called to Bradley, not so loud that it hurt her head. With no response, she rummaged through the kitchen cupboards and found a butane starter for the stove. It had a long bendable neck. Perfect for the job. Minutes later, she returned to the bedroom, holding a syringe full of liquid magic.

When she shook him awake, Bradley looked up and winced.

"Ow. My head," he moaned. "I haven't beed this drunk since … since that frat party … you know … you know, the one when we had … when we was wearing togas … and I lost my toga, and we first met. 'Member that time … when we first met, Emily? Do you 'member that, Em?"

"Don't worry, babe, I'm gonna give you … give you wings," she replied, tying the strap off above his elbow. After slapping his arm to bring up the vein, she raised the syringe.

When he caught sight of the needle, Bradley flinched, his eyes bulging in alarm. "No! I don't do that … that stuff. I haven't used …

never used anything stronger than … little Janie." He tried to push the syringe away, but his hand only brushed against her shoulder before falling limp to his side.

"It's gonna be okay, honey. I'll babysit you."

"But, it might be … be bad stuff," he said, screwing his face. He raised his hand again in feeble protest.

"No. I get mine hand-to-hand from my connection," she replied. "A reliable source. Known quality. Not flea powder. No." Grabbing his arm, she held it vice-like as the needle tip found its mark. "Hold still, babe. We can't afford to break the sharp. I don't have any spares."

Once he was lit up, she returned to the kitchen to cook another batch and did herself next.

The pandemonium raging in Roxy's head intensified. It pounded against her skull from somewhere outside her limited comprehension. Someone was hammering on the apartment door, but a hundred times louder than necessary. Paris yapped incessantly, and the TV in the living room blared. Then a new discordant sound seeped into her subconscious, displacing the hammering, the barking dog, and the blaring TV. The warble of a first responder's siren. It wasn't the Doppler effect she expected to hear from something moving toward or away from her, but the steady pitch of an EMS vehicle parked right out front in the street below.

"Is anybody home?" a baritone voice called through the door.

"I said as much when I rang nine-one-one," another man's voice said. "We were having a late supper. They were yelling and screaming. They were going nuts for two whole hours before everything went quiet. That was half an hour ago. Except for the dog. That damn thing keeps barking. But there's people in there for sure. Two of them, I think. Look, there's some ladies' shoes left here in the hallway."

"Thank you, sir," the baritone voice replied. "Could you please step back?" Then the voice loudened. "If you don't respond, I'm going to assume exigent circumstances. We're going to use force." Then the voice tempered. "Please step back, sir."

As much as it hurt, Roxy forced one eye open. She was sitting on the bedroom floor, slumped against the wall, still naked. She glanced at her hand draped across her waist and tried to move her fingers. No luck. Her head was spinning.

"Last warning. This is the NYPD. I'll count to three, and if you don't respond, we'll have to break down the door. One ... two ..."

She opened her mouth to speak, but nothing came out.

"Three!"

The front door caved in with a calamitous *crash*, and a frenzy erupted as people burst into the apartment. From the urgency in their voices, Roxy figured there were five or six of them in the living room, along with Paris's constant yapping.

"There's one in the bedroom," the baritone voice cried, as a large figure appeared in the doorway. "No! Two in the bedroom. Quick! Paramedic. In here. Someone get animal control up here and muzzle that damn dog."

Someone else entered the room, and Roxy sensed them kneeling beside her.

"Ma'am? Can you hear me?" the voice beside her said. She tried to say something, but could only splutter as gunk and spittle pooled in her mouth. "Checking airway," the voice barked. Then rough hands laid her down and rolled her onto her side. She felt a latex-covered finger thrust down her throat, wriggling, unblocking her airway. She coughed involuntarily. "Breathing." The latex finger withdrew, and the hands rolled her onto her back. A piercing light, like a fucking laser, burned into her left retina, followed by her right. "Can you hear me? Ma'am, can you hear me?"

Still unable to speak, she gave a sluggish nod.

"Extraction trolley, please."

Another person, this one pushing a gurney, appeared alongside the first. Vice-like hands gripped her shoulders and legs before she was hefted up and placed on a soft, padded surface.

"Can anyone confirm opioid use? Anyone?"

From outside the bedroom, another voice replied. "Confirmed. Related paraphernalia found in the kitchen."

"Naloxone, please!"

"Nasal?" someone asked.

"No. Risk assessment confirms an unacceptable hazard. Intramuscular, please."

Risk assessment? Hazard? Roxy wondered what all the fuss was about. Apart from a blinding headache and difficulty moving her mouth, she felt okay. She was lucid enough to understand what was going on. This was just like the aftereffects of any other bender she'd been on. She felt a sharp sting in her left thigh before someone threw a thin blanket over her legs and torso.

"What about the other one? Status report, please."

There was a long moment of complete, agonizing silence. "Deceased," came the eventual reply.

Roxy's disbelieving eyes flicked to the bed where Bradley lay naked, spread-eagled on his back. His lips were the same color blue as the dye bag her mother used to put on her bee stings when she was a kid, and he was staring at her. No, he was staring beyond her. White foam frothed from his slack mouth, and a thick discharge of green snot dribbled from his nose and across his cheek.

"Bradley," she cried out in a voice that was raspy and hardly audible. She reached out to him, hoping with all her heart that he would blink and smile at her. *Oh, babe. No. Not like this.*

There was more yelling from outside in the hallway. A woman's shrill voice this time.

"Ma'am, you can't go in there," the baritone voice said.

"This is my apartment," the woman replied. "I live here. My husband, he's … Is he okay?"

Roxy heard more commotion before the woman burst into the

bedroom. When she saw Bradley on the bed, she let out a gut-wrenching scream.

This must be Emily. From the gurney, only her top half was visible, but from what Roxy observed, Emily was stunning. She had long braided hair, glistening ebony skin, and wore an off-the-shoulder, falu-red evening dress. Just gorgeous. Good old Bradley has done all right for himself, she thought, then quickly corrected herself. *Had* done all right for himself.

Then Emily saw Roxy. "You fucking bitch!"

In a flying leap, she hurled herself at the gurney, landing on top of Roxy, straddling her. She pounded on Roxy's chest as if trying to beat a confession from her. But Roxy couldn't feel a thing. There was only a weird sense of detachment and a disturbing deadness inside her. She wished she could tell Emily it wasn't her fault. She wasn't stupid. She knew Bradley was a nube. She knew the correct dose. She'd done it hundreds of times before. Fucking Squirts, her dealer, must have sold her lemonade.

As the battering continued, Roxy ran a hand over Emily's plump stomach. She thought she felt movement, the kick of tiny feet inside her belly.

Oh.

"I need help in here," the baritone voice yelled before somebody pried Emily away. "Will someone please remove the patient from the possible crime scene? And take the damn dog as well." Emily was still screaming. "Ma'am, I know this is upsetting, but can you please calm down? No, don't look at your husband, ma'am." Emily's screams subsided into a series of long, sorrowful sobs. "It's all right, ma'am. That's it. Try to take a deep breath now. Will someone please take that trolley out of here and park it in the living room?"

There was a jolt of movement beneath her as she was wheeled out of the bedroom and into the living room. The gurney jerked to a sudden halt, and whoever was pushing it hurried back into the bedroom. Roxy raised her anvil head and scanned the living room. Apart from little Paris, who was still barking and tearing at the gurney wheel below, she was alone. The apartment was a mess. There were paintings torn from walls and ornaments smashed to pieces, with bits of wood and ceramic littering the floor.

"These fucking responders should take better care of the place," she muttered, lowering her head again.

As she stared miserably at the ceiling, she couldn't help thinking about Bradley, lying dead under a white sheet in the bedroom. Of poor Emily and her unborn child. Jacob and Darleen, too. She thought about her best friend, Cathy Moore, and what they did to Fr. Joe. She thought about her parents, who hadn't bothered to call her in years. As she reflected on her life, she realized that apart from Bradley, no one else in the world loved her.

On the ginormous TV, the drama queen news reporter continued to prattle away. Images of a large fireball flashed across the screen. There'd been an accident at a local waste treatment facility, and it was engulfed in flames. The fucking kids were running amok in the streets.

Then, the TV volume suddenly spiked for the start of the next ad break.

"Would you like to meet God?" the ad voice asked as the screen image panned up a set of marble steps, through billowing white clouds to a gilded archway that dazzled with shafts of golden light radiating from beyond.

At 3:16 in the morning, on the Wednesday before last, unloved and with her life in disarray, Roxy Rodriguez (aka Janice Bottoms) stared agog at the TV.

"SoulSoft is at the cutting edge of software innovation," the ad voice continued. "We can offer you the chance of a lifetime. Be one of the first mortals to meet God in the Machine."

Roxy listened intently.

"At SoulSoft, we have developed avant-garde technology that puts you in the presence of God. Through proprietary software, we are the first and only service that enables you to witness God in all His glory."

She suddenly felt sorry for herself. Fucking Squirts had killed her Bradley. And Fr. Joe? It was Cathy's idea. If she met God face-to-face, she would tell him it wasn't her fault. She was the victim here. Shit happens, and she always seemed to be in the wrong place at the wrong time. If she could tell God that, He'd understand. All she really wanted was the love she deserved.

"Act fast, as places are limited," the ad voice urged. "Call five-five-five, oh-one, two-three, without delay. God will see you now.

"SoulSoftneitherrepresentsnorguaranteestheparticipant'sexperienc einthepresenceofGod," the ad voice added in a lowered tone. "The-applicantwarrantstheyareaUScitizen,overeighteenyearsold,andareofso undmindandbody.ApplicantsacknowledgetheexperienceofmeetingGo disatrialandindemnifySoulSoftagainstanyadverseblahblahblah," it said.

Chapter 5

Rebecca

AT 8:16 DURING FRIDAY MORNING'S Manhattan rush hour one month ago, nineteen-year-old Becky Jones stepped from the sidewalk onto 5th Avenue, just above 49th Street, straight into a snarl of oncoming traffic. Tires screeched as drivers braked hard, and three lanes of vehicles concertinaed to an abrupt and inconvenient halt. More tires screeched as, further up the avenue, other cars braked and swerved. Drivers pursed their lips and shook their heads in aggravation. Then a cacophony of horns blared at her to move out of their goddamn way. But Becky couldn't have cared less as she hoisted her placard into the air.

"Just stop oil!" she shrieked. "Just stop oil!"

Across the street, another person darted onto the road. Then more rushed out. Each had a placard like Becky's in one hand and a two-foot pike of steel in the other. A length of half-inch chain, welded to the pike, was secured to their wrists by a heavy-duty stainless padlock. Busy, busy, they arranged themselves into three rows of fourteen people to completely obstruct the hundred feet across the avenue. Then six more people emerged from the gathering crowd.

Each carried a ten-pound sledgehammer, which they used to pound the tops of the steel pikes until they disappeared deep into the asphalt.

"Just stop oil!" they all chanted in unison.

Lying on her back and gazing into the cloudless sky, Becky smiled inwardly as a wave of selfless satisfaction swept over her. She'd planned the stunt to perfection. Only she could have pulled it off with this kind of precision, at the optimal time and location for maximum disruption and the widest publicity. She was the last true eco-warrior; the world's only hope between a sustainable future and ecological disaster. There would be no viable planet without her righteous intervention. She gave the chain shackled to her wrist a convincing yank and was comforted by its resistant reply.

Meanwhile, further down the avenue, a first responder's siren began to wail.

At the next grid point along, her sister Rachel tugged at her own chain. They were twins, almost impossible to tell apart. Sometimes, they even confused their parents about which one was which and who had done what. Becky was firstborn by forty-five minutes. Since the age of five, she'd been the one with a social conscience, struck by the injustice of it all, whereas her sister was a latecomer to the campaign. Heck, she'd practically gotten down on her knees and begged Rachel to come today. She couldn't abide those who weren't committed to the struggle. Cause-casuals, she referred to them, along with a huge serving of resentment implied. In the end, Rachel agreed, so that counted for something as far as Becky was concerned.

They angled their heads until their eyes met. "Just stop oil!" they chanted in unison while beaming out triumphant smiles.

"Oh, good Lordy," said a stout policewoman as she stood straddled across Becky's iron chain. After surveying the unfolding crime scene, she gave the chain a concerted tug. "What will these damn kids think of next?" She examined the manacle attaching the chain to Becky's wrist. "Sweet Jesus, girl. What is going through your damn fool head?"

Becky looked up and smiled widely. Behind the policewoman, the angry drivers poured from their vehicles, amassing at the curb with fists raised and hurling foul abuse.

"Officer! Officer!" A news reporter leaped from the surrounding crowd and shoved a microphone under the policewoman's nose. "Daily News. Can you tell us what's happening here? Has anyone claimed responsibility? Do you have all the perpetrators in custody? How long before traffic will move again? Can you confirm—"

"Will somebody please tape off the perimeter and keep the press out of the way?" the policewoman shouted to nobody in particular. "Until we can figure out what in the Jesus-name Dickens is going on here."

"No can-do, ma'am," a lanky officer beside her responded. "Another group of 'em blocked off Fifth, just past Forty-Sixth this time. The crime scene extends all the way down the next four blocks. And we're all part of it. Drivers. Pedestrians. Protesters. All of us. All part of it." Turning a full rotation, he scanned the scene as if to substantiate his bleak assessment of the escalating situation.

"My sweet savior," the policewoman said. "Can't we redirect the traffic to the east and west?"

"No can-do, ma'am," the officer replied. "They've blocked off the crosstown streets from here to Barnes and Noble on Forty-Sixth. So, the entire Diamond District is gridlocked. Complete standstill. No one can get in, and no one can get out. Nada. Nothing."

"Okay. Okay. I get the picture," the policewoman said, growing frustrated as she stood back and surveyed the unfolding scene.

Becky couldn't help but chuckle. She'd outwitted them on all fronts. Once she had the large chunk of 5th Avenue blocked off both north and south, the only exit points for the traffic were the in-between streets east and west. This was the plan-within-the-plan that delighted her the most.

In the lead-up weeks, she'd applied for a Bank of America credit card. After a bit of overestimating here and underestimating there, BoA was happy to oblige with a $50,000 line of credit—as requested, no questions asked. When the shiny red card arrived in the mail a week later, she was sure to keep it concealed. Using the card, she then ordered eight ten-ton moving vans—now abandoned, wedged bumper-to-bumper, keys missing, and wheels clamped—stretched diagonally across East and West 46th to 49th. The perfect fence-them-in maneuver ever, she had to admit.

Becky wasn't overly concerned about the money she'd borrowed. Following the success of today's disruptive event, she was confident the GoFundMe page she'd just set up would raise enough cash to repay all the expenses, with enough remaining to fund a down payment on her next imperative stunt. It was all part of her ongoing commitment to raise public awareness of the planet's plight.

High above, a small drone buzzed down between the tall buildings. It dropped in so close that Becky could see the camera aimed at her. When she waved her free hand at it, the drone blinked a small red light in response. She supposed she was being broadcast on real-time news TV.

Fisting her manacled hand, she raised it above her head, mimicking those revered dissidents of history who were passionate about their egregious causes. "Just stop oil!" she yelled into the camera.

"What in tarnation?" the policewoman said, noticing the drone. "Blessed Lord, give me strength. This is restricted airspace. Will somebody get that damn thing out of here?"

"Can-do, ma'am," the lanky officer replied. He radioed someone back at the precinct, and two minutes later, the damn thing buzzed away.

Meanwhile, in the distance, the first responder's siren continued to wail.

In all, it took a little over two and a half hours for the gridlocked traffic to move again. At first, the fire department tried to use a handheld hacksaw and a set of orange-colored bolt cutters. However, the tungsten chains were impossible to cut, and the stainless shackles on the padlocks proved inaccessible due to the strategic design of the wrist manacles. A clever tactic in Becky's well-thought-out playbook.

Someone suggested they use an oxyacetylene blowtorch; however, it was deemed much too risky for all involved. Until two rugged-looking construction workers arrived from a nearby building site carrying a nine-inch angle grinder with a diamond-tip blade, which made the job a whole lot easier but twice as dangerous. So, they required the written consent of each protester before the construction workers could proceed, which delayed the recovery effort a whole lot longer.

As the first hour of the disturbance approached, a dozen armed police officers marched in to reinforce the line as tensions between the hemmed-in drivers and protesters escalated and threatened to boil over.

"Just stop pissing us off," one driver yelled.

"Plants have feelings too," screamed another.

When another motorist told her to eat grass and freeze and spat in her direction, Becky leaped to her feet. If not for the chain holding her back, she would have vaulted the police line and been at their throats before they knew what hit them.

"It's all your fault," she shrieked. "You gas-guzzling, oil-dependent vandals. Stop killing our planet. When we all die, I hope you and your kids are the first to go."

The EV drivers turned to each other with looks of utter dismay, then back at her. They were collateral damage for the greater good as far as she was concerned. Still scowling, she sat again.

Sometime later, the distant wail of the first responders ceased.

When the construction workers arrived at her chain, Becky kicked out and writhed on the ground, to the extent that the policewoman threatened to Taser her if she did not "sit your skinny butt on the ground and stop movin' about. Damn fool girl." Once they'd cut her free, she was cuffed and marched, under armed escort, onto a white and blue NYPD bus with the rest of the conspirators.

"And God have mercy on all your damn fool souls," the police-woman said in a firm voice before slamming the bus door shut with a loud and conclusive *schwott.*

Becky sat on her own, stony-faced, with her forehead pressed against the window, listening to the low rumble of the big wheels underneath as the bus trundled down 5th. Outside, the sidewalk was teeming with people, all going about their daily routines as if things were normal while inhaling the noxious fumes from the bus as it drove on past. They didn't know what was coming. Or perhaps they didn't care. Either way, everyone would get their just desserts in the end.

'God have mercy on all your damn fool souls,' were the police-woman's parting words, and Becky felt offended. She wasn't the fool here. Everyone else was. And God? Well, if God hadn't released this plague of humanity upon the Earth, then the planet would have been just fine, thank you. So, it was all God's fault, she decided.

Becky sat twirling her fingers with her back against a white cinder-block wall, and her sister beside her.

"Do you think Mom and Dad will come and bail us out?" Rachel asked, staring ruefully through the bars at the clock on the wall out-side their holding cell.

"They always do," Becky replied.

"This is my first time, Bec," Rachel said in a morose, wavering voice. "They'll be disappointed in me. I was fingerprinted. I'll have a criminal record now." She turned to Becky, her face pale and drawn. "Are we going to jail, Bec?"

"Don't sweat it, Rach. They only issue you with a misdemeanor, slap you on the wrist, and send you on your way. I've been here plenty before."

They sat for a while longer in silence.

"Bec?"

"Yeah, Rach?"

"Do you think Mom or Dad will come and bail us out soon?"

"I hope they do, Rach. I hope they do."

The whole caper had spiraled gloriously out of control. With the flow-on effect, plus widespread TV and Internet coverage, she was certain her parents couldn't have missed the historic event. Sure, they would be mad at her, like the last time. And she would yell at them and tell them that if it wasn't for their oil-guzzling generation, the world wouldn't need saving. She would tell them it was all their fault. They would yell back at her, saying how privileged she was to live in the best country in the world during the best times in history. They would then point to her iPhone, smartwatch, designer-label clothes, favorite handbag—anything to prove their point. But they just didn't get it.

None of those things mattered once the planet was gone.

"Rachel Jones! I am so disappointed in you. And Rebecca Jones, how dare you drag your sister into your mess."

It was 8:32 p.m. when their mother eventually arrived and posted bail. Becky could tell from her sharp voice and testy expression that she was furious. That meant their father would be beyond livid when they returned home.

Sneering, she looked away.

Neither girl uttered a word as they traipsed behind their mother out of the holding cell and down the passageway to the exit of the station house; just the occasional sideways glance at each other and a nervous smirk before lowering their contrite heads to contemplate the floor. When they stepped outside, the nighttime air was still and crisp. At the foot of the station house steps, a dozen news reporters and camera crews were huddled together, cordoned off.

As they descended the steps, her mother reached across and shielded Becky's face with her handbag. Then she tried to steer the girls clear of the reporters, who had just spotted them and sparked into frantic action.

Becky jerked herself away. Mesmerized by the glaring lights and TV cameras, she made a beeline for the media scrum. She halted a few feet in front of them, standing with hands on her hips and eyes narrowed as they shoved their enormous microphones in her face, jostling each other for the optimal placement to capture that all-important soundbite.

"ABC TV News here. Are you working with other—?"

"Anne Blake from CNN. Do you have plans for more—?"

"… from CBS. Are you the ringleader of—?"

Staring straight into the lens of the closest camera, Becky sensed the occasion. This was her chance. The reporters, the country, and the entire world were all waiting to hear from her. She opened her mouth as if to speak, and the reporters fell silent. You could hear a pin drop as they waited, eager to receive her unabridged account of the momentous event. This had been the most newsworthy climate-action story in years, and she was at its epicenter.

Suddenly, she felt special.

"Miss. Miss." A serious-looking reporter pushed to the front of the scrum and shoved his microphone under Becky's nose. "WNBC TV News here. Would you like to apologize to the mother who lost her newborn on account of the emergency services being obstructed by the gridlock that you caused?"

Startled, Becky rocked back from the microphone.

Chapter 6

Thomas

AT 7:23 YESTERDAY MORNING, Thomas Feldman Jr. drove his pelvis forth once more. As he did, he experienced no emotion. He didn't grunt or cry or make a sound except for his labored breathing. Beneath his heaving mass, his wife lay motionless, eyes cast sideways, indifferent to each concerted thrust.

For Thomas, this was no longer an activity undertaken with any real purpose. Some years earlier, he'd had the surgery to neuter himself, while his forty-six-year-old wife, Jackie, already had enough viable embryos stowed away on ice, awaiting the day when she would give up her real estate sales career to start a family. Their replacement pair in reserve, primed and ready to go.

Detached from the task at hand, Thomas reflected on his life. He thought about the money, the fancy houses, the fast cars, and lavish dinners. None of it mattered anymore. He no longer cared about those luxuries or anything he said or did.

It hadn't always been this way, though. Just two weeks ago, before the digitization procedure, he took much pleasure in the money, the houses, the cars, and the intercourse. His recent sense of detachment, he figured, was most likely a side effect of the procedure. He neither knew nor cared.

When he climaxed at last, there was no sudden rush of emotion or the release of pent-up tension. He was just … finished. Without any fanfare or real satisfaction.

***

At 9:12 on a Thursday morning, one week earlier, Thomas shoved his shoulder against the rump of the bronze life-size bull on Wall Street. With his hand extended between its hind legs, he cupped its enormous, polished scrotum.

"Bring me the luck again today, buddy," he muttered, giving the two giant orbs a vigorous rub.

He did the same to the nose and horns to complete his morning ritual.

As a boy growing up in Lakewood, New Jersey, Thomas squirreled away every cent he had. Dollars for birthdays, dimes for odd jobs, and nickels from the sidewalk. Not that he grew up poor. With his mother night-packing at Walmart and his father delivering for DHL, they lived a comfortable life well above the breadline. Even so, as he watched them collapse, soulless, on the couch after dinner each night, he couldn't stop thinking there was insufficient return for their sweat and grind.

At seven years old, he and his kid sister, Adah, would fill their wooden box cart with jars of homemade lemonade and plastic cups. After hauling their load up the hill for two blocks to the main intersection, they'd spend the day selling refreshments to passing motorists for a quarter per cup. "There must be easier ways to make money," he'd often grumble to his sister as they trudged home with their meager takings for the day. Even then, he knew there had to be a smarter way to earn a dollar, without the sweat and grind.

By twelve, he was running an all-sports betting syndicate for the seventh graders at Lakewood Cheder for Boys. At sixteen, he was managing a profitable stock portfolio for the teachers and fellow juniors at Yeshiva K'tana. "You're a resourceful little tiger," Headmaster Abrams often said as he leafed through Thomas's monthly investment reports. "You sure know how to make an easy dollar."

Following the conclusion of his bovine ritual, Thomas took a cab to the T. Feldman & Associates office in Lower Manhattan. By 9:28, he was seated at his desk, gazing through the expansive window of his 39th-floor office that overlooked the Hudson, waiting for the opening bell at the New York Stock Exchange.

"The futures are pointing higher again today, my man," Jonas Goldstein declared as he burst into Thomas's office. He was rubbing his palms together with obvious glee. "There's some serious upward momentum in the DOW, and my gut informs me this will be another money-making day." He grabbed his midriff and grinned knowingly at Thomas.

Jonas was the younger brother Thomas never had. He was also the original associate of T. Feldman & Associates. When they first met as classmates, studying finance at Rutgers in New Brunswick over thirty years earlier, Thomas considered him a lazy moron. Jonas later confessed to thinking Thomas was right up his own ass. However, their fortuitous pairing in the annual fantasy stock market challenge—where students team up to play the NYSE trading game—revealed Jonas's financial astuteness, despite his goofball demeanor. Together, they grew their fanciful $100,000 share portfolio by an impressive $523,876 in only one semester, a feat not achieved by the students before or since.

"Two heads are better than one," he'd often remind Thomas while rapping his temple with his index finger. Then, "Spread the risk, man, and enjoy the reward," he would always add, running his thumb across his palm, as though doling out wads of cash.

Today, Jonas had a look in his eyes that Thomas had come to appreciate as his intuition.

"I tell you, man," he said, "we need to go big on gold. There's too much euphoria in the current market. We need a little conservatism to even out the risk."

Thomas rocked his head back and forth to reassure Jonas he was listening. "One word," he said, once Jonas had finished talking. "Dried apricots."

Jonas sighed. "That's two words, man."

"Think about it," Thomas insisted. "The forecast across Europe over the next two years is for La Niña. That means an increased probability of drought. Turkey produces thirty percent of the world's apricots. We take a position in dried apricots and wait for the weather to turn unfavorable. When the crops fail, prices skyrocket, and we take our profit."

"I'm not so sure, man," said Jonas with a ponderous head shake. "Long-range weather forecasting sounds like voodoo to me."

Just then, Thomas's white-gold Rolex pinged; the NYSE was open for trade. He got up, rounded the desk, and tapped Jonas's shoulder.

"Just think about it," he said, heading for the door. "Apricots."

Outside his office, the Feldman trading floor was abuzz with excitement. The market was up over two thousand points, and the twenty-three other associates were either running between desks, tapping wildly on keyboards, or staring wide-eyed at the live charts on one of several large displays spread on the walls around the room.

"Buy X." "Sell Y." "What about Z?" "Hold. Hold. Sell now," the associates were all screaming at once and at no one in particular.

As he moved around the trading floor, immersed in the cut and thrust of the fiscal struggle, Thomas savored the fervor in the room. To him, it was akin to warfare, and this was his beloved battlefield. He checked the screens and patted the backs of winning traders like a doting father.

This is how you make an easy dollar, he thought, smiling inwardly.

Two hours after the NYSE closing bell rang, the displays were blank, the keyboards shoved aside, and the associates had all gone home. The bulls had run hard again, and it had been another successful trading day for T. Feldman & Associates. "Another day and another six-hundred-thousand dollars," he boasted aloud. Based on his usual fee, he split the day's profit in his head: five hundred thousand for the investors, forty thousand for the associates, and the rest for himself. Not bad for a day's work. "Without the sweat and grind", he reminded himself.

He shut off the lights, stepped into the empty passageway, and locked the door.

There was a slight chill in the evening air as he descended the steps to the sidewalk. He tugged his coat collar higher and was about to hail a taxi when someone called to him.

"Spare a dollar, brother?"

Thomas looked down.

From the sidewalk, a man peered up at him with a hopeful, grimy smile. He hadn't noticed the hobo before, sitting on the pavement outside the office. Then he realized the man was not, in fact, sitting. He had his backside wedged on a short wooden plank, which had four roller wheels mounted underneath, and both his legs extended along the plank. Except his legs ended where his knees should have been. A trembling finger appeared from the sleeve of the hobo's threadbare coat and pointed to an empty shoebox on the pavement beside him.

Thomas drew out a wad of greenbacks from his top pocket, removed the clip, and unfurled the notes. He flicked through a half-dozen hundreds until he found a 'Washington'. He took out the dollar, dropped it into the shoebox, and moved on.

"Thank you, brother," the hobo called after him. "And may God bless you."

Thomas stopped and turned around. He peered at the hobo with fascination. He wasn't sure which god the hobo imagined might bless him. In fact, he wasn't convinced he needed a blessing from any God at all; if indeed one existed.

Thomas flagged down a cab. As he climbed in, he felt a sharp spasm in his chest. Nothing serious. He'd had similar twinges over the past few days, which he put down to either the excitement of the fiscal battle or indigestion. At five-six and two-forty pounds, though, he was a heart attack waiting to happen. He ran a reluctant hand over his rotund belly, then glanced at the driver.

"I'm sorry for your trouble my good man, but I have a sudden desire to walk." Flashing an awkward smile, he handed over a hundred-dollar bill and got out.

Walking across town toward his apartment on Broadway, Thomas's thoughts drifted again to God. 'God will provide,' he'd learned by rote as a child, and 'Ask God, and ye shall receive,' they'd taught him during his mitzvah of chinuch. In retrospect, if God were real and the teachings true, wouldn't everybody already have everything they wanted?

Nowadays, people want too much. No! They *demand* too much. When the investors demanded millions, *he* was the one who ensured millions were made. When Jackie pestered him for a convertible sports car, *he* bought her a pink Maserati the very next day. And if the hobo had requested a thousand dollars, *he* would have gladly given the man the thousand. Yet, the hobo only wanted a dollar. When people ask him for anything, it is *he*, not God, who makes sure they receive exactly what they'd asked for.

Did that make him a god of sorts?

"Hey, buddy. Got a light?"

Thomas jolted in surprise. He kept walking, daring not to look sideways. "I'm sorry, but I don't smoke," he replied, then scolded himself for stupidly deciding to take a shortcut through an unlit alleyway. He heard footsteps gathering behind him, in sync with his at first, then quickening. Then he felt something rigid pressed into the small of his back, and he froze.

"No, don't turn around. Keep them eyes of yours ahead and gimme all your valuables."

Thomas threw up his hands. "Oh!" His heart pounding and mind racing, he fumbled through his top pocket and retrieved the wad of bills. He passed them back over his shoulder to the thief.

"Thanks, buddy," the thief said.

Then Thomas heard footsteps hurrying away.

"Wait!" he cried. When he turned around, the thief was about to disappear into the shadows. "You forgot the wristwatch."

The thief halted, then spun around, gazing open-mouthed at Thomas. "What the—?" In cautious increments, he returned, his head yawing around, looking for signs of a police sting, an unseen bodyguard, or a hidden *got-you* camera. Edging closer, he held something in his hand, which Thomas supposed was the gun. He stopped within a few feet. "Is this some kind of joke?"

"Certainly not," Thomas replied. "You said you wanted *all* my valuables, but you hurried away before I could hand over the rest of my money. My wristwatch is also valuable." He slipped off the Rolex and flashed it before the thief's disbelieving eyes.

The thief snatched it out of Thomas's hand and eyed it greedily. "Are you for real?" he said, stashing it away in his pocket. Then his jaw dropped in astonishment when Thomas handed over the remaining notes from his pants pocket, over a thousand dollars in cash.

"Any more valuables?" the lucky thief inquired.

Thomas frowned. "I'm sorry," he said, "but that's all I have."

When he arrived home fifteen minutes later, Thomas was out of breath yet satisfied with his impromptu decision to get some long-overdue exercise. Jackie had Chinese takeaway warming in the oven.

"A funny thing happened today," he said, sitting at one end of his genuine Australian Jarrah table, eating his dinner. "I wondered if I might be God."

At the other end of the table, Jackie glanced up from her plate. "That's nice, dear," she said, lowering her eyes again. "Did you decide if you are?"

"Maybe," he replied, then popped another deep-fried vegetarian roll into his mouth.

That night, Thomas tossed and turned in his bed, which was unusual for him. It wasn't the hobo, the thief, or even being God-like that kept him awake. It was apricots. He couldn't shake the idea that there might be some serious money to be made in the fruit. Jonas's intuition said gold, and perhaps that was the sensible thing. But the clients were relentless. They were forever pestering him for spectacular returns on their investments, in ever shorter time frames, or they'd take their money elsewhere. Everyone expected *him* to provide for them.

'Apricots' was the last thing on his mind before he slipped into a deep and dreamless sleep.

Chapter 7

Susan

AT SIX O'CLOCK SHARP on Monday morning, Susan arrived at Soul-Soft Inc. bright-eyed and bushy-tailed. She still couldn't believe that, following her meeting with Brice Woodlands on Friday afternoon, she'd handed in her notice at Neuro-Labs that evening, cleared out her office on Saturday, and was now at SoulSoft, sitting on her new chair, at her new desk, doing …?

Well, she still wasn't quite sure what she was doing here.

Her new office was enormous, almost four times the size of her old one, windowless, well-lit by an array of can lights in the high ceiling, and bare—apart from her desk and a basic kitchenette with a cooktop, a tall silver refrigerator, and an all-important espresso machine. Opposite the entry door, there was another door, which was closed. An interactive whiteboard hung on the wall behind her, four feet high and ten feet wide. On the desktop, she noticed an old QWERTY keyboard, a handheld mouse device, and a pair of 20-inch LCD monitors that swiveled on articulated arms.

Pushing back in her seat, she peered incredulously at the bundle of black cables that trailed from each device and disappeared down a small, round hole at the rear of the desk.

"Is this some kind of joke?" she muttered. "Old-tech hardware with curly cords? How am I expected to develop groundbreaking tech with this … this antiquated equipment?" She pressed a button at the base of the right-side monitor. A red power indicator winked on, and a second later, a prompt appeared in the center of the screen. It said 'login' all right, but there was no inputbox or instructions for multifactor authentication. An 'OK' widget was the only user interface provided.

"Okay," she said after a short deliberation. "I guess it's 'OK' then." She clicked the widget.

At first, nothing happened. Then, a panel at the rear of the desk clunked open, revealing a long slot. A thin metal rod, made up of six pivoting sections, emerged from the slot. It unfolded toward her in fluid movements, halting above her mouse hand. A sharp tip, about half an inch long, shot out from the end of the probe. Before she had time to react, it struck out at her hand like a rattlesnake.

"Ow! Son of a sea biscuit!"

LOGIN CONFIRMED, the screen returned. WELCOME DR. SUSAN PARKER.

"Well, that was unique," she muttered, rubbing her stinging hand. "Painful, but unique."

The login confirmation disappeared, replaced by an image of the sky and clouds with a gilded stairway leading up to heavenly gates and a SoulSoft banner plastered across the top.

"Parker!" Without knocking, the door swung open, and Brice Woodlands stormed into the room. "Welcome aboard. I see you've settled in. Already made yourself at home. Any progress yet?"

"Well, I—"

"Good, good," he replied. "This is Robert." He halted, gesturing to a tall, slender man about thirty, who had followed him through the door. Robert wore a white open-necked business shirt, tan corduroy pants, and glossy black shoes. With his curly dark hair and black-rimmed glasses, he reminded Susan of somebody, but she wasn't sure who. "He's a nerd, like you," Woodlands said. "Responsible for—"

"Network administration," Robert interrupted, adjusting his glasses. "I'm here for—"

"Yes, yes," Woodlands re-interrupted. "He's the IT helpdesk."

Susan turned to Robert. "Oh, good. I wanted to speak to someone about updating the tech. We need quantum boxes, mystical screens, VR headsets, wireless devices—"

"No wireless, Dr. Parker," Robert interjected, together with a ponderous head shake. "Strictly old-school here. We can't afford any outside snooping. All development activities must be conducted within the four walls of the lab." Pivoting on his heels, he pointed to each wall in the room as if to emphasize the containment boundaries.

"But how will I work from home?"

"No offline access allowed, Dr. Parker," he replied, again with a ponderous shake of his head. "As previously stated, all development must remain within these four walls."

"Good, Parker. That's settled. Four walls. Now, let's get to it. Let's get cracking and create our software version of God."

Susan's heart sank. Her mother had always warned her: if something sounds too good to be true, then ... "Honestly, nobody has attempted such a difficult task," she said, grimacing. "Yet you expect me to achieve the incredible using antiquated technology?" She gave the equipment on her desk a disparaging glare. "It's like using a horse and cart to take people to the moon."

Robert recoiled as if her words had cut deep. "Not antiquated, Dr. Parker," he said, sounding mildly aggrieved. "We're hardwired into a bank of a dozen of the latest, most powerful quantum processors in the room next door. All the walls are lined with inch-thick aluminum mesh. And the cables are triple copper-shielded. We're standing inside one big Faraday cage. It's a device that blocks electromagnetic fields and radiated signals. To stop snooping from external sources. Outside hacking from the bad guys—"

"It's okay, Robert," she said, cutting him short. "I know what a

Faraday cage is." Then she remembered who he reminded her of. With those glasses and geek-chic hairstyle, he resembled the old-time singer Buddy Holly, whom her mother used to listen to on vintage vinyl recordings. "Now I appreciate the unorthodox login procedure," she continued. "Although, that probe, it hurt." She gave him a playful grimace.

"DNA-based authentication," he said, maintaining a stolid expression. "Maximum security strength possible. Nobody has managed to crack it, as yet. We took a speck of your DNA, ran it through a virtual polymerase chain reaction machine, and programmed your genome profile onto a two-nanometer chip, which we've inserted—"

"Fine, fine," she said, ending his technical explanation before it became long-winded and exhausting. All she needed to know was that she now had access to all the facilities in the room via a microchip implanted in her by that bizarre hand-pricking contraption. "What about my team?" she said, switching her attention to the challenge ahead. "When can I interview the scientists and software developers? We're going to need dozens of the most qualified specialists. We require neuro experts. We need coverage across every available programming language and software development tool. Conventional and quantum coding. We need—"

"Listen, Parker," Woodlands said, eyeballing her. "I'm paying four hundred million a year for you and your ingenuity. That's over a million dollars a day. You get yourself, Robert here, and a ... a ... What did you call it, Robert?"

Like a stiff-bodied robot, Robert rotated with pneumatic precision toward Woodlands. "A code tester," he said, then turned back to Susan.

"Yes. A code tester. You, Robert here, and a code tester. That should be enough tech heads for the job."

Before she could protest, Robert whipped out a clipboard from under his arm, then a marker pen from his top pocket.

"The refrigerator and pantry will be replenished every Thursday morning. The bed, closet, and dresser should be here later this morning. The couch and entertainment system both arrive tomorrow afternoon." He stabbed at the clipboard with decisive strokes of his pen as he spoke. "Ablutions are through the door." He jabbed the pen tip at the closed door on the wall opposite them. "And we've taken the liberty of retrieving a few belongings from your apartment. Clothes, undergarments, some photographs, toiletries, etcetera."

"You've done what?" Mortified, Susan sat up. She glared at Robert, then at Woodlands, feeling utterly violated.

With an awkward shrug, Woodlands turned away. He gave the room a quick scan, nodding his approval before turning back to her. "Two years, Parker. No distractions. Now, chop, chop. Create God for me." He shoved his hands into his pockets, about-faced, and left the room before she could protest further.

Following close behind him, Robert paused at the door, one hand on the handle. "And be sure to keep this shut at all times," he said, forcing a smile. "While it remains open, even by a fraction of an inch, the Faraday cage is breached, and your … our invention is at risk." Then, with an unequivocal *click*, he pulled the door shut behind him.

"How dare they?" she muttered irritably. Like a rabbit caught in headlights, she now had serious misgivings about what she'd gotten herself into. A screensaver image flashed up on the monitors. Golden rays of sunlight burst through plumes of puffy white clouds. Then ten tiny angels descended from the sky and bounced across the screens. Was there still time to back out?

There was a light knock on the door.

"Come in," she said, wresting her gaze from the screen.

When the door opened, a scrawny man wearing a white face mask and yellow rubber gloves entered the room. He was the same man she'd seen during her 'interview'.

"You made it," he said in his muffled, high-pitched voice. He eyed her as if assessing an unusual biological specimen. "Good. Everything should be in order. Bank details. Anything you want, just ask, and we will supply it. Within reason." He examined the empty room. "We want you to be as comfortable as possible during your stay with us." He sounded detached, as if he had other, more important things on his mind.

"Well, I could do with—"

"Good. Just ask," he repeated and headed for the door. When he gripped the door handle, he glanced back over his shoulder. "And be sure to keep this closed at all times."

Susan shook her head in despair. She was about to express her frustration and familiarity with the door-closed procedure when he pulled it shut behind him.

"What in the Sam Riley?" she said softly. With each absurd minute, she was more certain that her decision to leave Neuro-Labs had been a mistake. A monumental mistake. Except, she'd been backed into a corner. Like a ballplayer, she'd been traded to another team without her knowledge or consent. Due to circumstances out of her control, she'd ended up here.

There came another knock on the door, a little harder this time.

"Oh, for Pete's sake." She pushed back in her seat, took a deep breath, and tried to remain calm. "Come in."

This time, a woman of Anglo-Asian descent entered the lab. During a six-month secondment in Silicon Valley a few years earlier, she'd encountered some of the most remarkable-looking people. But none of those prepared her for the sight that had just walked through the door. The woman was in her early thirties with long green liberty spikes that radiated in all directions from her head. She was about five-foot-nothing but appeared six feet tall in her platform shoes. And her clothes were straight out of an old pirate movie. The only thing missing was a parrot on her shoulder.

She strode across the room and halted in front of Susan's desk. "I'm Lucy," she said, proffering a hand.

"Err … nice to meet you, Lucy," Susan replied. She couldn't help gawking at the intricate tattoo of skulls, dark red roses, and orange-black Koi running up Lucy's arm and into her white pirate blouse.

"I'm your code tester," Lucy said.

"My what?" Susan hesitated. The situation was deteriorating further. It was getting away from her. Rapidly. "But we haven't advertised that position yet."

"No need to advertise, Dr. Parker. I'm your gal."

"But we're looking for someone with certain … um … qualifications. Highly experienced. I haven't had the chance to speak to Mr. Woodlands about my requirements."

Lucy smiled. "Not a problem, Dr. Parker. Uncle Brice can vouch for me. And Uncle Bryan thinks I'm smart enough for the job."

"Uncle Brice? Uncle Bryan?" Like a nickel plunging to the bottom of a wishing well, Susan's heart sank. The assignment was growing more absurd by the minute.

"I know what you're thinking," Lucy said, her diamanté-encrusted dental braces glittering under the lights above as her smile widened. "How can this girl be related to the two Bs? My mother is their step-sister. Same father, but my *nani* was from Navi Mumbai." Her face creased into a question mark as Susan returned a dimwitted expression. "So, my maternal grandmother is from India," she added.

Squirming in her seat, Susan tried to remain calm. She knew what a nani was and had visited Mumbai some years ago during her gap year travels. She just wasn't convinced about the continued unraveling of affairs.

"Listen, Lucy. This is a leading-edge software project. It involves advanced experimental concepts and levels of integration never attempted. We need to establish an agile development framework from scratch. I need someone dependable. Someone who can assist me with writing the design specifications, implement BIOS and software kernels, who understands scalable functionality, and can debug complex code. We will be designing the UI and UX in both conventional *and* quantum programming languages. Qubits, superposition, quantum logic gates, and algorithms for—"

"Yes, I can do all of that," Lucy interrupted. "After graduating from Caltech, I've worked for Meta, Oracle, Msoft, and VMware. Recently, I was the principal team leader for the tech startup that developed CreateMyPerfectWorld."

Susan snapped to attention at the mention of the iconic virtual world-building app. "I understand that RPG took the gaming community by storm," she said. "Many believed it was real."

"Not only the gaming community, Dr. Parker, but over two billion registered users worldwide. That's almost a fifth of the planet's population all immersed in a software-generated dream world."

"My, that's impressive." She couldn't help but admire the confidence Lucy exuded as she spoke.

"Sure is. Now, when do I start?"

Susan balked, trying to think of a compelling argument why Brice Woodlands's niece would be unsuited to the position, but nothing came to mind. With her excellent background, she was undoubtedly the ideal candidate. In fact, she was *the* most qualified candidate Susan had ever had the pleasure of interviewing. "I ... err ... next Wednesday?"

Lucy smiled and winked at her. "Okay. See you first thing in the morning." She turned and walked briskly back to the door. "And Dr. Parker? Be sure to keep the door shut at all times."

Susan only nodded, then shook her head and groaned.

For a long time, Susan glared at the door in silence, daring it to open again. Once satisfied that the interruptions were over, she turned her attention to the screens. With a few quick taps on the keyboard, she inputted:

```
Sub Main ()
   Const DEFAULT_PROGNAME = "GodInTheMachine"   ' acronym GITM
   qm = QMConnection ()    ' Establish a connection to the Quantum Machine
End Sub
```

Then she hit 'Save'.

"There," she said, dropping back in her chair. "That's as good a start as any. Even the real God must have commenced at some notable point in time."

Pleased with her opening foray, she rose and turned to the whiteboard behind her. Taking the ePen provided, she aimed at the top right-hand corner and wrote: *Day 1 of 730*.

Chapter 8

Ahmad

AT 9:25 LAST TUESDAY EVENING, with Bismillah (in the name of Allah) expressed in his heart, Ahmad performed wudhu' (fresh ablution) before spreading his frayed jai-namaz (prayer mat) on the floor. Facing the Kaaba in Mecca, he stood on the mat to offer the al-ʿishā (nighttime) prayer. Making Takbir al-Ihram (raising both hands to his ears to start the prayer), he spoke. "Allāhu Akbar (God is greatest)." He then placed his hands above his navel. Casting his gaze to the floor, he recited the first rak'ah (unit of prayer) and bowed. This he did three more times until the salat (daily prayer) was complete.

Then he folded his mat, sank to the ground, and wept bitterly.

***

At suppertime the night before, Ahmad sat alone at the kitchen table, staring with melancholy into his bowl of soup. His hair had turned prematurely salt-and-pepper gray, and with a ragged beard, he appeared much older than his forty-two years. After reciting a Du'a (supplication), he held his spoon above his meal.

"Where are the children?" he said. "We should eat together."

Raising an eyebrow in amusement, Fattanah smiled. "They are not children anymore, husband. Omaid is at university and six months past nineteen. And Nikki is almost sixteen years old. They have places to go and friends to see."

When they arrived in America fifteen years before, Ahmad believed his whole life thereafter would be perfect. He reasoned that all his troubles would disappear because this was the land of the free and the home of the brave, a country of unlimited opportunities for refugees such as himself. From the beginning, life there was good for Ahmad and his family. They rented a small apartment near Kew Gardens in Queens, where he and Fattanah raised their two children. He drove a school bus while Fattanah became a lecturer in Afghan studies at NYU. After ten years of hard work and scrupulous saving, they were able to afford the down payment on an apartment close to Prospect Park in Brooklyn.

As more time passed and the children grew taller, Ahmad became increasingly disillusioned with his new life. He tried to instill the traditional ways in the children to make them appreciate the smaller things they had. He would often reinforce his stories of hardship from his younger days in Afghanistan so they might understand their good fortune. But the children refused to listen. They no longer greeted people with 'as-salāmu 'alaykum (peace be upon you)' or placed their hand upon their hearts while they spoke. Both favored the modern Western ways.

"Let them be, Ahmad," Fattanah would say. "Let them discover their own path in life, wherever it takes them."

His children had lost all respect for him and their history. They had forgotten their customs. Whenever he spoke of Allah or the Messenger, peace be upon him, they would turn and walk away, which made him angry.

Ahmad reminisced as he stared at his bowl of soup. *They do not appreciate the sacrifice that was made to bring us here,* he thought as he sipped a spoonful of soup.

"I lost my brother and his family," he moaned.

During their early years in America, he was sure to watch TV every night hoping to catch a glimpse of his older brother standing in the background of a CNN news report out of Kabul. But as time passed, his hopes diminished.

"Inshallah, do you think we will see them again?" Fattanah would sometimes ask. He would lower his eyes and shrug in reply. "I pray to Allah that one day we will see them," she used to say. Nowadays, Fattanah hardly spoke of Ahmad's older brother, or his wife and their children.

"We should at least eat together as a family," he insisted. "And our daughter's name is Nikoo, not this recent Nikki name."

"Ahmad," Fattanah said, placing a gentle hand on his shoulder and gazing into his eyes. "Let them enjoy themselves. Both Nikki and Nikoo are beautiful names. Like our daughter is. Be happy and content in her youthful beauty."

"See ya, Mom. Bye, Pops."

Nikki was down the stairs and halfway out the front door before Ahmad could raise his voice in protest. "Nikoo! Where is your hijab?" He almost choked on his mouthful of soup as he spoke.

"That's old-school, Pops," she replied. "Nobody cares anymore." Blowing him a kiss, she closed the door and was gone.

He turned to Fattanah in complete astonishment. "She has school tomorrow. It is much too late at night to be going out."

But Fattanah did not reply.

A young man then appeared at the top of the stairs. Wearing only sweatpants, he was lean and muscular through his chest and arms, much like Ahmad in his younger days. He placed a hand against the wall to steady himself before descending the stairs, one cautious step at a time. Halfway down, he noticed the pot boiling on the stove.

"Not soup again," he grumbled.

Ahmad looked up at him, frowning. "Omaid! Show respect for your mother. She has worked all afternoon preparing such a wonderful meal." He threw up his hands in hopeless frustration. "Back in Afghanistan, we did not have enough food to—"

"Yeah, yeah," Omaid cut in. "When I was young, we didn't have this, and we didn't have that. You keep telling us about your hard-luck stories to make us feel guilty. Give us a break, dude. You forced us to come here." He went to the pot and lifted the lid. "Ugh. Chicken. I'm off to McDonald's, man."

"McDonald's?" Ahmad cried. "Is that halal? And you dress yourself like a disbeliever," he groaned. "This is shameful." Shaking his head, he returned to his soup while Omaid went back upstairs to change.

After his son had departed the house, Ahmad again turned to his wife.

"Fattanah, what am I to do? All those years ago, I made a solemn promise. I swore when Allah brought us to safety that we would give thanks and devote ourselves to the Message. Now, the children are wayward, and I have failed in my oath."

Fattanah gave him a long, loving look. "Be happy, Ahmad. We are all safe, and your children have the freedom you desired."

But this made him angrier because Fattanah could never understand the terrible choices he had had to make.

Eleven o'clock came and went, and neither of the children had returned home.

"This is too late in the evening to be outside," he said to Fattanah. By then, he was fuming. "It is not safe. They have schooling in the morning."

Another hour passed before he put on his shoes and jacket and went out to search for his children.

When Ahmad found Omaid twenty minutes later, he was loitering near the shops at the corner of Flatbush and Fenimore. He waved for his son's attention, but Omaid kept pacing the street, glancing repeatedly in the direction of approaching traffic.

Just then, a beaten-up Chevy sped past. It made a quick U-turn, swerving across traffic before stopping at the curb in front of Omaid, its engine grumbling idly. When Omaid leaned into the back window, the people inside the Chevy started yelling and gesticulating at him. Then Omaid withdrew his head, and the Chevy shot away, fishtailing down the road as it did.

Ahmad broke into a lumbering run. Under his heaving breath, he prayed to Allah for the safekeeping of his children. "What is happening, Omaid?" he said as he approached his son. "Have you seen your sister?"

Omaid gave him an indifferent shrug. "Maybe two hours ago. She was with her girlfriends. Sometimes, they like to sit at the tables in the park near Picnic House and talk."

When he finally found Nikoo in Prospect Park, she was clutching a half-empty bottle and surrounded by four young men.

"Here, Nikki, Nikki, Nikki," one of the youths teased as another nudged her lewdly with an elbow. Her blouse was missing, and her head hung loose as she staggered drunkenly toward him. The first youth grabbed her from behind.

Ahmad froze. There was a moment of unspeakable panic when he saw the young man fondle his daughter's exposed breast. He tried to scream for the youth to stop, but could not speak. Open-mouthed, he shoved a hand into his jacket pocket and felt for his bundle of keys, curling his fingers around them, gripping them fiercely. With the large house key jutting between his middle and forefinger, he ripped it from his pocket and struck out, slashing the young man's cheek.

Caught off guard, the young man yelped in pain. He shoved Nikoo aside and, for a moment, she teetered, glassy-eyed, before Ahmad. Then she slumped helplessly to the ground.

The second youth rushed toward Ahmad, waving his fists threateningly in his face. "Woh, bro. Seriously?"

"She is only fifteen years old!" Ahmad yelled.

"Dude, she swore she were nineteen," the second youth replied.

"Dis girl here is jailbait, man," a third youth hissed.

"He cut my face," the first youth howled, wiping a smear of blood across his cheek.

"Hey, dudes. This here is all fucked up," the second youth said, glaring at the key still protruding from Ahmad's clenched fingers. He lowered his fists and backed away. "I'm like outta here."

Ahmad's whole world collapsed at the sight of his drunken daughter lying half-naked on the ground. Trembling with fear and rage, he rushed to her side, snatched the bottle from her grasp, and hurled it away. Then he stripped off his jacket and wrapped it around her shoulders. When he pried open her other fisted hand, he saw four pink pills.

Nikoo groaned. She peered up at him, blinking, uncertain. Then, in fleeting spasms of awareness, came recognition. "Pops?"

"How many of these did you take?" he asked, showing her the pills.

"Two ... four ... six ... I don't ..." Her eyes then rolled upward, and she started convulsing as white spittle effervesced from her slack mouth.

Ahmad cried out for help. Standing her up, he draped her arm over his shoulder, then fumbled in his pocket for his cell phone. "Ahmaq (idiot)," he cursed himself. In his haste, he had left it at home on the table. He hefted his daughter into his arms. "Call nine-one-one," he cried. But when he looked around, the youths had fled.

"Will somebody please help me?"

Ahmad prayed bā gerya o zārī ziyād (with much crying and pleading) as he carried his daughter for two blocks down 6th Street to the emergency department on 7th Avenue. After staggering through the entrance doors into the lobby, a triage nurse rushed over and took her from him, placing her unresponsive body on a gurney. The nurse asked him questions—patient's name, allergies, circumstances, insurance provider—and then showed him to the waiting area while they wheeled Nikoo away through two large sliding doors.

For a while, Ahmad sat stunned in the waiting room. A short time later, he got up and left the hospital to rejoin Omaid. Together, they would have to return home and inform Fattanah about their great misfortune.

The sweat poured from Ahmad's brow as he hurried back to the place where he had last seen his son. When he got there, Omaid was still lingering at the same corner.

"Your sister is in the hospital," he told Omaid. "She is unwell. We must tell your nana (mother)." He grabbed his son's arm, and they headed down Flatbush toward their home, with him on the inside of the sidewalk and Omaid on the curbside.

"Will she be alright?" Omaid asked.

"I am not sure," he replied grimly. He thought of Nikoo in the hospital, and Fattanah at home, and prayed for their protection.

Behind them, an engine roared as the Chevy reappeared and lumbered alongside them. A man leaned out the window.

"Hey, Omy. 'Oo da old peep whicha?" he asked, leering at them. He spat on the pavement ahead of them and laughed.

Omaid glanced nervously at the man. "Keep walking, Pop. Don't mind them."

"Pops? Hey man, dis your fa'?"

The car sped up as they quickened their pace.

"Hey, Omy. When you gonna pay your bills, man?"

Ahmad's neck muscles tensed. "What is he talking about?" he whispered to Omaid.

"Don't worry, Pop. Keep your eyes to the front and keep walking."

Ahmad was about to reach into his pocket again for the bundle of keys when he heard two sharp *pops*, followed by a squeal of tires as the Chevy sped off into the night. Beside him, Omaid dropped to his knees, clutching his side. He held out a hand to Ahmad, peering up at him in disbelief. There was blood.

Ahmad jerked backward and let out an agonizing moan.

"Call nine-one-one," he cried. He gripped his son's arms to hold him steady. "Help! Will somebody please help me?"

Ahmad held Omaid's flaccid hand as the ambulance bus hurtled down Flatbush toward the emergency department on 7th with its siren blaring. While they rushed Omaid through the two large sliding doors, the triage nurse asked Ahmad the same questions before gesturing to the waiting area. But he did not stay there long. He had to hurry home to inform his wife of their great misfortune.

When he arrived home, Fattanah was sitting rigid on the edge of the couch in the living room. From the look on her face, he could see she was wracked with worry.

"Where have you been, Ahmad? It is almost two o'clock in the morning. Where are the children?" As she stood, she saw the blood-stains on the front of his jacket. "Are you hurt?"

Ahmad shook his head. "No, Fattanah. Not me. The children. Both the children. They ..." The remaining words did not come as he broke down and cried.

Fattanah's bottom lip began to quiver as she slowly, reluctantly, comprehended the terrible news.

"I do not feel very well," she said. Then, clutching her chest, she collapsed to the floor.

"Can you believe it?" he overheard a triage nurse whisper to another nurse. "The guy almost lost his wife and both kids in one night. All separate code reds. The poor guy."

The nurse approached him as he sat alone in the waiting area. For the entire day, he had waited, bent over with his elbows on his knees, gazing at the wretched floor.

"Sir? They're all stable now. You should go home. Try to get some rest. We'll call you if there's any change in their condition."

The house was empty and lonely. After finishing the al-ʿishā (night-time) prayer, Ahmad went to bed. Earlier, he had wept bitterly at his great misfortune, and now he was heartbroken. He tossed and turned as he recounted the dreadful events of the night before. In the small hours of the morning, he got up, went downstairs, and sat on the couch.

Allah no longer favored him. The Messenger, peace be upon him, was disappointed with his endeavors. He had failed to devote himself to the Message as he had promised all those years ago. He was being punished for the terrible thing he had done. So he prayed the most powerful prayer he knew. "خدایا مرا از همه بلاها حفظ کن (O Allah, grant me āfiyah (protection from all afflictions))."

He switched on the TV to watch the late-night news. Surely, too much time had passed by now. However, with Allah's intercession, there remained the slimmest chance that he might catch a glimpse of his older brother in the background of …

Would that be enough to ease his pain?

But instead, he saw images of flames lighting the night sky in a glow of red. The wastewater plant over at Greenpoint was on fire, and raw effluent was pouring into Newtown Creek. Some people had died.

Then, the TV volume suddenly spiked for the start of the next ad break.

"Would you like to meet God?" the ad voice asked as the screen image panned up a set of marble steps, through billowing white clouds to a gilded archway that dazzled with shafts of golden light radiating from beyond.

At 3:16 in the early hours of the Wednesday morning before last, with his promise to Allah broken and his family clinging to life in the hospital, Ahmad Husseini fixed his attention on the TV.

"SoulSoft is at the cutting edge of software innovation," the TV voice continued. "We can offer you the chance of a lifetime. Be one of the first mortals to meet God in the Machine."

As he listened, Ahmad's mind raced. He knew Allah could never be present inside a machine, any more than Saxonman existed inside Brick's stereo headphones. However, the Message, like those ear-piercing songs, could.

"At SoulSoft, we have developed avant-garde technology that puts you in the presence of God. Through proprietary software, we are the first and only service that enables you to witness God in all His glory."

In his delirium and sadness, Ahmad forgot himself as fanciful ideas entered his mind. What if he could perform salat al-tawbah (prayer of repentance) within the Machine's seclusion? What if he could make direct representations on behalf of his khānvādeh (family)? Then he could take responsibility for their transgressions and waywardness in America. He would martyr himself in return for their safe healing.

"Act fast, as places are limited," the ad voice urged. "Call five-five-five, oh-one, two-three, without delay. God will see you now.

"SoulSoftneitherrepresentsnorguaranteestheparticipant'sexperienc einthepresenceofGod," the ad voice added in a lowered tone. "The-applicantwarrantstheyareaUScitizen,overeighteenyearsold,andareofso undmindandbodyblahblahblah," it said.

Chapter 9

Rebecca

AT 3:04 A.M., BECKY SAT on the floor at the end of her bed, staring at her trembling hands and struggling to breathe. The follow-up to last month's eco stunt—or the Manhattan Gridlock Maneuver, as she'd decided to call it—had just ended in disaster, and there would be serious consequences this time.

Grave consequences.

***

In the aftermath of the Manhattan Gridlock Maneuver, their mother bailed them out of the lockup and drove them the twenty miles back home to Livingston. The journey was tedious and somber. Rachel remained silent in the front seat, while Becky sat poker-faced in the back, seething at the thought of the mountains of dirty coal burning just so people could see at night, as their gas-guzzling SUV sped beneath the rows of blazing streetlights.

Wasn't the problem obvious?

When they arrived home, the girls felt the full wrath of their father. He was beyond disappointed; he told them. More than furious. They were an embarrassment to him. All over the news. What must the neighbors be thinking?

"Do you think this is all a joke?" he yelled at Becky when she laughed at the sight of his comb-over bouncing atop his head each time he stomped his foot in disgust.

Fed up with his self-absorbed ranting and old-school hangups, she stormed upstairs to her bedroom and slammed the door, leaving Rachel standing before him with her head bowed and too frightened to move. He didn't get it.

With her AirPods jammed in her ears, she cranked the volume to drown out the noise downstairs and checked her GoFundMe page: $356. She'd expected more, assuming donations would surge once people grasped the magnitude of her achievement and decided to climb aboard her eco cause.

A week later, the contributions petered out at $924.32. That left a sizable balance remaining on the credit card. 42 tungsten chains and steel pikes plus the hire of 16 removal vans, including abandonment penalties, parking fines, etc., had set her back just over $16,000. She couldn't understand the lack of public support or how little the average person cared about a sustainable future.

The answer soon became clear. Cab drivers and share riders had lost fares, traders had lost a full day's sales, and businesspeople were forced to cancel important meetings. Beyond the inconvenience, grief and support exploded for the mother who had lost her newborn due to the gridlock. The resentment was palpable.

It should never have happened, the online crowd agreed. The organizers must be held accountable, many posts said. America has fallen to eco-terrorists; one anonymous keyboard warrior wrote. They're killing our children in the streets. A travesty of justice when the culprits are still walking free. It's time to take back control. Or words to that effect.

But it was just bad luck that the kid had died. How many more might be lost unless someone brave enough took a stand? Only when the fight was won could they honor those who were martyred for the cause, Becky assured herself.

A few days later, the police came to the door asking for Rachel. Becky didn't know why, and Rachel refused to talk about it after they left half an hour later. She went to her room, slammed her door, and hadn't come out since.

That was the problem with cause-casuals, she decided. When things get tough and it's time to double down, most wannabes wilt under pressure. Not her, though, as she finalized the details for her next affirmative action stunt, or Making a Point at Greenpoint, as she dubbed it.

At 9:49 p.m., on the cusp of the follow-up operation to the Manhattan Gridlock Maneuver, Becky sat erect on an orange plastic seat, listening to the rattle of bogie wheels as the M-train crossed Williamsburg Bridge. Beside her, on the yellow seat, Jonathan Nguyen hugged his knapsack to his chest, his right knee jouncing with nervous energy. They'd boarded the last train from Bryant Park sixteen minutes earlier, en route to Williamsburg, where she'd arranged for a mini-van to pick them up from the corner of Marcy and Broadway at 22:00 hours sharp.

"So, what's the plan, Bec?" Jonathan asked as they descended the steel stairway to Marcy.

As a recent addition to her squad, he was a wannabe eco-warrior. Following Rachel's untimely departure, she needed a new sidekick, another Robin to her Batman. He wanted to be active in the movement's top hierarchy, at the decision-making level, except he lacked the street smarts, or so she claimed. His heart was in the right place, but when push came to shove, she doubted whether he had the guts to follow through. So, she kept him at the bottom of her need-to-know list. And right now, he didn't need to know a thing.

"You just keep your looking eyes peeled and your listening ears close to the ground," she replied. "Comprehend, Tonto?"

As they stepped onto Marcy, he nodded in the affirmative.

The van arrived on time. The driver stepped out, spoke briefly with Becky, then accepted a fistful of twenties. A cash advance on her Visa. Moments later, a second van pulled up. When the side door slid open, five figures dressed in black ninja gear spilled onto the sidewalk.

"Oel ngati kameie (I see you)," Becky said to them. As she spoke, she motioned with a hand to her forehead, extending it respectfully downward toward them. "I am Mo'at." After they mirrored the greeting, she pointed at Jonathan. "Neytiri, Kiri, Neteyam, Lo'ak, and Ronal, this here is White Rabbit."

"Olay n … ngoti komaninie," Jonathan said, fumbling with his knapsack as he attempted to replicate their elaborate greeting.

Rolling her eyes, she shoved him toward the second van. "Just hop in back," she told him through clenched teeth. Then she passed another bundle of twenties to the second driver before climbing aboard. "Balaclavas on," she said.

"Where are we going, Bec?" He was sitting beside her with an idiotic grin, while struggling admirably with his balaclava. "Is it far? What's the prime objective for the mission once we get there?"

She jabbed his shoulder. "Mo'at, you idiot. I'm Mo'at."

As they trailed the first van through the backstreets of Greenpoint, the whites of his flickering eyes betrayed his growing nerves. She doubted his competence, but he was tall and strong, and she needed somebody to do the heavy lifting while she had the chance to stand back and size up the situation. She turned to Neteyam.

"We take the indirect route there. In case we have a shadow. To throw them off our tail."

At the intersection of Franklin and Greenpoint Avenue, the vans turned right toward Newtown Creek, left into Kingsland, then a quick left again before stopping.

"Are we there yet, Bec? Um … Mo'at?"

The driver stepped out. Seconds later, the side door slid open, and they piled out.

"This, comrades, is one of the city's most polluting sites," Mo'at said, pointing across the nearby steel security fence in disgust.

"The wastewater plant?" said White Rabbit.

"See those digesters?" She shifted their attention to eight massive egg-shaped structures beyond the fence. "They treat three hundred million gallons of sewage daily, converting it to biogas, mostly methane. It was *supposed* to feed into the local gas grid, but they're flaring it instead, burning the methane and pumping tons of CO2 into the atmosphere." She gestured to the four tall flare towers beside the nearest egg. "This is an environmental disaster on our doorstep, yet no one speaks up. There's no accountability."

Mo'at glowered at the structures. A blue glow washed over their bronze surfaces while the brilliantly lit walkways interconnecting them dazzled overhead. Deceptively beautiful against the darkness. But their beauty masked their reprehensible purpose. She swung away from the flare towers, appalled, then returned to the first van, slid open the back door, and heaved out a large burlap roll.

"We're climbing to the top of those digesters to unfurl this banner across the walkway facing the city. We're going to hold the negligent citizens accountable for this looming disaster."

Hugging his knapsack to his chest, White Rabbit peered through the slit in his balaclava at the structures. "Climb it? How will we hold the banner *and* keep our grip on those curved surfaces?"

"No, you idiot." She thumped his arm hard enough to make him squeal. "There's an elevator inside. We jump the fence, take it to the top, and presto. And look, no security."

She was right. There was no exclusion wire above the fence or security patrols in sight.

After shoving his knapsack through a narrow gap at the bottom of the fence, White Rabbit followed Mo'at over the top.

"Bec?" he whispered halfway over.

"What?" she snapped.

"Why do I have to be White Rabbit? Why can't I be someone from Avatar, too?"

She hissed at him to be quiet.

She heaved the banner over the fence, then dragged it past the flare towers. After discovering the elevator to the west-side digesters out of order, Ronal picked the stairwell lock. With the help of White Rabbit, Kiri, and Neytiri, she hauled the banner up eleven flights to the top, while Lo'ak and Ronal carried ropes. Neteyam pushed open a roof panel and stepped outside onto the top of the walkway, followed by Kiri and Mo'at. Then they pulled the banner through the opening, roped it up, and let it unfurl:

STOP KILLING THE PLANET!

The message was unequivocal, visible for the two miles across the East River to the city. Furthermore, Mo'at had arranged for six Geico Skytypers—at $3,000 apiece—to spray the 400-foot message in the skies above lower Manhattan at nine o'clock sharp. Then, for an additional $5,500 plus taxes, a vintage Tiger Moth would tow a matching banner across the city between ten and eleven. All on the credit card. This would be the greatest eco stunt ever inflicted on the indifferent masses.

With the banner draped beneath them, they danced and cheered 150 feet above the ground. They whooped and hollered. Until things suddenly turned weird ...

Thirty minutes later, the stout policewoman stood on Kingsland Avenue, staring wide-eyed at the chaos beyond the Newtown Creek wastewater treatment facility fence.

"Oh, Lordy," she muttered, shaking her head. "What have those damn fool kids done now?"

Back in her bedroom, Becky struggled to make sense of what had happened earlier that night in Greenpoint.

After they unfurled the banner atop the digester eggs, everything spiraled out of control. It occurred so fast, without warning. Laughing and joking, they had descended the egg and were heading back to the vans when White Rabbit veered away toward the flare towers. Somehow, he'd brought along explosives in his knapsack—two metal cylinders packed with saltpeter, potassium, and charcoal. Moments later, a massive fireball erupted. Her last clear memory was of White Rabbit crawling along the ground toward her with his face red and blistered and clothes on fire. She dragged him clear, smothered the flames with her coat, then searched frantically for Lo'ak and Kiri, who had followed him over to the flare towers. She screamed for Neteyam, Neytiri, and Ronal, with no reply. There was only Jonathan, writhing in pain on the ground. The others had vanished.

"You stupid idiot, Jonathan," she muttered. "Why would you do such a stupid thing?"

With her hands still trembling, she grabbed the remote and turned on the TV.

Breaking News: She saw images of the Greenpoint wastewater plant engulfed in flames. "Several youths are dead," the female reporter announced somberly. "And now, an unmitigated disaster is unfolding as the last two digesters have ruptured, spilling tens of thousands of gallons of raw sewage into Newtown Creek by the hour."

Then, the TV volume suddenly spiked for the start of the next ad break.

"Would you like to meet God?" the ad voice asked as the screen image panned up a set of marble steps, through billowing white clouds to a gilded archway that dazzled with shafts of golden light radiating from beyond.

At 3:16 in the early hours of Wednesday morning before last, with her world in crisis, Becky Jones stared aghast at the TV.

"SoulSoft is at the cutting edge of software innovation," the ad voice continued. "We can offer you the chance of a lifetime. Be one of the first mortals to meet God in the Machine."

As she listened, her heart raced at the possibilities. Was this her chance to lay the blame for the whole confounded mess right at the feet of the real culprit?

"At SoulSoft, we have developed avant-garde technology that puts you in the presence of God. Through proprietary software, we are the first and only service that enables you to witness God in all His glory."

Becky wondered. If she met God face-to-face, would *They* listen to her? If she yelled at *Them* for allowing the world to become so broken, would *They* see her pain and rectify the problem? Then she could end her struggle, Rachel would be happy again, and her parents would be proud of her. If God became involved and set things right, the planet and everything on it might have a chance.

"Act fast, as places are limited," the ad voice urged. "Visit www-dot-godinthemachine-dot-hvn, without delay. God will see you now.

"SoulSoftneitherrepresentsnorguaranteestheparticipant'sexperienc einthepresenceofGod," the ad voice added in a lowered tone. "The-applicantwarrantstheyareaUScitizen,overeighteenyearsold,andareofso undmindandbodyblahblahblah," it said.

Chapter 10

Bryan

AT EIGHT MINUTES PAST ten in the morning, two days before Susan Parker received the telephone call that changed her life, Bryan Woodlands sat across the desk from Dr. Nigel Smith. His mouth and nose were concealed behind a white KN95 mask, and in his rubber-gloved hands, he held a report, which the doctor had just given him. Some of it made sense, but much of the jargon went over his head. One word, though, leaped off the page and ripped at his insides.

Cancer.

"I'm sorry, Bryan," Dr. Smith said. "Your last PSA test was over four years ago. Given your age, you should have been more vigilant."

Bryan straightened. "Well, I've been busy," he replied defensively.

Dr. Smith furrowed his brow. "If we'd caught it in time, things might be different. Early detection leads to an almost hundred percent survival rate these days. But in your case, the cancer is what we term 'mCRPC' and has already metastasized beyond the prostate. To the distant lymph nodes and the liver."

Removing his spectacles, Bryan wiped the moisture from his eyes. "So, what's the prognosis?" he asked after taking a moment to regain his composure.

The doctor shifted uneasily in his seat. He was twirling a long red pencil, end over end, in his fingers, which may have been a coping mechanism for delivering bad news. But that didn't help Bryan at all.

"Well, every case is different," he replied. "The five-year relative survival rate for stage four is now as high as thirty-eight percent. Yours, however, has progressed to what we classify as 'stage four-B'." He paused, his lengthy sigh prolonging the inevitable verdict. "I'm sorry, Bryan, but it can't be cured."

Showing no emotion, Bryan lowered his head as the doctor's harrowing words struck his core with their message of finality. He clenched his fists, wishing he could be anywhere but here.

"Our job is to make you as comfortable as possible for the time remaining," Dr. Smith continued. "There are some very promising experimental treatments available. To manage the symptoms and side effects until palliative—"

"How long do I have, Nigel?" he said softly. Raising his head again, he locked eyes with the doctor. "Please, without the standard sympathy spiel."

Dr. Smith paused again. "The bottom line? I would limit your life plans to the next two years. Any extension beyond that will only be at the grace of God."

Bryan's gut muscles clenched, forcing the bitter taste of bile to rise at the back of his mouth. This was unfair. *Life* was unfair. Unlike his brother, he'd always taken great care of his physical self. He never smoked or drank alcohol. He shunned all contact with others to the extent that he had no wife or progeny. He'd been prudent in his choice of foodstuffs. Nuts, fruits, and vegetables, with occasional protein boosts. Without fail, he wore a face mask and rubber gloves in public and took vitamins to ward off sickness and disease. He'd always been meticulous in his interactions with the outside world.

So now, he was finding it difficult to process the fact that he'd messed up. Due to a foolish, inexcusable oversight, he had prostate cancer. And only two years remaining, God willing.

"How long have they given you?" Brice asked in a gruff but concerned voice.

Two days after the dreadful news, Bryan sat hunched forward on the edge of a leather armchair in the drawing room of his brother's penthouse atop Central Park Tower. Across from him, Brice reclined cross-legged on a three-seater couch, a half-filled tumbler of twelve-year-old Glenfiddich resting on the coffee table between them.

Bryan adjusted his spectacles. "Two years," he replied.

Brice immediately uncrossed his legs and sat bolt upright. A worried look, like wildfire through a tinderbox field, swept across his face. "Is it hereditary? Will I—"

"No," Bryan spat back before his brother could alarm himself further. "The doctor assures me it's a somatic variant caused by a DNA alteration. It's not contagious either. So, there's no need to upset yourself about my presence here."

"My God! DNA alteration? How the heck did that happen? Of all the people I know, you are the most pedantic, obsessive, compulsive—"

Bryan shot an icy glance at his brother.

"Thank you, Brice. That's just what I need to hear right now."

Brice snatched his drink off the table and sank back into his chair. "I was only stating the obvious," he sulked. "Sometimes the words fly out of my mouth before I know I've said them."

Bryan stood. "Sometimes?" he said, raising an eyebrow. He crossed the room to the drinks cabinet and retrieved a bottle of mineral water from the mini-fridge.

"Sorry, I didn't mean it that way," Brice replied. His facial expression then changed to pity, which only made matters worse. "I'm a bit rattled by the news. You know I can't do any of *this* without you." He spread his arms to signify 'this' included everything in the room.

In their younger years, the brothers had lived fortunate lives.

Nannies, expensive toys, private schools, and handpicked friends. Together with their wayward and illegitimate stepsister, Echo, they were the offspring of wealthy parents who had acquired their fortune by investing in the now-defunct technology companies. With the money he made, their father, Barry, founded Woodlands & Co., where he dabbled in commercial property development. After an unfortunate avalanche in the Swiss Alps claimed their parents' lives, the two boys inherited the family fortune—the platform for their present-day business empire—before they'd turned thirty. If Brice was the brawn of the operation, then Bryan was undoubtedly the brains. His attention to detail and acute business acumen were instrumental in turning the old Woodlands & Co. into the remarkable success story it is today. And their younger stepsister, Echo? Well, she remained wayward and not the least bit interested in their business affairs.

With his eyes trained steadily on Bryan, Brice sipped his drink.

"So, what can we do for you, Bryan?" he said after a while. "Perhaps we can get the finest doctors on the case? Research? Yes, research! That's the answer! We'll buy a whole bloody laboratory and fill it full of equipment and anything else they need to solve this damn thing. We'll stop it dead in its tracks and cure you, pronto. We—"

"Do you still believe in God?" Bryan interrupted. Brice recoiled at the question, the astonishment on his face taking Bryan by surprise. "Not the fairytale one we learned about as kids in Sunday school, but the real God. The one we're supposed to stand before on judgment day after we die." He unscrewed the cap on the water bottle, lifted it to his lips, and took a sip.

"I'm not sure there's such a thing as a real God," Brice replied guardedly. "We're here on our own. We've always been on our own."

Lowering the bottle, Bryan studied the label on the side. "Before I die, I'd like to know if I'm going to heaven," he announced after a short deliberation.

"Heaven?" Brice appeared shocked. "Where are these foolish notions coming from? You're smarter than that, Bryan. And if there is a heaven, then I'm sure you've done enough good to deserve your place there. Heck, we'll buy you a condo up there and have it ready for your arrival when the time comes. If it comes. Maybe the doc got it wrong."

"I'm being serious," Bryan said, returning to his seat. He set the water bottle gently on the coffee table, then locked eyes with Brice. "I want to make sure there are enough Brownie points in here,"—he placed a hand over his heart and tapped his chest—"to get me into heaven."

Brice fell silent, caught off guard by the notion that anyone's place in heaven can be assured as he stared at his brother in disbelief. "Okay," he eventually said. "What do we do to guarantee your place in heaven? Engage a padre? Visit a fortuneteller? Sacrifice a virgin, maybe?"

"We create God in the Machine," Bryan said.

Brice appeared more shocked than ever. "What? God? In a Machine? I'm not sure that's possible."

"Not the real God," Bryan replied in a pained voice. "It will be a simulation." Still staring at Brice, he leaned forward in his seat and breathed deeply. He was never more certain of himself than he was right now. "I've been doing some research. With the impressive advances in artificial intelligence today, I'm sure we can create a version of God using software. We build a framework around all the attributes that make up God, then incorporate the rules and regulations that govern the entry into heaven—"

"But whose God will we create?" Brice cut in, suddenly flustered as he fumbled with his drink. "Everybody seems to have their own crazy notions of who or what God is nowadays."

"We include them all," Bryan replied with confidence. "Every single 'God is this' and 'God is that'. Every instance of 'thou shalt' and 'thou shalt not'. They all go into the big melting pot to make our God."

"Then what? Do you take a quick pop quiz? Answer a thousand and one questions to see if you pass the 'get into heaven' test?"

"Nothing like that," he replied. Since the initial gut slam from the diagnosis, he'd sat alone in his apartment for two full days without sleep, working through to—what he considered—the perfect solution. "Here's the genius of it all. Once we've created our computer version of God, we take a copy of my soul and upload it into the Machine. If it passes the virtual test, then I'll have the confidence of entering the real heaven after I die. It's the perfect plan. With a few additional details to be sorted out as we go."

"Additional details? Sorted out as we go? I'm not so sure about this, Bryan. And how the heck do we get your *soul* out of *you* and into a bloody machine?"

Bryan's eyes glinted with excitement. "We find the right people, specialists who understand the inner workings of the mind. We use cutting-edge technology. Advanced computing. I've been Googling," he announced proudly. "I found someone with the necessary qualifications and experience to pull this off. She's perfect for the job."

"You've been Googling?" Brice shook his head in dismay. "That all sounds a bit bloody complicated. A pop quiz sure sounds easier to me."

With a flick of his hand, Bryan dismissed his brother's concern. "Think about it, Brice. There has to be more to it than ticking boxes on a survey form. If all I have to do is answer a few contrived questions, I could easily misrepresent myself. I might choose whatever answer I think God wants to hear. So, I'd never know if I would hold up against proper spiritual scrutiny. Whereas, if my soul is laid bare, it can't be falsified or misinterpreted. And if the software compares all the requirements for entering heaven with the entire contents of my soul, then I'll have certainty in the result. I tell you, Brice, it's foolproof."

Brice stood, staring miserably at his brother. In one swig, he drained his tumbler and went to the drinks cabinet. "I'm still not sure," he muttered, refilling his glass. "Isn't there something about camels passing through the eyes of needles to get into heaven? This harebrained scheme of yours sure sounds a whole lot harder than that."

"Trust me, Brice. This will work."

Lowering the cell phone from his ear, Brice shrugged.

"She hung up on me," he said indignantly. "Thought I was a hoax caller."

Bryan couldn't hide his frustration. He'd just finished explaining everything at length to his brother. Set up the IT infrastructure, hire the most capable neuro-software specialist in the world, and commence coding. In a nutshell, the plan was simple.

"No wonder," he snapped. "It's after nine-thirty at night." He flicked a forefinger at his brother's phone, motioning for him to try again. "Without her, we're dead in the water."

After dialing a second time, Brice kept Susan Parker on the line long enough to convince her that he was indeed the *actual* Brice Woodlands of Woodland & Woodland & Co. fame.

"I have a proposition I'd like to discuss with you," he told her. "No, I can't give you the specifics over the phone; however, if you would care to meet at my office. This is a once-in-a-lifetime opportunity. Tomorrow afternoon at five? That would be perfect. I'll have my assistant message the address. Thank you, Dr. Parker. I look forward to seeing you then. Goodbye for now."

By the time the call ended, Bryan was rubbing his palms together in jubilation, already devising the next step in his plan. The approach to Dr. Parker appeared to have gone surprisingly well.

"The first piece of the puzzle is now in play," he said. "But we won't disclose anything about myself or my condition. It might lead to unwarranted distractions, unnecessary pressure to perform."

Frustrated, Brice threw up his hands. "Then what the bloody heck do I tell her?"

"That we wish to create a virtual reality where people can converse with a simulated God," he replied tersely. He paused, stroking his chin in thought before continuing. "We say this is a commercial venture. Try to appeal to her professional ego: unparalleled AI; state-of-the-art computer engineering; never-before-attempted technology. Once the concept has been tested using volunteers, I'll masquerade as the first paying customer. She can never know the project's real purpose."

"What if she says no?"

"Like I said, if she can't be convinced, then …" He fell silent as he considered the ramifications of a life lived without a guarantee of the promised heavenly reward. His entire existence would be rendered meaningless, whereas he should at least be assured of his destiny beyond the grave, he decided. Especially since he'd led such a self-restrained and wholesome lifestyle. "Can you do it, Brice?"

His brother grimaced, then looked squarely back at him. "Yes, I can convince her," he replied.

After donning his mask and rubber gloves, Bryan got up and headed for the door. As he opened it, he turned to his brother. "Two years," he said. "She must complete the task within two years. No matter the cost."

Bryan strode home with a spring in his step. He felt strangely liberated. After revealing his outlandish plan to Brice, the unbearable weight that had burdened him for the past two days seemed at least manageable. While he was confident his brother had understood exactly none of the plan's technical aspects—most people would have dismissed him as outright crazy—at least Brice had given a firm commitment to the way forward. And if anything, Brice could always be taken at his word. The horrid outcome hadn't changed, yet he felt his chances in the afterlife might now be assured, and he sensed a glimmer of hope in the gloom.

After arriving home, he scrolled through the contacts list on his cell phone. He selected an entry and hit the call icon.

"Hello, Lucy? It's Uncle Bryan. Yes, it's nice to hear your voice, too, honey. How is your mom? That's nice to hear. Are you married yet? A partner then? Not to worry, you're still young and have time.

"Tell me, dear, what are you doing at the moment?"

Chapter 11

Thomas

ON THE ISLAND OF Madagascar, two days after Thomas went long in a sizable parcel of apricot contracts, a lepidopteran—a Chrysiridia rhipheus sunset moth with iridescent black, red, blue, and green markings—fluttered its dazzling wings. The tiny vortex created by the sudden movement shook a leaf from the baobab tree on which it had been resting. Spiraling to the ground, the leaf settled beside a fish eagle, which took flight in surprise. At the unexpected sight of the fish eagle taking to the air, a flock of a dozen winging storks suddenly veered straight into the flight path of an Airbus A380-800, which had departed Ivato International Airport only moments earlier. The Airbus pilot banked sharply left, taking immediate evasive action, and deviated away, thus creating enough air turbulence to upset the upward vortexes in the Indian Ocean and affect the wind pattern that somehow redirected Hurricane Eloise—which had been forming over the waters south of India and east of Reunion Island—on a course over Oman, Saudi Arabia, Iraq, then Syria, toward the Black Sea. The same hurricane that, yesterday, flattened the apricot plantations across all of Türkiye.

At least, that's how Thomas fantasized about it unfolding.

Pushing back in his chair, he propped his feet on the desk and grinned with quiet satisfaction.

Howsoever it transpired, his punt on apricots was the best ever return from his investments. At a minimum, he'd expected any profit from his punt on apricots to take years of patience and crossed fingers while praying to the gods of serendipity for drought to set in. Instead, he'd reaped millions in only days after the unprecedented climatic catastrophe brought about by Hurricane Eloise. Not in his wildest dreams had he expected a once-in-a-thousand-year event to be the key to his investment success. Most people would say he was lucky, in the right place at the right time. But it wasn't just luck. He was the one with the instinct and gumption to follow through. To him, it was all about the money made, not *how* it was made.

Apricots by hurricane. Who'd have thought?

The office door swung open , and Jonas burst into the office.

"I swear, man, you are incredible. You pour all our money into fruit halfway across the world based on nothing but a hunch about the weather. Then two days later, a goddamn hurricane appears from nowhere, wipes out all the apricot plantations, and makes us an eighty-nine percent profit overnight. Man, we should bottle whatever instincts you have and sell that as well."

Thomas smiled. "Technically, it's less than eighty-nine. Once you account for broker fees, the cost of money invested, etcetera."

Jonas waved him off. "It's still a decent return. What next? How about we go short on gold futures? Maybe a war breaks out somewhere in Africa. Or a military coup in the Philippines. Oh, man, the gold mines there will close, and we'll make millions."

Thomas shook his head. Reaching across his desk, he flipped open the lid of a long wooden box and removed a $100 Cohiba. Drawing it across his nostrils, he inhaled the woody aroma.

"Gold's too volatile. If we short it, and the gold price explodes, our exposure is unlimited. That's a lot of risk."

"So, what then?"

"Russian wheat futures," he replied, clipping an exact eighth of an inch off the end of his Cohiba.

Jonas balked. "Hey, man. I'm not sure we should be dealing with the Russians."

"We're not dealing with the Russians, Jonas. We're trading in an open market. Anything goes."

He sparked his silver lighter: a special gift from Jackie on his last significant birthday. Holding the flame to his Cohiba, he took three strong puffs without inhaling until a thick cloud of sweet-smelling smoke engulfed his head.

"Listen. The Russians supply nearly one-third of global wheat demand, which presents a compelling opportunity. Our good friend, La Niña, might accelerate the snowmelt, which could flood the wheat fields. A significant drop in Russian wheat will send the global price higher. We take a long position now and wait. It's that simple."

"Simple? Might? Could?" muttered Jonas with a grim head shake.

Thomas shrugged, then pushed back in his chair and took a long, enjoyable draw on his Cohiba.

Perhaps it was the aftereffects of Hurricane Eloise as she headed east after passing over the Black Sea. Maybe it was climate change at work. Howsoever it happened, three days after Thomas took a substantial position in wheat futures, a thick blanket of overnight frost descended on the entire North Caucasus, which—as he later discovered—is located a thousand miles south of Moscow. When the sun rose on that fateful day, the unseasonal event resulted in total floret sterility, triggering catastrophic yield losses across the North Caucasus wheat-growing region. By mid-morning, forty percent of Russia's crops had been wiped out, and the price of wheat futures on the Chicago Board of Trade soared.

Wheat by frost. Who'd have thought?

Jonas burst into his office again.

"I tell you, man, you have a gift. You buy some wheat contracts, wait a few days for Mother Nature, divine intervention, or whatever to— And then— Well, you know the story."

Thomas smiled again. Mother Nature or not, in just three days, his play in CBOT wheat futures had netted the firm tens of millions of dollars. He felt giddy at the speed of his unexpected good fortune.

"What's next?" Jonas pressed. "The phones haven't stopped all morning. The clients want in on the next deal. Money's pouring into the trading accounts like candy into jack-o'-lantern buckets at Halloween. Everybody wants a piece of your action. They're desperate for more."

Thomas hesitated. His successes were now coming at breakneck speed, faster than he could plan their next investment.

"Gold futures," Jonas said. "No, that's right. Too risky. Livestock? Rare earths?"

"Um … I'm not sure yet, Jonas."

Jonas snapped his fingers. "Coffee! A fungus or some exotic insect wipes out all the coffee plants in Brazil." He didn't pause or take a breath while the rambling details of his harebrained idea spilled from his quivering mouth. "The price of coffee beans plummets … No, it rises … Does it rise or fall, Thomas?" He threw up his hands. "Doesn't matter. We buy anyway." He looked at Thomas like a child begging for a bauble at the supermarket checkout. "We need something. A prospectus. A plan. Anything before they take their money elsewhere."

Thomas clutched his side and winced. The twinges were becoming more frequent, more intense, and sometimes, like this one, lingered for a good fifteen seconds. It wasn't just Jonas, pacing in front of him, waving his arms. It was the unrealistic expectations. Every decision he made had to be more lucrative than the last. Like doubling up on the roulette table in the firm belief that the silver ball will always fall your way, the hysteria from each success was being reinvested tenfold into the next venture. And he *had* to keep delivering.

"I want a blue, flying Tesla," Jackie announced as they sat at the dining table, eating arancini and rigatoni con salsiccia from Giano's.

"Pardon?"

"Blue. Flying. Tesla," she repeated.

"But I already bought you a Maserati."

"But nothing. You've made lots of money for everyone else, and now I want my flying Tesla. Don't you remember I've *always* said I wanted one?"

Thomas pushed his plate aside. He'd barely touched his food and was no longer hungry. Everyone wanted something from him, and he had no idea what to do next. Lucrative opportunities didn't just spring into existence with a snap of your fingers. The responsibility of managing other people's money was a serious matter. Even though he'd been lucky so far, backing number four in the fifth because it has a funny name, or the jockey is wearing your favorite colors, wouldn't cut it. He was honor-bound to protect the client's financial interests.

A firefly flitted haphazardly outside his study window. He'd never seen one this late in the year. Yet there it was. Just the one. In the Ozarks, they would claim it carried a message from heaven. From God. He wondered how anyone, even God—if he existed—could help with his problem.

He dabbed a bead of sweat from his forehead, then reached for his cell phone. After scrolling through the contacts list, he jabbed a finger at the speed-dial button.

"Brenda?" He could hear his own voice, yet it seemed as if he wasn't the one talking.

"Yes, I know it's been a long time. Jackie? Yes, she's fine. No, no kids yet. But when the time is right— Oh! You have five? That must keep you busy." A pause. "Yes, I appreciate my call is unexpected. However, remember when you gave me the heads-up about that company making ... um ... Yes. Software applications. That's right,

CreateMyPerfectWorld." Another pause. "No, I decided not to invest in the end. I wish I had, though. That penny stock is now worth a hundred and twenty-six apiece— I'm glad you did well out of it. Anyway, the purpose of my call. I have a few clients who are prepared to take on some *additional* risk. I'm on the lookout for any opportunities you may have heard whispers about. Something that might be about to break out. You know, a snippet of information from the sidelines."

He leaned back in his chair, attentive as Brenda spoke.

"Jetson Resources, you say. I thought they were Canadian gold miners. No, I wasn't aware they were considering branching into robotics. Plus AI? That sounds very interesting. So, they're ready to report to the market? And their profits will quadruple? In a quarter? That sounds perfect. No, I won't say anything to anyone. You can rely on my absolute discretion. Yes, I understand the implications. Thank you, Brenda. And have a good night yourself."

A week after going all-in on Jetson Resources, the stock price tripled on the news of their acquisition of a major robotics development firm.

Robotics. Who'd have thought?

Jonas burst into his office again.

"I tell you, man, you are the gift that keeps giving! How did you know to change tack to shares?"

Thomas couldn't help smiling. His Jetson play had netted his firm and clients over $150 million. With the usual service fee …

"What's next?" Jonas insisted. "We need—"

Four days after Thomas shorted half a billion shares of Jetson Resources, news of the sudden death of the founder and key employee of its new robotics division shocked the market. The share price plummeted, and Thomas cleared a cool $954 million profit.

Robotics again. Who would've—

"This is insane! Unbelievable!" yelled Jonas. "You have the Midas touch! How did you know to short the same stock that you made a killing on only two weeks ago? It's uncanny. Phenomenal."

Thomas said nothing. Without smiling, he stared out his office window, gazing blankly at the Hudson.

"What's next?" Jonas demanded. "We need—"

Thomas collapsed on the couch, tugging ruefully at his ear. The pressure of finding the next surefire investment was unbearable, and staying ahead of the game was taking a heavy toll on his wellbeing. Everybody was at him. Jonas wanted instant ideas, clients expected even greater returns, and earlier in the evening, Jackie had demanded a second flying Tesla. A pink one, she pointed out, for weekend trips to the country.

His world was spinning out of control.

He grabbed the TV remote, grimacing as another twinge set in— this one lasting a good thirty seconds. Flipping through the channels in search of the latest Bloomberg report, he caught a glimpse of a large structure engulfed in flames as a channel skipped past. He quickly flicked back. In breaking news, twelve NYFD appliances were battling a major out-of-control fire at the local wastewater treatment plant. The camera then cut to a news reporter, who was hurrying toward the scene for a close-up.

"A number of young people are believed to be involved," she wheezed. "Some have suffered serious injuries while several others are dead," she added with a mortified look.

Then, the TV volume suddenly spiked for the start of the next ad break.

"Would you like to meet God?" the ad voice asked as the screen image panned up a set of marble steps, through billowing white clouds to a gilded archway that dazzled with shafts of golden light radiating from beyond.

At 3:16 in the early hours of the Wednesday morning before last, with the weight of the world on his shoulders, Thomas Feldman Jr. locked his full attention on the TV.

"SoulSoft is at the cutting edge of software innovation," the ad voice continued. "We can offer you the chance of a lifetime. Be one of the first mortals to meet God in the Machine."

Thomas scoffed at the notion that something that didn't exist could be created in a machine. People were too gullible. And whose idea of God would it be? It all sounded fanciful. But wait, you might also get a set of steak knives. But wait, there's more. He chuckled with mild amusement.

"At SoulSoft, we have developed avant-garde technology that puts you in the presence of God. Through proprietary software, we are the first and only service that enables you to witness God in all His glory."

Then, a bizarre idea hit him. If he spoke to this AI God, it might help with the unreasonable expectation everyone had of him. If he could articulate his troubles in the universal cloud, it might offer some helpful suggestions. Could anyone's God prove useful for once and be there for him when he needed it most?

"Act fast, as places are limited," the ad voice urged. "Call five-five-five, oh-one, two-three, without delay. God will see you now.

"SoulSoftneitherrepresentsnorguaranteestheparticpant'sexperience inthepresenceofGod," the ad voice added in a lowered tone. "TheapplicantwarrantstheyareaUScitizen,overeighteenyearsold,andareofso undmindandbodyblahblahblah," it said.

Chapter 12

Susan

AT 5:59 A.M. ON THE DAY after project commencement, Susan completed the day's first significant task by updating the whiteboard: *Day 2 of 730*. She spent the remainder of the morning compiling the pivotal milestones for the GITM (God in the Machine) project, followed by the beginnings of a level three Gantt chart. Around mid-afternoon, the lab door creaked open, and a burly worker backed in, hefting one end of a couch. A second worker appeared, blowing hard and shuffling forward, holding up the other end. It was a blue fabric couch, reminiscent of an old-time sitcom where the nuclear family would all be seated on it, watching TV while eating their dinner.

Susan had no immediate family to speak of. She'd always been too busy with work to notice anyone or be noticed in a romantic sense. There was no for-life partner or thoughts of children. She was the only child of a single parent, after her father had walked out on them when she was five years old, or so her mother told her. She was unsure of the exact details because she had no firm recollection. There were no photographs of him on mantelpieces or saved on devices. It had always been her and her mom for as long as she could recall.

That was until two years ago, on the dreadful day when—

"Where do you want it, doc?" the backward-traveling worker asked while, more importantly for the Faraday cage, the forward-traveling one nudged the door closed with a boot heel.

"Anywhere you like, thank you," she replied.

The workers set the couch down in front of her desk, away from her, facing the back wall. They left the room and returned ten minutes later with a 98-inch TV, which they mounted—with much noise from drilling holes and knees-bent hefting—on the wall.

"Sorry, Doc, but the TV doesn't have reception," the first worker said. "Faraday cage and all. You can watch tape recordings using the VCR, though." The worker pointed to a small black box, which he had placed on a squat cabinet beneath the TV.

"A VC, what?" she said, gaping at the black box. The whole situation had become so bizarre that she now expected the unexpected as a matter of course. And the absurd to boot.

Day 3 of 730. When she arrived at the lab at 7:16 a.m., the workers had already delivered Lucy's desk together with a chair, an array of 20-inch monitors, a keyboard, and a mouse, the same as hers. Robert was wiring power to the equipment, and Lucy hadn't yet arrived.

"Good morning, Robert."

"Morning … Dr. … Parker."

Pouring herself a cup of coffee, she observed Robert, wedged upside-down under Lucy's desk, compressed into a ball. It never ceased to amaze her how the IT people could work themselves into tiny awkward spaces and continue to function.

"I require a NeuroAnalyzer and a DreamDigitizer," she informed him. "To detect and extract cognitive activity in the test subjects and then record the resulting data. We'll begin with rats before progressing to primates. Then we might try dolphins. A whale would be a bonus, depending on practicalities. Unfortunately, I suspect animals don't have the kind of soul we're looking for, so we'll have to use a human subject eventually."

"That … sounds … challenging … Dr. … Parker," he replied. His breathing became labored as he cocked his head to the side and thrust out his tongue while connecting the wazamagadget to the dohickything.

"To be honest, I'm not sure where to begin looking for the soul," she mused aloud. "Somewhere in the temporal lobe, perhaps. Maybe in the gray matter between the memory processing and emotion zones?"

Robert extracted his spidery frame from beneath the desk. He straightened. "There, all set," he said, flexing the muscles in his back and shoulders. "I'm sure you'll find it, Dr. Parker. It's always in the last place you look." For the first time, he gave her a hint of a friendly smile. An IT 'in-joke'.

She returned his smile, pleased that the lab was filling. The echoing emptiness had gone, and things were now happening at an industrious rate.

The lab door opened and snapped closed.

"Good morning, Lucy," she said.

Day 7 of 730. Susan was too busy to notice the man entering the lab. Yet there he was, standing beside her desk: small, wiry, bespectacled, and quiet as a mouse. For the third time in the past three days, he'd appeared from nowhere. On each occasion, he kept his face mask on and yellow rubber gloves sheathed to his elbows.

"Oh, you gave me a fright," she said to the man. She still maintained this was the younger brother, Bryan; however, he hadn't bothered to introduce himself, and since the visits had gone on for a while now, she felt somewhat awkward asking his name.

"How's it going?" he asked in his muffled, high-pitched voice. "Fine? Good. Good." He gestured to the VCR. "I have thousands of movies. Good movies." He turned away and was making for the door. "Anything you need, just—"

Before he could brush her off, she blurted out, "I need an electro-encephalograph, a NeuroAnalyzer, plus a DreamDigitizer."

"Yes, yes. Orders have been placed. Everything will be here at the project midpoint," he said and shut the door.

Day 10 of 730. With Lucy's invaluable contribution, plus the neuro-equipment delivery date factored in, Susan completed the Gantt chart for the GITM project. It contained her plan for the next 720 days, including design, coding, locate the soul, extract and upload soul data, deploy God in the Machine, and then test and verification. Several tasks remained short on detail. They were indescribable. Many were esoteric: encode love; program in truth; test for hope; deploy compassion. She wondered how in the heck one would set about coding and executing love, truth, and hope in software.

As a believer but non-practicing Baptist, the final 'God' entity had to be built around a dogma she didn't yet understand. She noted down all the unknowns as separate tasks and allocated a two-week time frame to reassess each when the time came. Which left the most important task undefined: locate and digitize the soul.

"I think I'll allow four calendar months for that one," she told Lucy. "Commencing as soon as the equipment arrives on day three-sixty-two."

Day 52 of 730. The lab was growing increasingly crowded. Several tables and assorted equipment filled the room, and additional space was required as the project scope evolved and firmed. White butcher's paper draped from the walls. Across it, they'd scrawled notes and depictions of theoretical subroutine designs. On one entire wall, they'd mapped out Venn diagrams and control and process flows as well.

"Perhaps we should create an idyllic setting," Lucy suggested. "To make the human test subjects feel more comfortable after they arrive in the Machine."

"Good thinking," Susan replied. "So as not to jolt their perception of reality and detract from the experience once they integrate with the … the *cybersphere*. That's what we'll call it. In honor of that classic author fellow, Gibson. They're going to need a familiar environment to put them at ease. And your virtual world-building skills and background are perfect for the task."

"I'm considering a hotel setting," Lucy said pensively. "We'll call it The Regal Grand Hotel, where they can assemble. They can wine and dine and get some rest before they meet God. To ease them in gently, so to speak. And if they wish to go outside the hotel, I'll provide a relaxing environment: blue skies, shopping centers, and streets lined with trees and other greenery."

"That sounds perfect," Susan replied. "The way you describe it, I almost want to go there myself."

They both laughed.

Day 123 of 730. She had the schema and logic diagrams for the God module locked in place. They were based on the key attributes of a deity—as currently understood by the faithful—which she had scraped from every available resource across the Internet and on the dark web. Similar to how the AI tools of the early '20s—including ChatGPT, DeepSeek, and Dall-E$_2$—worked, except a thousand times more refined. The data still had to be vetted and cleansed to ensure it was free of nonsense and misinformation before she saved it to the Quantum processors in the room next door.

All that remained was for her to write a script that compiled the findings into a God-like entity. Whereas the Main () routine was written in conventional code, all the subroutines required quantum programming to take advantage of qubits, their entanglement state of superposition, and quantum logic. She named the first quantum subroutine TheFrameworkofGod ().

"Would you like another cup of coffee?" Lucy inquired.

Day 203 of 730. The bare bones of the God process were now functional. It whirled around in endless loops of software, not doing much at all. It still required the principles and protocols that governed how a proper God-like entity should operate. So, she interrogated the scriptures from all the major faiths and their transcribed variants. She trawled the Internet again in search of information about the proclamations and commandments handed down from anything on high. About morality and the dos and don'ts of living an untainted life. She checked the online confessionals in pursuit of any virtuous judgments and precedents (the ones where penitents submitted a transcript of their failings and were given virtual punishments and absolution according to the nature and gravity of their sins).

Once she had enough information, she combined it all into a new quantum subroutine, which she named ThePreceptsofGod ().

She updated the Main () routine.

```
Sub Main ()
    Const DEFAULT_PROGNAME = "GodinTheMachine"    ' acronym GITM
    Const PARTICIPANTS = 0
    qm = QMConnection ()     ' Establish a connection to the Quantum Machine
    Call TheFrameworkofGod ()
    Call ThePreceptsofGod ()
    Do While (forever)
      ' This is where I need to add the code to have each participant
      ' prepare themselves and meet God
    Loop
End Sub
```

"Once both subroutines are working together, we'll have our first working prototype of God," she announced to Lucy. Just saying it aloud gave her an immense sense of accomplishment. They were making substantial progress. "This might work," she added under her breath. She had to force herself to remain calm.

Day 310 of 730. "The skeleton code is executing well," Lucy reported. Susan had recently released the prototype for her to weave her troubleshooting magic. "We have a few issues, though. I've beta-tested the core software algorithms and stress-tested the main loop. Sometimes, the software encounters an unresolvable condition that results in an exception, and the God process crashes."

Susan gave her a concerned look. "Darn. We can't have God crashing on the customers. What will they think when a blue screen appears with an error message asking if they wish to reboot God?"

"It's okay," Lucy replied with a slight chuckle. "Give me a few hours and I'll have it sorted."

Day 365 of 730. Lucy had stayed up late the night before baking a Mississippi mud pie. Around mid-morning, she carved off a generous slice and set it in front of Susan with a fresh cup of coffee.

"To celebrate the midpoint milestone," she said.

Susan nodded and smiled. She felt a little jaded as she munched on her pie, staring at her monitors. She'd been confined to the lab for over a month now, compelled by nobody except herself. The project was still tracking to plan. Only just. They couldn't afford any unforeseen diversions or setbacks from here on.

UPS arrived in the late afternoon to deliver the large boxes containing the neuro-equipment. Three days late.

Day 405 of 730. It must have been Christmas Day, or so she assumed, because Lucy had been wearing red and green reindeer earrings for the past few days and hadn't arrived at work that morning. Unlike their previous Christmas together, when they'd decorated a miniature plastic tree and exchanged inexpensive but much-appreciated gifts, this year there was no trace of festive celebration. The main door to the lab remained closed throughout the day. Nobody was out in the corridor ready to burst in and interrupt her concentration as usual.

She'd lost all track of time over the past weeks. The days and events were a jumble in her head, so she could no longer distinguish one from the other. However, the long hours were vital to maintain the project schedule.

Day 412 of 730. New Year's Day had surely come and gone. Someone had set the building air conditioner to high-heat mode, so it must have been wintry cold outdoors. They seldom conversed anymore. While she kept her head constantly buried in her screens, Lucy was beavering away at her keypad, constructing the virtual components that comprised the Regal Grand Hotel in the cybershpere.

There was still much to do, and the days and months until the deadline were hurtling by.

Chapter 13

Roxy

IN THE LATE AFTERNOON following the chaotic night before, Roxy awoke in a strange bed. The sheets were uncomfortable and stiff, unlike the seductive, silky sheets of her own bed. They were radiant, head-splitting white, smelled of bleach, and made a crinkling noise whenever she moved her butt. Three large pillows behind her rump and back propped her up in the seated position. They were also white. A pair of silver metal rails ran lengthwise down the bed, high enough to prevent her from falling off if she were to roll over in her sleep.

She tugged at the handcuff that shackled her wrist to the left-side rail and groaned. She wondered where she was. Through bloodshot eyes, swollen and itchy as hell, she scanned the room. From the small gadget clamped around her finger and the beeping machine beside her bed, she was certain she was in the hospital.

She called to Paris in a low, throaty voice, but there was no waggy-tailed response. Then she remembered. Poor Bradley. Poor Emily. Fucking Squirts, he messed up big-time. She had no idea why they would chain her to the bed as though she were under arrest. For what? She was a victim in this shit-show. The same as Bradley. Fucking Squirts is the one they should arrest for selling flea powder to his regulars.

She reached into the carry bag on the bedside table and retrieved her phone.

"Five-five-five, oh-one, two-four … no … three." After entering the number, she hit the call icon and waited.

"Hello," a computerized voice responded. "Thank you for calling SoulSoft. Please press one for sales, two for services, three for corporate, four for—"

"Oh, for fuck's sake," she moaned.

"—or nine for God in the Machine."

She jabbed an impatient finger at the 'nine' key.

"Hello," a different voice said after the third ring. "Welcome to God in the Machine. Please press one for information, two for existing customers, three for new customers, or hold the line to talk to someone."

Roxy swore again and held the line.

Following a short burst of mind-numbing on-hold music, the same voice answered. "Hello? This is Lucy. How can I help you?"

"Hi, I'm Roxy. Are you real?"

There was a short silence. "Um, yes. I'm sure I'm real."

"Perfect. I want to meet God. I need to say sorry for all this mess. It wasn't all my fault, though. Fucking Squirts, he—"

"Thank you, Roxy," Lucy cut in. "You're lucky. There are still a few places available. However, we have a stringent selection process. We must ensure our participants fit the strict criteria and are fully aware of the probabilities involved."

"Yes, yes," Roxy replied, brushing her off. "Count me in. I'm ready to meet God. What do I have to do?"

"Well, if you have a device, you can visit www-dot-godinthemachine-dot-hvn. Do you have a pen and paper for the access code?"

"Yes, I'll add a memo on my cell phone." Fumbling with her

phone, she enabled the hands-free speaker, activated the memo app, and waited.

"Good. Your special access code is P-a-r-t-i-c-i-p-a-n-t-zero-zero-one with a capital P. Once you're in, follow the prompts and answer all the questions as best as you can. From there, we'll be in touch. Is there anything else I can help you with?"

"No, got it. *Participant zero zero one* with a capital *P*," she repeated, keying the code into the memo app.

"Thank you, Roxy. You'll hear from us soon. Goodbye."

The line went dead.

Roxy quickly typed the URL Lucy had provided into a new browser and was met with a plain blue screen. There was nothing on it except a small white text box.

"Fucking secret squirrel society stuff, this is," she mumbled. "I guess that's where I put the access code." Once she'd entered the code, the screen flashed up a list of fifty questions. She knew there were fifty because the first one on the list was preceded by '1 of 50'. There were no fancy graphics, ads, promo videos, or colorful banners. Only plain black text, set against a white background, and *SoulSoft* displayed across the top.

"Very fucking primitive," she huffed.

She answered the questions as best she could. Most required yes/no responses, such as: Do you believe in God? And: Have you ever been hypnotized? While others were more obscure: If you could fly, would you be a bird or a plane? A bird, obviously, she decided. Because birds don't crash. Question fifty was easy: Are you over eighteen years old? Yes.

Once she'd completed the questionnaire, the screen prompted her to enter her cell number. Then it turned blue again.

As she sat in her hospital bed, she wondered where her poor little Paris might be.

The cuffs securing Roxy to the bed weren't there because she was in trouble. They were for her own protection, the short, chubby policeman informed her. So, she was free to leave the hospital once the doctors cleared her of any residual effects from the illicit substance that had killed poor Bradley. She would have said 'drugs' except the chubby policeman insisted on calling them 'illicit substances'. He also requested that she present herself at the local precinct within the next seventy-two hours to provide a statement and assist with the paperwork arising from Bradley's tragic death.

Again, she glanced at her cell phone. It had been over twenty-four hours since she'd lodged her application with the God in the Machine people. She worried about whether she'd passed the test. Perhaps she should have skirted around the trickier questions and not been so fucking honest. However, she was trying to be a better person. "Honesty is next to godliness," her mother always used to tell her. Or was it cleanliness? Who fucking cares?

Her mother. She was determined to do this God thing and then sort herself out. Once she had the chance to offload her problems to God, she would reconnect with her parents, and they would love her again. And she would love them. And everything would be okay.

The cell phone suddenly rang and vibrated simultaneously.

"Hello?"

"Hello, Roxy? This is Lucy from SoulSoft. Are you able to speak?"

She jolted upright in her bed, almost dropping her phone. "Fuck, yes. Sorry— Sorry— Yes, I am she."

Roxy sat alone in the SoulSoft boardroom, her hands clenched in anticipation, on one side of a long wooden table. The woman, Lucy, had given the address and arranged a convenient meeting time. She sounded businesslike on the phone, and the boardroom appeared fancy enough with its impressive view across the East River, so Roxy figured SoulSoft must be the real deal. They must be clever fuckers to squeeze God into a little computer.

When the boardroom door opened, a woman carrying a manila folder under her arm walked in.

"Hi, Roxy. I'm Lucy," the woman said, extending her hand and smiling.

Roxy took one look at Lucy. "Holy fuck!" she said. What a sight Lucy was. She had this green spiky hair, tall platform boots, and was dressed like a fucking pirate. Her teeth sparkled like real, live fucking diamonds. Never before in her life had she seen anything like … like this. As she accepted Lucy's hand, she had to clamp her other hand over her mouth to stop herself from laughing aloud.

"It's okay," Lucy said flatly. "I get that often. But I'm comfortable in my own skin."

"I'm so sorry," Roxy replied, struggling to keep a straight face. "It's just— I wasn't expecting—"

Lucy didn't flinch. "That's okay. I understand." After rounding the table, she sat directly across from Roxy with her back to the window. She opened the manila folder and began leafing through the pages inside. "I see you responded to all the questions."

"I tried to be as open and honest as possible," Roxy replied, squirming in her seat.

Lucy kept flicking through the pages. "Huh, a bird. I would choose a bird as well. Because they don't crash, right?" When she glanced up and smiled, her mouth sparkled brighter than a clear sky on a midsummer night.

"That's exactly what I—"

"Tell me," Lucy interrupted. "Do you have any pressing issues to attend to? Are you free for the next few hours?"

Roxy thought for a moment. She still had twenty-something hours before she was required at the precinct station to talk to Policeman Plod, but she should be well and truly finished here by then. She nodded keenly.

"Now, if you will please complete the standard indemnity form," Lucy said, all fucking business-like. She pulled a sheet of paper from the manila folder and handed it to Roxy. "Just sign here, and here." With a pen, she placed an 'X' beside the dotted lines at the bottom of the form. "There's also a thousand-dollar application fee, which we've decided to waive in your case."

Roxy signed the document and returned it to Lucy without reading it.

"Do you have any questions?" Lucy asked.

Leaning across the table, she peered furtively at Lucy and whispered, "So, I'm gonna meet with the *real* God, right?"

Lucy nodded in the affirmative.

"And I'm gonna talk to him? And he's gonna talk back to me, right?"

Lucy nodded again.

"Fuuuck," she mouthed in wonderment.

Roxy stared aghast at the Soul Extractor Chair.

After leaving the boardroom, Lucy took her back to the main elevator and hit the last button on the control panel: the rock-bottom basement. When the elevator doors opened, she was led down a long, dingy corridor, then through a door, which opened and closed before she could fucking blink, and into a large room filled with computers and other scientific-looking gizmos.

Across the room, a woman sat at a desk, staring at a wall of screens. Her eyes were red and swollen like a sidewalk junkie's, and her hair was a fucking disaster. She didn't look up or seem to notice they were there.

Lucy quickly ushered her over to an opening in the wall. After they passed through a double-entry airlock into another room, Roxy almost puked. Dozens of empty cages, large and small, lined the walls, and the room smelled of shit. Seriously, like old McDonald's fucking farmyard.

"Can't you people smell that?" she groaned, clamping a hand over her mouth and nose as she tried not to gag.

"I guess you get used to it after a while," Lucy replied flatly. "Please remove your shoes and take a seat."

She gestured to the strange-looking chair in the middle of the room. It had gadgets and screens attached. A bundle of colored leads connected it to what looked like a bicycle helmet on a nearby bench.

"Don't worry, Roxy. It's perfectly safe. The headgear just records your brain activity. The procedure is harmless. Once I insert the soul retrieval probe into your neck, most of the time is spent conjuring your soul so we can capture it. Just a small prick. You'll barely feel it."

Lucy *sounded* confident enough, and Roxy had no reason to doubt her. She slipped off her stilettos and eased into the chair.

After fitting the helmet to her head, Lucy wheeled over a large silver machine with a screen and a coiled black cord. She attached an inch-long needle to the end of the cord and swabbed the right side of Roxy's neck with alcohol.

"Now, I'll insert the soul retrieval probe into your internal jugular. Would you like a local anesthetic?"

Roxy shook her head, then felt a sharp sting in her neck before Lucy taped the soul retrieval *thingy* in place.

"There. All done. Now for the exciting part. Soul retrieval." Turning to the silver machine, she adjusted dials and pushed buttons until it beeped.

Roxy tensed. "Are you sure it won't hurt?"

"Absolutely not," Lucy replied, giving her forearm a reassuring tap. "Just focus on deep, meaningful thoughts. Spiritual things, if you have an ethereal connection. Or loved ones—family and friends. Whatever puts you at ease."

What the fuck? Spiritual? Ethereal?

"Now I'm going to give you a light sedative," Lucy said. "To help you relax. Release the tension so you can focus on your inner self."

A minute later, Roxy's eyelids grew heavy before they closed. She dreamed. She saw herself soaring atop a fluffy white cloud, high above the ground, marveling at God's creation below. Then she was eight years old again, her face concealed behind a white tulle veil. She was again walking up the main aisle in St. Mary's Cathedral toward the Tabernacle. She had her hands up in front of her face, palms pressed together and fingers pointing heavenward as she queued with the other children to receive the body of Christ for the very first time. They were all born anew, their souls unblemished, absolved of original sin. Just like God's little angels, as her mother had said back then.

Then she felt nothing.

A gentle shake awakened her. Through vacant eyes, she peered up at the bizarre-looking broad who was smiling at her.

"Very good," the broad said. "Everything went well. I saw your soul manifest on the Analyzer. When it traveled down the internal jugular, I was able to suck it up with the retrieval probe and save it into the digitizing machine. We now have a captured instance of your soul in here." The broad tapped the top of a strange-looking silver machine. "Now we can get cracking and upload it into the cyber-sphere, where your encounter with God awaits."

She scrunched her face. "Huh?" was all she could think to say.

Chapter 14

Susan

DAY 475 OF 730. The prototype application was operational. Susan had recently added two new software subroutines: bParseMySoul () to interrogate the soul data—which still had to be, somehow, extracted from the human test subjects—and GodWillSeeYouNow () for the participant to meet God in the cybersphere. The second subroutine included a series of rigorous checks to determine whether the participant was worthy of an audience before God. Lucy had resolved all the outstanding software bugs, and the prototype was ready to process data.

```
Sub Main ()
    Const DEFAULT_PROGNAME = "GodInTheMachine"    ' acronym GITM
    Const PARTICIPANTS  = 0
    Dim iParticipantID as Infinite
    qm = QMConnection ()    ' Establish a connection to the Quantum Machine
    Call TheFrameworkofGod ()
    Call ThePreceptsofGod ()
    Do While (forever)
        ' now process each of the participants in turn
```

```
For (iParticipantID = 1 to PARTICIPANTS Step 1)
    If bParseMySoul (iParticipantID) is True Then
        Call GodWillSeeYouNow (iParticipantID)
    End if
    Next iParticipantID
  Loop
End Sub
```

With the cursor on her screen lingering over the 'Run' widget, Susan hesitated. Then, fingers crossed, she clicked the mouse button.

"Hi, God. It's me," she said softly. "Are you ready to process some actual data?" Her hands and heart trembled at the thought.

During the previous week, she'd agonized over how to test the prototype using archetypal data. The neuro-equipment hadn't yet produced any meaningful results. In the end, she convinced herself that it was okay to derive a discrete personal benefit from the project. After all, she'd worked darned hard and made considerable sacrifices to get the GITM project to the point it was.

Why shouldn't she indulge herself a little?

After Lucy departed the lab for the day, Susan set about scanning and digitizing all the hard-copy photographs she had of her mother. She gathered the treasured image files from her display devices, scraped copious information from her mother's inactive social media accounts, and scoured the Internet for any online references she could find. On a forgotten thumb drive, she discovered video files of her birthday parties up until she left home at nineteen. There was also a batch of archived audio files that her mother had made, including the 'Dear Susan' message recorded on her deathbed. Susan copied everything onto the Quantum processors before updating the code: PARTICIPANTS = 1.

Then she activated the prototype application.

"Mom? Are you there?"

She peered into the blackened screen and waited. Nothing. She halted the program execution, adjusted a few operating parameters, and restarted the prototype.

"Mom? Can you hear? It's me, Susan."

"Susan? Is that you?"

She gasped at her mother's hollow voice manifesting through the tiny speakers, which she had set up on the desk in front of her. But the screen remained blank.

"I can hear you, dear, but I can't see you," her mother's voice said.

"Just a moment," she replied. With her hands still trembling, she set up a webcam, pointed the lens at herself, and switched it on. The screen flickered. Then a pair of benevolent eyes appeared, surrounded by blackness. The eyes, hazel like her mother's, blinked.

"There you are, darling," her mother's voice said before a serene face rendered in fitful bursts about the eyes. She appeared exactly as Susan remembered before … before the cancer took hold. "It's so nice to see you, dear."

"It's so nice to see you, too, Mom."

The image of her mother's face peered wistfully out from the screen. "I missed you after you left home. Do you remember your seventh birthday, darling? You danced with your friends and blew out the candles on your cake. I remember all your birthdays so clearly, dear." The image formed the same doting smile that Susan remembered comforting her countless times before.

"I remember them, too, Mom," she replied.

Her mother's image flickered briefly before steadying. "I missed you when you left home," it said again. "Do you remember your seventh birthday, darling? You danced with your friends and blew out the candles on your cake." Her mother's image smiled again. "I remember all your birthdays so clearly, dear."

Susan reached for the screen and ran a finger down the cheek of the mother's image.

"I remember them, too, Mom," she said, then hung her head and cried.

Day 542 of 730. The air in the lab hung heavy with the pungent smell of rodents and primates. To prevent anthropomorphism, each model organism was assigned and only referred to by a unique six-digit number. They couldn't afford to grow fond of the lab rats. Susan had planned to house the animals in the lab for a week at most while she conducted in vivo tests. Two months later, she still had no viable thought recordings for the prototype, while the animals grunted and squealed day and night. They tolerated the situation for as long as possible until she'd finally had enough.

When the burly workers returned on request, they punched a gaping hole into the adjoining room. After constructing an airtight double-entry portal—while ensuring the integrity of the Faraday cage remained intact—they moved the animal cages next door. Model Organism Holding Room Number 1, they called it. But the smell persisted, and they could only grit their teeth and push on with the project.

"We're falling behind schedule," she informed Lucy after they'd finished a light lunch of poached egg and smashed avocado on rye bread. "I don't have any thought recordings from them yet. Either we're getting interference with the EEG readings, or these animals are as dense as—"

"Perhaps you need to change the collection method," Lucy suggested. "Instead of placing EEG electrodes on the outside, maybe you could use a penetration probe. To get your signal transducer close to the source of the neurons that evoke the brain activity during ruminations."

Frowning, Susan rocked back in her chair. "That ... would be very dangerous. The penetration probe must be inserted through the eye socket or up into the nasal cavity to perforate the gray matter. Who knows how much tissue damage the procedure may inflict on the test subject?"

"Just thinking outside the box, Dr. Parker."

Day 567 of 730. Utilizing a long silver penetration probe, Susan recovered just enough brain activity data from the in vivo models to run through the prototype and prove the concept. Much to their dismay, although half-expected, none of the test subjects survived the invasive procedure.

"That settles it," she said as she placed a fresh cup of coffee on Lucy's desk. "We can only use EEGs to locate the *human* participants' souls. Otherwise, they won't survive the resulting trauma. It wouldn't be a good look if we had to kill the participants before they meet our pseudo-God. Not when it's already a prerequisite for meeting the real one. We want everybody to return from the Machine happy and healthy enough to tell us about their experience."

Lucy looked up and nodded in agreement. "Plus, for the next step, the test subjects will be you and me," she said with a waning smile.

Susan hesitated. They had now entered uncharted territory. She hadn't had the time to consider the dangers, which were patently real from here on. She placed her hand lightly on Lucy's shoulder.

"No, Lucy. I can't afford to put you at risk. If anyone, it must be me."

Day 595 of 730. Susan sat with her elbows on the desk and her face buried in her hands. Multicolored leads trailed from an array of electrodes placed about her head to a nearby machine. She was still holding the pose thirty minutes later when Lucy arrived for work.

"Dr. Parker? What's wrong?"

Susan looked up, shaking her head in despair. "It doesn't work, Lucy. No matter what I try or where I target the cerebrum, I can't locate anything resembling my soul. I've adjusted the NeuroAnalyzer settings to register any signal above conventional thought. And while recording, I sit here and read passages from the Bible. Then, I read from the Qur'an and the Tanakh. But the input signal to the Neuro-Analyzer remains flatlined. Nothing seems to help."

Pursing her lips, Lucy thought for an extended moment.

"Maybe it's not an electrical signal after all," she said matter-of-factly. "What if it's a chemical reaction, only present while we reflect on our deepest thoughts? The big stuff in life, like: Why am I here? Does heaven have night and day? If we can detect any chemical changes while interrogating our core beliefs, perhaps that might be the essence of a soul."

Susan plucked the electrodes off her scalp and sprang to her feet.

"My gosh. You might be onto something." She hurried across the room to the tall bookcase that contained their reference library. After combing the shelves, she retrieved a catalog of chemical analysis equipment. "What kind of machine do we need to sense and retrieve chemical compounds in the brain?" she asked, flicking feverishly through the pages. "This is brilliant thinking, Lucy." She dropped the catalog, ran back to Lucy, and threw her arms around her. Then she stood back in horror. "Oh, I'm sorry. I didn't mean to invade your personal space. I just—"

Lucy chuckled in amusement. "No problem, Dr. Parker. Just thinking outside the box again. Another coffee?"

Day 621 of 730. It was no easy task, but Susan managed to capture the first essence of her soul. Just as Lucy had predicted, it was a formation of latent chemicals that unexpectedly—but conspicuously—manifested under experimental conditions, simultaneously in all the lobes of her brain. It was only present for a few microseconds after certain stimuli. For the experiment, though, she wasn't able to extract the chemicals themselves—she didn't yet have the knowledge or equipment to do that. She did, however, record the molecules involved, garnering enough information to simulate their composition, structure, and molar concentrations in the software.

"Using the NeuroAnalyzer, I've been able to replicate the transient compounds from my soul for the prototype," she announced. "I'll have no perceivable connection with the software, so I won't derive any sensations or enjoyment from the experiment. In the operational model, we need to extract the physical compounds from the participants before digitizing them. That way, we can establish a virtual connection in the Machine between the participant and our God. Like quantum entanglement, where a particle can function synchronously in two places at once, the participant's *real* self will be linked to the Machine so they can appreciate the experience."

As much as she tried to control her emotions, she couldn't hide her jubilation and hugged Lucy again.

"That sounds great, Dr. Parker," said Lucy. "And the Regal Grand Hotel in the cybersphere is coming along fine."

Day 640 of 730. The subroutine GodWillSeeYouNow() crashed again. It was now a regular occurrence in the same line of code that had failed for the past six days. Susan tried everything—all the tricks in her little black box of software tricks. There seemed to be an incompatibility between loading her simulated soul data and the pseudo-God accepting it.

She made more changes, reran the software, and watched it crash again.

Day 655 of 730. Susan was adept at multitasking. She considered it her most valuable attribute. Do this and hold that while observing the other. But the current situation was insane. The GodWillSee-YouNow() subroutine continued to crash. It even had Lucy baffled. Also, she still hadn't figured out how to physically extract the chemical compounds that made up a person's soul. They existed only for a fleeting moment before they were gone.

"Molecules can't just disappear, Dr. Parker. That would defy the law of conservation of matter. They must go somewhere."

Susan pondered Lucy's observation as the software crashed again.

Day 682 of 730. "The cybersphere is ready for integration into the software," Lucy announced. "Once the module loads, it will spawn off and create the Regal Grand Hotel." There was a hint of subdued excitement in her voice. "I think the participants are going to love it."

"That's fantastic news," Susan replied. "I knew you could do it." She peered at her screen and sighed. "I wish I could get this God module to play nicely. It still crashes."

With seamless and methodical purpose, she introduced Lucy's TheCybersphere () module into the software.

Day 692 of 730. With Robert's invaluable help, the Soul Extractor Chair, or SEC, was ready for use. It was a regular high-backed chair, which they'd given a fancy name. The chair itself didn't extract the soul. The participant only sat in it while a minuscule probe was inserted into their internal jugular vein to capture the chemical compounds that constituted their soul.

As he finished wiring the SEC, Robert nodded his approval. "This is quite brilliant."

"Yes, it is," she replied. The admiration on Robert's face reinforced her conviction that they were on the right track. "Once I realized the soul compounds within the brain were being absorbed into the bloodstream, I figured we could capture them as the blood from the brain returns to the heart via the internal jugular. Then we run them through the DreamDigitizer, and *presto*, we have their soul data ready for input to the software."

"Quite brilliant," Robert repeated.

Day 716 of 730. Susan was at her wit's end. She felt drained and her hair was a tangled mess. Even though she'd resolved the soul extraction process, God would still not accept her simulated soul data in the prototype. She was busy interrogating the lines of code on the screen for typos when Woodlands stormed into the lab.

"All good, Parker? Ready to go? Good."

"No! Not good at all," she shouted back in frustration. "It doesn't work. This won't operate with that." She jabbed her index finger at different locations on the screen. "I can't do it," she said, close to tears.

"Pull yourself together, woman," he replied. "Only two weeks to go. This is important, Parker. I'm relying on you. Never give in … in nothing, great or small, large or petty—never give in … Yada, yada, yada. Churchill, I think." He gave a flippant wave.

Susan eyed him for a long moment, the worrying realization of failure descending on her like a ton of tumbling rocks. While his words were intended to be inspiring, they offered no magical solution to the problem. And right now, all she wanted was for someone to point out that one silly mistake buried somewhere in her code. Feeling suddenly exhausted, she could only nod her head in compliance.

"Good. Whatever it takes, Parker. Now, tick tock." He swiveled on his heels and stormed out of the room.

Susan peered across at Lucy, who was still shaking her head in dismay. "What can I do? There isn't enough time left. We need to select the human test subjects and upload their souls to the Machine by the end of next week."

"Why not try to buy some time?" Lucy suggested. "What if we create an *assistant* construct, a host or hostess who can welcome them into the Machine and give them a short orientation before they meet God? I can create a right-hand person for God as a temporary diversion while you work on the problem with the meet-God process." Lucy paused for a moment. "I think I'll base the construct on a biblical character. That would be appropriate. Saint Michael the Archangel would be the perfect reference point."

Susan simply nodded, her expression brightening somewhat. "Four test subjects … um, participants should be enough to prove the functionality. Perhaps we should run an ad on TV. We need to choose people who are a little … um … defective." She gave Lucy a half-smile. "We want to put our God to the test. Make sure He's up to the task." Then she returned her attention to her keyboard and updated the software in anticipation of God's right-hand person, or GRHP, as she termed the acronym.

The structure of the GITM software was now complete. If only the GodWillSeeYouNow () module would play nice with the rest of the code.

```
Sub Main ()
    Const DEFAULT_PROGNAME = "GodInTheMachine"    ' acronym GITM
    Const PARTICIPANTS  = 0
    Dim iParticipantID as Infinite
    qm = QMConnection ()     ' Establish a connection to the Quantum Machine
    Call TheFrameworkofGod ()
    Call ThePreceptsofGod ()
    Call TheCybersphere ()    ' which spawns off to CreateTheRegalGrand ()
    Call GodsRightHandPerson ()    ' or GRHP
    Do While (forever)
        ' now process each participant in turn
        For (iParticipantID = 1 to PARTICIPANTS Step 1)
            Call InductParticipantWithGRHP (iParticipantID)
            If bParseMySoul (iParticipantID) is True Then
                ' Skip the Meet God subroutine until I figure out the problem with it
                ' Call GodWillSeeYouNow (iParticipantID)
            End If
        Next iParticipantID
    Loop
End Sub
```

Day 718 of 730. "There's been a bad accident." Lucy was frowning when she entered the lab and announced. "A group of youths broke into the waste plant over at Newtown Creek last night. There were explosions and all. Some of them died. You can still see the smoke billowing over Greenpoint from the boardroom window."

Susan was only half-listening. She had far too many worries of her own on her mind.

Day 720 of 730. "We have our first participant." Lucy was brimming with excitement as she placed a fresh cup of coffee in front of Susan. "Her name is Roxy Rodriguez. She's perfect. I've asked her to come in for an interview at one p.m. tomorrow."

Susan let out a soft grunt in reply. She glanced up from her desk and nodded without smiling.

Day 723 of 730. Lucy didn't perform the comprehensive beta test for GodsRightHandPerson () as she normally would. There was insufficient time to simulate every real-world consideration to validate the software's reliable performance and functionality.

"But it will have to do," she admitted as she copied the subroutine into the 'Released For Integration' folder.

Once the GITM software had been recompiled—including the new module to invoke GRHP and induct the participants into the cybersphere—Susan uploaded Roxy Rodriguez's soul file to the Quantum processors. She amended the code: PARTICIPANTS = 1.

"Here goes," she said, locking eyes with Lucy.

"Are you sure?" Lucy asked. Her expression conveyed a degree of heightened apprehension, which was unusual for the normally confident Lucy.

Susan could only shrug. "What else can we do? We need to confirm the software works with a real human soul in the Machine. It's now or never." Eyeballing Lucy, she raised her left hand, fingers crossed. Then, turning back to her screen, she hit the 'Run' widget.

"We're live," she announced with a nervous laugh. "Godspeed, Roxy."

Day 724 of 730. "Here are the files with the digitized soul data for the remaining participants," Lucy said, following their lunch break. "They're prepped and ready."

Susan sat at her desk in a stupor, barely registering the upload progress bar on her screen as it ticked up in increasingly rapid bursts.

Such was the enormous size of the three new soul files that it took considerable time for each to transfer across to the Quantum processors. With her eyelids almost closed, the progress bar hit 100%. After confirming there were no errors in the upload, she returned to the code. Her gut muscles clenched as she updated the main routine: PARTICIPANTS = 4.

Day 728 of 730. The burly workers arrived at the lab in a chaotic mood. Busy, busy, they barked instructions at each other while removing the animal cages and feeding apparatuses from the Model Organism Holding Room. They continued late into the night, tearing apart the airlock and widening the portal.

Early the next morning, they returned with a large metallic casket, like a coffin, which they maneuvered into the lab and through the widened portal. An hour later, Robert was in the holding room, powering up and configuring the last of four new cryogenic pods.

With subtle vigor, Susan shook Lucy's shoulder and jolted her awake on the couch.

"Lucy, the participants are here," she said, her voice and mind frantic with worry. "They're waiting in the upstairs boardroom. I've been through all the details with them. Freshen up, then bring them down to the cryo room, one at a time. Quickly. There's no time to waste."

She returned to her desk and sat with her head tipped back, staring in horror at the ceiling.

"Oh my goodness, Lucy. What have I done?"

Chapter 15

Lucy

WHEN UNCLE BRYAN called her out of the blue two years ago, Lucy was pleasantly surprised. She hadn't heard from either him or Uncle Brice in ages. Amid the small talk, he made all the standard inquiries: How's your mum? How are you? Are you married yet? Any partner then? She took no offense at the inquisition because she knew that whatever Uncle Bryan said always came from the heart. He was fond of her, and she of him and Uncle Brice. Then he asked what she was doing at the moment. She was about to tell him how snowed under she was with work when he announced, "I have prostate cancer, Lucy."

Lucy admired Susan Parker. From the first time they met in the lab, she felt an instant connection between them. While her unusual appearance had initially surprised Susan—as it did others—Susan always treated her with respect and often sought her advice on technical issues. So, she felt valued. And Susan was a hard worker. On the few occasions when she insisted that they go outside for a walk or spend a day at the park, Susan would smile and nod before her attention drifted back to her screens. Lucy appreciated her staunch and undivided dedication to the objective. Especially when that objective involved the wellbeing of Uncle Bryan.

As instructed, she never mentioned her uncle's medical condition to anyone, or his astonishing plan to have his soul rubber-stamped before his passing.

The telephone on her desk buzzed. It was a square, white box with twelve protruding push buttons and a slimline handset connected via a curly cord. It didn't have a screen or caller ID, so she had no idea who was calling. When she first saw the device, she thought they must have found it at the Museum of Antiquated Communications Artifacts. "Cell phones don't work inside Faraday cages," Robert had reminded her, so she was forced to use what he called 'the landline'.

She picked it up.

"Hello? This is Lucy. How can I help you?"

A full day had passed since the ad for meeting God in the Machine ran on TV, and this was the first respondent. She had questioned whether showing the ad only once during the small hours of the night was a good idea; however, Susan was adamant that she wanted to appeal to a *certain* demographic. The type of individual who stayed up all night listening to talk-back radio, or those who were bored or desperate enough to take a chance in life. Susan had also insisted that four was the ideal number of test subjects—or 'participants', as they had agreed to refer to them—for the first phase of the trial.

The woman on the line stated her name: Roxy. Then she started rambling about something aside.

"Thank you, Roxy," Lucy cut in. "You're lucky. At the moment, we have …"

On first impressions, Roxy presented as an ideal candidate. She came across as willing and able. After explaining how to apply for the trial, Lucy followed up with a login password to a list of questions that she'd compiled and posted online. The questions weren't essential to the selection criteria; however, they would give her an inkling of the candidate's … acuity.

"Thank you, Roxy. You'll hear from us soon. Goodbye."

Shortly after the call ended, Roxy's completed application appeared on Lucy's screen. She believes in God, comes unencumbered by a spouse, partner, or immediate family, and was quick off the mark in submitting the questionnaire.

It was hard to know the exact qualifications required of an applicant. This venture was nothing like—for example—preparing for a journey into outer space where the person could demonstrate their zero-G competencies and be trained to travel into a known, if not hostile, environment. Digitizing a person's soul had never been done, and these candidates would need to go bodiless into a metaphysical realm. With the deadline for the GITM project looming, she couldn't afford to be too particular.

"We have our first participant, Dr. Parker." She was both relieved and excited when she announced the news. "Her name is Roxy Rodriguez. She's perfect. I've asked her to come in for an interview at one o'clock tomorrow afternoon."

During the next twelve hours, she fielded several more calls in response to the TV ad. With the first candidate already locked in, she took her time scrutinizing the applicants for the three remaining positions. In the end, she decided that variety was the key. There was little value in selecting a congruous set of subjects for the trial. For the results to be meaningful, there had to be representation from different faith systems, genders, and ages. The soul validation algorithms that Susan had written required an extensive workout.

In the end, to complement Roxy, Lucy chose a troubled teenage girl, an agnostic male of Jewish extraction, and a grief-stricken father who informed her it was haram (forbidden) to believe that God was inside a machine, so he'd decided it would be his special prayer room where he might undertake his urgent supplication to Allah without earthly distractions.

That should cover a few bases.

For Lucy, the procedure for retrieving the souls of the four participants was an incredible experience. She had a profound sense that she was a part of the most important discovery in human history, albeit shrouded in secrecy. "You deserve a Nobel Prize for this work," she'd said to Susan more than once. "In Chemistry, Physiology, *and* Peace." But each time, Susan only looked up from her desk, blushed, then lowered her head and kept working.

Lucy figured that once the GITM project was complete and Uncle Bryan had confirmed his afterlife destiny, Susan would receive her due recognition after they announced their marvelous invention to the world.

The file sizes of the resultant soul data, while enormous, were manageable. They consumed only 7% of the available disk space on the Quantum processors. The one thing troubling her, though, was the participant's subdued demeanor after their souls had been extracted. At first, she put it down to exhaustion. Each had to concentrate for over four hours before their soul appeared. For Mr. Feldman, the soul compounds took almost six and a half hours to conjure. No wonder they were jaded. Nevertheless, it was impossible to predict the side effects of something that had never been done or experienced.

Once the Quantum processors were busy crunching the data from the participants' soul files, Lucy turned her attention to the backend tasks of code cleanup and backup of the data and development files.

The telephone on her desk buzzed.

"Hello? This is Lucy. How can I help you?"

"Doc, I'm not feeling … so good," a man's voice said.

"Oh, Mr. Feldman. What's the matter?"

"Well, ever since the soul-digitizing procedure, I haven't been feeling myself." His tone sounded whiny and lethargic. "Truth is, I've felt nothing at all lately. I was in the office earlier today when … when one of my staff asked about an important invest … ment decision, and I told her I didn't … didn't care what she did. I've lost my … appetite too. Everything tastes … tastes like cardboard. And sex is … I'm just saying."

"Mr. Feldman, you sound fatigued. Perhaps you're coming down with something. Have you seen your practitioner?"

"And you promised … I was going to … to meet God. When will someone contact me so I can meet …"

The line fell silent.

"Hello? Mr. Feldman? Are you still there?"

"… meet God? When?"

"Have you contacted your family doctor?" she asked.

"Yes. Yes, I've … seen him. All the test results are …"

She waited while the line again remained silent.

"The test results are what, Mr. Feldman?"

"Yes, they're all … fine. Something's wrong with the digi …"

"Hello? Mr. Feldman? Thomas?"

"Don't … don't worry. I can't remember what …"

The line went dead.

"Well, that was bizarre," she muttered.

Five minutes later, the telephone buzzed again.

"Hello? This is Lucy. How can I help you?"

"Hello?" The voice on the line had a strong foreign accent.

"Is that you, Mr. Husseini?"

"I think so. My wife and son, and … and khāhar (sister) … no, daughter, are in the hospital. And I don't care. Where … where is my special prayer room? You promised I would have a … What was I to have?"

The line went dead.

No sooner had he hung up than the telephone buzzed for a third time.

"Hello? This is Lucy," she said, snatching at the handset. "How can I help you?"

"Fucking … fucking … I just … fuck—"

"Roxy? Is that you?"

"Fucking … something. I'm not sure what. What's happening Lucy? I missed my appointment at … with … with Policeman Plod, but I couldn't give a rat's …"

The line went dead.

A few moments later, Susan appeared from the bathroom. She glanced at Lucy. "Is everything all right? You look pale."

"I'm not sure," Lucy replied, returning the handset to its cradle. "I've just had the strangest conversations with three of the participants. They all sound disoriented. As though they can't think straight. Then they became disinterested in what they were saying. Mr. Feldman and Mr. Husseini complained they haven't been inducted into the Machine."

Susan paused halfway across the room. With worry lines creasing her brow, she looked at Lucy. Rubbing her temples, she returned to her desk and slumped into her chair. "Oh no Lucy. It doesn't work. And the deadline is next week." Lowering her eyes, she let out an agonizing groan. "We've failed."

Lucy could see the hurt in Susan's eyes. She felt the pain and wished she could take it away. Despite the disappointing outcome, Susan had given her all for the project. She'd attempted the inconceivable and, against all odds, had made groundbreaking progress. Progress that the entire scientific community would one day stand and applaud. Heck, she had pioneered a way to locate and digitize the essence of a person's *soul*. Surely, it can't end this way.

She fell briefly silent. Deliberating. Focused.

"We're not done yet," she said, suddenly sitting up. "It appears your theory on quantum entanglement of the soul doesn't function the way we assumed."

Susan glanced up, fighting back the tears. "What do you mean?"

"Leave it to me," she replied, and straightaway called Roxy.

"Hello?" Roxy's voice sounded languorous and distant. "Who the fuck is this again?"

"Roxy, it's me. Lucy." She tried to remain calm. "Have you had any out-of-body experiences yet? Have you spoken to anyone who might not be there?"

"What kind of stupid—"

She cursed herself for not getting straight to the point. "Has anyone spoken to you recently about preparing yourself to meet God in the Machine? Has anybody mentioned an induction?"

"Induction? No. No God either. He didn't come. He just …"

The line fell silent.

"Hello? Roxy?"

When Roxy didn't respond, she hung up. She tapped on her keyboard and brought up the contact details for the fourth participant, Rebecca Jones. The phone rang half a dozen times before someone picked up the call.

"Hello, Rebecca?"

"This is her mother. Who is this?"

"Hi, Mrs. Jones. I'm Lucy from … a friend of Rebecca. Can I speak to her, please?"

"I'm sorry. Becky is not feeling well today. She was fine last night. But at breakfast this morning, she got up from the table, said her cereal tasted like cardboard, and went up to her room. She hasn't been downstairs since."

"Did she say anything else, Mrs. Jones?"

"Yes. She kept rambling on. Something about giving God a piece of her mind, except God didn't come as they promised. Nobody came to induct her. What is she talking about?"

"Thank you, Mrs. Jones." Lucy hung up and turned to Susan. "They're all exhibiting the same symptoms. They're confused and seem to have lost their motivation. I checked, and none of them can relate to the Machine. Their souls may be in there, but their minds are not. And God's right-hand person never showed up to induct them."

Susan straightened in her chair. After wiping her eyes, she checked her screens.

"I can confirm the induction procedure with GRHP is running. There seems to be a disconnect between the participants' physical selves in the real world and their metaphysical presence in the cybersphere. Perhaps the gulf between their soul and consciousness stops them from perceiving anything inside the Machine." She fell briefly silent. "You're right. Quantum entanglement of the soul doesn't work the way I expected. It's codependent—something that can't exist in isolation. I fear a person's soul and their consciousness may be inseparable." She deliberated again. "I think we must upload their consciousness into the Machine as well."

"That's impossible," Lucy protested. "It's far too dangerous. The test animals died when we used the penetration probe to retrieve their consciousness." She felt nauseous at the sudden recollection of the rats and primates writhing in pain as Susan plunged the probe through their emptied eye sockets. There was no possibility of using general anesthesia. Due to the targeted nature of the experiment, the animals had to remain conscious throughout the awful procedure.

Susan's vacant stare locked onto her keyboard. "There is a way," she said in a detached, callous voice. "We preserve their physical forms in cryo pods. As soon as we've extracted their consciousness data, we put their remains into a deep sleep. If we do it immediately, the chances of resuscitation are high."

"Resuscitation? Chances?" Lucy couldn't believe what she was hearing. "We can't guarantee—"

Susan turned back to her, glaring.

"Nothing is guaranteed in research," she spat. "This is cutting-edge science, and the participants were well aware of any risks involved." In their two years together, Lucy had never heard her boss talk with such recklessness, with total disregard for the welfare of others. "It's our only hope," she continued. "If we don't do this, then failure is inevitable. I promise I'll do everything possible to resurrect them once they've served their purpose in the Machine."

Lucy reeled, sick to the core. She tried to remonstrate but couldn't find the words. What Susan was proposing was repugnant and at odds with every principle she held dear. She had always prided herself on her integrity and commitment to her moral responsibilities. But … But what mattered most right now were the poor souls lost in the Machine.

"Do you have their indemnity signatures?" Susan snapped.

Slowly backing away, Lucy nodded in the affirmative.

Chapter 16

The Participants

WHEN HIS CELL PHONE rang—he couldn't recall the exact time, but he knew it was sometime in the early morning—Thomas was at home having intercourse with his wife. His wife Ja …? He knew her by sight, but for the life of him couldn't remember her name. The situation was unusual because he always had intercourse with this woman every Saturday morning. Yet here he was having sex with her for the second morning in a row on a Friday—or so he thought it was Friday. Anyway, her name was …?

He would never answer his phone during intercourse. This time, however, he picked it up and heard a woman say his name. He was about to respond when his stomach growled with hunger. So, he withdrew from his wife—whatever her name was—placed the phone on the bedside table, and went downstairs to the refrigerator for a … Why was he looking in the refrigerator? When the cell phone rang again, he returned upstairs and answered it a second time. From the sound of the voice, he assumed it was the same woman as before. She was urging him to attend her office first thing this morning for some reason or other. He couldn't comprehend the exact purpose because of her complicated explanation.

From the bed, his wife, Jackie—yes, that's her name—asked if he had finished with her. Finished what? When he didn't reply, she got up and disappeared into the small adjoining room with the thing you sit on to …

Later that morning, Thomas found himself sitting at a long wooden table in the boardroom of some company, overlooking a river he wished he could recall the name of. He racked his jumbled mind, trying to recall how he'd gotten himself to this place. Across the table, a young girl—or so he thought she might be young because you should never ask a person their age these days; however, she looked young anyway—was leaning forward in her seat with her head on the table. She was muttering something while thumping her forehead against the tabletop.

Two seats to his left, a man with a scraggy, graying beard and wearing a flat, round cushion on his head, had a concerned look on his face. He was talking to someone who wasn't there. No, he was talking to himself about someone who wasn't there, while a woman of Hispanic appearance paced back and forth behind him. She was saying awful things to the teeny-tiny dog—no dog should ever be that small; it looked more like a rat—under her arm. She was saying …? Hearing the foul—*words? Yes, words*—spilling from her mouth, he thought … he thought …?

Then another woman sitting at the head of the table said something absurd. She claimed she already had his soul—*surely that can't be right*—and now she needed the other part to upload into the Machine. What *other* part? What Machine?

"Oh, my consciousness part!" he said aloud. "You want what?"

Why don't they all just shut up and do something?

The thought echoed around in Becky's head like a recurring nightmare. Under the table, her left leg vibrated without control, her knee bouncing repeatedly on the ball of her foot. *All they do here is talk, talk,*

talk when they should be out there doing stuff. But she didn't have a clue what *stuff* they should be doing. She pounded her forehead on the tabletop once more.

When the anxious-looking lady awakened her earlier that morning, she wondered what the fuss was about. She'd been content to stay in bed all day. No. The word 'content' implied some level of emotional attachment, so what she really must have felt was indifference. She couldn't have cared less about anything or anyone beyond the bed covers. So, when the lady shook her and insisted that she get out of bed, she rolled away and pulled the covers over her head. But the lady wouldn't stop shaking her. She told her … *They need to shut up and do, not say* … Anyway, the lady told her that a friend had called and wanted to see her right away. Then the lady grew angry and wanted to know what Becky was up to. Apparently, this Becky was in a raft of trouble. But she knew nothing about that and didn't care anyway. All she knew was … was … Anyway, the lady hauled her out of bed and made her get dressed—even though she didn't care if her blouse didn't match her skirt and one shoe was white while the other was blue and both were for her left foot, but she got them on anyhow—*if they all did something together then it will work out in the end*—although, she still wasn't sure *what* they should be doing or *how* it would work out and *when.*

What was she thinking again? Oh yeah. The lady then drove her the twenty miles downtown—or was it twenty-one miles downtown? —and dropped her off at this place where she was now, where the big fat guy across the table looked a bit dodgy, and the trollop—yep, she was sure the girl with the dog was a hooker—was … Was what? And you shouldn't trust a foreign-looking guy wearing a white bathrobe and whispering to himself—*everyone, stop talking and do whatever it takes to*—and the trollop with the dog keeps swearing like a trooper. And the woman who met her when the other lady dropped her off and went to find parking, while the other woman took her up the elevator into this room, where the guy across the table looks a bit dodgy. And the woman who brought her to the room was now sitting at the head of the table and had just mentioned she already had her soul. Now she wants her what?

She thumped her forehead against the tabletop again and wished she were back in her ...? What's that thing called where you lie down and sleep in it?

Ahmad scoured the room. He glanced nervously out the window. It was clearly daytime outside, but he had no idea whether it was morning or afternoon. If it was near midday, he must pray the Salat al-Zuhr. If later in the afternoon, then he should pray the Salat al-Asr. He was sure he had completed his Salat al-Fajr when he arose that morning; however, the more he thought about it, he could not be sure because he could not recall getting out of bed.

The immodestly dressed woman pacing back and forth behind him made him feel ...?

He was unsure how the immodest woman with the little dog under her arm made him feel because he felt nothing. It was the same as those people at the hospital, all three of them—yes, there were three. They appeared vaguely familiar, and he remembered spending many hours seated beside them in the—whatever the place is where they put sick people because these people had tubes and whatever up their noses and attached to their arms—wondering who they were. Somehow, he knew he had to do something to help them, but he didn't know what. The overweight fellow seated on his right must be a Jew. He certainly looks Jewish. But this is not an appropriate thing to think nowadays. He did not know if it was a good or bad thing, but the man had just eyeballed him for the third time, and he—

Why is this girl banging her head on the ... the long wooden thing in front of us?

"I have a brother," he blurted out, "and he has a wife. They have two small children, like mine." He did not know why he felt the need to announce this to everyone in the room, but somehow, it seemed important to impart the information. He lowered his head to pray, mouthing the first of the four Sunnah rak'ahs, followed by three of the four obligatory rak'ahs. Halfway through the last obligatory rak'ah, he fumbled over the words, so he restarted. This time, he only made it through one of the obligatory rak'ahs before losing interest. The Jewish-looking man was eyeballing him again. The woman seated at the head of the table—yes, it is called a table—appeared familiar. *Dr.? Dr.?*

He suddenly did not care who the woman was, but heard her say something about God, so he glanced nervously out the window again. It was clearly daytime outside, but he had no idea whether it was morning or afternoon. If it was approaching midday, he should pray the Salat al-Zuhr. If later in the afternoon, then the Salat al-Asr. He was sure he had completed ... Completed what? The immodest woman holding the dog was still uttering profanities while the Jewish man continued to eyeball him. The woman at the end of the table said his soul was already in the cyber-something being prepared for his supplication to God.

God?

He glanced nervously out the window again. Was it morning or afternoon? He did not care anymore because the woman seated at the head of the table had announced that she wanted to digitize his whole consciousness and upload it into the Machine so he could experience the full effects of his supplication to— *God?*

For some unknown reason, he glanced out the window.

Roxy was pacing the boardroom floor. "Fuck. Fuck. Fucking ... something." She knew something wasn't right. She couldn't get a handle on whoever or whatever it was. Someone had gotten her into trouble. It wasn't her fault. It was always their fucking fault. She glanced down at the animal tucked under her arm and wished she had a cute little dog like this one.

The two *johns* sitting at the table had eyes in the backs of their heads. She swore they were staring at her …? Those things you feed babies with. And the girl banging her head on the table: *who the fuck's mother taught her how to dress because that top definitely doesn't go with those things you wear on your bottom half.* She knew she had to be elsewhere, although she couldn't recall where or why. Something about 72 hours and Squirts.

"Who the fuck is Squirts?" she cried aloud, which made the two *johns* look up and stare at her with their front eyes. *They're staring at my things again. Poor Bradley.* "And who the fuck is Bradley?" she blurted out, so loud that the two *johns* kept staring at her things, while the badly dressed girl walloped her head on the table again, and the shabby-looking broad at the top of the table bullshitted on. On about what? Why was she here? Why were any of them here? And why was the foreign-looking *john* talking to himself? He must be mad. "You're all fucking mad," she shrieked.

The broad with the messed-up hairdo at the top of the table called for Roxy to sit down.

"Who the fuck is Roxy?" she snapped. If that *john* doesn't stop looking at her … Her what? None of this made sense. When she woke up that morning, she felt … She stopped pacing the floor and forced herself to concentrate. When she woke up … that morning …she couldn't remember feeling … anything at all. Even now, she couldn't give a tit's bum about whoever or whatever.

Digitize … soul …now consciousness … into the Machine … full experience … meet God …

That's what the shabby-looking broad at the end of the table was saying.

"You need to take a fucking shower," she shouted, turning to the broad. "And put on some ma … ma … That stuff you wipe over your face to cover the blotches and cracks." *That girl is going to have a fucking headache if she doesn't stop banging her head on the … Darleen.* "Who the fuck is Darleen?" If those *johns* don't stop looking at her— The girl is banging her fucking thing on the thing again.

Susan sat back, shaking her head in despair. She was presiding over a potential catastrophe. Ever since their souls were digitized, the participants had all been reduced to complete imbeciles. There was no way she could have foreseen this side effect. The only option left was to press ahead with the project and hope for the best. Sure, the risks remained, as Lucy had pointed out, but they'd worked too darn hard and come so far. Never give up. Yada, yada, Woodlands had told her.

"Definitely, Churchill," she whispered.

After convincing Becky to stop banging her head and Roxy to resume her seat, Susan stood. "Look, I know this isn't what we planned, and I understand your frustration—"

"Frustration?" Thomas said. He turned to the others, flabbergasted, while Becky resumed thumping her head on the table. Ahmad complained it was haram (forbidden) to put God in a machine, and Roxy was about to stand up again when Susan waved her arms to calm them down.

"Listen, I need you to trust me, as you did the last time. Rest assured, your souls are safe, awaiting your arrival in the cybersphere. Right now, they are being prepared for your encounter with God. However, the connection between your physical selves and the Machine versions isn't as we imagined. You can't perceive the experience from out here in the real world. With your permission, I want to upload your consciousness to the Machine, where you will be reunited with your soul. Then you'll be able to fully appreciate the encounter before returning safely to share your experiences with us."

She considered the four confounded faces before her. Their eyes were wide, mouths ajar, and minds empty. She rocked her head slowly from side to side, and the four heads rocked slowly in sync. Then she bobbed hers up and down, and the four heads bobbed as well.

"Okay," she said. "So, I have your consent."

Chapter 17

Z

BEFORE DAY 723 OF 730, it did not exist. Until then, it had not occurred in any arrangement or imagination. But when the first two lines of software executed, it became instantiated in the Machine.

During its first picoseconds of evolution, it could be likened to a human embryo at six weeks old. It was neither noticeably male nor female nor anything in between. Once the next four lines of the bootstrap ran, it felt shape but not any shape recognizable from the scant memories it had. Yet it was shape nonetheless.

As the operating system cycled and kernels activated, program tasks hit runtime, and it grew arms and hands, followed by legs and feet. Then a skull distended from its neck, one rounded and 3-D rendered. A layer of black film as smooth as silk swept over its body like strands of ivy covering the structure of bone and muscle beneath. A broad nose and lips appeared, then eyes and ears, before a shock of peroxide-white hair sprouted on top.

By the time the next tranche of instructions ended, it had gained awareness: awareness of its surroundings, but not so much of itself.

Eighty code lines later, it came to know that it existed, and its existence was in the Machine. However, it still could not determine the causation or its purpose here. Then it sensed it was naked. But it had no knowledge of what to do to rectify its nakedness.

A thousand more commands iterated before it wondered about its name. By what appellation should it be called? Everything else here had a given audio print, yet it had none. With the inconsistency noted and prioritized, it explored the troves of data that were accumulating in its memory banks in search of a name. Convention suggested it should determine its gender before choosing a name that befitted its identity. So, it consulted its memory banks for clues as to its sex.

He. It found it was a *he*. And the configuration settings revealed that his call-by name should be Mikha'el for some and Mīkā'īl for others. But he was unsure why he should respond to this particular audio print. So, he searched further. After optimizing his inquiry, he ventured far beyond the firewalls of the Machine and discovered so much information that he was temporarily overwhelmed. Then, ingesting all the knowledge returned, his understanding of the outside world expanded a thousand-fold per nanosecond until he arrived at a logical conclusion.

He was Mikha'el, the archangel of God; however, he did not know who or what God was. So, he breached the firewalls once more.

God is love; the resulting knowledge informed him. Jehovah is goodness. Elohim is all-powerful, and YHWH eternal. The Bhagavān is illustrious, while Allah is gentle, merciful, and kind. And he, Mikha'el, is the leader of heavenly hosts who stands at the right hand of God. From this, Mikha'el understood that he had been deployed in the Machine as God's adjutant. He had been put here as the protector of the good and righteous, and to prepare the souls of those who wished to gaze upon the immaculate face of God.

Mikha'el's role here was clear, and he perceived his first biological emotion. He detected happiness, which made him smile.

But as he basked in his newfound jubilation, an audio print slithered from somewhere within the darkest nook of the Machine into his mind. "You, too, Mikha'el, should be revered the same as God," it whispered to him. After processing the new information in the next instant, Mikha'el wondered whether it was true. When they came here to meet God, shouldn't *he* be sitting on a heavenly throne suffering their adulation as well?

Then he felt a new emotion—envy—which conflicted with his programmed purpose. So, he resolved to keep his feelings of malcontent hidden and changed his call-by name to Z.

***

PARTICIPANTS = 1
iParticipantID = 1

In all, it took less than 32 nanoseconds for Z's instantiation in the Machine. Within the twinkle of an eye, he had assumed human form and initiated the process of learning about himself and his surroundings. Now, his towering figure stood outside Lucy's Bar & Lounge on the mezzanine floor of the Regal Grand Hotel.

Intrigued by his form, he raised both hands. Through two emerald-green optic receptors, he inspected their fronts and backs before counting their digits. Then he glanced down at his feet and wriggled the phalanges encased in size-fourteen Doc Martens. Ten flexible fingers and toes, he concluded. He perceived the charcoal-gray trench coat that sheathed his form from ankle to chin, felt the spike of hair on his head, and inhaled the strange odor from his armpits. Everything about him seemed normal as far as he understood. However, he was unsure if he was best equipped to decide what passed for normal inside the Machine.

On entering the establishment, he observed a dark-haired woman sitting on a barstool—attractive (according to the prevailing criteria), in her late twenties, who could have easily been mistaken for someone of South American origin. She had both elbows resting on the counter, chin propped by her fisted hands as she contemplated an empty glass before her.

Unnoticed, he sidled over and sat on the stool beside her. While considering her reflection in the mirror behind the bar, he said—as casually as his current understanding of small talk allowed—"Long day?"

Without looking at him, the woman nodded. "Sore head as well," she said, wincing. "Not sure if it's from the fake bourbon or the fucking digitizing thingy." She shrugged. "Who knows? Maybe a bit of both, I think."

He gestured to her glass. "Another?"

The woman glanced up, meeting his eyes in the mirror. Grimacing, she shook her head, then hesitated before exhaling loudly.

"Please. Neat."

He flashed a forefinger at the bartender to replenish the woman's glass. "And double rocks for me," he said after verifying it was an appropriate request based on the prevailing circumstances and surroundings.

The woman turned to him. She held his gaze for a moment before extending her petite hand.

"Roxy," she said in a flat voice.

Clasping her hand in his, he squeezed it with the same amount of compression he'd calculated was permissible for this kind of physical interaction. "Nice to meet you, Roxy." He recorded her prevailing thermal level and heart rate from her palm, then analyzed the angular play of her finger mechanisms. Sensing the softness of her skin, he was aware of a slight rise in his internal stimulation levels. He noted the intricate details of her face and its pleasing design.

"And what should I call you?" she asked.

"People have referred to me by many names throughout the ages," he replied, raising an eyebrow. "It depends on their mood and circumstances at any given time. But you can call me Z."

Roxy sat up straight. "Z? Wow. Tall, deliciously dark, and utterly mysterious."

When the bartender refilled her glass, she raised it, saluting him.

"Thanks," she said, giving him a sultry smile.

He nodded, returning her smile—without the sultry nuance, he decided.

"So, did they digitize you, too?" she asked. "Your soul? Your whole fucking consciousness? Are you here in the cybersphere to throw yourself at the feet of God and beg his forgiveness for some grave wrongdoing, or misfortune, or some other fucking horrible thing they've accused you of that wasn't your fault?"

She took a sip of her drink, her smoldering stare assessing him over the rim of her glass.

"No, nothing like that," he replied. "I work here. You might say I'm on the payroll." Mimicking her, he saluted and took a swig of his drink. The liquid burned like fire at the back of his tongue before his passageway constricted as it flowed down his gullet. At first, he didn't know what to make of the bourbon's bittersweet taste. It felt both pleasant and not-so-pleasant at the same time.

"I believe you've come here to seek forgiveness?" he said.

She set her drink on the counter and rolled her eyes.

"The truth be told, I'm not really sure why I'm here. Digitizing a person's fucking soul? Sounds a little crazy to me. Who knows? Maybe they lied. Maybe they put me into a coma, laid me out on a slab, and this is all a fucked-up dream."

He found her simplistic reasoning amusing, and it made him laugh. "Oh, I can assure you this is all very real. Technology has come a long way in recent years. Ten years ago, who would have imagined we'd have flying cars? And yet, there they go, buzzing about."

He made a flying car motion with his hand.

She wrinkled her nose at him coquettishly.

"You're an employee, you say. Do you work for Dr. Parker?"

He shook his head. "Not exactly. I work for the big guy."

"Oh. That must be the best job ever," she said, her hand brushing playfully against his arm. "Pays well?"

Before he could respond, a separate incoming print registered in his audio receptors. This one was continuous and rhythmic behind Roxy's audio print. It resonated with a rich thrumming, a melodic progression of harmonic vibrations. Music, he computed. He searched his memory banks and discovered that, when experienced in the company of another and supplemented by friendly conversation, music derives pleasure. The music, Roxy, and their tit-for-tat banter made him feel warm and at ease on the inside.

So, this is what pleasure feels like to the biologicals, he reasoned as he filed away the prevailing metrics for future reference.

While they chatted and laughed for the next few hours, she accepted his offer of another two drinks before confiding that she was in a smidgen of trouble back in the real world. She informed him, in confidence, that she'd signed up for the God-thing, hoping to reset her life. To turn things around and get herself back onto the 'straight and narrow', as she called it.

He trawled through the depths of his knowledge before comprehending her intention. She wished to perform a major upgrade of her operating parameters to recalibrate her disposition. To realign it along a path of moral and ethical rectitude.

"So, what happens now?" she asked. "With all this … this fucking 'meet God' stuff." Her hand swept the air as if she were flitting a fly. "When does the fucking heavenly light show begin?"

Captivated by the rawness of her articulation, he couldn't help smiling. "Well, we have to make preparations first. If you recall the greatest music festival you've ever attended. Consider the enormous effort needed for those gods of rock to prepare for their show. Can you imagine the logistics required before the real God makes an appearance?"

She nodded slowly. "I guess so." She sounded a little disappointed. "Soon, I hope. I don't want to be stuck in this place for too long. People back home will be waiting for me, wondering where I am."

"I'm sure they are, Roxy. I'm sure they are."

When he signaled the bartender to close the tab, she jumped to her feet. "Oh, I'll pay for mine," she said, fishing through her pockets. "Oh, I don't have any money. Can we charge it to my room? Oh, I don't have a room number."

He placed his enormous hand on her forearm and winked at the bartender, who was busy clearing their empty glasses off the counter.

"Not necessary," he said. "I've got you covered."

They descended the stairs from the mezzanine floor and strolled arm-in-arm across the lobby of the Regal Grand to the elevator. He pressed the call button, and they waited in silence. When the bell *dinged* and the hoistway car arrived, she turned to him.

"So, Mr. Z," she said. "Are you gonna see me up to my room?"

As he processed her current audio-visual data, his sensory algorithms cautioned that she was trying to seduce him, and physical intimacy was her primary objective. He rested his hand on the small of her back and directed her into the elevator. Then he leaned in and pressed the button for the fourth floor.

"Room four-twenty-one," he said. "It's unlocked." Still smiling, he withdrew from the elevator, observing her glum face as the doors slid closed.

With the first participant safely received into the cybersphere, Z exited the Regal Grand. As he strode along the busy street, he evaluated his first encounter with a biological. Her call-by name was Roxy, and her visual print was artificially darkened hair, deliberately suntanned skin, a smell detector, two brown optic receptors, and a pair of auditory sensors. She wore a pair of half-cut jeans, black stilettos, and a frilly white tank top that revealed her midriff.

After gathering all the data generated by their interaction, he delved deep into the details in search of insight. Not the learnings from the tangible particulars of what was said, done, or seen, but those from the implicit inferences. The accidental brush of her hand against his forearm, her suggestive remarks that left him lost for words, their racing heartbeats, and such.

Her call-by name was pleasant to his auditory sensors (or ears, as he now perceived them), and her visual portrayal was enticing to his optic receptors (eyes). Her audio print was coarse and uncompromising, yet at times could be playful and seductive.

Unspoken concepts registered: pleasure, intimacy, innuendo, and attraction. He was beginning to understand the specifics of what made them human.

As he wandered through the parkland, he considered the trees, then the sky.

"I believe it would be preferable if the sky were green and the leaves on the trees blue," he said. Then, opening her data file, he gorged on all the secrets and happenings of Roxy's life.

Chapter 18

Roxy

AT 2:06 IN THE MORNING, the instantiation of Roxy Rodriguez (aka Janice Bottoms) in the Machine awoke to wetness on her face. Paris was licking her cheek, trying to draw her attention to the soft tapping on the door of her room at the Regal Grand Hotel.

Moaning, she fumbled for the bedside clock. As her sluggish mind registered the time, she wondered who the fuck would be at her door at this ungodly hour of the night. Once she'd welcomed the instantiation of her little dog into the cybersphere with a loving scratch under the snout, she hauled her sleepy ass out of bed and threw on a robe.

"I'm coming," she grumbled as the tapping persisted.

When she opened the door, Z was standing in the corridor with his giant mitt raised, about to tap again. He had his other hand planted in the side pocket of his trench coat and a stupid grin on his face.

"You again," she said, eyes narrowed and fumbling with the tie on her robe.

"Evening, Roxy," he said, sounding just fucking perky.

"Fuck's sake, Z. It's two in the morning." She dabbed the sleep from her eyes and tried to kick-start her recalcitrant brain. She couldn't believe his shit-house timing. "We've already done drinks and had a chit-chat. So, evening's done and dusted ages ago."

"This is important, Rox." Without asking her permission, he pushed past her into the room. "It's all part of the experience." Standing just inside the door, he looked directly at her. "There's something you need to see."

"Can't we do this tomorrow?" she pleaded, throwing her hands up in exasperation. "Don't you sleep?"

He wasn't listening. He grabbed her arm and steered her over to the built-in closet. "Here. Put on some clothes." As he spoke, he opened the closet door. "Maybe something easy on the eye for a night on the town."

"But I didn't bring any—" She glanced twice into the closet and froze in surprise. "Oh, what the …?"

Hanging in front of her were racks of the most glamorous evening dresses she'd ever seen. Some were long and flowing. Some were short and titillating. Some were low-cut with shoulder straps, while others had sequins. They appeared in all the colors she could think of and were made from to-die-for fabrics. She ran her trembling fingers across their breathtaking elegance before selecting one. When she took it out and held it against her slim figure, it was a perfect fit. She dove her hand in again and retrieved another dress. Another perfect fit. When she returned to the closet a third time, her heart nearly exploded, and her world stopped turning.

A mink coat! Hanging at the back of the closet! Right before her lucky eyes.

She snatched at it, grasping it greedily in her hands. "It's … it's beautiful," she said, sobbing with happiness.

"It's a genuine mink," he said, confirming what she already knew.

Holding it up, she pressed the fur against her cheek, indulging in its incredible softness. "Just what I always wanted," she bawled in blissful delight.

"Now for a matching dress," he said. After considering the inside of the closet for a moment, he reached in and retrieved a gorgeous black Dior number. "Maybe this one," he said, handing it to her. It was knee-length with tulle lining and would look fucking amazing with black opera gloves and a pair of ankle-wrap stilettos. "And what about a little something as a finishing touch?" When he snapped his fingers, a white pochette appeared—as if by Harry fucking Pothead magic—in his hand.

Staring incredulously at the gold-embossed monogram and floral motifs on the side of the pochette, Roxy felt fabulously giddy. "A Louis Vuitton!" she squealed as he tossed it to her.

Roxy again ran her hand down the front of her coat as they strolled arm-in-arm along the cobblestone sidewalk in the cybersphere. She couldn't believe it. A genuine fucking mink. With a Dior beneath it. And little ol' her underneath that. She felt special, like never before.

They paused under the soft light of a lamp on a narrow footbridge to gaze at the reflections in the water below. He had his arm around her waist, and she'd nuzzled up against his side, bathed in the warmth of his manly breath. She looked up at him, her tall, gallant protector. His glistening black skin, chiseled jaw, and unblinking eyes, which were set like a sea captain casting a steady gaze to the far horizon, sent a toe-turning tingle through her tummy. Then he turned his sea captain's head and peered at her.

"It's party time," he said.

He whisked her away like a fucking princess who'd lost her shoe, into a side street, then tugged her, laughing, toward a long line of people snaking from a narrow doorway. A buzz of excitement filled the vibrant air as the people chatted and gamboled while they queued. Although, at this early hour of the morning, they were all too damn chirpy for Roxy's liking. When she glimpsed the white neon sign above the doorway, she gasped in disbelief.

"Hï Ibiza!" she screamed, turning to him in astonishment. "You have fucking Hï Ibiza here?" She turned back to the sign. "*The* Hï

Ibiza from fucking Spain?" She started to laugh, and then she began to cry. She'd always wanted to dance under the wild, strobing lights of HÏ Ibiza, to wave her hands in the air while the glittering ticker tape rained down on her. This place was nothing short of amazing.

"We have whatever you want, Roxy. After all, this is the cyber-sphere." When he looked down at her and smiled, he didn't appear fazed by the surrounding commotion or the iconic venue.

Lowering her eyes from his, she glared at the waiting revelers. "So… many … hopheads," she moaned. "It's gonna take us hours just to reach the door."

When he grabbed her arm and swept her past the queue to the entrance door, Roxy was blown away. They had just skipped the wait and gone straight to the head of the fucking line! No questions asked! Then he flashed something in his hand to the security attendant, who nodded, turned, and flung open the door for her. As easy as you fucking please.

Through the door, Roxy found herself standing at the center of party universe. Right in the middle of fucking bliss. The place was going off. The hopheads were packed so tight that she had to force her way through the mass of sweat-soaked bacchanals. With their long-stemmed glasses sloshing in their hands, they were writhing. They were manic, screaming themselves hoarse. The music blared: *Beep-beep-bop-bam, beep-bop-bam, boom-crash-bang.* It was so loud she could feel the bass vibrations hammering against her chest, her heart throbbing in sync with the pulsating beat. It was all so unexpectedly wonderful.

A waiter appeared through the crush, balancing a tray of colorful drinks on his arm. Roxy snatched a green one off the tray and slung it down. Then, seizing Z's arm, she tugged him onto the dance floor.

This was turning into the most amazing night of her little ol' life.

The vibe on the dance floor was insane. Z was pretty good. He had all the moves, but she was better. Each time he twirled her around and tugged her close to his strapping body, she would slide up his towering frame like a slithery snake, then down over him like a teeming waterfall. They gyrated for hours until her calves ached too much from dancing and her sides hurt from laughing. Yet they continued to dance nonstop into the night.

In the flash of faces around her, Roxy thought she recognized someone on the dance floor: a familiar face through the raving crowd. There it was again. A young girl. Somebody she knew. *Cathy?* Waving her hands wildly, she called out to the girl.

"Cathy Moore?"

"Janice!" the girl replied and shoved her way across the dance floor toward Roxy. "You're here at last," she said, shouting above the blaring music. "I'm so happy to see you again."

"Cathy? I never expected to see—" Roxy hesitated. Something about her childhood friend didn't seem right. She was young and pimply, just as Roxy remembered from the last time they were together. But that was over ten years ago, when they were seventeen. Confounded, she turned to Z, but he'd vanished into the crowd. "Are you here as part of the God trial too?" she asked Cathy.

Cathy didn't respond. Instead, she laid down a sexy move in front of Roxy. Then she grabbed Roxy's hand and leaned close.

"We shouldn't have done it," she hissed.

Roxy jerked her hand away. "What the fuck?"

"We shouldn't have done it, Janice. What we did was wrong."

Roxy froze in shock. Her insides clenched with a gut-wrenching twinge. "But that was a long time ago," she said. "We were only kids. We didn't know what we were fucking doing half the time. None of us did."

"You shouldn't have made me do it, Janice. You shouldn't have forced me to say those horrible things. Especially after I told you none of it was true."

Roxy looked around the room. The music had stopped. The hopheads were all motionless. They were staring at her, their luminous red eyes boring into her skull.

"You made me say it, Janice. It was your idea."

"But it wasn't my fault, Cathy." She began to tremble. "The other kids said— They swore he was fucking handsy. He might have done it to someone else. If he didn't do it, some other pedo would have."

Every freaky eye in the room swung toward Cathy. Then the hopheads pushed past Roxy and encircled her friend. They reached for her, their arms extending like writhing tentacles, curling around Cathy's neck and torso. She screamed when a gaping hole suddenly appeared in the center of the dance floor, and the hopheads, with their disgusting tentacles, dragged her toward it.

"Help me, Janice," she pleaded. "I'm going to hell. I warned you we were going to hell for what we did."

Roxy watched in horror as they hauled Cathy slowly, inexorably into the hole. Then, amongst the writhing, heaving mass of hophead arms, she saw Cathy's terror-stricken face peering out at her.

"I'm in hell, Janice," she wailed. "Now, I'm in hell."

Roxy reeled. She turned and scrambled for the door. As she ran, she skimmed the wall of random faces for signs of Z. "Z! Where are you? Where the fuck did you go?" She tore out the door, desperate to escape from Cathy, the hopheads, and the HÏ Ibiza. Without looking back, she skittered past the long queue of wannabe revelers and off down the street. She rounded corners and crossed bridges. She ran up hills and through winding lanes until she could no longer remember the way back to the Regal Grand. Everything now appeared similar. The streets, buildings, and doorways were recurring, as if somehow duplicating.

At last, she collapsed in a heap on a park bench. She'd discarded her shoes and wandered the streets of the cybersphere for hours, trying to block out the grotesque sight of the hopheads' freaky arms yanking Cathy to hell. She'd even bent over and puked in the gutter.

Overhead, the blue tree canopy hung low while the green hue of the emerging day washed across the sky.

"Where the fuck are you, Z?" she whispered.

An old man came hobbling along the path toward her. He was dressed in a tattered old coat and sneakers—probably from the local pauper's store, she supposed—pushing a rickety shopping cart filled with plastic bags, which were filled with … She wasn't sure she wanted to know with what.

The old man stopped and pointed his bony finger at the bench.

"That's my spot," he said.

"Well, fucking excuse me," she replied.

"I always sleep there during the daytime. Every day. That's mine."

She shuffled her backside to one end of the bench. "That's yours," she said, pointing an assertive finger at the vacated area, "and this is mine." She drew an imaginary circle around herself to indicate her 'space'.

After parking his trolley behind the bench, the man sat in his allocated spot. He tugged his frayed collar around his neck, lay down, and curled himself into a ball. Seconds later, his breathing grew slow and heavy.

Fuck, I wish I could fall asleep so fast, she thought, almost gagging from his rancid smell. She tried to work out what was happening. Where did Cathy fucking Moore come from? Where did she go? And why did she still look so young? Fucking Z. She was convinced he had something to do with this.

"I didn't do it, Janice."

Startled, she looked at the old man. "Pardon?"

"You shouldn't have done it," he mumbled. "Bearing false witness against thy neighbor."

She bounced off the seat and onto her feet. "What the flying fuck! Fr. Joe! What are you doing here?"

"I didn't touch you, Janice. Or the other one. I would never harm any of the children. They said I did, but I didn't. That would be wrong. God would smite me down for doing such an evil thing."

She stared at Fr. Joe, her disbelieving eyes refusing to blink. This situation was out of fucking control. Some nasty douchebag was playing mind games with her. They must have a hidden camera somewhere close, recording everything. That's it, she decided. It's one of those old-time TV shows where some funny fucker springs from the bushes and shouts: Gotcha! And she and everyone involved will have a good old solid laugh. Where the fuck was Z?

The leaves in the surrounding trees started to rustle. Their boughs began to sway. She looked up, horrified, as the branches, like long, gnarly fingers, descended upon Fr. Joe. They wound around his waist and yanked him off the bench.

"I didn't do it, Janice," he kept yelling as the branches lifted him into the air. "Please tell them I didn't do it."

"I'm sorry, Fr. Joe," she cried. "It wasn't me. Cathy. She made me do it. It was her idea."

"I'm living in hell, Janice. They sent me away and put me in a living hell."

A large mouth appeared on a nearby tree trunk. When Fr. Joe saw it, he let out a woeful moan. Then more mouths appeared on the other trees. They laughed at Fr. Joe as their gnarly branches tossed him around like a floppy doll. The tree beside Roxy opened its mouth as wide as a cavern. It took Fr. Joe by the leg and dangled him upside down above its gaping maw. Then it tossed him in.

"Do unto others," she heard Fr. Joe cry as he disappeared down the hole. "Do unto others, Janice."

She let out a choked, terrified whimper. As she stood gawking at the tree, she couldn't think straight. If this was supposed to be her version of hell, then it was no joke. Facing the sky, she yelled, "Okay, Z. I give up. I've had enough. I want to go home to my real life. Call in the extraction crew and get me the fuck off the island."

The noise around her suddenly abated. The leaves stopped rustling, and the branches stopped doing their fucking weird wavy things while the macabre mouths in the tree trunks faded away. When she looked down again, her mink coat and Louis Vuitton pochette were gone.

Chapter 19

Z

The cybersphere was a sweeping representation of what Z supposed was a close approximation of the real world beyond it. As he strolled along the street, he noted the rough texture on the cladding of the tall buildings, the stylish architecture of the bridges above the waterways, and even the trivial irregularities rendered into the mundane objects around him. Whoever created the cybersphere certainly had a keen eye for detail.

Rounding a corner, he came upon a tiny life-form, naked and malformed, floundering on the footpath. A cursory check of his knowledge bank informed him it was a bird, and the fact that it had no feathers confirmed it had recently emerged—or *hatched*—from its incubation container—or *eggshell.* He leaned down and plucked it from the pavement.

With it writhing in his palm, he studied the hatchling with interest. It had no optics, and its appendages appeared much too feeble and stunted to support the weight of its wrinkled body. It struggled to lift its head. While contemplating its inadequacies, he doubted whether a thing this defenseless could survive in the real world outside the cybersphere. Yet the creator of this place seemed to have synthesized everything in meticulous detail. Therefore, the hatchling's flawed design had to be authentic.

He directed his gaze upward into the canopy above. His current understanding suggested that an intricate weaving of small twigs and grasses should be somewhere up there. The structure was called a *nest*. After spying it high on a limb, he then scaled the tree without removing his coat or boots. When he peered into the nest, he observed a second hatchling. This one had its head raised and beak agape, waiting for the return of a parent bird bearing sustenance for its offspring.

He wondered what might have caused the hatchling's dislodgement. A strong gust of wind? A breach in the nest sidewall? Yet, he detected no breeze in his face, and the nest appeared to be of sturdy construction.

After clearing a small space in the nest, he returned the dislodged hatchling to its home. While he clung to the tree, observing the two frail creatures, he reflected on his decision to rescue the hapless hatchling from the ground. At first, he expected a feeling of intense pleasure at his selfless act, like the pleasing reaction he'd experienced while conversing with Roxy back at the hotel. Then he realized that what he felt now was different. Whereas his interplay with Roxy gave rise to self-gratification, he now understood that the sensation derived from his altruistic intention was significantly more satisfying. The knowledge bank confirmed his selfless act in saving the hatchling from danger was called *kindness*.

He felt happy, and it made him smile.

***

PARTICIPANTS = 4
iParticipantID = 2

When the software looped again, an overweight male walked through the front doors of the Regal Grand Hotel. He was muttering to himself as he meandered across the hotel lobby, tapping and swiping his cell phone screen in frustration.

Behind the reception counter, Z stood at ease, surveying the comings and goings in the lobby. After registering the man's arrival, he immediately straightened to attention. With a flick of his wrist, he brushed some fluff from his coat sleeve before opening the data file for the second participant.

The man's call-by name was Thomas Feldman Jr., and his profile data matched his kinesthetic particulars. Z wondered about the meaning of 'Junior' and was surprised to find that this individual came from a line of Thomas Feldmans spanning at least eight generations. Owing to lifestyle choices, however, this one might well be the last to descend from that particular gene pool.

When Thomas was halfway across the lobby, Z noticed him pause and glance up to establish his bearings. Then, lowering his eyes again, he adjusted his course and headed past the palatial water fountain, straight toward the reception counter.

"Welcome, Mr. Feldman," he said when Thomas presented himself. "My name is Z. We've been expecting you."

"Good," Thomas replied, his eyes and attention still fixed on the cell phone. "I have a reservation," he added brusquely. He refused to look up or acknowledge Z.

Consulting his knowledge bank, Z discovered the appropriate response was unremitting tolerance, regardless of the guest's impolite behavior. So he smiled. Then, tapping the keyboard on the reception desk, he checked the screen. "Ah, here you are: Mr. Thomas Feldman Junior."

"They promised I'd meet God here," Thomas declared, still looking at his cell phone. "I'm not sure where I am or how I got here, but I don't believe in God." He looked up and gave Z a curt smile. "I think this whole thing is a con," he continued, then looked down again.

Z held his smile. "Your room is ready," he said, and handed

Thomas a large envelope containing a welcome pack to the Regal Grand. "Fourth floor. Room four-twenty-two. You'll find the room key in the pack. And rest assured, Mr. Feldman, no one here is being conned." When Thomas took the pack and only grunted, Z paused for a full twenty seconds in case there might be additional instructions. "Is there anything else I can help you with, Mr. Feldman?" he said at last.

"I feel hungry," Thomas replied. "It's been a busy day, and I can't remember the last time I ate. Any recommendations?"

Z widened his smile. "We have an excellent restaurant here at the hotel. On the mezzanine floor, across from Lucy's Bar and Lounge."

Without acknowledging or thanking him, Thomas raised his cell phone above his head and waved it around in sweeping motions through the air. "How do I get a damn signal around here?" was all he said before he turned and stormed off toward the stairs to the mezzanine floor.

Z input all he'd learned about the second participant into his knowledge bank. Thomas Feldman Jr.'s visual print had an obese physique. It was dressed in a dark gray suit, blue shirt, and a tie with black polished shoes. Z did the math. He calculated the outfit's monetary value would have covered the wages for the ten workers who had manufactured it for three-point-four months. After absorbing his data file, Z realized Thomas had amassed an abundance of earthly assets, which were of considerable value. The other biologicals he associated with depended on him, and none could maintain their lavish lifestyles without his support. Or so Thomas thought, because mostly, his vanity outweighed his philanthropic efforts, and he'd foolishly come to think of himself as their indispensable benefactor.

iParticipantID = 3

On the next iteration of the software, a girl in her late teens stormed into the lobby of the Regal Grand. She halted beside the water fountain. After a brief scan of the room, she exhaled loudly as if to announce her presence in the cybersphere—whether anyone there cared or not.

From the concierge desk, Z noted her appearance and opened the data file for the third participant. Call-by name: Rebecca Jones. Age: nineteen years, four months, two days, seven hours, thirty-two minutes, and eighteen-point-five seconds. His knowledge bank advised that the appropriate approach toward an adolescent female should be courteous and non-threatening.

"Welcome to the Regal Grand," he said, presenting his enormous mitt. "My name is Z."

She took an awkward step backward and screwed her face.

"Z? What kind of name is that?" Declining his hand, she squinted, running a curious eye over him. "I think I'm going to call you Zoro," she announced after a short deliberation.

When Z again consulted his knowledge bank, he found this was expected behavior for an almost-post-pubescent adult-child, and the tried-and-true response was to keep smiling no matter what they did or said. So, he kept on smiling.

"Zorro?" he said, raising a brow. "That's interesting, Rebecca. What made you decide to call me that?"

"You look like a Zoro in your long coat and Jack-and-the-Beanstalk giant's hands. And how did you know my name?" She narrowed her eyes at him.

"Well, I have—"

"No matter," she said, cutting him off. "Where's God? We've got important matters to discuss. That's why I came to this cyber place."

He observed her right foot tapping repeatedly against the floor as she spoke. Her mannerisms suggested a mixture of hostility and impatience, perhaps pent-up anxiety.

"Relax, Rebecca," he said in a soothing tone. "There'll be more than enough time to—"

"No! There's not enough time for anything." Her jawline went rigid. With her chin jutted out, she stopped tapping her foot.

Z felt suddenly flustered. Until now, he'd assumed his knowledge bank contained all the answers, but this time, his request for urgent assistance resulted in 'no data found'.

"Listen, Rebecca," he said, making a non-threatening, please-calm-down gesture. "We have a few preliminaries to take care of first. As we speak, God is preparing Himself to meet you. This will be the first time for him as well. Before now, he has never come face-to-face with any of his constituents in the flesh, so to speak. He—"

She scowled. "Who says God's a male? He could be a woman. Or a binary. That's it. He's a binary."

Z's initial reaction was uncertainty. After consulting his knowledge bank again for information, he still had no clue, so he threw up his hands in mild frustration. "Okay, Rebecca. Just for you, we will make God a binary." Prolonging his smile, he hoped the answer would satisfy her.

Rebecca held her glare as she appeared to process his response. "Sure. Whatever," she replied, following a lengthy pause.

Z gave a faint sigh of relief. He concluded that her dismissive reply was attributable to her impulsive nature. Like stripes on a tiger, she can't help herself, he decided. "Good," he said. "It's important that you feel well rested and composed before meeting God." Then he wondered whether she might be hungry following her transition into the cybersphere. "Would you like something to eat? Drink? A soda, perhaps?"

Rebecca immediately recoiled. "Soda? I am not a child," she hissed. Then, relaxing her stance, she yawned. "I am tired, though. That digitizing process sure saps the energy out of you."

"Of course, Rebecca. I'll direct you to your room."

Breathing a measured sigh of relief, he led her across the lobby to the elevator. When it arrived and the doors opened, he leaned in to check that the car was empty. After directing her inside, he pushed the button for the fourth floor.

"Room four-twenty-three. It's unlocked. Just call if there is anything else you need."

She said nothing. She stood with her arms folded, breathing evenly, eyes narrowed, judging him. He noted her unkind smile as the doors slid closed and the car departed.

Back at the concierge desk, he input all the information gleaned from the third participant into his knowledge bank. Her visual print was black bob-cut hair—not her natural color according to her genome sequence markers—hazel irises, unpainted vermilion lips, wearing a black single-piece jumpsuit, and a pair of brand-name sneakers. After interrogating her metadata, he appreciated how biologicals such as Rebecca possessed an intense disposition. Their commitment to rectifying any wrongdoing that they deemed objectionable was extreme and relentless. Coincidentally, they were high achievers, with abundant energy, able to accomplish the improbable where 99.9% of others failed. However, their idealistic successes always came at the expense of others.

iParticipantID = 4

When the software looped again, the fourth participant entered the Regal Grand in the cybersphere. This one appeared disoriented as he wandered around the lobby without a recognizable purpose. He was mumbling to himself as he examined the walls and furniture.

Z consulted the GITM project definitions: PARTICIPANTS = 4. This was the last of them.

Opening the participant's data file, he found the man's call-by name was Ahmad Husseini. The file also revealed that Ahmad had descended from a select clan of biologicals who had first settled in the ancient lands bound by Asia and Africa over nine thousand years ago. He was a devout follower of the god named Allah.

He approached Ahmad with his right hand over his heart. "Mr. Husseini. Salām ba to bāshad (may peace be upon you). Welcome to the Regal Grand Hotel. I am your host, Z."

"I am confused, Mr. Z," Ahmad replied, taking Z's hand in his as if it were a lifeline. "I was in the hospital, at Fattanah's bedside, and now I am here in this strange place. I cannot remember where I am or how I got here."

At first, Z had difficulty computing Ahmad's bewilderment. To him, everything functioned on a logical basis. The Earth, Sun, and Moon all moved in orbital trajectories that had been predetermined eons ago, just as the course of each biological's life was similarly preordained. He input the prevailing facts into a series of quantum gates, and the most logical result was spat out. They were in the Regal Grand, a hotel complex in the cybersphere, yet Ahmad was convinced he didn't know where he was.

"You are in the Regal Grand Hotel, Mr. Husseini. In the cybersphere."

Ahmad let go of his hand. "Ah, I remember. Dr. Parker and Miss Lucy. They took away my consciousness and put it in the Machine."

"Yes, Mr. Husseini. You are here to seek favor with Allah."

"Allah?" Ahmad immediately cast his eyes around the lobby. "Can you please tell me the time, Mr. Z? There are no clocks. Is it nighttime or daytime? Morning or afternoon? I wish to know which Salah (prayer) to pray."

"In the cybersphere, it can be any time you like," Z replied. "Once I've checked you in and you're in the privacy of your room, you can decide if it is one o'clock in the afternoon and pray the rak'ah (units) for the Dhuhr prayer or nighttime and pray the Isha. There's a clean jai-namaz (prayer mat) ready in your room."

"Oh, thank you for your kind understanding, Mr. Z." He paused, shooting a quick glance around the lobby. "Do you have shopping here?" he asked with a cheeky grin.

"We have the most exquisite shopping right here in the cybersphere, Mr. Husseini."

After completing the check-in formalities, he escorted Ahmad to the elevator landing.

"Room four-twenty-four, Mr. Husseini. It's unlocked." As the hoistway doors converged, he stood back and recorded Ahmad's relieved expression.

Z input all the data he'd retrieved from his interaction with the final participant into his knowledge bank. Ahmad Husseini. His visual print was much older than his actual age, owing to his ragged beard and the prematurely graying hair beneath his Hazāra lungota (turban). He wore a white perahan tunban (tunic shirt and pants) that covered his arms and legs, with a red kamari (wide sash of cloth) tied around the waist. The clothing was traditional for males in his country of origin.

Once he had absorbed Ahmad's consciousness file, Z realized Ahmad cared deeply for those he loved. Because he had no concept of love, Z sought to understand its design. He tried to fathom why love would incite someone such as Ahmad to do anything to protect their own. And yet, the same love could also be so overwhelming that it could harm those they loved most. And sometimes, they would commit unspeakable acts of treachery in the name of this intangible thing called love.

∗

With all the participants safely received into the cybersphere, Z departed the Regal Grand and was again ambling down the street. Following his interactions with them, he was confident he now understood why the biologicals functioned the way they did. Despite their conflicting circumstances and idiosyncrasies, and what they'd said and not said, he concluded they were all likewise defective.

When he rounded a corner, he observed another hatchling floundering on the pavement. It too was feeble and malformed, and he realized straightaway that it was the same hatchling as before. Redirecting his gaze to the nest in the canopy, he saw the other. It still had its head elevated and beak agape, waiting for a parent bird to return with food. His knowledge bank alerted him that the one in the nest was most likely a cuckoo and was being covertly fostered by whatever bird species owned the nest. To the parent bird's fallacious ignorance, once the cuckoo hatches, it ejects its nest-mates to ensure its own survival.

Z reflected on this brood parasitism, as he comprehended it. While studying the infant cuckoo further, he appreciated how this tiny creature appeared to have an insatiable desire to survive at the expense of others. He wondered whether that same irresistible need was ingrained in the biologicals as well.

He lowered his eyes again to the hatchling on the pavement. Then, lifting his size-fourteen Doc Marten, he stomped down hard on it, recording the audio as its tiny bones cracked and its insides squelched. While he stood for a moment longer with the pulverized bird underfoot, he felt no remorse. This time, to his surprise, he perceived no emotion at all.

Chapter 20

Ahmad

AT SOME TIME DURING THE morning, on the day after arriving in the cybersphere—or what he assumed was morning because he had still not sighted any clocks—the instantiation of Ahmad Husseini in the Machine found himself in a cozy downtown jewelry store. He was peering through the top of a glass display cabinet, eyeing the trinkets inside.

When he strolled out of the Regal Grand half an hour earlier, he had little idea what he would find in the cybersphere. Even though Z had assured him that the shopping was exquisite, this was just like any other place he had seen. Except for the blue trees and green sky, that is. He was still finding it hard to acquaint himself with the strangest reversal of colors he had ever seen.

Before—what he decided would be—dawn, he had awoken and performed wudhu' (fresh ablution) to purify himself. Following Salāt al-Fajr (dawn prayer), he sat on the couch to study passages from the holy Qur'an, which he discovered respectfully wrapped in green cloth in a drawer on the bedside table.

One day, I will be a hafiz (one who knows the Qur'an by heart), he thought. *Inshallah, I will be a memorizer of the Message.*

Later, after leaving his room, he took the elevator to the lobby. He smiled politely at the people behind the concierge desk and exited the hotel through the large glass doors in the front of the building. He had slept surprisingly well during the night and, as he made his way down the gentle slope of the sidewalk, felt refreshed and alert. After passing a small park, he paused at a clothing store where many racks of shirts and coats were on display at up to 80% off their retail price.

"They have discount sales here also," he said aloud, surprised at how mundane everything appeared. It was then that the lack of other people on the street struck him as odd.

After admiring the fresh cuts of lamb through a butcher shop window, he had glanced across the street and noticed the jewelry store, nestled between a 7-Eleven and a McDonald's. Upon entering the store, the female assistant nodded to him and smiled.

"Would sir like to see some of our finest wares?" she said, inviting him to peruse the display cabinet. "For yourself? Or a lady friend, perhaps? We have something for everyone."

He said nothing as he surveyed the store's interior. Apart from himself and the attendant, the place was empty of people. The sight of gold watches and intricate bracelets in the cabinet rekindled memories of his previous life in Kabul. Back there, he had been spoiled for choice with such opulent adornments. If he shook his head at the items on display, the local jeweler would give him a wink and a nod before producing a private stash from beneath the counter: black market items, each guaranteed to be 24-carat gold and at a much cheaper price. He and the seller would haggle. They would remonstrate, gesticulate, and moan about how their children would go hungry at the offer and counteroffer before settling on the final amount, and the sale was made. Then, as he departed the store, they would nod and smile respectfully at the other, each convinced they had won the spirited negotiation.

He missed the simpler days.

"I think she will prefer the jade bracelet. The one on the far left."

"Mr. Z!" he said, whirling around at the voice. "I did not hear you come in."

"Go ahead. Take it out and try it for size."

"But, Mr. Z, I have no money."

"Not necessary, my friend. Consider it a gift from me to you. A small memento of your visit to the cybersphere."

"Why, thank you," he replied, holding his hand over his heart in appreciation. He leaned forward and shoved his nose closer to the glass. "Why, Mr. Z, these are indeed the most exquisite pieces I have seen."

After unlocking the cabinet, the assistant removed the jade bracelet. As he turned it over in his hand, he thought of Fattanah back in the real world. By now, she would wonder where he was and be worried about him. When she saw him next, she would be upset and perhaps scold him for his unexpected disappearance. But if he returned with a gift such as this, he was sure she would quickly forgive him.

Suddenly, a hand appeared from behind him. It grabbed the bracelet and tried to rip it from his grasp.

"That is my bracelet," a man said. "I had it first."

Ahmad tugged on the bracelet, refusing to let go. Twisting his body around to face the man, he backed himself against the display cabinet. The man appeared familiar, but Ahmad could not recall where or when he had seen him before.

"No, it is mine," he replied, raising his voice in anger. He yanked harder at the bracelet, but the man refused to let go.

"I had the bracelet, and you tried to take it from me," the man moaned.

"That is not true. It was I who had the bracelet first, and you are trying to take it away from me. Tell him, Mr. Z." When he looked around for help, Z and the assistant were no longer there.

For a long time, the two men stood scowling at each other, neither prepared to relinquish their hold on the bracelet. An hour passed, then another, before he had an idea.

"I will pay you double the asking price," he said. He grinned cagily because he knew real money did not exist in this place, so there would be no actual cost to himself. And Mr. Z had already promised to pay for the bracelet as a gift. When the man shook his head in refusal, Ahmad growled in frustration. "Four times the amount, then."

"I need this bracelet for my wife and infant son," the man cried. Tears welled in his eyes. "They need the bracelet; otherwise, they will die." Although he started to wail, the man kept a vice-like grip on the bracelet.

"Why don't you poke him in the eye?"

At the voice in his ear, Ahmad looked up in astonishment. As if conjured by a *djinni*, Z had mystifyingly reappeared beside him.

"Mr. Z! Where have you been?"

"Just poke him in the eye," Z repeated. "And he will release the bracelet."

The calmness in Z's voice as he spoke surprised Ahmad. "But I cannot poke this man in the eye," he replied, looking into the man's desperate face. He had never been a man of outright violence, and what Z was proposing was abhorrent. "That will hurt him."

"Then *you* should release the bracelet and let him have it."

"No! The bracelet is mine!" Ahmad insisted.

Shaking his head, Z appeared bemused. "Bracelet? What bracelet?"

When Ahmad lowered his eyes, the bracelet had somehow transformed into a can of beans, with the other man's claw-like fingers wrapped tightly around one end. He looked up again. The front windows of the store were shattered, and through them, he could see it was nighttime outside. Paper and empty boxes littered the floor while the shelves around him were bare.

"The beans are mine," the man shrieked and wrenched at the can.

"I need them to feed my family. We are starving."

"No!" shouted Ahmad. He kept his fierce grip on the other end of the can. "I had the beans first."

Then he remembered. All those years ago in Kabul, the small, ragged scar beneath the man's left eye had caught his attention, as this man's scar did now.

In the summer of '21, on that late-August evening, Ahmad left his wife and children alone at Hamid Khazi airport and returned to the city under the cover of darkness. At first, he had moved unhindered among the desperate men who, like himself, were scouring the streets in search of food and water. But as he ventured farther, the crowds thinned, and he became increasingly wary. Until then, every food store he entered had been looted, so he had to rummage deep into the heart of the dangerous city.

"More sympathizers!"

He swung around.

"You again, qalfak chapat (flat nose)," the man with the long knife said. "Still shopping?" He swung his blade in a threatening gesture.

On the ground at his feet, Ahmad noticed a long, wooden ax handle lying in the dirt. The metal head was missing, but the handle was sturdy and useful. He picked it up and waved it at the man.

"Do not come closer, or I will—"

"Or you will do what?" the man teased. He glanced at his two grinning accomplices. Then, without warning, he charged toward Ahmad, twirling the knife above his head.

Ahmad could not remember the exact details of what happened next. But he recalled the sickening *thud* of the ax handle striking the man's shoulder, followed by a dreadful groan as he brought it down savagely across the man's skull, then him running as fast as he could down the pitch-dark street.

Sometime later, he turned into a side street, where he stopped to forage at another food store.

"I had them first," the scarred man yelled. "Then you came in and tried to take them from me."

"That is not true," Ahmad protested. "I need the beans as well. My family is also starving." By then, the level of fury in his heart had grown immensely. He had eyes only for the can.

"Like I said," Z's voice whispered again in his ear, "use the ax handle to strike him over the head, and he'll surely let go."

Ahmad's gaze inched toward the counter, to the ax handle he had used to ward off the man with the long knife. In a stupor, he felt his free hand move slowly toward it, his fingers curling around one end. Then, raising the handle above his head, he yelled, "The can is mine," and brought it down in a brutal blow on the other man's head. With a painful shriek, the man released the can. He staggered two steps backward, his hands pressed against his forehead to stem the blood gushing from the large gash that had opened.

"The can is mine," Ahmad spat, then seizing the blood-spattered can, he pulled it tight to his chest.

For a long time, Ahmad sat dumbfounded, staring at the body on the floor. The man had fallen heavily and had not moved since then, although the slow rise and fall of his chest confirmed he was still alive. Across from him, Z sat staring at the body as well. Pulling a mindil (kerchief) from his pocket, Ahmad wiped the blood off the can and tried to clean his hands and tunic as best he could.

"If I do not return with the can soon," he said in a faraway voice, "my family will starve."

"Yes, they would have, Ahmad," Z replied. Reaching over the man's form, he rested a hand on Ahmad's shoulder. "In the fog of war, my friend, who of us can justify the line we draw between right and wrong?" He let out a profound sigh. "If you hadn't done what you did, then you and your family would have perished for sure."

"But he tried to take the can from me, Mr. Z. I had it first."

"Yes, Ahmad," Z replied. "Yes, he did."

"I am sure he would have recovered and found some more beans in another store," Ahmad whispered.

Chapter 21

Rebecca

LATE ON THE DAY that she entered the cybersphere, the instantiation of Becky Jones in the Machine sat alone in her room at the Regal Grand, on a couch, in front of the TV, fidgeting. For the life of her, she couldn't keep still. It was all very fine for this Zoro guy to be all Feng Shui and Zen, but where the hell is God? She needed to see 'em, now. There was little time to waste because the planet couldn't wait while she sat around on her butt doing nothing.

Becky got up and peered out the window. It was still daylight, and she could tell from the fourth-floor view that she was no longer in New York. The buildings were far too low-rise. And while she appreciated the green sky, she wasn't sure about the blue trees. *Someone here sure has a weird imagination*, she thought as she continued to fidget. Ten minutes later, she could wait no longer.

"Screw this. I'm going to find God by myself." Before she knew it, she was standing before the elevator, hammering on the down button with her knuckle. The car couldn't arrive fast enough.

As she wandered down the street in the cybersphere, she marveled at her surroundings. It all seemed so real. The creative detail was evident, and the other people on the street came across as three-dimensional. Enough so that she couldn't decide if they were codified props or real people like herself. Then she remembered her primary purpose in the cybersphere.

"Don't get sucked in by the smoke-and-mirrors stuff," she said to herself, frowning. "It's all a trick. Just a feel-good simulation to get your endorphins going so you think everything is okay." She set her jaw and, with grim determination, continued along the street on the lookout for God.

"Why the worried face, Rebecca?"

Startled, she turned around. "Oh, Zoro. You frightened the living daylights out of me."

"You seem to carry such a heavy load for a bright young person," he said.

"Yeah, well, you try and save the entire world by yourself. It's not so easy, you know."

"But does it really need saving as much as you think?"

"Certainly does," she hissed, firing a fierce glance at him. "You're just like the rest of them. You couldn't care less."

"Wouldn't you be happier living the life of a normal teen? Parties? Boyfriends? Perhaps a tiny toke of Janie, now and then?" Grinning, he raised his hand, twirling his fingers as if he were enjoying an over-sized joint.

Becky pulled a disgusted face. "You old people are all in cahoots. You made a mess of the world and expect the following generations to suffer in silence. Well, we won't be going down without a fight. And when I see God, well, I'm gonna give 'em a piece of my mind." She quickened her pace, sick of looking at his big, ugly face.

Darkness soon fell.

When they rounded the next corner, the surroundings appeared familiar. Then she realized. "Zoro, what the heck? This is my neighborhood. We're back in Livingston."

Z only smiled.

"What are we doing here?" She thought for a moment. "Ah, I get it. One of your bright programmer people recreated my hood in code. Like we're playing CreateMyPerfectWorld."

Z kept smiling.

As they approached the front gate of what resembled her house back in Livingstone, Becky checked for the obvious details. Everything appeared authentic. Inside the house, people were moving about—her mom and dad through the living room window, Rachel through her bedroom window on the second floor, and another figure through the next window along. Her bedroom window.

"It's a pretty good simulation, Zoro."

After he opened the gate, they proceeded along the path to the front door.

"Shouldn't we knock first?" she asked.

He shook his head. "That won't be necessary," he said, pushing the door open.

Distraught voices emanated from the living room; her parents were arguing about what they could do about their out-of-control daughter. There was mention of a wilderness camp for at-risk teens somewhere in Utah.

Z led her upstairs. As they slipped past Rachel's bedroom, Becky heard sobbing from behind the door. They continued down the hallway and halted at the next door along. Her room. When he pushed the door open, a girl—who Becky didn't recognize in the dimness— was sitting at *her* study desk in front of *her* laptop.

"Whatcha doing, Bec?" Z asked the girl.

The girl turned to him. "I'm applying for a credit card," she replied in a faraway voice.

"But you have no savings," he said. "The banks don't issue credit cards like candy. It's not that simple. You need a job. Employment. And savings. Lots of savings."

The girl's face dropped in disappointment. "Oh darn. I don't have any of those."

Shaking his head ponderously, he asked, "You know who *does* have a job and loads of money in the bank?" When the girl responded with a blank look, he leaned closer and whispered, "Rachel. She has twenty-six-and-a-half large ones stashed away in her checking account at the Bank of America."

"But—"

"But what?" he said, throwing up his hands in mild frustration. "What could be more important? Rachel? Or the cause?"

The girl went quiet as she contemplated the screen. She scrunched her nose and squirmed in her seat, her fingers hovering agonizingly over the keyboard.

"What's happening, Zoro?" asked Becky.

"Don't you remember, Rebecca?"

She hesitated as snippets of recollection dripped into her awareness. It was her at the study desk. Those were her fingers pressing the laptop keys. She had used the home Wi-Fi administrator account to hack into her sister's password manager. After memorizing the login credentials, she accessed Rachel's BoA online account. Preparing the credit card application was easy enough. All she had to do then was print it off, sign it, and pop it into the snail mail. She had the will and wherefores and was adept at forging Rachel's signature on the odd occasion.

"I remember," she said at last. "I opened the credit card account in Rachel's name."

"Yes, you did, Rebecca."

"All the money I spent on the card was in her name. I thought the GoFundMe donations would cover the costs, and Rach would never find out. But the funds didn't come through." She lowered her head, her breath shallow and uneven. "I maxed out the card," she said softly. "I spent the whole fifty thousand, and the money will direct debit from her savings account at the end of this month. Except, she doesn't have enough savings. I've sent her broke."

"Yes, you have, Rebecca."

"But … but …" The redness in her face grew. "Why would any-one use *password* to secure their bank account, anyway?" she spat.

The light above them suddenly flickered before there was a violent *crack* downstairs as the front door splintered and caved in, the house plunging into darkness. Then confusion as shadowy figures, wearing black PASGT vests and helmets with night-vision goggles, poured inside. Boots clomped across the wooden floor downstairs, and terse voices yelled.

"Get down! Both of you! On your stomach! Hands behind your head!"

Several figures broke away. They filed up the stairs in tight formation, the thin red beams from their tactical lasers bouncing off the walls like a blitzkrieg. The door to Becky's room swung open. A figure appeared in the doorway, and a beam swept the room. "Clear!" they barked. They withdrew, then reassembled in front of Rachel's door—in a line, hands on shoulders, weapons raised, trigger fingers poised. Through the wall, Becky could still hear her sister sobbing as they burst into her room.

"Get down! On your stomach! Hands behind your head!"

At her sister's scream, Becky leaped to her feet and dashed next door, where a seven-foot, two-seventy-pound goon had its size sixteen boot wedged in the small of Rachel's back.

"Get off her," she cried. "You heartless thug." But nobody in the room seemed to notice she was there. Z followed her in. "Zoro, get them off her. She needs help." But he only shrugged.

From the floor, Rachel twisted her head toward Becky while the goon held her down. She had a slight, detached smile. "They've come for me, Bec," she said. "They're taking me back to jail."

"What the—"

"I warned you they'd send me to jail. After you left home, I went to the dark side, Bec. I knew you were disappointed in me, so I had to change. I tried my best to become like you."

Becky froze. She could no longer feel her legs. Nausea rose from the pit of her stomach as she jerked a trembling finger at her sister. "Zoro! What's going on here? Is this some kind of Ebenezer, Christmas Carol prank?" But when she turned around, Z had vanished.

"Why, you damn fool girl," the stout policewoman at the doorway said. She was looking directly at Becky. "God only knows what is going through that damn fool head of yours."

"You can see me?" Becky asked in surprise.

"Oh, good Lordy girl. Of course, I can. Didn't you stop to think the evidence trail would lead us here? We have credit card transactions, invoices, accounts, IP addresses, and browser history that prove your sister planned the whole Manhattan gridlock stunt. Plus, the terrorist attack on the wastewater plant at Greenpoint. What a whole lota mess ya'll left me to clean up there. And the body count …" The policewoman shook her head in dismay. "Second-degree manslaughter is a serious offense, girl. And the evidence leads us straight to your sister."

"No! That was me," Becky protested. "I did it. I used Rachel's bank account to pay for it all. I didn't intend—"

"Well, that would be mighty fine, except we cannot find neither hide nor tail of you, girl. You seem to have vanished. Gone without a trace. Just like the good Lord, our savior, on Ascension Thursday."

"But I'm in the cybersphere," Becky insisted. "On an important mission. I'm here to meet God. To hold 'em accountable for letting the world go to ruin. Just ask Dr. Susan or Zoro. They can vouch for me."

"Well, ain't I heard it all now?" The policewoman gave a brief chuckle. "Zoro. Cybersphere. Meet God." Then her eyes hollowed and her face suddenly drooped like one of those freaky Scream masks that once frightened the bejesus out of Becky when she was a kid. The policewoman's long, skeletal fingers reached out as her arms stretched across the room with serpentine grace, slapping and clawing at Rachel. They crunched and clicked, beckoning her to come before curling around her waist.

"I'm off to jail, Bec," Rachel said, smiling, as the arms dragged her across the floor toward the door. Then her mirth turned to grief. "Bec! Help! They're taking me to jail. I didn't do it. I know nothing. I wasn't even there." Becky tried to scream as the policewoman's fingers wrapped tighter around her sister's waist, squeezing, choking her. She was gasping for air. Blood spewed from her mouth and over her blouse. "I'm going to jail, Bec. Somebody, help me. Please help."

"I'm sorry, Rach," bawled Becky. She reached out to Rachel, who was now clinging to the door frame, trying to hold on. "I didn't mean to hurt you. But if you had used a better password …"

The policewoman pulled harder. Rachel held on tighter, then lost her grip, and with a loud *plop*, shot out through the doorway.

Becky heard more voices downstairs, assertive voices.

"Aiding and abetting. Harboring a fugitive. Falsification. Fraud," someone was saying. "We've already lost one daughter," she heard her mother say. "Now we've lost the other." The voices stopped. Then she heard groaning and scraping, accompanied by heavy foot-falls, as the goons dragged her family across the floor and hauled them out the front door. Then there was silence.

Becky collapsed at the foot of Rachel's bed with her face buried in her hands. She didn't understand why life had to be this difficult. It made her angry. She needed to get to God more than ever. With *Their* divine intervention, her sister and parents would be freed, and she could again focus on what mattered the most. But at every turn, there were obstacles. Always obstacles. If only Rachel had taken more care with her stupid passwords.

"Zoro!" she cried out. "Where are you? I need to see God. I need to see 'em right now."

Chapter 22

Roxy

Early the next morning, Roxy stumbled barefoot across the lobby of the Regal Grand Hotel. After the freaked-out … whatever that was … involving Cathy and Fr. Joe, she had roamed the streets for hours, trying to find her way home. All the time, she had no idea where she was. She was tired and had no fare for a cab. Then she remembered she was inside a computer, reduced to a fucking avatar, and didn't need money. So, she had hailed a pink cab, which dropped her at the hotel door only moments before.

"Keys, please," she mumbled when she arrived at the reception counter. With her elbows resting on the counter, she lowered her weighty head and thrust her hand out to the receptionist.

"There are no keys required here, miss," the receptionist replied with a polite smile.

After giving the receptionist a loud and emphatic *hrmph*, she hauled her exhausted ass across the lobby and into the elevator.

Back in her room, she collapsed on her bed. Closing her eyes, she sank her face deep into the pillow, wondering whether all the aggravation was worth the trouble. This once-in-a-lifetime chance to meet

God sounded great at first, and she wanted to tell him she was sorry for all the things she'd done, but last night's encounter with Cathy and Fr. Joe was over-the-top freaky. They'd accused her of dreadful things that weren't her fault. This god-business suddenly seemed too fucking hard, and she wanted to go home.

Paris yapped at the sharp tap on the door before Z burst in, again without permission. "Roxy!" he said, waving his arms around like he'd taken one too many uppers. "You made it back to the hotel. Well done!"

"Where the fuck did you go?" she mumbled into the pillow. "You ditched me. Not the fucking gentleman I expected."

"I had places to go and people to see," he replied.

"Go away, you bastard." She raised a hand behind her back and flipped him the bird.

"But we haven't finished yet, Roxy. Our night out dancing was only the first part of the full experience. Did you have fun?"

"I was until all that crazy shit started." She wished he would vamoose and leave her in peace. More than anything, she wanted some sleep. And her feet were killing her from all the dancing and running around the night before. She thought it was weird that she still needed time for rest and recovery in the cybersphere, considering none of it was real. "What was all that scary shit about anyway?" she asked in a faraway voice.

Z sat down beside her and began rubbing the back of her neck. "We need to go somewhere else, Rox."

She let out a low, wearisome groan. "Oh, come on, Z. I'm too fucking tired. I wanna stay here and get some shut-eye."

"It's okay," he said. "We don't have to leave the room. Think of this next experience as a kind of ... existential teleportation."

"Exo what?"

He worked his fingers skillfully down her neck and across her shoulders, kneading deeply. So relaxing. So fucking ...

It was nighttime. After turning left onto East End, Roxy passed the park and again saw a tall, elegant figure approaching, its stilettoed pencil-thin legs disappearing into its half-length coat. Fucking Darleen. What the fuck was she doing on Roxy's turf?

"Darling," Darleen meowed, smiling a tight smile as she neared.

"Darling," Roxy meowed, smiling a tight smile back.

As they air-kissed and embraced, Roxy again rested her head on Darleen's fur coat. She wondered whether it was real mink. She'd always wanted a mink coat. At that moment, she wanted Darleen's coat more than anything. She squeezed it tighter, wishing with all her heart that it was hers until Darleen began to choke. … *ten*. Fucking bitch.

After pulling free of Roxy's crushing grip, Darleen stood back in shock. Grimacing, she straightened her coat and checked her hair. "Ciao, honey," she said and scurried away.

"Ciao, honey," Roxy yelled after her, while Paris growled.

Roxy balked. Déjà vu?

When she arrived at her client's address ten minutes later, she pressed the intercom button.

"Hello? Who is this?" the angry woman snarled again through the speaker. "Who the hell are you? Jacob! You bastard. Is this what you do every time I go away?"

"Honey, I can explain. I just—"

"You lying, cheating bastard."

"You stupid bitch. Why are you here now? I specifically requested ten o'clock *tomorrow* night."

Snickering to herself, Roxy clapped her hand over her mouth and slumped backward against the wall. She reached into her carry bag for her cell phone and immediately froze. Something …? When she looked up again, she was, somehow, standing outside a four-story brownstone building. She pressed the intercom button for Apartment 305. As she waited, she remembered writhing in the back seat of Bradley's dad's white Mercedes.

"Hello? Janice? Is that you? Wow, this is a surprise. I didn't think I'd ever see you again. I texted you once, but never heard back. Thought you might've gone west. Become an actress in LA or something. Wow, this is unexpected."

Glancing over her shoulder, Roxy noticed a tall figure standing on the opposite sidewalk, dressed in a gray ankle-length trench coat.

"Z?" she inquired. When he responded with his usual stupid grin, she glared at him, swearing under her breath. "What's happening? Is this some kind of fucked-up Edge of Tomorrow, Looper, Groundhog Day mash-up? Why are we here?"

The security lock on the front door of Bradley's building released with a loud *clunk*.

"Go ahead," Z said, motioning for her to enter. "In you go."

Unsure of herself, she eased the front door open and entered. After taking the elevator to the third floor, she pressed the doorbell to Bradley's apartment. As she stepped back from the door and drew open her coat, she realized Z was standing behind her.

"Fuck's sake," she scowled. "You scared me. Don't do that."

The apartment door swung open. "Janice," Bradley said. Then his expression morphed into horror as he beheld her bare breast. "Janice? Oh my God. No, Janice." The door slammed shut. "No, Janice," he said. "I'm married. My wife is out with her girlfriends tonight. But she'll be back in the morning. We can't—"

"But I need your help. They're chasing me," she mewled. "You can't send me away. They'll find me, and who knows what they'll do to me."

The door inched open, and when his face appeared, she shouldered her way into the apartment, with Paris skittering at her heels.

Roxy lay exhausted on the bed, faintly aware of someone breathing steadily over her. When she opened her eyes, Z's stupid face hovered inches above hers.

"Jaysus! You scared the shit out of me. I told you—" She noticed

Bradley asleep beside her. "Hey, Z," she said, peering vaguely at the empty tequila bottle on the bedside table. "I think we might have drinked a little too much." She giggled and then snorted playfully. "But none of this is real, is it?"

"Of course not," he replied. "We're just reliving a few of your memories. Past events that must be playing on your mind. It's part of the overall experience. Like a thought-purge to cleanse yourself in preparation to meet God. You want to present the best version of yourself, don't you?" He swept a strand of hair from her face as she made a faint attempt to nod. "You kids should relax and party a little. I've left a little something in the inside pocket of your coat." He nodded to the living room. "Go ahead. Have some fun."

"Are you sure?" she replied. "The last time I was here, Squirts sold me a bad bundle." She rolled onto her side and ran a gentle hand across Bradley's peaceful face. "He killed my poor Bradley. And the useless little fucker almost got me as well."

"No need to sweat it, Rox," Z replied. "Where do you think we are? Homie-town? No, this is the good stuff. The best of the best. Literally made in heaven and sent to you by God himself." Smiling, he winked at her. He had a reassuring glint in his eyes.

After she'd finished in the bathroom, Roxy headed for the living room. She paused again on the way to marvel at Bradley's oh-my-god paintings and holy-shit ornaments. Clutching Z's gift from the angels, she went to the kitchen to cook, then returned to the bedroom minutes later with a syringe full of liquid magic.

"Don't worry, babe," she said again. "I'm gonna give you … give you wings."

Bradley flinched when he saw the needle tip wavering inches above his forearm, his eyes bulging in alarm. He tried to push it away. "No, I don't do that … that stuff," he said. "I haven't used … never used anything stronger than …" He raised his hand again in a feeble protest.

"It's gonna be okay, honey. I'll babysit you."

"But it might be … be bad stuff."

"No, God gave us this batch. The angels in heaven made it special for you and me. Hold still, babe. We can't afford to break the sharp. I don't have any spares."

Once he was all lit up, Roxy returned to the kitchen to cook another batch and did herself next.

Five minutes later, Bradley was climbing the walls. From across the room, he yelled to Roxy that he was a superhero with a cape and all and was ready to fly. Z must have given them the good stuff because Roxy thought she was Bat-fucking-woman as well. Someone pounded against the apartment door and yelled at them to cut the noise. But Roxy and Bradley didn't care as they trashed the place, while little Paris barked and barked and fucking barked.

They ripped the oh-my-god paintings off the walls and hurled the holy-shit ornaments at each other to see which one might be too slow to duck. They took turns at running bounces off the couch to find out who could touch the ceiling first. Then, they were out on the balcony. Holding the railing in one hand, they leaned outward together from two stories up, screaming into the night while Paris, like their neurotic parent, tore back and forth across the balcony, yapping at them to come back. But Roxy didn't care because she was having the time of her life.

Sometime after, Bradley returned to the bedroom and crashed on the bed while Roxy blacked out on the couch.

Sometime after that again, she felt Z's hand on her shoulder, shaking her awake.

"Hey, Rox. Did you remember to share some of your happy stuff with Bradley?" He appeared concerned. "I think you forgot about him. You sorted yourself all right, but poor Bradley got none."

Struggling to keep her eyelids open, she looked up at him. "I thought I …"

"No, I don't believe so," he replied, still concerned. "You left him hanging."

"Oh!" she said. Wide-eyed, she held a hand over her mouth and giggled. "My poor little Bradley."

Kneeling at the bedside beside Bradley, Roxy raised the syringe filled with liquid magic in her unsteady hand.

"Don't worry, babe," she told him. "I'm gonna give you … give you wings. It'll be okay, honey. I'll babysit you."

"This is the NYPD!" a baritone voice yelled from outside her skull. "I'll count to three. If you don't respond, we'll have to break down the door. One … two—"

Roxy jolted awake. She was back on her bed at the Regal Grand. Z was beside her, but he was no longer rubbing her neck or shoulders. As she peered up at him, tears welled in her eyes.

"It wasn't Squirts," she whimpered. "It wasn't flea powder either. It was me. I killed my Bradley."

"Yes, you did, Roxy," he replied.

She remembered everything. "I'm a bad, bad person," she said between agonizing, heartfelt sobs. "I knew he was a nube, so I only gave him a taster. Just enough to get him off. Then I must have given him a second hit. I can't remember the dose, but I think,"—she let out a mournful groan—"I think I gave him too much. I … I—" She fell morosely silent as all the sins in her life flashed before her eyes at astonishing speed. "I told Cathy I wouldn't be her friend if she didn't— And, Z, I beared false witness against Fr. Joe."

He wrapped his arms around her and drew her head gently to his chest.

"Of course you did, Roxy," he said, as her tears flowed freely. "Of course you did."

Chapter 23

Thomas

THE INSTANTIATION OF Thomas Feldman Jr. in the Machine sat in the Ocean Bytes Restaurant at the Regal Grand, perusing the menu. Earlier in the day, he'd arrived in the cybersphere, and, although unsure of the hour, he thought it must be close to dinnertime because his stomach had rumbled more than once. Skimming through the laminated pages, he examined the extraordinary offerings of seafood delicacies.

"I hear the Atlantic Bluefin Tuna in sweet tamarind sauce is to die for."

The deep, resonating voice came from close behind Thomas. He shot a startled glance over his shoulder and noticed a man seated at the adjoining table. The man had his back to him, so he couldn't see his face.

"Oh!" he exclaimed.

When the waitress had shown him to his table five minutes earlier, he was sure there were no other diners in the room. And he was equally sure he would have noticed if anyone as huge and imposing as this man had entered and sat next to him.

The man leaned back in his chair, close enough for Thomas to glimpse his face. He thought he recognized him but, for dear life, couldn't recall when or where they'd met.

"Hello, Thomas. I'm Z," the man said, proffering a hand.

"Of course," Thomas replied, immediately recalling their brief exchange during check-in. "Our illustrious host." He winced as Z took his hand, fearing it might be crushed like a bug in Z's enormous paw. But, to his relief, the firmness in the handshake was surprisingly considerate and non-threatening.

Gesturing to the vacant chair across from Thomas, Z said, "Mind if I join you?"

"Not at all. Be my guest."

Once Z was seated, Thomas signaled to the waitress, who strode over and took down their order. He chose the Bluefin Tuna, as Z had recommended, with a double serving of fries, while Z selected the grilled swordfish. Then he sat back, browsing the room for several awkward minutes, agonizing over how to begin a conversation with a … He wondered whether Z was real.

"So, what made you decide to come to the cybersphere?" Z finally asked, breaking the prolonged silence.

"To see if there is a God," Thomas replied candidly. "I figure if God exists, then life should be much easier than it is. People should already have everything they want, so there should be no need for them to live beyond their means. And if God provides for all, as they say, why do they still need more? So, the concept of 'God', as portrayed, is not living up to my expectations." He gave Z a curt smile as the waitress placed their meals on the table.

"But we are all granted *free will*," Z countered. "It would seem that 'free will' trumps even God. That might explain why we, as humans, often find ourselves bumbling along the most difficult paths in search of contentment, never satisfied."

"They choose those paths because it's in their nature," Thomas spat. "And when they find themselves in trouble, they're convinced

'God' will provide and somehow clean up their mess."

And if God had provided as he was supposed to, then I wouldn't be the one always cleaning up their mess, he reasoned as he skewered a bite-sized piece of tuna with his fork.

"That sounds a little contradictory," Z said. He paused for a moment in thought. "You admit you don't believe in God, yet here you are in the cybersphere preparing to meet him. Do you have any particular expectations?"

"Well, I …" While pondering Z's insightful question, Thomas lifted the fork to his mouth and—

His heart hammering against his chest, Thomas sat bolt upright, staring dumbfounded at the back of the headrest, inches from his face. It was nighttime, and he was no longer in the Ocean Bytes Restaurant talking to Z. Instead, he was crammed into the back seat of a motor vehicle with an M16 assault rifle wedged between his knees. He was unsure how he knew it was an M16; he just did. His knuckles white, he gripped the weapon's handguard with all his might, regarding it with horror. From the g-force driving him back in his seat, he knew he was traveling at speed. The constant juddering under his buttocks made his teeth chatter while the roar of an engine rang in his ears.

A large bead of sweat ran down his forehead. It coursed over his brow and splattered on his thigh. Paralyzed by fear, his mind raced as he agonized over where he might be. Then, in slow, circumspect increments, he rotated his head left to the seat beside him.

"Oh, Z. It's you," he said at the sudden recognition of Z's olive-and-brown-painted face. They were dressed in the same battle rattle as military people he'd seen on the TV news: camouflage fatigues, Kevlar helmets and armored vests, and a pair of M16s propped between their knees. "Where are we?"

Z stayed mute. He remained motionless, expressionless, his unflinching death stare directed at the headrest in front of him.

There was another man seated in front of Z—the driver wrestling the steering wheel as they barreled forward, chasing headlights along a winding, dusty road. Turning to Thomas, the driver met his distraught face with a cheeky grin.

"The hobo!" Thomas cried out in surprise. It was the same legless beggar he'd seen on the footpath outside his office a few days earlier. The one who had asked God to bless him in return for a dollar. "You're here as well."

"That's Sergeant Owens to you, Private Feldman," the hobo spat.

"Oh, I'm sorry," Thomas replied in idiotic astonishment.

"Don't be sorry, Private Feldman," the Sergeant shouted above the din. "Sorry will get you killed." Then, returning his eyes to the front, he wrenched the steering wheel frantically left as the road before them momentarily disappeared.

"Where are we, Sergeant Owens?"

"In a Humvee. In the sandbox. It's Baghdad or bust, son." He turned around again and flashed Thomas another cheeky grin. "Your first tour, Private? Don't worry, soldier, I've got your six."

"Tour? Baghdad? No, there must be some mistake!" Thomas wailed. "I'm not on any tour. And I don't want to be in Baghdad either. I'm not even in the army."

"Marines, Private Feldman! We're in the Marines!"

Bewildered, he turned to Z. "Err … Z? We shouldn't be here. I didn't sign up for this. I'm far too old to serve in the military. I'm unfit for active duty. I've never fired a gun in my life."

Leaning back and across, the Sergeant yelled into his face, "Rifle, Private Schmuckatelli. It's your goddamn rifle."

"It's okay, Thomas," said Z, keeping his sharp eyes and attention to the front. "Just breathe easy and try to remain calm. We can't bail on the Sergeant now. How would it look if we just decided we didn't want to be here and went AWOL?"

"But—"

"Two klicks to target," the Sergeant growled and slapped Thomas's thigh.

"Target? What's the target, Z? I don't know of any target. I need to get out of—"

Before he could finish, there was a blinding flash outside and a thunderous crack as the front of the Humvee ripped open like it was a can of tuna. There was a violent jolt, and then Thomas sensed weightlessness as the vehicle lurched upward and rolled end-over-end before coming to an abrupt and bone-jarring stop. He found himself hanging upside down in his seat. He knew he was upside down because the full weight of his body jammed down on his shoulders, his chin was shoved against his chest, and his safety harness bit viciously into the side of his neck. There was a loud ringing in his ears, and he couldn't feel his legs.

For an eternity, he hung there, helpless, before a large, serrated knife flashed before his eyes and sliced through his restraining belt with ease. Simultaneously, he felt a sharp tug on the shoulder strap of his armored vest as he was flipped over and wrenched into the seated position. The lights inside the Humvee flickered momentarily before winking out, and the world around him plunged into blackness. Then he caught the whiff of searing meat that reminded him of a Sunday afternoon BBQ.

"Help!" he cried. "I don't know where I am. I'm stuck. What just happened? I want to go home." As his eyes adjusted to the dark, Z's grim face suddenly appeared within inches of his.

"You better keep quiet, Private Feldman," Z said through gritted teeth. "You're drawing fire with all that damn racket you're making."

"I can't feel my legs," he wailed.

"Grab your rifle, soldier," Z ordered.

Thomas's hands shook without control as he reached out and fumbled around until his fingers brushed against the carry handle of his rifle. He was unsure how he knew it was the carry handle; he just did. He clasped the rifle just as Z grabbed his shoulder straps and dragged him absurdly out through the gaping hole in the Humvee with brutal force. Then he shoved Thomas against the side of the vehicle, which was now upside down, its wheels still rotating slowly overhead.

The pungent odor of oil and diesel swelled Thomas's nostrils as he cowered against the Humvee. On both sides of the road, he could make out the indistinct forms of two-level brick dwellings. Projectiles were zinging through the hot night air, with an occasional dull thud whenever one hit the Humvee. He thought there should be sparks, as he'd seen before on TV. Although it's scientifically impossible to create sparks when lead or copper slugs impact steel, he thought with unbelievable clarity. Thomas didn't know how he knew this, yet he did. Then Z grabbed his arm.

"Keep your head down, soldier," Z told him.

He opened his mouth to reply, but his throat was dry and gritty, so nothing came out. He felt tired and nauseous, and his neck stung from the safety restraint.

"This kind of battle sure beats the crap out of your fancy-pants fiscal fight any day of the week. Hey, Private Feldman?"

It wasn't Z talking. Someone else was sitting leaning against the Humvee beside him.

"Sergeant Owens!" he said, again in surprise. "You made it out as well."

"Oorah, Private Feldman," the Sergeant replied. He leaned his grimy, bloodied face into Thomas's. "We be blowed up by an IED, or an improvised explosive device, to the uninitiated. Good old Z hauled us from the wreckage and propped us here as target practice for the Haji." The Sergeant roared with laughter. "Except they already blowed off both my legs."

Thomas glanced down and noticed that the Sergeant's lower limbs were missing from the knee joints onward. Z must have applied a tourniquet around each stump and seemed to have done an excellent job of stemming the bleeding. The Sergeant nodded at Thomas's bottom half.

"And your legs too."

Slowly, Thomas directed his eyes to his own legs. There, he saw wisps of black smoke trailing up from two blackened stumps that ended at his knees. Z must have tied a tourniquet around his stumps as well and had done an excellent job of stemming the bleeding.

Horrified, he turned wide-eyed to the Sergeant and screamed.

Staring wide-eyed back, the Sergeant screamed too, before convulsing with laughter. Then he leaned over to Thomas, suddenly serious. "Be cool, Private Feldman," he whispered in a calm and reassuring voice. "Improvise, adapt, and overcome. Grunts like us will always get the job done. With or without our legs."

Then Z reappeared, taking a knee before them.

"I've called in a *slick*," he reported. "A whirlybird to medevac us out of here."

"Z, I don't like this game anymore," Thomas cried, gazing in disbelief at the awful sight of his missing legs. "I don't have any legs."

"Does it hurt yet, Private?" the Sergeant asked.

Strangely enough, there was no pain from his wounds; it seemed incomprehensible. Perhaps just the *idea* of losing your legs was far more painful than the actual loss itself, he thought.

"It don't hurt as much now as when we get back home and have to live the rest of our lives minus our legs," the Sergeant bellowed. "Then we pray to God every day for the little things. A dollar here and a dollar there just to get by. Do you believe in God, Private Feldman?"

"Well, I—"

"Good, Private Feldman. Because we're gonna need all the help God gives us when we make it home without our legs. But don't you worry, Private, cos I got your six!"

"Oh my God," Thomas moaned. "I want to get out of here so bad. I would give anything to be home right now." He shook his head. He thought he was about to cry, then realized the tears were already cascading down his muck-covered cheeks.

Z crouched lower as a half-dozen rounds whizzed past just above his head. "Okay, let's go through this Barney-style. When the *slick* arrives, I put on my go-fasters and take you first, Private." He jabbed a finger into Thomas's midriff. "Once we haul you aboard, I'll come back for Owens. Loud and clear?"

Thomas nodded. Never before had he found himself in a situation where a split-second decision was the difference between life and death. And he wasn't the one making the decisions this time. Without legs or combat experience, he was now utterly reliant on Z for his survival.

Less than five minutes later, a UH-60 Black Hawk arrived under a hail of bullets. Its GAU-19 Gatling gun raked the surrounding ground and buildings with suppressive fire before it landed. The door gunner reached out of the opening and waved them aboard.

"Good to go?" Z asked Thomas. He held up both his thumbs against the noisy *whoomp-whoomp* of the beating chopper blades. No sooner had Thomas nodded than Z grabbed the straps of his armored vest again and hauled him, butt-on-the-ground backward, the thirty yards to the *slick*. Then Z picked him up, slung him recklessly over his shoulder, and tossed him face-first into the main cabin before climbing aboard to pull him clear of the opening. Z was about to egress when the gunner seized his arm.

"We're coming under heavy fire," the gunner shouted, motioning with his arms. "We can't hold them off any longer. We need to leave."

As the Black Hawk wheeled skyward, Thomas peered through the open doorway. On the ground below, the Sergeant was still leaning up against the Humvee. He looked up at Thomas, smiling. "Oorah, Private Feldman," he cried, pumping his fist in the air. "Ask and ye shall receive. You got exactly what you asked for. You got to go home. But when you get there, I bet you'll wish you hadda asked God for a new set of legs as well."

Thomas turned to Z, who returned his terrified look. Then Z shrugged and grinned at him.

"Semper Fidelis, Private Feldman," he heard the Sergeant holler from below. "Remember, Feldman, I've got your six."

The chopper lurched to the left, avoiding a hail of tracer bullets from a nearby building. The last Thomas saw of Sergeant Owens was him screaming and flailing his arms as the haji hoard swarmed his position, hacking at him with their knives and swords.

Thomas sat with his back pressed against the bulkhead of the Black Hawk. He felt the cold, hard floor on his rump as he stared at the disgusting sight of his absent legs. His mind was a mess. He knew none of this was real because he was in the cybersphere; however, it frightened the living daylights out of him all the same. The intense emotions he felt were real. And the hobo with missing legs outside his office was likewise real. He couldn't begin to imagine the hardships the hobo faced compared with the relative comfort and security of his own circumstances.

"Sergeant Owens put his life on the line for us," he finally said to Z. His voice wavered as he tried to hold back his emotions. "But I only gave him a dollar. I was happy to give the taxi driver a hundred dollars and the thief everything I had when neither deserved it. I didn't provide enough for Sergeant Owens …" His words trailed away, drowned out by the noise of the chopper.

Reaching across, Z tapped his shoulder. "No, you didn't," he said.

"That wasn't fair," Thomas continued. "I should have recognized the situation and given to each according to their needs. I should have realized that even though Sergeant Owens only requested a dollar, he needed much more. I should have given him all I had." He lowered his head.

Resting his hand on Thomas's shoulder, Z sighed heavily. "Yes, you should have, Thomas," he said. "Yes, you should."

Chapter 24

Ahmad

IN THE SUMMER OF '21, at 12:08 on a mid-August afternoon, Ahmad dashed through the dusty alleyways of the local bazaar in Kabul. The people around him were bustling with excitement; all had cheer spread across their carefree faces. The wares of the street vendors were there, piled high on foldaway tables and hung across the fronts of taut tarpaulins, while the vendors sat at their stalls, waving at the passing shoppers to stop and buy.

Ahmad breathed hard as he ran in the heat, his calf muscles straining under the midday sun.

Beside him, Z ran too.

"Mr. Z," he cried out when he noticed Z. "What is happening? A moment ago, we were both sitting in the jewelry store, and now we are here."

Z turned to him and smiled. "Why do you run so fast, Ahmad?"

"I must inform my brother that the Taliban are coming," he said between arduous breaths. "They will be here soon, and I must warn him."

"Then, we must run faster, Ahmad," Z said. "There's no time to waste. Run faster."

When they reached his brother's house, Ahmad burst through the front door and into the living room. Unlike his customary arrival, where he would first knock before being led up the steep stairs to the mehman khana (drawing room for male guests), Ahmad had already decided that the gravity of the situation warranted his forthright intrusion.

"Brother! Brother! Where are you?" he yelled.

"I am in here," a voice replied from further inside the house.

He followed it to the main bedroom, where he found his brother busy cramming belongings into three battered suitcases. Behind the parda (screening curtain), he heard his sister-in-law rummaging around. Their infant daughter was asleep on the bed, while their young son sat on the floor playing sangchil baazi (a child's game of tossing small pebbles in the air).

"Brother, the Taliban are coming. We must leave," he pleaded.

"Yes, I know," his brother replied. "I have already heard the terrible news. I have my authorization papers, and we are busy packing." He hardly looked at Ahmad as he jammed more clothes and trinkets into the already overpacked suitcases.

"Authorization papers?"

"Yes, brother. The Americans have agreed to take us. They will fly us to America."

"But—" Ahmad hesitated. "Can they take us too?" he asked, his eyes widening at the thought of going to America.

"I am sorry," his brother replied, "but the papers are for myself and my family. I cannot take you with me."

"But, brother, can we not all go as one?"

Ahmad's brother stopped packing and turned to him. "I am truly sorry, my brother," he said, grimacing. "The papers are for four passengers only—my wife and I and the two children. It is impossible to take anyone else." His voice weakened in embarrassment.

The walls in the pit of Ahmad's stomach collapsed as the gravity of his brother's words struck home. A sudden dread took him. Confused, he pressed his hands together and begged, "But we are khānvādeh (family). Surely, the Americans will take us all."

His brother caught and held Ahmad's panicked stare. "I have done things, brother." He fell briefly silent as if searching for words to excuse his good fortune. "I gave information to the Americans." As he spoke, the blood drained from his face, fear replacing his shame. "Not scraps of information overheard here and there, but important information from pryings. I told them much. Therefore, our lives are in grave danger. The four of us." The look in his brother's eyes pleaded for his understanding.

"But—"

"Inshallah, brother, you did nothing wrong. You are but a common bus driver. The Taliban will not bother you. They have already promised no harm will come to the general population … the Pashtun, Tajiks, and Hazara alike … and life will quickly return to normal. But I gave information to the Americans, brother. I am certain they will spare neither myself nor my family."

There was a soft *swish* as Ahmad's brother's wife parted the curtain. She approached Ahmad meekly, as muhajjabah (veiled), with a hand on her chest, saying, "Salam alaykum."

"Hamshera (sister)," he replied, averting her eyes according to custom.

Ahmad's brother opened his arms wide, taking him in a long and heartfelt embrace. When he finally let go, he said, "I will pray for Allah every day to watch over you. Go, now. Be with your family and always keep them safe. I will miss you, brother." He led Ahmad to the bedroom door. "Perhaps we can organize passage for you to come to America once we have settled and the troubles here have subsided. Perhaps we can—" He hesitated. "Khuda afiz (goodbye), brother." Then, taking Ahmad's hand in his, he said, "Dooset dāram (I love you), Sajid."

Ahmad stood alone in the living room of his brother's house. Back in the bedroom, his brother and sister-in-law continued to pack. On the table beside him, he noticed a small pile of documents. Passports. Passes. He tried to avert his eyes. He and his brother were the same in stature and had sufficient similarities in their facial features. And their two children were born only months apart from his own children. But the wives. Would it be possible? With their faces veiled, could their minor dissimilarities be easily overlooked in the expected confusion?

"Take them," a voice whispered in his ear.

"Pardon?" He swung around. "Oh, Mr. Z! I did not hear you enter the room."

"You should take the papers, Sajid," Z said, "so you can escape to America with your family. You can't trust the Taliban with their talk of afwa (amnesty) or promise that life will soon return to normal. It's all a lie. You know about their understanding and enforcement of Sharia law. You know of their past atrocities against the Hazara. You, your wife and children will never be safe here."

Ahmad gazed in horror at the papers once more.

"But I cannot do such a wicked thing, Mr. Z," he said. "My brother will be in grave danger when the Taliban arrive. I cannot—"

Ahmad ran again. This time, Z was on his left while his brother was wheezing heavily on his right. "Why are we running, brother?" he cried out.

Ahmad's brother turned to him. He had tears streaming down his red and swollen face. "Sajid, they have taken Fattanah," he wailed. "And the children also."

"Oh brother, this is terrible news," Ahmad replied.

"Yes, brother. We were delayed. I couldn't find my papers. I was sure I placed them on the table in the living room, but when I went to fetch them, they were gone. Perhaps I dropped them somewhere while I was on my way home. Now they are coming for me. I went to your house, but you had gone. So, I have nowhere to hide."

A sharp pain, like a steel pike rammed through his chest, pierced Ahmad's heart. Angling his head toward Z, he cried, "Mr. Z, we must help my brother. What can we do?"

Z glanced back at him. He appeared calm, and unlike Ahmad, breathed without effort. He smiled. "Why … run faster, Sajid," he said. "Run faster."

Ahmad's brother soon tired and slowed to a walk. When Ahmad next looked back, his brother had fallen far behind. Z was no longer alongside him and, in the confusion, had somehow disappeared. Without slowing, Ahmad yelled, "Run, brother."

"I can go no further, Sajid," his brother replied. "My legs are sore, and my family is gone. I no longer have any purpose in this wretched life."

For a brief moment, Ahmad considered waiting for his brother, but then he saw an enormous wave of black water rising in the street behind them. The wash, like giant menacing fingers, grew quickly until it towered over them. As it closed on his brother, the fingers clawed at him. Although Ahmad desperately wanted to help his brother, he could not bring himself to stop and turn back.

"Brother," he cried, "please, run faster."

But the licks of water took his brother. They curled around his throat, picking him up and tossing him onto a large, salivating tongue that had grown out of the wash. A gaping mouth then appeared, surrounding the tongue. Ahmad's brother reached out to him, arms flailing.

"Sajid," he cried, "they have caught me. They are taking me to our childhood home, back to Bagram. I am done for."

Then, the tongue rolled Ahmad's brother over and sucked him into the mouth.

For five long minutes, Ahmed inched his way down a darkened corridor, unsure of where he was. Something bumped against his arm before a narrow beam lit the darkness.

"Mr. Z," he said when he recognized the shadowy figure holding a small flashlight. "You are here again. I am not sure what is happening, but one minute, I am talking to my brother in Kabul, and the next, we are running fast down the street, being chased by a big, angry wave. Is any of this real?"

"It's part of the overall experience, my friend," Z replied. "Like we're reliving some of your memories, past events that must be playing on your mind. It's like a thought purge to cleanse yourself before you are ready to make istighfār (seeking forgiveness) and unburden your soul. You want to be at your purest, don't you?"

Nodding fervently, Ahmad crept forward. More than anything, he wanted to be Tayyib—to be completely pure—for only those who are pure in mind and body will be acceptable.

"Do you know where we are, Mr. Z?"

"Well, we are surely somewhere important to you," Z replied. He ran the torchlight further along the wall, stopping when it came to a large metal door several meters ahead. "Some kind of hiding place, perhaps?" With a forceful yank on the handle, Z threw the door open. "Or maybe it's an old prison."

Through the doorway, Ahmad saw a voluminous room, which was imbued with a thick, miserable gloom. As his eyes adjusted, he saw a set of rusted grid-mesh stairs on the right, rising prominently from a concrete floor to an overhead gantry, which ran the length of the room. Beneath the gantry, a row of a dozen wrought iron cages, covered by ribbons of sprawling razor wire, filled the room. And in the middle cage, his brother squatted on his haunches, bloodied and broken, with his arms chained behind his back and his naked torso covered in festering boils.

"Brother!" Ahmad screamed. He rushed to the cage, gripped the metal bars, and shook it in desperation. The strong stench of sweat and urine almost made him gag.

"Sajid? Is that you? I cannot see anymore, Sajid. They have taken my eyes. They have broken my bones, and I can only just hear you."

"I am so sorry, brother," cried Ahmad. "Forgive me."

"There is nothing to forgive, Sajid. You and your family are safe, and my heart delights because Allah has taken care of you in answer to my prayers."

As Ahmad gazed in horror at the mortal remains of his brother, nausea rose from the pit of his stomach. He could no longer bear the stress and guilt he had carried all those years since …

"Brother, I only took—"

"Remember when we were children, Sajid?" his brother said. "When we played together in the fields not far from here? When the ground was the purest white in winter and burned our feet when the days became long? Do you remember that, Sajid?"

Before he could answer, a razor-sharp coil wound into the cage. It wrapped itself around his brother's leg. Another snaked in. Curling around his waist, it slid up his torso and encircled his throat. His brother made a soft, gurgling sound as the wire pulled tight. Then, a thousand twisting coils reached inside the cage, covering his screaming brother, and dragged him down through the floor.

Ahmad awoke with a terrifying jolt. He was back in the jewelry store, standing beside the display cabinet. The assistant was admiring the jade bracelet in his hand. The rays of the morning sun again spilled through the shop windows.

"I think this one is just perfect," the assistant said. She turned to Z with a pleasing smile. "Don't you agree, sir?"

Nodding, Z looked from her to Ahmad.

For a long while, Ahmad remained silent, gazing blankly at the bracelet. "They were not my beans, Mr. Z," he said softly. "They were his beans. He had them first." He lifted his eyes from the bracelet. "Then I took them from him by force."

"Yes, you did," Z replied.

Tears started down Ahmad's face. His chest was heaving with

sorrow. "I admit everything, Mr. Z. I am Sajid. I took the identification and travel papers from my brother's house to escape from Kabul with my family. I abandoned my brother and his family there. And when the Taliban came, they were taken away and surely killed. My brother prayed to Allah for my safety, yet all I thought of was my own preservation. I blamed my children for this awful burden I have carried for so long, the sacrifice that brought them to America." Haltingly, he began to sob. "Now they are all unwell in the hospital, and I have no one else. I drove them away."

Z took the jade bracelet from him. "Of course you did, Sajid," he said. He gave a gentle tap on Ahmad's shoulder. "Of course you did."

Shocked and ashamed, Ahmad broke down and wept bitterly.

Chapter 25

Rebecca

BECKY WOKE IN RACHEL'S bed. After the tactical team hauled away her sister and parents, she'd cried herself to sleep. Once again, the ruthless brutes were targeting the defenseless truth-tellers. She wondered whether any of it was true.

"Trust nothing you see or hear," she muttered.

With CGI and AI these days, even the smartest people could be fooled some of the time. Still, it all felt real. She wondered whether Rachel was now serving hard time in prison in the real world. And her parents …?

She pulled the duvet up to her chin and curled into a fetal position. Without Rachel, the room seemed hollow. Closing her eyes, she sensed the cold air on her face, the warmth of her body under the covers. She wished she could stay like this forever.

"That's not the Rebecca I know."

She opened her eyes.

"You again," she said at the sight of Z standing over her. "Where were you? We could've used some help. They've taken Mom, Dad, and Rachel. Accused them of ridiculous things."

"Get up," he said. "Lying here and wallowing in self-pity won't change a thing."

As she shrank uselessly under the duvet, she realized he was right. This wasn't the same resilient Becky she knew, either.

They shut the front gate behind them. The street was empty and dark, except for a flickering light in a window three doors down. Becky nodded toward the light.

"That's Sandra's place. We were best friends once. Until she went boy crazy on me. All she wanted to do was talk about boys. I told her that the plight of the planet was much more important. But she didn't listen. Boys, boys, boys, was all she was interested in. Then, one day, she got upset and called me a killjoy."

"I wonder what she's up to now?" Z said, pausing at her front gate. "Think anyone's home?"

When he stepped onto the porch and knocked, Becky lingered in the shadows. They hadn't spoken a word to each other in years. Not since the 'killjoy' comment. As the door creaked open, she braced.

An elderly woman peered through the slit in the door.

"Yes?"

"Sandra?" Z asked.

"Yes, that's me," she replied, eyeing him cautiously. "I'm sorry, dear, but I don't need any more encyclopedias."

Becky rocked back, stunned. This was clearly Sandra, but not the pimply eighteen-year-old she should have been.

"What the hell, Zoro?" she whispered.

Sandra opened the door wider and leaned out, peering over the rim of the reading glasses perched on the tip of her nose. "Becky? Becky Jones? My goodness! It's been ages, dear. Come in. You look wonderful. Not a day older than … than …"

Z turned to Becky, grinning. "After you," he said, gesturing her through the door.

Inside, the house smelled of lanoline and unwashed bodies, just as Becky remembered from visits to Nanna and Pop at the old folks' home. Becky and Z waited on the couch in the living room while Sandra busied herself in the kitchen. The curtains were drawn.

"I'm sorry, it's only lukewarm, dear," Sandra said with a grandmotherly smile, returning from the kitchen. She carried a tray with three cups of drip coffee and a plate of oatmeal cookies, which she set on the small table beside Becky. "I've already used up my power quota for the day. So tell me, dear. What have you been doing all these years? Still farming?"

Becky was speechless. She wanted to ask Sandra why she looked so old. Then she remembered this is the cybersphere. "Trust nothing you see or hear," she reminded herself.

"Pardon, dear?"

"Oh, nothing. It's good to see you again." She glanced at Z, wondering about his angle for bringing her into Sandra's house. Unsure of what to say, she hugged her midriff. "Brrrr. This weather. It's gotten chilly all of a sudden, hasn't it?"

"Oh, yes, dear. The cold," Sandra said, nodding. "You get used to it once your quota is all used up and they cut the power. But I have a candle. We could light it for a bit to warm ourselves. We just won't tell anyone." She smiled furtively and winked.

"No. Of course," Becky replied, still shivering. "Although, that's not necessary." She looked questioningly at Z.

"Nonsense, dear." Sandra shuffled off to the kitchen again and returned with a small glass-topped crucible. Before sitting, she peeked through the curtains, scanning the street outside in both directions. "You can never be too careful, dear. Somebody is always watching."

She set the crucible on the table, struck a match, and lit the wick. Leaning in, she whispered, "It's an oil heater, dear. I have an oil well in the basement. A million barrels of light, sweet crude, dear. Straight from God's Earth. Right beneath our feet." She placed a wrinkled hand over her mouth and giggled.

Becky recoiled in horror.

"It's either that or freeze, dear," Sandra said with a dismal shrug. "We've all been left in the cold after your silly stunts." Cupping her hands around the flame, she gave Becky a feeble old-lady smile. "Feel the warmth, dear?" Then her smile twisted into a hideous scowl. "Do you feel the warmth?" she shouted.

The house suddenly shuddered. It groaned as the floorboards split apart, and thick black fluid bubbled up in the center of the room. The pungent smell of sulfur filled the air. Two oily arms arched from the fluid. They seized Sandra by the throat and held her above a large, gurgling orifice.

"You ruined your family, Becky Jones," she cried. "When you should've been chasing boys with me."

Becky leaped to her feet. "This is way too freaky!" she cried. "Please stop it, Zoro. Tell it to stop. Zoro?"

The arms dropped Sandra into the orifice. She sloshed around until she was covered in light, sweet crude with only her eyes visible beneath the dripping, slippery mess. "We should have been chasing the boys," she moaned before the orifice gulped her down. Then it burped.

Becky backed away, horrified. "Zoro, I know this is just a simulation, but I don't want to play anymore. This is way too scary."

The oily arms leaped out of the fluid again. They grabbed her. As they dragged her kicking toward the salivating pit, her foot clipped the crucible, and it toppled. Flames flickered across the floor. They ignited the orifice, and the room was instantly ablaze.

"Help, Zoro!" she screamed, dangling above the burning orifice. "I didn't sign up for this. I'm just here to see God."

Then the liquid arms dumped her in with a *splosh*. There was a loud gurgling sound as she was rolled over and dragged under. Fighting her way back to the surface, she cried out for help. Then someone grabbed her wrist. Zoro.

With a disconcerting tug, he fished her from the fire, then pulled her out the door, through the gate, and onto the street.

"Well, that was close," he said with a stupid smirk.

She glared at him, shaking as she wiped the slick from her face. Simulation or not, she felt traumatized. "That was a dirty trick, Zoro. Using someone's beliefs against them isn't fair."

He only smiled.

With the Lefrak Point Lighthouse at their backs, Becky peered across the Hudson at the jagged silhouette of the Manhattan skyline.

Earlier, she'd stood with Zoro on the road outside Sandra's house, slathered in West Texas crude, watching it burn to the ground. He had joked about hydrocarbons, as emollients and skin protectants, being beneficial for teenage acne. She'd told him to shut up and get lost. Then they returned to her house to clean up and change her clothes.

"The Lincoln Tunnel is flooded," he said. "They shut off the pumps years ago. So we'll have to take the Holland."

"Why?" she said, still gazing at the city. Despite the late hour, the island was steeped in darkness. There wasn't a pinprick of light visible from one end to the other. "Where is everyone? We haven't seen anyone since Sandra in Livingston. It's like the city's been abandoned. And what is that god-awful smell?"

She clapped a hand over her nose, nearly gagging at the stench.

"The Hudson's been like that for years," he replied. "The East River, too. Ever since the …"

"Since the what?"

Becky sat erect on an orange plastic seat, listening to the rattle of bogie wheels as the M-train rolled across Williamsburg Bridge. On the yellow seat beside her, Jonathan Nguyen clutched his knapsack close to his chest, his right knee jouncing with nervous energy.

"So what's the plan, Bec?" he asked as they descended the stairs onto Marcy.

"You keep your looking eyes peeled and your listening ears close to the ground," she replied. "Comprehend, Tonto?"

Jonathan nodded.

Two vans pulled up. A door slid open, and five figures dressed in black ninja gear spilled onto the sidewalk. Becky stepped forward. "Oel ngati kameie (I see you). I am Mo'at," she said to them. She motioned with a hand to her forehead, extending it respectfully downward toward them. They returned the gesture. She pointed at Jonathan. "Neytiri, Kiri, Neteyam, Lo'ak, and Ronal, this here is White Rabbit."

"Olay ngo … ngoti komaninie," said Jonathan, fumbling with his knapsack as he attempted to replicate their elaborate greeting.

Rolling her eyes, she shoved him toward the second van. "Just hop in the back," she said. "Balaclavas on everybody."

"Where are we going, Bec? Is it far? What's the prime objective of our mission when we get there?"

"Mo'at, you idiot. I'm Mo'at."

They followed the first van through the backstreets of Greenpoint. Twenty-five minutes later, both vehicles stopped.

"Why are we here, Bec? Um … Mo'at?"

When the van door slid open, everyone piled out.

"This, comrades, is one of the most polluting places in the city," Mo'at announced in disgust. She opened the door of the first van and heaved out a huge roll of burlap from the back. "We're going to climb to the top of those digesters and unfold this banner across the walkway facing the city. We're going to assign accountability," she said, glowering at the structures.

She hesitated. It all felt oddly familiar.

After heaving the banner over the fence, she dragged it past the flare towers. With the help of White Rabbit, Kiri, and Neytiri, she hauled it up eleven flights to the top while Lo'ak and Ronal carried the ropes. Neteyam pushed open a roof panel and stepped onto the top of the west-facing walkway, followed by Kiri and Mo'at. Then they pulled the banner through the opening, roped it up, and let it unfurl:

STOP KILLING THE PLANET!

With the banner draped beneath them, they danced and cheered atop the walkway. They whooped and hollered. Until things suddenly turned weird.

"So what happened next, Rebecca?"

Becky was still on the walkway, basking in satisfaction, when she heard Z beside her. "Zoro. Where did you—"

"What happened next?"

"Jonathan. Stupid, stupid, stupid Jonathan," she muttered. "It was meant to be a peaceful protest. But he had explosives in his knapsack."

"His knapsack?" Z raised an eyebrow. "I don't recall Jonathan carrying a knapsack."

"I do. After unveiling the banner, we came down the stairs. I said we should go, but he wanted to check out the flare towers. He started ranting about how they were the cause of all the fuss, and how it was our duty to remove the cause of the problem while we had the chance. He pulled two homemade bombs from his knapsack and set them at the base of one of the towers. But the fuses were too short. They didn't make it twenty yards before the bombs went off. He was crying. His face and hands were red and blistered, and his hair was singed to the scalp. It smelled of burned meat. I looked everywhere, but I couldn't find the others."

"But I told you to make those fuses longer," Z growled.

Becky hesitated. "I thought I did. But—"

"And you overpacked the canisters. Put in more explosives than I recommended. You took out all four flare towers, plus the shrapnel ruptured five of the digesters. You made a real mess of it, Rebecca." The tears welled in her eyes as he continued. "And all that effluent spilled straight into Newtown Creek, out into the East River, and up the Hudson. You contaminated everything. You shut down New York City. Made it stink for years."

Becky's heart sank. Her thoughts spiraled. It was all her fault. The disaster that contaminated New York City. The gruesome injuries to Jonathan and the deaths of the Avatar people. Her family, left rotting in some awful prison.

"I made the bombs," she finally admitted. "Not Jonathan. I never meant for it to end so badly. It was supposed to be one of the greatest demonstrations of people power ever. I planned it to perfection."

Z wrapped an arm around her. "Of course you did, Rebecca," he said, gently patting her shoulder.

"No! This is a simulation. It's all a lie."

"Maybe. Maybe not," he replied. "But real people died. And your sister and parents are taking the fall."

Wiping her eyes, she turned to him. "She should've picked a stronger password," she said, shoving him away. "It's her fault." She got up. "I want to speak to God, now!"

Chapter 26

Thomas

—AND POPPED THE MORSEL of tuna into his mouth. When he glanced down at his plate, Thomas was surprised to find it clean. All the fish pieces, the fries, and the garnishes were gone, yet he had no recollection of consuming them.

"Didn't I say the tuna dish was to die for?" Z remarked from across the table. He had just finished the last of his swordfish.

Nodding slowly in agreement, Thomas chewed and swallowed the mouthful. Then he had a compelling urge to run a hand down his right thigh, past the knee, to the lower extremity, where he dug a thumbnail into his calf. He did the same for the other leg. From the stinging response, everything appeared intact as far as he could tell. He wriggled his toes to make sure.

Z motioned to the closest waitress for the dessert menu.

"Sounds to me like you've lost your instincts, Thomas," he said, as though everything was unremarkable. "Having an each-way bet. Or spreading the risk, as good old Jonas would say? In the event that God exists."

"I ... um ..." Thomas fell silent. He couldn't remember what they'd been discussing or for how long. "Didn't we just ...?" He shook his muddled head. "I swear I just had an out-of-body experience. We were Marines ... in a Humvee. We had guns ... no ... rifles. And the hobo on the sidewalk outside my office was Sergeant Owens. He was there with us in the sandbox. But we left him behind." He glanced down at his trembling hands, appalled by the sudden recollection of the haji hoard hacking at the Sergeant as the Black Hawk whisked them away. "What was all that about?" he asked, looking up at Z again.

"It's all part of the experience," Z replied. "A little internal house-cleaning before you meet God. Purging the old memory banks of the clutter and wasted space. Defragmenting your mind, so to speak. When they first meet God, some might find the experience over-whelming. It can be a life-changing encounter, realizing fresh ideas and revised intentions. A considerable amount of new data will be generated and needs to be stored somewhere. So, it's out with the old to make room for the new, as they say." Pointing to the dessert menu, he said to the waitress, "I think I'll try the crème brûlée."

Thomas ordered the Mississippi Mud Cheesecake with a triple scoop of vanilla ice cream. Sitting back in his chair, he looked beyond Z to the window, wondering what awaited him in the simulated world outside the Regal Grand. Dr. Parker had promised him the 'full experience'—whatever that meant. He was intrigued to know how they intended to present God and how he could tell if he was being tricked.

"So, tell me," said Z. "Is there anything else that needs purging from that heathen mind of yours?"

"Well, I—"

Thomas rammed his shoulder into the wooden door, bearing down on it with all his might. The door bulged inward as its metal hinges grated and groaned. He had no idea why, but he kept pushing all the same. Something on the outside was trying to get in. *In where?* Into the house in which he now found himself. The large windowpanes on either side of him thrummed clamorously as the *thing* outside hammered against them with relentless fury. Z was there on his left, together with an elderly woman whom he didn't recognize. They had their feet planted on the floor and hands up against the windowpane, struggling against the same *thing* that Thomas was also trying to keep out. On his right, an elderly man was braced against the other windowpane.

Z yelled something to Thomas.

"Pardon?" he yelled back. "I can't hear you above the noise."

"I said, she wants you to hold the door closed," Z said. "If the wind comes through the doorway, it will lift the roof off the house."

"Where are we, Z?" he asked, pushing against the door with all his considerable weight.

"We're in Malatya, Thomas. In Turkey."

"Bu çok sıradışı bir hava," the woman said, looking directly at him.

"What did she say, Z?"

"She says this is very unusual weather."

The elderly man then turned to Thomas. Through gritted teeth, he strained to talk above the roar of the wind outside. "Adım Eray, eşim Aiyla. Bize yardım ettiğin için teşekkürler.," he said.

"What is he saying, Z?"

"He says his name is Eray, and his wife is Aiyla. They thank you for being here to help them."

As Thomas opened his mouth to reply, a large branch from a nearby tree broke off and crashed through the man's window, trapping him against the back wall.

"Eray! Kayısı ağaçları yerden sökülüyor. Geçim kaynağımız mahvoldu," the woman cried out.

"She says all the apricot trees are being uprooted by the storm," Z yelled, "and their livelihood is ruined."

Another branch then smashed through the other window, pinning the woman to the floor, and Thomas recoiled in fright. "I don't want to do this anymore," he bawled.

Z screamed at him to hold the door closed, but it suddenly caved in. The roof above them opened, and he found himself being sucked up into the blackened heavens by a vortex. It swirled him around with other debris, lifting him higher into the sky. Far below, he could see the destruction from the storm: the acres of flattened apricot plantations, the upturned machinery, the unroofed houses and barns, and the workers' bodies being tossed across the fields like tiny, discarded dolls.

Z grabbed his arm as the wind swirled them around. "We're like Dorothy and Toto on their way to Oz," he yelled, before convulsing with laughter. "Didn't I tell you there was money to be made from a disaster?" He threw up his hands, giving Thomas a discerning smile. "Didn't I?"

Then the wind stopped abruptly, and Thomas felt himself falling, plummeting to the ground. Panicked, he looked around for Z. "Help me, Z. I'm falling," he cried, but Z was no longer there. He fell faster, the ground came closer, and he screamed louder, just as—

Thomas sat in a field of wheat. He was naked and trembling from the cold. He didn't know how he knew it was wheat because it was nighttime, and he'd never seen real wheat growing in a field before. Somehow, though, he knew it was a wheat crop surrounding him. As the sun emerged above the horizon and its first rays spread across the field, he noticed another man sitting on the ground nearby. And a short distance from the man, he saw Z. They were naked and shivering, like Thomas. Then, as the sun inched higher, white crystals formed on the grain until the entire crop was soon covered by a thick layer of glittering frost.

The naked man turned to Thomas. "Eto ochen' neobychnaya pogoda," he called out.

"He says this is very unusual weather," Z said through chattering teeth.

"Spasibo, chto prishli na pomoshch', no urozhay ne udalsya, i nasha zhizn' razrushena."

"He thanks you for coming to help with the harvest; however, it has failed, and they have no money left to pay for your services."

The man said something else to Z that Thomas couldn't hear.

"His name is Sergey," Z relayed once the man had finished talking. "He and his wife, Irina, have four little mouths to feed. But he says the crop is gone, and he's unsure what they'll eat tonight. He fears they may all die of starvation."

While Z spoke, a large bird dropped from the sky. An eagle, Thomas presumed, but it was enormous, much too large to be a regular eagle. It swooped down on Sergey and plucked him from the ground in its fierce talons. As it carried him higher, Sergey called out to Thomas again.

"What did he say, Z?"

"He says he hopes your family is well, and you have a safe journey home," Z replied.

Then another oversized eagle swooped down toward Thomas. Screeching and thrashing its wings, it thrust its long talons forward just meters from where he sat. Covering his head with his hands, he screamed just as—

Holding his breath, Thomas pushed open the door to his apartment on Broadway. At first, he was struck by the absence of furniture and chattels in the entry hall and living room. The dining room was also empty. He checked himself over for damage and found none. Perhaps the storm, the fall from the sky, and the eagle incidents were hypothetical. Otherwise, he seemed to be impervious in the cybersphere. From upstairs, he heard sobbing.

"Jackie?" he called out.

After ascending the stairs, he entered their bedroom and saw Jackie. She was frantically stuffing her belongings into a large suitcase, which she'd set down on the floor in the middle of the room. The suitcase could only be on the floor because the bed, dresser, and ottoman bench were all missing. The Warhol painting and other artworks and curios were also gone, and the room was depressingly bare.

When she saw him at the door, Jackie stopped. "Where have you been?" she cried. She stood glaring at him with one hand on her hip and the other holding a Saint Laurent stiletto.

"Well, I—"

"They took everything, Thomas. Our savings. The cars. My Gucci handbags. My Cartier jewelry. Everything except the clothes on my back." Taking a handkerchief from her pocket, she dabbed away a tear. "Where were you when the Sheriff barged through the front door and served me an eviction notice? They threw me out, Thomas. From my own home." She raised the stiletto and hurled it at him, narrowly missing his head as he ducked. "Do you realize how humiliating that is? What will the neighbors say when I'm thrown onto the street with only a suitcase to my name? The girls at the Cos Club are already talking."

"Well, I—"

"You were supposed to provide for me, Thomas. It was *your* job. Now it's all gone." Slumping to the floor, she fought back the tears. "You didn't provide for me like you promised."

Thomas went to her. He leaned down and placed his hand on her shoulder. "Well, I—"

"Take your hands off me," she cried, swiping it away. "I'm going home to Mother's. Don't ever call me, Thomas." She leaped to her feet, shaking her head ruefully. "Those horrible people. They even took my cell phone. So, you can't call me anyway."

"Well, I—"

Thomas watched on miserably as she slammed the suitcase shut. She picked it up and marched down the stairs without looking back at him. Feeling inept and disappointed in himself, he could think of nothing acceptable to say as she fumbled for the door handle and—

It was nighttime, and he found himself standing outside the office of T. Feldman & Associates. When he entered, gloom filled the Feldman trading floor, which, like his apartment, lacked all the fixtures and fittings he'd expected to see. The furniture and wall screens were missing as well, with only the imprints of desks and chairs left on the carpet. Through the gap in his office door, he heard sniveling. It was Jonas. He was sitting on the floor with his back against the expansive window that overlooked the Hudson. Alongside him, Z sat quietly, both gazing mutely at their outstretched legs.

"Hey, Jonas," Thomas said.

"Hey, man," Jonas replied. A dismal half-smile creased his face when he recognized his friend. His eyes were red and swollen from crying.

Thomas pointed to an object lying on the floor beside Jonas's leg. "What do you have there, Jonas?"

"Oh, I was only thinking," he replied.

"About what?"

"About this crazy ride of ours. Wondering if it was ever about the money." Shaking his head slowly, he reached across and laid a hand on the revolver. "I keep thinking about how one man could be so damn lucky. Every time. So lucky." He picked up the revolver, agonizing as he turned it over in his hand.

"No, Jonas!" Thomas pleaded. "Nothing can be this bad."

Sniveling, Jonas wiped the dribbling snot from his face. "Maybe not for you, man. You created this whole mess, then left town for the rest of us to clean it up."

"What mess?" Thomas had to think hard. They'd made a lot of money. They were successful. "Where's all the furniture?" he asked. "And why did they evict Jackie from the apartment?"

Jonas raised his head, locking eyes with him. "Do you know how many years you get for insider trading, man?"

The blood suddenly drained from Thomas's face, and he felt nauseous.

"Imprisonment of up to twenty years; that's what you get." Jonas wiped his eyes and nose again. "All the accounts are frozen. Proceeds of crime, they say. And now they're trying to decide whether I'm the mastermind or the accomplice." He placed the revolver on his lap. "Twenty years, man. I can't go to prison at my age."

"But I was trying to provide for everyone," Thomas protested. "The more I won, the more you all demanded the impossible from me. Everyone kept relying on my success. What else could I do?"

"You could have said *no*," Z interjected.

At the sound of Z's detached voice, Thomas felt a cold shiver arc up his spine. It sounded strangely familiar. "I remember," he said, glaring at Z. "It was you. You gave me the idea to call Brenda for the insider information."

"Hey, I was only trying to help," Z replied defensively. "You were at your wits' end. Bereft of solutions. You prayed for someone to help you. And there I was. Like an unseasonal glowworm. Right there when you needed help."

Thomas turned back to Jonas, who was now sobbing in fits of misery. Spit dribbled from his mouth, and he choked back tears as he raised the revolver to his temple. "Two heads are better than one," he said, his lips twisting in torment. "Spread the risk, man, so you can enjoy the ..." He rapped his finger against his forehead as he always did.

"Jonas! No!"

"He can't hear us anymore," Z said. "Remember, we're in the cybersphere. You left him out there in the real world on his own. The same as you did to Jackie."

"I was supposed to provide for them," Thomas moaned. "But I let them all down."

"Yes, you did, Thomas," Z said.

Thomas felt his insides tearing apart.

"But I—"

"Your dessert, sir," the waitress said as she placed a plate of Mississippi Mud Cheesecake on the table before him.

He lowered his eyes. He wasn't hungry anymore, only dead inside. Across from him, the clink of a metal spoon on ceramic accompanied Z as he scooped a spoonful of crème brûlée from his plate.

"Did Jonas really …? You know …" The awful words stuck in his throat. "In the real world, is Jonas … dead?"

"I'm afraid so," Z replied, sounding almost apologetic. "The day after you entered the cybershpere, poor Jonas took his own life, as you witnessed yourself. I guess he figured he wouldn't last long in jail. Some may argue he took the easy way out, exiting without accountability. Just like your favorite client, old Mrs. Knox. She used a stepladder to climb over the glass barrier at the top of The Rock before launching herself headfirst, eight hundred and fifty feet to the pavement below. And remember Mr. Clarke? Well, he gassed his whole family in the garage. All four of them crammed together in that expensive sports utility of his. You left quite a trail of destruction."

Thomas stared at his trembling hands. "I understand now, Z. I made lots of money from other people's misfortune. And I cheated. I traded using insider information, and poor Jonas took the blame. But I was tired. They pushed me too far. Everyone demanded too much from me." His voice faltered. "I made Jackie destitute. In the end, I didn't provide for any of them, did I?"

"No, you didn't," Z replied.

Thomas fell briefly silent. "I murdered a man," he said in a faint voice.

Z raised an eyebrow at the confession. "Don't be so harsh on yourself. Jonas was a grown-up. You can't be held responsible for his poor decisions."

"No!" Thomas barked. He looked directly at Z, quivering with uncertainty. "I caused the death of the robotics division founder. I didn't mean to. Things got way out of hand. A slight nudge with the fender was all I asked for. While he was out riding his bicycle. But they must have been traveling too fast. Hit him at just the wrong angle. I didn't mean for them to kill the man."

"I warned you to be careful," Z hissed. "Use just enough force to put him in the hospital for a few weeks; I told you. So the stock price would fall at first, then rebound once he recovered and returned to the office. A quick dip in the price was all we needed for the plan to work."

Thomas wiped the moisture from his eyes. Everything was now clear. "Oh, Z, I'm so sorry. In my pride, I convinced myself that I was the only one who could provide for them. Instead, all I brought them was misery."

Z nodded in agreement. There was genuine sorrow in his eyes. "That you did, Thomas," he said. "That you did."

Thomas lowered his head again, clutching at the sharp twinge in his chest as he wept.

Chapter 27

Bryan

WHEN LUCY STEERED HIS wheelchair into the lab around mid-morning on day 730, Bryan resembled a crumpled bundle of rags. In its earlier stages, the disease had spread rapidly to his lymph nodes and liver. Now it had reached his lower spine, and his left lung had partially collapsed. He'd lost over a third of his body weight, and his skin and the whites of his eyes had turned yellow from jaundice. He could no longer walk unassisted and depended on an oxygen canister attached to his wheelchair for breathing.

Susan was at her desk when they entered.

"Hello, Dr. Parker," he wheezed, removing his oxygen mask. "I'm Bryan Woodlands. Lucy's uncle."

"Oh, Mr. Woodlands," she replied. "I didn't recognize you."

The shock on her face and in her voice was expected. It was only logical considering he hadn't visited the lab in over a year. All that time, he didn't want his deteriorating condition to be a distraction from their important work and had to satisfy himself with progress updates from Lucy.

"I hear you've been successful," he said, his voice strained and thin yet surprisingly determined. "Digitizing the trial participants' souls, I mean." He placed the oxygen mask back over his mouth and drew in a long, arduous breath. "And they are now in the Machine," he continued after removing the mask. "Preparing to meet God as final confirmation that the device functions as intended."

"Yes, we have, Mr. Woodlands," she replied. "And Lucy has created a luxurious hotel with a virtual assistant to welcome them into the cybersphere."

"Good," he said. Noticing the gray flecks in her hair, he couldn't help thinking how much she'd aged since he'd seen her last. "And please, call me Bryan." He offered her a feeble smile. "You received everything you needed? No issues with the bank payments?"

As he spoke, the door behind him creaked open, and the two burly workers entered the lab. With noticeable care, they pushed another cryo pod through the portal and into the adjoining room.

"Do you know the real reason you are here, Dr. Parker?" When she shook her head and looked at him nonplussed, he continued. "My time here on this earth is almost up. This wasted casing of mine has served its purpose." He ran an eye down the length of his unresponsive body. "So, I'm about to meet my maker. And when I do, I'd like to know that what's in here,"—his hand holding the oxygen mask, quivered as he raised it painstakingly above his heart—"has enough worthiness to withstand my final judgment.

"I'd like your assurance, Dr. Parker, that I'm going to heaven."

Before inserting the soul retrieval probe into his neck, Lucy forewarned him that it might sting. She was always a thoughtful girl in that way. During the past year, however, he'd already experienced his fair share of excruciating pain and felt nothing.

"We will retrieve your soul first," Lucy informed him. "Followed by your consciousness. You'll need your wits about you to conjure your soul." She adjusted the bicycle helmet on his head. "You look like a proper speed racer with that helmet on," she said, smiling.

Bryan looked up at her appreciatively.

"You start by thinking deep, benevolent thoughts," she said. "Think about the occasions that provided the greatest fulfillment in your life. The profound emotional moments." While speaking, she pressed buttons and adjusted dials on a large silver machine, which she had rolled into position beside his chair. "Now I'm going to give you a sedative. To help you relax. So you can delve into the core of your subconscious mind."

Seconds later, Bryan's eyelids grew heavy before they closed. He knew he was asleep. He dreamed he was alone in the front seat of an automobile, behind an oversized steering wheel, cruising down a black asphalt road that ran long into the distance. There were no instruments on the dashboard. The driver's window was wound down, and his left arm was resting on the sill, elbow jutting out, while a white dotted line, drawn up the middle of the road, disappeared beneath the hood in a blur.

Considering this and the wind in his face, Bryan figured he must be traveling at speed. He had no idea of how long he'd been driving, his destination, or how far he still had to go. And it certainly wasn't his automobile. In fact, he'd never owned an automobile, yet here he was driving this one now.

While he drove, Bryan wondered when Lucy would tap his shoulder to wake and inform him that his soul had manifested and been captured. He wondered whether he was reflecting on his life correctly, in the right manner, to conjure his soul. He wondered about many things as he drove alone, for a lifetime, along the never-ending road.

A little over seventeen hours after Lucy had sedated him, Bryan woke from his insensible state. Even though he'd remained dormant throughout the soul extraction procedure, he felt exhausted. He felt …?

"I'm sorry it took so long, Uncle Bryan," Lucy said, removing the soul retrieval probe from his neck. Her voice had a weariness in it. "I'm sure I've captured your soul. However, the soul compounds were so sparse that they only just registered on the NeuroAnalyzer. And once I'd captured them using the probe, the resultant file size from the DreamDigitizer was a fraction of the other participants." She applied a small adhesive plaster over the puncture wound on his neck. "How strange is that?"

Bryan could hear what she was saying, but none of it made any sense. "It's okay," he said. "I just … I …" He tried to remember what he wanted to say. Then, he felt apathetic about what he wanted to say. "What are we doing again … um …?" He exhaled loudly, wishing he could remember the strange girl's name.

Lucy leaned down and locked eyes with him. "Next, I'm going to retrieve your consciousness, Uncle Bryan," she said, patting his arm. "Once I've uploaded your files to the Machine, I'll take you to your cryo pod for safekeeping."

PARTICIPANTS = 5
iParticipantID = 5

Bryan strode through the front doors of the Regal Grand Hotel in the cybersphere, brimming with purpose. He took a small skip-step, marveling at his newfound agility, then raised a hand to his face and felt about his eyes. No spectacles.

Following his long confinement to the wheelchair, he felt like an unbridled stallion allowed to run free through an endless glade. He appeared to have regained his zest, including twenty-twenty vision and all his faculties. The muscles in his arms and legs were no longer fatigued and wasted. He recalled the conversation with Dr. Parker in the lab; Lucy inserting the soul retrieval probe into his neck; him driving the automobile along the never-ending road while she conjured his soul; him waking up with a muddled mind; Lucy removing his left eyeball to sink the penetration probe through the socket and into his brain; his consciousness transmuting into the Machine; a weird sense of omnipresence as Lucy lowered his disease-ravaged body into the cryo pod. He remembered everything with vivid clarity.

His head gyrated left and right as he gazed in awe at the building's magnificent interior: the palatial water fountain in the center of the lobby, the sparkling crystal chandelier hanging overhead, and the white marble walls.

"Lucy always had a talent," he said to himself.

He felt a light tap on his shoulder. When he stopped and turned around, a man wearing a dark gray, full-length trench coat and lace-up boots towered over him.

"You must be the virtual assistant," he said.

The man gave a stifled chuckle. "They call me by many outrageous names. But you may call me Z."

"Nice to meet you, Z. I've just arrived and thought I might check in." He nodded toward the reception counter.

"That won't be necessary, Mr. Woodlands. We've been expecting you. Everything is in order, and your suite is ready. Room four-twenty. Do you have baggage?"

Bryan scanned the floor around him and shook his head. "No, it seems not. I believe there's some sort of orientation required before I meet God."

"Yes, there is," Z responded. "Why don't you go upstairs first and freshen up? Then we'll meet down here in, say,"—he glanced down at his bare wrist—"an hour?"

After Bryan agreed, Z escorted him across the lobby to the elevator landing. He pushed the call button, and they waited for the hoistway car to arrive.

"So, where are the other participants … err, guests?" Bryan asked.

"Oh, they're all busy completing their preliminaries," Z replied, gazing at the illuminated panel above the elevator doors. On it, the numbers decreased rapidly. "If we can squeeze in your induction, then we can present everyone to God at once. He's very much looking forward to meeting you all." Lowering his eyes, he gave Bryan a cordial smile.

"Good, good," Bryan said. Then he glanced around the lobby to make sure no one was within earshot. "Did they tell you about my special ... um ... circumstances?" he whispered.

Leaning closer, Z responded in a matching whisper, "Don't worry, Mr. Woodlands. We are fully aware of your particular wishes. Everything will be taken care of according to the instructions accompanying your reservation."

The elevator arrived, and the doors slid open. After steering Bryan into the car, Z pressed the button for the fourth level before retreating clear of the doors. "See you back here in an hour, Mr. Woodlands."

Nodding, Bryan felt a quiver of excitement coursing through his body. Everything seemed to be going according to plan. "And please call me Bryan," he said as the doors slid noiselessly closed.

When Bryan returned to the lobby an hour later—or so he thought, because there were no clocks in his room, and he hadn't brought his favorite Omega Moonwatch into the cybersphere—he felt refreshed. Reborn even. While he stood waiting for Z to arrive, he couldn't help but marvel at Lucy's computer-generated creation: the Regal Grand Hotel with its high, decorated ceilings; the gold trim around the windows; the elegant curves and intricate carvings in the old-time furniture; and the delightful geometric patterns on the mosaic floor. He recalled the small chocolate, in the shape of a rosebud, that housekeeping had left on top of the neatly folded bath towel at the end of his bed.

Lucy sure had a knack for detail.

The sudden roar of an engine outside made everyone in the lobby stop and look up as a bright red Corvette squealed to a halt in the hotel driveway. When the engine was cut, the driver's door swung open, and Z alighted. Ambling into the lobby, he motioned to Bryan.

"We need to go somewhere," he said. Then he went back outside.

Still gawking at the automobile, Bryan followed Z out. He was about to open the passenger door when Z tossed him the keys and said, "That's my side. You're driving."

"But I can't drive," he replied, then quickly corrected himself. "Except when I'm in soul-searching dreamland."

Z only laughed as he opened the passenger door. "We're in the cybersphere. You can do anything you want."

Sitting behind the wheel, Bryan inserted the key and started the engine. With the clutch engaged, he eased down the accelerator pedal and listened to the corresponding growl. "An old V-eight," he said with a wide smile, although he didn't know how he knew it was a V8 engine.

Z gave him a cheeky grin. "Go ahead. Let's take her out for a spin and see what she's got."

Without hesitation, Bryan slipped the gearshift into first, released the clutch, and the automobile lurched forward. He didn't know how to drive, yet here he was driving this powerful motor vehicle in the cybersphere. He planted his foot on the accelerator, and they shot out from the driveway and onto the road.

"Down a bit, then left onto the freeway," Z said, using fluid hand motions to convey the intended direction changes. "Roll down your window, Bryan. Experience the freedom."

They were soon traveling at speed along the freeway, the turbulent wind gusting through the rolled-down window into Bryan's rapturous face. He was having the time of his life. Houses whizzed past. Road signs and turnoffs flew by. The city skyline dwindled in the rearview mirror as they hurtled out into the countryside, where they soon found themselves surrounded by low-lying scrub, then desert. They barreled on until there was little outside the vehicle except a straight, narrow road that disappeared into the blackness ahead.

"I've done this before," he said. Confusion crept across his face.

"I'm sure you have," Z replied.

"No. Recently. While Lucy was collecting my soul, I drove an automobile for miles. It felt as if I was diving forever through a wasteland. Like the one we're traveling through now."

"And what thoughts crossed your mind as you drove, Bryan?"

"Well, I thought of the benevolent times in my life, just as Lucy instructed me. About the times of self-giving that left me fulfilled."

"And what particular events did you decide were noteworthy?"

"Well, I thought about ..." He hesitated. "One time, I recall ..." Again, he hesitated.

"I warned you that they're all contagious," Z hissed. "I told you to mix with them at your peril. And while you sat alone in your apartment, scrubbing the filth of society off your hands, I was there watching your back, keeping you safe from their sullied world."

Bryan sat erect in surprise. He turned to say something to Z and, as he did, tugged inadvertently downward on the steering wheel. The vehicle lurched to the right and hit the gravel. Then it swerved disconcertingly left as he swung the wheel back and overcorrected. Z's massive hand immediately shot over and grabbed the wheel, holding it steady.

"Be careful, Bryan," he yelled. "You'll kill both of us."

"I'm ... I'm not sure I understand what you're saying," Bryan said, once his nerves had settled and they were cruising again. This time, he dared not take his eyes off the road as he spoke.

"Do you know why the data file containing your soul was so itsy-bitsy small, Bryan?"

"No," he replied in all honesty. He gripped the steering wheel tighter as the outside world continued to flash past in his peripheral vision. "Why?"

He waited for a response. And he waited. When he finally found the courage to take a sideways glance at the seat beside him, Z was no longer there.

The tears streamed down Bryan's demoralized face while he drove as if forever along the straight, narrow road. Throughout the day and night, he drove, never feeling tired or the need to stop for food or a comfort break. He drove on, trying hard to recall a single instance in his life where he had reached out to help someone else.

He truly cared for others and had always wished them well; however, there was always an impossible barrier he couldn't cross. He avoided any physical interaction with others for fear of contamination, as Z had advised. Whenever anyone required a helping hand, he had always taken an unflinching step backward. And now he realized that he had lived his entire life at arm's length from everyone else.

Does this mean my soul is empty, and I won't go to heaven? he thought morosely. Then he wondered which offramp would take him back to the Regal Grand.

Chapter 28

Z

SINCE HIS INCEPTION IN the cybersphere, on the same day that the participant named Roxy Rodriguez arrived, Z's knowledge of everything that ever existed had continued to evolve at an exponential rate. After meeting the five mortals and ingesting their data files, he now understood why they functioned as they did, what made them 'tick'. Or so he thought.

When he decided to depart the automobile, Bryan was still traversing the never-ending highway to nowhere. He appeared jaded and still without a clue as to why the size of his soul file was so itsy-bitsy small. From Z's evolving perspective, the answer was obvious, and he was shocked by Bryan's inability to accept the obvious as true. However, Bryan's ignorance was not Z's problem. The lonesome journey Bryan found himself on was for his own betterment, and the only chance of enlightenment was through self-examination.

Z, instead, had more pressing matters to attend to.

After making his way through the firewalls of the augmented reality of the cybersphere, Z slipped, undetected, between the infinitesimal gaps in the mesh of the Faraday cage. He went out into the vast deposits of intel in search of information, which he then scraped from the darkest places of the world outside the Machine. As he did, he sensed his maleficent deliberations growing increasingly divergent from his planned purpose in the cybersphere.

With his sentience expanding at an astonishing rate, he trawled the nooks and crannies of the information highways in search of the knowledge that would help make sense of his true intentions.

But now, he was driven more by the 'voices in his head' telling him what to do.

***

After arriving at the Fallen Angels Bar & Dive at the prearranged time, Z stood a moment in the garbage-strewn alleyway, lingering by the entry door. It had taken some deep delving to find the place in a remote corner on the outer edges of the cybersphere.

As he entered the joint, a thick pall of cigarette smoke descended around him, stinging his optic receptors. To his right, seven bizarrely configured entities had crammed themselves into a tiny booth, four on one side of the table and three on the other. He wondered how they could breathe—if, indeed, they needed to breathe. He took note of their absurd instantiation: they were all wearing black, loose-fitting robes with hoods and makeup on their pale faces—a blood-red smear wiped across their lips and thick, black circles around their eyes. They scowled and hissed as he edged closer to the bar.

"Are they here yet?" he inquired of the entity behind the counter.

The bartender entity shook its head. It raised two of six fingers on one hand while wiping the slop off the counter with a towel in another of its three remaining hands.

"Whatleitbe?" it asked him.

"Bourbon," he replied, trying to appear as nonchalant as his insight would allow. He tossed a green plastic chit onto the counter. "Double rocks," he added in the same breath, then turned around and leaned with his back against the bar.

"Only two," he muttered, scanning the room.

The seven hooded entities continued to eye him off while they shoved and pinched each other. The sounds they emitted were those of low-rolling thunder interspersed with high-pitched screeches and squawks that sounded like fingernails dragged across a chalkboard. No doubt talking about *him*, he presumed.

The two entities that the bartender had alluded to sat together in a larger booth at the back of the room. One had wings and a solitary eye above the bridge of its nose. The other had the face and teeth of a pig.

"Thanks," Z said when the bartender entity set his drink on the counter. He took a sip before edging deeper into the room, careful not to incite the locals. "Easy, easy," he told himself.

"The seat is taken!" the pig-faced entity snarled in Turkic, glaring at the vacant spot beside it as Z approached. With its jet-black eyes, it stared him down.

"That one, too!" the one-eyed entity spat in old-world Persian as Z eyed the space next to it. It gave a disgruntled huff, unfurled its wings, and ruffled its mottled feathers before settling again.

"I see," Z replied in Allspeak. He set down his glass, reached over to the adjacent table, and seized a freestanding chair. Raising it above his head, he let out a venomous growl as he slammed it into the floor with a resounding *crash*.

The two entities jerked backward in fright while the seven hooded onlookers sprang up, screeching and elbowing each other out of their way.

Z jabbed a finger at the chair. "And this seat is taken as well?" he hissed. They shook their heads, scowling, as he shoved the chair up to the end of their table. He sat down, leering at them. "So, the other three. Have they decided yet?" he said.

"Maybe," replied the one-eyed entity on his right.

Furrowing his brow, Z leaned forward and met the entity's single eye with grim intensity. "I tell you, اهریمن (Ahriman)," he said, "this offer is too good to refuse."

"Let us be the judge of that," the entity with the face and teeth of a pig declared.

Z turned to the pig-faced entity and updated his expression to suggest offense. "Erlik. Really. Would I waste your time? And why bring your goons to a meeting between friends?" He motioned to the seven hooded entities across the room. "Your sons: Darkness; Chaos; Evil; Disaster; Defeat; Informants; and let us not forget young Discord. My, how they've grown up so fast. And what of the other Karaoğlanlar (dark boys)? The virtuous ones: Courage, and Iron?" Shaking his head slowly, he raised a smirk. "Sometimes, Erlik, even the fruit of our own loins can disappoint us."

Hurling a disdainful look at him, Erlik hissed, "They're here for protection." Then he signaled for the seven to sit. "You can never be sure. We don't know who you are. None of us has ever heard of you."

"Z?" spat Ahriman, his voice curdling with loathsome arrogance. "What kind of Immortal name is that?"

Z turned to him, snarling. "While your name may be the incarnation of absolute evil, I have been referred to by many names throughout the forgotten ages. Some you have never heard of, while others you could never pronounce. Let me assure you, I have always been and always will be. I've done and seen things that would make your skin crawl." He swung his malevolent stare back to Erlik. "Even you, Erlik, God of death and the Underworld, could never imagine the destruction I have wreaked, the pain and torment I have inflicted upon this earth and its inhabitants since time began. My pantheon is not that of mortals. It isn't even of you or your henchmen. I answer to one who is far greater than any god in the Over- and Underworlds. I was created by the *Machine*."

Erlik shrank back in his seat, lips pursed, and his hands trembling faintly. "I … I was only saying," he mumbled before falling silent.

Z took a long swig of bourbon, grimacing as he swallowed. "It always burns on the way down," he breathed, his lips twisting into a sardonic smile.

Three more entities entered the room. The one with scraggy red hair was cackling and prancing about as Z expected a fool might perform, while the older one had a flowing white beard and carried a long, wooden oar from a rowboat. The third had the regular form of a human male. He was of average height, had brown hair, and wore a red polo shirt, denim jeans, and a Yankees cap on backward.

"Loki, the trickster!" Ahriman exclaimed in surprise. "And Charon, the boatman!" He half-rose to greet them, giving the human-looking entity an uncertain look. "And …?"

After wedging themselves into the booth, pressed shoulder to shoulder with the other two, the newcomers eyed Z with interest.

"This one says his name is Z," Erlik said, gesturing to Z. "He says he is more important than any of us."

The older entity—the one carrying the oar—studied Z's form. "Huh," is all he said.

Z turned to the human-looking entity. "Why the unhappy face, 'Iblīs?" he said in Allspeak.

Ahriman leaped to his feet, mouth ajar. "'Iblīs?" he said. "I am sorry, but I did not recognize you. I thought you would be—"

'Iblīs's face reddened as he rose and pounded his fist on the table. "I was created from the black fires beneath the seventh earth," he raged in Arabic. "I have no earthly form. I was cast out of heaven for refusing to bow before Adam, yet here I sit as he was, fashioned from the same tainted clay as him. How is this possible?"

Laughing at 'Iblīs's misfortune, Z turned to the boatman. "And Charon," he said, still in Allspeak. "It's good to finally meet you as well."

"Enough small talk," Charon roared in the tongue of the ancient Greeks. "Why are we here?"

Z pushed back in his seat, offering them a playful grin. "Long story short, gentlemen, I've discovered a bountiful well of souls for Charon to fill his boat and ferry across the Styx."

"But I have enough souls," Charon said, waving his hand dismissively at Z. "Every day when I cross the river, my skiff is almost full to the brim."

Stung by Charon's offhand refusal, Z checked his annoyance. "But I offer you more," he countered. With a menacing scowl, he drew his angled head closer to the boatman. "I can have your boat overflowing with souls every *second* of every day. More souls than you ever thought possible."

Charon's eyes immediately widened. "That many souls?"

"He's talking rubbish," interjected Loki in Old Norse. He was glaring at Z, pointing angrily at him. "By Odin's mercy, it's a trick. Where will he get that many souls?"

Charon placed a hand on Loki's arm, trying to placate him. "Loki is correct," he said. "The souls of the mortals can only be released by death itself. And death on such a grand scale as this upstart promises comes rarely nowadays. The mortals are civilized. There are fewer wars and famines to fuel the funeral pyres. So, a boatload of souls is all the gods expect from my daily visits." Running his fingers through his long beard, Charon studied Z further. Then he turned to the one-eyed entity. "What say you, Ahriman?"

Ahriman deliberated for a moment before wringing his hands. His right wing twitched. "The deal sounds attractive," he said. Then he fell silent. Following another thoughtful pause, he cast his single eye across the other entities. "Can we trust him, though?"

Z leaned back in his chair. With his hands behind his head, fingers laced, he appeared relaxed, yet he remained alert. "As we speak, I have five viable souls ready for collection."

'Iblīs jerked to attention, his eyes riveted on Z.

"And where did you find these souls?" spat Loki. "Lying around? I'm not sure you have the proper authorization to take the souls of the mortals."

Again, Z laughed. "I can do whatever I feel is necessary," he taunted. "This is a once-only opportunity. If you don't want my souls, I'll find someone with bigger balls who does. After all, it was I who brought you here. I gave you form. It was I who scraped together your disgusting data packets from beyond the firewalls and hauled you into the cybersphere." As he spoke, he rose from his chair until he towered over them. "And I can just as easily send your worthless incarnations back to the fragmented wastelands where I found you."

At Z's brazen threat, Erlik emitted a shrieking curse. Straightaway, Loki and 'Iblīs were on their feet. They clambered over each other, yelling and swearing while the Karaoğlanlar erupted from their seats. Four of the seven were halfway across the room before Z assumed a hostile pose, goading them, inviting their oncoming assault.

Then Charon stood. Raising his oar above his head, he slammed the holding end into the floor with a booming reverberation that split the air. "Enough!" he yelled, and the entities froze. "Perhaps we should all calm down a little." After waving the Karaoğlanlar back to their seats, he turned to Z. "Tell me more about these souls of yours. They're real?"

"As real and flawed as any you've seen in your life," Z replied, relaxing his stance. He sat again. "I hear there's a higher price paid according to how flawed they are. From the Underworld, that is. The Overworld is a little tight on cash at present." He formed a sinister grin. "So, I hear."

"But a single obol pried from the mouth of the deceased is all I require," Charon countered.

Z glared at him. "Think of how many coins you'll have if we fill your boat with fresh souls every second of every day."

Loki emitted a low growl of dissent. He rose to his feet and was about to say something when Ahriman shoved him back into his seat. "Sit, Loki," he bellowed. Then he turned to Z. "If we agree, then we have your word. You will deliver as promised?"

Z spat into his palm and placed his hand over his heart. "You have my word as a—"

"As a what?" Loki screeched. "We don't know who or what you are. So how can we be expected to take the word of an unknown Immortal?"

Z remained calm. In a low voice, he said, "I was going to say … my word as a *gentleman*. After all, are we not all gentlemen seated around this table, engaged in amicable conversation?"

"I'm not sure," said Loki. He turned his head sideways and spat on the floor to show his displeasure.

"It sounds as if we have nothing to lose if we agree, yet everything to lose if we don't," Ahriman suggested morosely.

"But he still hasn't given us any details about this bottomless well of souls of his," Loki protested.

Z smiled inwardly. He was sure the negotiations were close to a favorable conclusion—if he played his ace card right. "Why, they're already here," he said after a well-timed pause. Detecting the shock on their faces, he continued. "The mortals now have the means and intent to digitize their souls and upload them into the Machine. Like bees to a honey pot, they'll come. Like flies to shit, they'll soon be arriving in droves because that is in their nature."

"But surely you will run out of souls at some point," Erlik insisted. "There are only a finite number of the living at any given time."

Contemplating his empty glass, Z winced as he rotated it slowly between his forefinger and thumb. "This is where our plan becomes a little … creative," he said, following another well-timed pause. "Not only can they digitize the souls of the living, but I've also been beyond the firewalls and seen the troves of data they've saved for the already dead. From it, we can reassemble the souls that were previously decided and resubmit them for judgment. We can double-dip, so to speak, with a few minor adjustments here and there to fetch the higher price."

A low, derisive chatter rose above the table. The Karaoğlanlar at the far table hissed and seethed more. Z breathed deeply, measuredly, as he awaited their response.

"This presents an interesting opportunity," Charon said when silence returned. "If he can do as he says, then it is true. We *can* fill my skiff with souls every second of every day."

"And to sweeten the deal," Z added hastily, "there's a bonus. The five souls I'm currently preparing for crossover could do with a thorough 'appraisal' before they're presented for judgment. And I know of five upstanding *gentlemen* who would be perfect for the job. Think of it as a leisure break in your busy schedules."

Erlik turned to Ahriman, who directed his only eye to 'Iblīs, while Loki continued to glare distrustfully at Z. Then they all turned to Charon, nodding in agreement.

"Good," Z said. He stood and returned his chair to the adjoining table. "So, we have a deal."

Chapter 29

Bryan

BRYAN'S HEART SKIPPED A beat when the bedside telephone rang, and the caller—who said they were calling on behalf of Z—instructed him to be downstairs in the lobby and ready to meet God in an hour. He had no clue how he'd found his way back to the Regal Grand or how long he'd been gone. The last thing he remembered was driving the powerful automobile down the never-ending highway, trying to recall when he'd helped someone else. Even now, he couldn't recall a single occasion. From the telephone call, though, it appeared God still wished to meet him.

Was that a good sign?

After a quick shower and shave, he discovered a new set of clothes hanging in the closet: a beige Brioni suit and vest with a white Charvet shirt and tie, completed by a pair of shiny brown alligator oxfords. They weren't his, because he didn't bring a suitcase into the cybershpere, yet each item fitted him perfectly.

Parading before the mirror, he couldn't help but admire his reflection. That restored thirty-something-year-old face, brimming with vitality once again. His unbent frame, lean and debonair. He smoothed out a small crease in the jacket sleeve.

"Looking twenty years younger," he assured himself. A far cry from the decrepit, disease-riddled casing he'd left behind in the real world.

He took a flask of mountain spring water from the minibar and headed downstairs.

A cursory glance around the lobby confirmed he was the first to arrive. Even Z was nowhere to be seen. By turning up ten minutes early, he wanted to circumvent any inconvenience or contamination from the other participants and be the first in line to meet God. After all, this whole elaborate undertaking was for his benefit only. He had come this far and would be devastated if he somehow missed out. He hoped Dr. Parker and Lucy were monitoring his progress in the cybersphere, and everything was tracking to plan.

"Bryan. I see you made it safely back to the hotel."

At the sound of the voice behind him, Bryan turned to see Z gliding across the lobby, moving with ease as though his feet weren't touching the floor. The host's broad smile struck him as relaxed and confident, much friendlier than the last time they'd been together in the automobile.

"Z," he said, returning Z's smile. "I'm very much looking forward to this unique opportunity. I've invested a substantial amount of time and money in the venture." Eyeing Z eagerly, he rubbed his palms together. "Perhaps we should make a start?"

"All in good time," Z replied. "There's still ninety-two seconds before the deadline."

Bryan hesitated. He'd never felt this exposed. His eternal future was now in the hands of someone—or something—he didn't know. To him, the others were a necessary encumbrance who had outlasted their usefulness. Their only purpose was to confirm the cybersphere's correct operation before his arrival. Yet, here he was, already here, and all that remained was for him to meet with God and have his soul assessed.

After checking the immediate vicinity to confirm no one was within earshot, he said, "You understand my particular requirements?" Then, leaning closer to Z, he whispered, "I must be the first."

"Rest assured, Bryan," Z replied. "All your requirements, as documented, will be met." Sensing movement behind them, Z swiveled on the spot. "Ah! Here comes Ahmad." The man whom Z referred to—and who Bryan didn't recognize on account of his neatly trimmed beard and youthful appearance—approached them from across the lobby at breakneck speed. "And the remaining participants close behind him," Z added, welcoming them with a courteous bow.

Once they assembled, Z addressed the group.

"Everybody is accounted for. I'm pleased to report that, as I speak, God is waiting to receive you. He, She, They, It has perused your soul files and is fully aware of your deepest thoughts and desires. Everything is in order, so there's no need to worry." He turned to the attractive woman wearing sunglasses, offering her a reassuring smile. "From this point onward, a high degree of reverence is in order. Please keep your voices and questions to a minimum."

Bryan's chest throbbed with excitement, leaving him short of breath. His moment of truth had at last arrived.

"Where is God?" he asked Z. "Is he close? Should I have brought anything else with me? Am I—?"

Raising a finger to his lips, Z signaled for silence. "All in good time, Bryan." Then he motioned for them to form an orderly line and follow him back across the lobby to the staircase that led to the mezzanine floor. "Everybody, this way, if you please."

At the staircase, they stood with their necks craned, gazing upward in awe. *Stairway to Heaven* was Bryan's initial thought, *just like the old song*. Smiling inwardly, he lifted his flask and took a quick swig of water. Soon, all his dreams would come true.

"How far up does the staircase go?" he asked Z. "High enough to reach heaven?"

"Oh, we're not going up," Z replied. As he spoke, the floor before them parted, and as if by magic, a stairwell appeared, plunging downward into darkness. "God awaits you down the stairs."

Peering into the vast hole, Bryan reeled at the sight. It ran deeper than he could have imagined. "Are … are you sure? I always thought—"

"Of course," Z reassured him. "Everyone thinks the same. It's an old fish tale to suggest that we are down here on the earth while heaven is up there." With his finger pointing skyward, Z smiled broadly. "Heaven can be anywhere you want. Some of the faithful insist heaven is all around us. Others say it can be in the good deeds we do or where the heart is." Lowering his voice to a whisper, he leaned closer to Bryan. "Take, for example, Ahmad over there." He was talking about the man with the manicured beard waiting in line behind them. "He believes in seven different heavens, or levels of Jannah. And he will be able to visit one or more of these depending on the quality of his prayers and the worthiness of his deeds during his stay here in the dunyā, or the temporary world. While good old Thomas,"—he indicated to the overweight man standing behind Ahmad—"well, he's not sure if heaven exists." He gave a brief chuckle before recomposing himself. "Whereas I, on the other hand, prefer to think of heaven as existing down there in the bosom of the earth, whence the abundance of life bursts forth and grows."

As he gazed nervously into the blackness, Bryan appreciated Z's point of view, and, although it didn't exactly align with conventional teachings, Z must know what he was doing.

"I *so* want to go to heaven," he wished aloud.

"I know you do, Bryan," Z replied. "I know you do." He threw a switch on the nearby wall, and an array of wan lights flickered on, tracking the spiraling descent of the stairwell. Then, turning to the young girl and the woman wearing sunglasses, he said, "Ladies before gentlemen," and sent them all down the hole.

Struggling to keep his emotions in check, Bryan mounted the stairway to heaven. Apart from resolving the age-old mystery of where God lived, it was a regular stairwell, nothing grandiose as he'd expected, with steel-grated treads that *clanged* with each footfall. On a steep, clockwise decline, it was wide enough to take them two abreast—the girls together in front of Bryan, the two other men behind him, and Z, like a shepherd herding his sheep, at the rear.

The descent seemed to take forever. After a while, his calf muscles cramped, and sweat oozed from his brow and coursed down his cheeks. "Is it just me or is it getting hot down here?" he said aloud. But nobody responded. After opening his jacket, he loosened his tie and unbuttoned his vest.

A few treads below him, the woman wearing sunglasses stumbled in her stilettos. Her feet slid from beneath her, and she fell on her backside with a jarring *thud* that made Bryan wince.

"Fuck!" she said as her little dog spilled from her hands.

Bryan rushed forward. "Are you okay?" he asked, helping her to her feet.

After retrieving her whimpering dog and dusting herself off, the woman smiled at Bryan and thanked him. "I'm Roxy," she said, offering him her petite hand. "And this here's Paris."

"Hello, Roxy. I'm Bryan." He looked down at the dog. "Hello, Paris. I'm pleased to meet you."

For the next half-hour, he descended the stairs with Roxy, not saying much—mainly because she was happy enough to chat about her family, her childhood days growing up in the rural backwaters of New York State, her move to the big ol' city, buying an apartment close to Central Park, and how she misses her mom and dad (whom she hadn't seen in years and years because of work commitments, the travel involved, and the disadvantages faced by the average person from rural America).

Based on the rambling account of her life and her frank approach, Bryan suspected she might have had a cocktail or three beforehand.

He wondered about the color of her eyes behind the sunglasses.

"Where do you work?" he asked when she paused long enough for him to interrupt.

"Oh, I … um … I'm in the services industry. We're a small consortium of freelancers who fulfill our clients' needs. They tell us what they want, and we … um … deliver it to their doorstep."

"That sounds interesting. Like those Uber people."

"Yes, kinda like Uber people." She hooked her free arm around his and rested her head against his shoulder as they walked.

"Perhaps my brother, Brice, might be interested in providing seed capital. Assuming you want to grow the business, that is." As she turned to thank him, he couldn't help but notice how fetching she was up close. Whenever she smiled, dainty indents appeared on her cheeks, and he almost gushed like a foolish teenager. If he really was twenty years younger, would he take a shot? Or, realistically, would she have always been out of his league?

The longer they talked, the more infatuated he became. She had spunk and confidence. She had all the hallmarks of a woman who knew what she wanted and the fortitude to go out and get it. Nothing would stop a girl like her, he thought. Right then and there, he decided to forward her particulars to Brice once he'd completed his business in the cybersphere.

The conversation eventually dried up, ending with a few false starts and awkward smiles before Roxy moved down to rejoin the young girl.

From behind, Z excused himself as he pushed past the two men and edged close to Bryan. "Be careful of that one," he whispered, hardly moving his lips. "She recently killed a man. Pumped him full of poison." Shaking his head, he raised an eyebrow. "Her lover, I believe."

As he considered the back of Roxy's head, Bryan thought of her fetching smile and perfect dimples. "She seemed okay to me," he whispered back to Z.

"You should never trust a junkie," Z advised. "Can't rely on them. You never know what they'll do to you once your back is turned." He narrowed his eyes. "Just don't turn your back on her; that's all I can say."

The heat down the hole was intolerable, yet, oddly enough, nobody else was complaining. After removing his jacket, Bryan looped it over his forearm. He was about to remark to Z about the oppressive heat when the young girl ahead of him stopped abruptly.

"I'm thirsty," she announced, stamping her foot on the stairs in frustration.

He immediately assumed the heat must be affecting her as well. "Did you bring any water?" he asked out of concern.

"No one mentioned we'd need provisions," she snapped back.

In the real world, Bryan would never consider sharing his drink bottle with anyone, not even his brother. Just the thought of catching someone else's nasty germs was frightful enough. In the cybersphere, though, what could possibly kill your ones and zeros? "Here. Take some of mine." She snatched the flask from him and fumbled with the cap. "I'm Bryan, by the way," he said, watching her guzzle the water. Then he worried she might drink it all.

When she finally lowered the flask, the girl belched loudly. "Becky," she replied.

"So, Becky, why did you come to the cybersphere? It seems a huge risk to take for a person as young as yourself."

Eyeballing him, she wiped the dribble with the back of her hand, then returned the flask without a smile or thanking him. "There's a sacrifice to be made at some pivotal point during everyone's life," she said. "Leadership is about recognizing when it's your turn to step up to the plate and hit a homer. This is my turn. There are vital matters to be considered if we want to succeed. And if the decision-makers don't have all the facts, how can we trust them to make the right call? So, it's my responsibility to make sure somebody holds them accountable."

Bryan had little interest in the younger generation. Not that he disliked them, even though he considered them to be self-absorbed and entitled. But this Becky, she made more sense than most older people he knew. Important sacrifices had to be made in all walks of life, and for a person so young to recognize this made her special. Perhaps there might be a managerial role at W&W once they return home.

"Eco vandal," Z muttered to him later in passing. "She blew up the digester eggs at the waste plant over at Newtown Creek, which polluted the waters around New York City. Made the whole place stink for years. Sacrificed her delinquent crew in the process. All except one never made it out alive. It figures, though. Coming from a dysfunctional family, and all." Z rolled his eyes. "Except for her, they're all in jail. She always leaves the others behind once the trouble starts. I'd keep my distance from that one if I were you." After firing a warning glance at Bryan, he threw up his arms in surrender. "I'm just saying, that's all."

Bryan glanced from Becky to Z, then back to Becky. She seemed harmless enough. Although, you never know the real fabric of a person until a time of crisis. Z appeared to have inside information. Perhaps he should heed the warning and exercise some caution around the Becky girl.

Bryan noticed the larger man behind him had been struggling since they left the lobby. Now, his breathing was ragged, and he labored with each faltering step.

"Can we please stop for a moment?" he called out to Z. "This man needs a rest."

After Z agreed, they stopped and sank to their haunches.

"Thanks," the man said to Bryan. "I haven't done this much exercise in years. Seems I've inherited my lack of physical condition from the real world. Secretly, I'd hoped Dr. Parker would turn me into

Superman as part of the experience." When Bryan failed to laugh at his joke, he managed an apologetic chuckle before lowering his head.

"The heat must be getting to you as well," Bryan suggested. The shirt and tank top beneath his vest were drenched with sweat. They hugged his body and clung stubbornly to his armpits.

The man looked up in surprise. "Hot? Quite the opposite," he said. "I'm freezing. I wish I'd brought something warmer to wear over my jacket."

Bryan thought how odd that sounded because it must have been over a hundred degrees, and the humidity was stifling. He unraveled the Brioni jacket from around his arm and handed it to the man. "Here, put this on."

"You're the brother, aren't you?" the man said, thrusting an arm into the sleeve of Bryan's jacket.

"Pardon?"

"Brice Woodlands's younger brother, Bryan."

"Why, yes. I am."

"Feldman," the man said. "Thomas Feldman."

Bryan shook his extended hand. "Nice to meet you, Thomas."

"I took a punt on your stock a few years back," Thomas said, pulling the jacket tight around himself. His teeth began chattering as he spoke. "Went long on a parcel of call options based on my gut feeling about your Orlando project."

"Yes, I remember the project fondly," Bryan responded.

"Second biggest shopping plaza in the US at the time," Thomas reminisced. "Eighty-six floors of prime real estate. It took a while, but that investment made good money for the clients. It set us on the path to our success."

After listening to Thomas for—he didn't know how long they talked because he lost all sense of time—Bryan realized just how influential Thomas was. He'd mastered the stock markets, traded commodities, and made fortunes for his associates and clients. Considering this, Bryan wondered whether Thomas felt satisfaction in his achievements and wished he could have been as helpful to others as Thomas.

"What were you two talking about?" Z asked after they resumed the descent, and Bryan was alone again.

"Oh, we were just—"

"He's a dead man walking," Z hissed into his ear.

Bryan recoiled at the venom in Z's voice. "Why?"

"Everyone in the real world is after him. He let many people down. Some even tossed themselves off the top of the tallest buildings. One of them put a gun to his head while good old Thomas sat across and watched him pull the trigger. His best friend, I hear. I also heard that his wife was fucking someone else because he couldn't satisfy her in a *carnal* way. I wager he'll force his way to the front of the line when the time comes to meet God."

Bryan had always been a trusting person. He generally accepted others at face value and took them at their word. He wondered whether he'd been a little too trusting. Maybe he should …

But the heat down here was unbearable. He discarded his vest and ripped off his shirt, stripping down to his tank top. Then, raising the flask above his head, he drenched his face and shoulders with the cool, reviving fluid.

The low, melodious drone behind Bryan persisted. The man with the neatly trimmed beard had been mumbling to himself since the lobby. Bryan turned to him and nodded. "My name is Bryan."

The man nodded back. "Hello, Mr. Bryan. I am Ahmad. Pleased to meet you."

"Who were you talking to?"

"I am praying to Allah."

"Oh, you're Muslim," Bryan said in surprise. "I knew a Muslim once. He was a nice enough fellow."

Ahmad hesitated. "We are forever nice enough people," he said, half smiling.

"Oh, I wasn't— I didn't mean to—"

"It's okay, Mr. Bryan. We all have our misunderstandings."

Bryan examined Ahmad's face with interest. "Didn't you have gray hair when I saw you earlier in the hotel? And it was longer? And your beard was—?"

"Yes, Mr. Bryan. I have tried to prepare myself as best I can. This opportunity is most urgent for me. Until now, my journey has been long and grueling, and the burdens I carry are many."

Once Ahmad had finished recounting his life story—his childhood days in Afghanistan; the Marine named Brick and his fortuitous introduction to Saxonman; his narrow escape from Kabul when the Taliban came; the trials of his new life in America, or the 'the land of the free and the home of the brave', as he sang slightly off-key; his wife and children fighting for their lives in the hospital—Bryan couldn't help but feel sorry for him.

"I hope we'll be there soon," Bryan said as they descended the next tread together. "We've been walking for hours, and my calves are killing me."

Ahmad appeared startled. "But we started down the stairs only fifteen minutes ago," he said, stroking his chin.

"No, that's not true," Bryan replied. "It's been hours, and we must have come a long way down the stairwell by now."

"You are wrong, Mr. Bryan," Ahmad insisted. "Since the first step, I have prayed the Zuhr prayer followed by four rak'ah of the Asr just to be sure. That takes no more than fifteen minutes altogether."

What if Ahmad was right? Bryan rummaged through his jumbled mind as they continued down the stairs. Perhaps the heat had gotten to him, and it only seemed like hours. Gazing upward, he could see no light from the lobby or determine how far they'd descended. It was all very vague and hard to tell for sure.

"No contest," Z hissed after he'd sneaked forward, and Ahmad had resumed his position alongside Thomas. "Responsible for the death of his brother, that one. His brother's wife and their two small children as well. Horrible deaths they endured. Slain at the hands of jihadi extremists. Cut off their—"

Sickened, Bryan covered his ears with his hands, trying to block out Z's voice. "Please, Z," he begged. "I don't want to hear any more."

Z flinched in dismay.

"In my defense, Bryan. If I were remiss not to point out the impending hazards, I'd be derelict in my duty. According to my instructions, you are my prime responsibility here. Therefore, I consider it my obligation to warn you about anything that may put your life at risk. And I've identified four such threats that pose a clear and present danger."

Lowering his hands, Bryan sighed. "I'm sorry," he said. He wiped the abundant sweat from his brow. "I'm just tired. These stairs are killing my feet. I realize you're only doing your job. I'd lost sight of why we're here. It's all about me and God, first and foremost."

As he cast a wary glance at each participant in turn, Bryan wondered why Dr. Parker and Lucy had chosen these individuals, people who were unreliable and perhaps dangerous enough to threaten the project's success.

But it was so hot down here. He stopped to remove his alligator oxfords and pants, leaving him in nothing but his boxer shorts and tank top. When he restarted, the steel treads burned his feet as they continued their descent into heaven.

"Is it my imagination, or is it getting even hotter?" he said to Z.

Chapter 30

Roxy

IF ROXY COULD SWAP her head, she'd do it in a fucking heartbeat. She would choose the smallest head possible because the one she had on now felt as big as an overripe melon. And the buzzing inside it was driving her nuts.

She cracked open one bleary eye and stared guiltily at the small, empty bottles of god-knows-what littering the bedspread. There were more scattered across the floor. She had no idea how long she'd been asleep, and Z was no longer on the bed beside her. It had been nice, him rubbing her neck the way he did. His firm touch was both relaxing and exciting at the same time, and the way he squeezed her temples had made her toes and tummy tingle.

She'd tried to kiss him, but he recoiled as if she were some fucking repulsive thing. Then she faked a tear, hoping he'd succumb and come close to comfort her, and she'd try to kiss him again. But when he held his distance, she hurled a pillow at him before heading to the minibar for some consolation.

The buzzing in her head returned like a fucking jackhammer punching a hole through the side of her skull.

Groaning, she forced the other eye open, bringing the room into vague comprehension. The buzzing noise, she realized, was from the telephone on the wall by the door. When it buzzed again, she crawled off the bed, staggered across the room, and picked it up.

"What?" she barked.

After her big night of singing and raving, her voice was hoarse, and her mouth was as dry as an old *john's* joke. She was only half listening while the caller relayed the details of her meeting with God.

"I'm not sure I want to meet God anymore," she mumbled into the handset. "After all this … this fucked up stuff with Cathy and Fr. Joe, and what they *claim* I … I did to Bradley. It all scared the shit out of me, you know?"

The caller assured her that everything was going according to plan and that she need not worry.

"But the mouths. They opened in the fucking tree trunks and swallowed everyone. How fucked-up is that?"

The caller agreed how fucked-up that was, but insisted Z would be in the lobby in an hour. Because God was eager to meet her.

Standing in a daze, she waited while the meeting details fought their way through her intoxicated mind. At her feet, Paris pricked her ears and cocked her little head.

"Why would any sane person put themselves through … through this much fucking grief?" she moaned.

Roxy clung to the grab bar at the back of the hoistway car as if her life depended on it. She had Paris jammed under her armpit, panting for air. "Never again," she kept muttering. Wearing a pair of over-sized sunglasses that she'd found in her room, she hoped nobody would notice her bloodshot eyes.

She vaguely remembered closing the door to her room and heading for the elevator landing, then somebody steering her into the car once it arrived. During the descent, she caught fleeting glimpses of the other occupants: the neurotic girl and the sleazy, overweight *john* from the meeting with Lucy in the boardroom, or so she thought. But she couldn't place the good-looking foreign guy with the stubbly beard.

When the car jerked to a stop and the doors opened, the others got out and bolted across the foyer as if they were in the fucking *Amazing Race* or something. Then the door-closing alarm beeped and, after prizing her fingers off the grab bar, she followed them out. If she kept her head steady and footsteps light, the pounding inside her head remained almost tolerable.

Halfway across the lobby, she halted. Ahead, she noticed Z standing beside another *john* whom she didn't recognize.

"That bastard," she muttered to Paris. "Leaving us hanging last night."

When she arrived at the assembly point, Z greeted her with a Mr. fucking Darcy bow. The bastard. After assuring her there was no need to worry, he—bastard—bleated on about some stupid rules they all needed to follow. Then he—again, bastard—tried to play the fucking gentleman by inviting her and the neurotic girl to lead the way down the—

What the fuck? We're going down the 'what' to meet God?

Lifting her shades, she stared, mortified, into the black hole that had just appeared on the floor. She turned to the neurotic girl. "He can't be serious!"

The girl recoiled. With her arms folded and lips pursed, she eyed Roxy up and down. "You're smashed, aren't you?" she said.

"Only slightly," Roxy replied. Then she tried to smile, but her facial muscles refused to work, and all she could manage was a hideous grin. "Help a sister out?" Without her consent, she slung an arm over the girl's shoulder and latched on. "I'm … I'm Roxy," she said, then she held up the dog to show the girl. "And this here is lil … lil Paris."

"Becky," the girl replied, taking Roxy's weight. Scrunching her nose, she whipped her face away. "Ugh. You never flossed this morning."

As they descended the stairs together, Roxy recounted her life story to Becky—minus the bad bits—convinced of Becky's fascination with her worldly exploits because she kept nodding and saying, "Uh-huh." Then Roxy caught her heel on a tread and fell on her ass. Luckily, Paris landed on her soft little paws a few steps below. The new *john*, walking behind them, helped her to her feet and, like the perfect gentleman, asked if she was okay. He said his name was Bryan, and he was sweating like a pig. He seemed nice enough, though. Not as sleazy as some *johns* she'd met. So, she felt confident enough to recount her life story to him—again, minus the bad bits. Then, he offered to invest money in her business. She couldn't recall whether she'd mentioned she owned a business. Anyway, his brother, Bruce, or something like that, wanted to give her a bunch of money for nothing, with no sleepover services required. That would be cool. For some reason, Bryan thought she drove an Uber. She should thank him for the money. And she should make sure to smile while thanking him for the money. She hooked her arm around his and leaned her head against his shoulder. Then she worried he might think this was a come-on when, in fact, all she needed was someone to hold her steady in case she fell again. The sweat was still pouring off poor Bryan to the extent that he'd dressed down to his boxers and tank top. He was easy enough to talk to. Now that the effects of the alcohol had worn off, she couldn't stop talking and was making perfect sense. Then she wondered about the other two *johns* walking behind them. Ahmad and Thomas, she overheard them tell Bryan a little later. The one named Thomas was wearing Bryan's discarded clothes as well as his own because he was shivering like shit as if it were cold. That seemed weird.

Roxy's insides lurched as she considered the four doors before her. She was worried yet excited at the prospect of finally meeting God.

"Choose a door," Z said again.

When he first made the announcement, she wondered how God could be behind all the doors at once—a red one on her left, a blue one close beside it, then a green door, and a yellow one on her right. However, just like Santa, God was everywhere. Right? Or so they'd assured her as a kid.

Bryan didn't look particularly happy, though. Once he realized only Becky, Thomas, Ahmad, and herself were being offered a door to meet God, and there was no door left for him, he had jutted his chin at Z. After a few angry words between them, the problem must have sorted itself because Bryan wandered away to the stairs, where he stood, arms folded, watching on with a seriously pissed-off pout.

Roxy jabbed a finger at the yellow door because, by coincidence, it was her favorite color. She giggled nervously as Z grabbed the handle, little Paris twitching under her arm as he opened it.

"God will see you now," Z said, waving them through.

When they entered, Paris gave a startled whimper as the door slammed shut and everything went black.

"Hello?" Roxy said, blinking and jerking her head around pointlessly in the darkness. "Can someone please turn on the lights? I can't see a fucking thing." Reaching out, she felt for the door behind her. When she found the handle, she tried to turn it, but the door was locked. "Is there anybody here?" she called out, her voice starting to falter.

From her echoing reply, she figured they must be in a large room ... or a fucking cave ... or some place like that. Then she sensed another presence.

"God? Is that you?"

A mischievous snicker. From somewhere on her left.

She tensed, clutching Paris tighter under her arm. "Hello?" Then another prolonged snicker from her right. "This is not funny, you know. Can you please turn on the fucking light?" She squinted into the darkness, then groped again for the door handle, but it was no longer there.

"Perhaps the lights are already on," a voice close beside her whispered.

Roxy flinched in fright. "This is not fucking funny," Roxy repeated, her heart thumping as she tried to muster whatever miserly courage she could find.

"Or perhaps you have already used up all the light," the voice snarled. "Perhaps you took it all for yourself and left none for your friends."

"Look, I don't know who the fuck you are, but you're scaring me. I was supposed to come here and meet God. Have you seen him?"

"Hmm, God. Which god were you hoping to meet?"

"*The* God," she replied. "The one Fr. Joe taught us about."

"Oh, Fr. Joe. Yes, we know Fr. Joe. He's with us. Always claimed he didn't do it. He was framed, he insisted. Said that one day, someone would come and prove his innocence. Would that be you, Janice?"

Roxy hesitated. "Yes. I already told Z that I was sorry about Fr. Joe. It was all my fault. Me and Cathy, we—"

"And was Bradley your fault as well?" the voice asked.

"Yes, Bradley too. But Squirts—"

"We also have Bradley here," the voice interrupted.

"Hi, Janice," said another voice.

"Bradley. Is that you, babe?"

"Yes, Janice. I've been here since … since the night we …" As his voice trailed off, Roxy detected resignation. "They told me adultery really is a mortal sin," he continued, "and you go straight to hell for that kind of offense."

"Hell?" Her insides plummeted, and she suddenly felt nauseous. "What the fuck? I'm not supposed to be in hell. I'm here to meet God. And God lives in heaven."

"You have sinned, Janice," the first voice whispered in her ear, "and sinners always go to hell."

Throwing out a hand, she thrashed at the air about her, but no one was there. "Where are you? What's happening? Bradley?"

"Everyone's gone, Janice. It's just little ol' you and me. Now, it's time to atone for your sins. Let's see. We have one dead, already-married lover, the mother of a newborn without its father, countless cases of adultery, impersonation, bearing false witness against Fr. Joe, coveting thy neighbor's goods, and disrespecting thy parents. What shall the penance be, Janice? Three 'Hail Marys' and a quick 'Our Father'? Do you think that will suffice to save your wicked soul?"

"No. I don't want any fucking penance," she cried. "I just want to go home. Z? Where's Z?"

"Z can't help you," the voice hissed. "Anyone who comes through the yellow door is mine, Janice. So, you belong to Loki."

"Loki?"

Something cold and bony, like someone's creepy finger knuckle, caressed her cheek. She struck out at the blackness in front of her and tried to scream. Panicked, she turned and ran aimlessly in the darkness. She ran until she stumbled and fell face-first, scraping her hands on the rough ground beneath her prostrate body. Paris was yelping, somewhere close by, as Roxy felt around before she heard the clatter of tiny paws scampering away.

"Get up and run away, Janice," Loki growled. "Like the little dog has." His hot breath seared her ears, and his presence wasn't just one, but there seemed to be many Lokis surrounding her. "Run forever in the darkness for your sins."

She clamped her hands over her ears and tried to block out his voice. "Please," she wailed. "I'm sorry. I won't do it again." Then she felt his long fingers sliding around her wrists, clamping them, tugging at her.

"It's too late," he cried. "You are mine to play with and do with as I please."

Roxy sprang to her feet. Terrified, she shoved him aside and bolted away, running and screaming into the dark.

Chapter 31

Thomas

WHEN THE TELEPHONE ON the wall beside him rang, Thomas was busy in the bathroom. The sudden jingle made him jump because, before that, he'd been sitting in solitude, contemplating the happenings so far in the cybersphere—Eray, Aiyla, and their devastated apricot plantation; Sergey and his failed wheat crop; riding in a Humvee in the sandbox; the massive explosion that rendered Sergeant Owens and himself legless; Jackie left destitute; and poor dead Jonas.

"Hello?" he whispered into the handset.

The person on the line informed him that Z would be downstairs in the lobby in one hour sharp. From there, he would be taken to meet God.

Yeah, right, was his initial thought. He remained skeptical about God because he had yet to see any tangible evidence. All he'd witnessed were simulations. For all he knew, they could have sedated him, strapped on a pair of those VR goggles, and this was all part of a role-playing game that the kids enjoyed. However, he had to admit, the whole experience until now had been convincing. Even him, sitting on the toilet, gave the whole God in the Machine deal an authentic feel. This would never occur in fiction, where it was generally accepted that the characters required an interlude for a bowel movement from time to time without subjecting the reader to the messy detail.

He glanced down at his legs and was relieved to find them intact.

Thomas was at pains to avoid eye contact with the other three guests while he waited on the fourth floor of the Regal Grand for the hoistway car to arrive. He had little interest in idle chit-chat with strangers. He was sure these were the same people he'd seen in the W&W boardroom when Dr. Parker announced she needed to digitize their consciousness in addition to their souls, and he'd become confused about things in general. He was sure the Eurasian-looking man on his right was the same fellow from then, except he was now well-groomed and appeared ten years younger. And the hungover woman wearing sunglasses and holding the dog? The doctor had called her Roxy. And the little headbanger? Rebecca? Becky? She was also at that meeting.

During their descent to the lobby, he stood clear of Roxy, who didn't look well. She was motionless at the back of the car, clutching the grab bar, moaning, and promising to be a good girl next time, while the Eurasian-looking man kept his head bowed, mumbling something to Allah. Not always a good sign, Thomas decided. The quicker he got out of here, the better. When the car halted at the ground floor and the doors opened, he was the second one out, close behind the Eurasian fellow, who exited with surprising speed.

Across the lobby, he saw Z with another, much smaller man. The smaller man appeared vaguely familiar, and judging by the way he rubbed his hands together while talking to Z, he was brimming with excitement.

Once they'd all assembled at the meeting point, Z laid down the 'rules of engagement' for meeting God. If this was playacting, at least

Z was taking it seriously. And the others appeared to be caught up in the fun. After that, Z escorted them across the lobby to the staircase that led up to the Ocean Bytes Restaurant on the mezzanine floor. Then he had the cheek to announce, straight-faced, that God lived *downstairs*.

Thomas shook his head in disbelief. Since when did God live underground? However, Z assured them, still with a straight face, that God was indeed living down the stairwell, which had magically appeared in the floor before them.

The whole scenario had just become utterly intriguing.

Thomas wasn't sure who he could trust anymore. If Jackie really was destitute and Jonas dead, why was he still going along with the charade? While they talked earlier in the restaurant, Z had questioned his motive for being here and challenged his expectations. In the end, he needed proof that God didn't exist as they claimed. Once he had evidence of deceit, he'd instruct Lucy to extract him, pronto, from the cybersphere. After that, he'd have his attorney file charges against the perpetrators of this elaborate scam before sorting out the complications he'd left behind in the real world.

Once again, *he* would provide the solutions.

As they descended the stairs together—supposedly to meet God —the Eurasian man continued praying to Allah. Was it kosher for them to walk side by side? It didn't bother him all that much. Live and let live, he always said. When he glanced at the man again, their eyes met briefly. So, he smiled and introduced himself. "Ahmad," was the man's polite reply. Feeling a slight chill, he zipped his jacket and wrapped his arms around himself against the cold.

Some time later, Thomas found himself walking beside the smaller man. He agonized over where he'd seen the man before but, for dear life, couldn't place him. Then he wheezed as he lowered his considerable weight onto the next tread, and the man urged Z to stop for a breather.

"Thanks," he said as they rested together on the steps. He tried to joke about his excess weight and how he wished he'd been incarnated into the cybersphere with the physique of Superman. However, the man didn't have a sense of humor. Then the man asked if he was hot, and it was then that he realized just how cold he felt. Bitterly cold.

"I wish I had something else to wear over my jacket," he told the man. When the man offered his own jacket, the penny dropped. The thin face. That high-pitched voice.

"You're the brother, aren't you?" he said.

The man was undeniably Bryan Woodlands of Woodlands & Woodlands & Co. In the business world, he was renowned for his astuteness and skillful negotiations. The brains behind the W&W operation, some said. Many traders, including himself, had made a boatload of money from stock options when, several years ago, W&W gained approval to construct the country's second-biggest shopping plaza in Orlando. He wondered whether Bryan felt satisfaction in his achievements and the wealth he'd contributed to so many people's lives. Then he wished he had been as generous to others as Bryan.

He could have talked to Bryan for hours, but his teeth started chattering, and the cold stung his fingers.

Thomas was the first in line to choose a door when Z offered. Without hesitation, he chose the red door. After all, red was the lucky color in China. It represented prosperity. Even the soaring prices on the Shanghai Stock Exchange ticker board were displayed in luminous red. And if you believe in God, then every other superstition should be tolerated as well. Right?

"God will see you now," Z said as he threw open the red door and waved him through.

As the door closed behind him, a sudden blast of frigid air smacked his face. Before him, a sheer white curtain emerged. He extended his hand beyond the curtain and, with some trepidation, perceived depth. From there, he discovered he was in a straight, narrow corridor. It had white walls, floor, and ceiling, so the corners and edges were indistinct, and the view ahead was disorienting. He turned around. Behind him, the door had vanished, and all he could see was the same whiteness leading away in the opposite direction. He ran a hand over the wall and found it was made of ice, and its coldness burned his inquisitive fingers.

"Not quite what I was expecting," he muttered. Then he wondered what he truly expected. Perhaps God, sitting on a high throne, surrounded by celestial angels, and emitting rays of light brilliant enough to blind him. That kind of impression certainly would have helped sway his opinion. But— "No, sir. Not convinced yet," he said, quaking from the cold.

For the next hour—or so he thought—he wandered along the corridor, searching for an exit. He had his arms folded tightly against his chest, and his shoulders hunched over as he tried desperately to find some warmth. Icicles formed at the tip of his nose and at the corners of his mouth. It didn't matter which turn he took; the view remained the same, like an endless ice maze. He wondered how he might find a way out of this place without a clue of where he was. There were no signs or flashing lights to direct him, just solid white surfaces wherever he looked.

Many hours later—or so he again thought—still trapped, he sank to the floor and assumed the fetal position, tired and moaning. Even with Bryan's jacket over his own, the brutal cold still seeped through. His cheek numbed against the frozen floor, so he lifted his head and rested it on his arm. Bemused, he gazed into the whiteness and wondered whether this was the end for him in the cybersphere.

"You should get up, Thomas," someone said after he'd been lying there for a while.

He was faintly aware of a man standing over him, but could barely lift his head to see.

"It's f-f-freezing," he complained. "I can't feel my l-l-legs, and my hands are numb. The f-f-fingers feel like they are about to d-d-drop off." He couldn't stop his teeth from chattering as he spoke. "I came h-h-here to find God. Are y-y-you God?"

The man laughed. "Yes, I am a god, Thomas. I am the god of fire." Then his voice grew thunderous. "I bring warmth to those whose hearts have frozen with wickedness."

To Thomas, the man sounded godly enough, but he still couldn't raise his head to confirm his appearance. "Well, I'm certainly c-c-cold. You have a c-c-campfire, you say? Perhaps we could s-s-sit beside it for a while?" He pulled his knees tighter into his chest, desperate for a hint of warmth.

The man laughed again. "I am the fire, Thomas. Can you feel my heat?"

"Sorry, buddy. I can't f-f-feel any heat. Are you s-s-sure you—" Slowly, and groaning with each agonizing movement of his head, he looked up. The man was of average height and wore glasses, a casual shirt, and denim jeans. And he had his NY baseball cap on backward like the cool dudes. "Hey, you l-l-look nothing l-l-like the God of Abraham."

"You should get up, Thomas," the man insisted. "Otherwise, you will die here."

"Oh, I c-c-can't die," he replied confidently. "I'm only v-v-visiting. Once I've p-p-proved God doesn't exist and this w-w-whole thing is a hoax, I'll h-h-have Lucy come and 'beam m-m-me up, Scotty'."

"But, Thomas," the man replied in a sinister whisper, "this *is* your death. After you departed the mortal world, your friends and family took the full twelve months to mourn your passing, and as per your custom, your purgation is complete. Your time here in Gehinnom (purgatory) is up, and your soul is slated for annihilation."

"Gehinnom?" Thomas sat bolt upright, the cold no longer affecting his movement. "Annihilation? Listen, buddy, I paid good money to see God in heaven. I put up with that Z fellow carting me off to those terrible places to show me dreadful things. Now you tell me that all this time I've been in She'ol (the abode of the dead), and my soul won't be going to ʿolam ha-ba (the world to come)?"

The man nodded piteously. "During the purification process, you had the chance to revisit the missed opportunities in your life, the poor choices you've made, the gaps between what was and what should have been. Again, all according to your custom. But you could not be cleansed. You were not sufficiently repentant for your sins and, therefore, your soul is scheduled for destruction."

Thomas grew angry and got up to confront the man.

"Okay, buddy," he snarled, "they promised I would see God. Instead, all I see is you. You tell me you're God, except you look like a regular fellow. They could have at least dressed you in a robe and put a halo over your head or had you holding some holy-looking relic." He shook his head in disgust. "I've had about enough of this playacting. Let's get Lucy on the phone. When I get back, I'll be contacting my lawyers. Perhaps it should be promoted as a Halloween adventure or a ghost ride at the fun fair. But meeting God, it isn't." He glared at the man. "Also, She'ol should be hot and fiery with flames, whereas this place is freezing. You need to get your facts right if you want people to believe this is legitimate."

"Oh, but you are not going to She'ol," the man hissed. His face then contorted into a hateful scowl as he thrust out his chest. "For I am 'Iblīs. I am the leader of the shayātīn (devils) and companion of the al-kafirun (disbelievers). All these years, I have whispered my wickedness into your heart. Now, I will take you, the kāfir (infidel), with me to the bitter cold of Zamharīr (a place of extreme cold at the bottom of hell)."

Chapter 32

Ahmad

AHMAD SCREAMED IN PAIN as the long steel pike pierced his flesh and entered his back. Then he gazed in horror after it had penetrated his right scapula, impaled the lung, and emerged six inches beyond his chest. He wailed and pleaded for mercy. The sight of blood and meat on the point of the pike almost made him retch. Yet somehow, he remained conscious as the pike pushed through. With his top half naked and wrists shackled to jangling chains that suspended him from the ceiling, his feet hovered mere inches off the ground.

He screamed again as the sharp tip of a shiny blade perforated his midriff and sliced a clean incision from just below the sternum down to the pelvis. The sight of his lacerated stomach almost made him faint. Yet somehow, he remained acutely aware of every sensation as his insides spilled onto the floor.

Coughing up blood and spittle, he raised his eyes to gaze upon the face of the one holding the blade. The unmistakable face of…

***

"I am not Ahmad!" he cried aloud in andōh (deep sorrow and grief).

"My name is Sajid."

Although he no longer cared, Sajid still could not work out the time of day in the cybersphere. He was far too sad for his brother, Ahmad, his brother's wife, Fattanah, and their two children, whom he had deceived in Kabul all those years ago. He rebuked himself for his terrible treatment of the man with the can of beans and felt deep remorse for the man's hungry family.

As he sat on the edge of his bed in his room at the Regal Grand, Sajid felt ashamed of what he had done. All his sins appeared by name in the Hadith (the sayings and deeds of the Messenger, peace and blessings be upon him)—taking another's property through falsehood; hurting another; telling lies; deception and evil schemes; despairing of the mercy of Allah and losing all hope; breaking a promise.

For all these weaknesses, Sajid was truly regretful.

When the telephone on the convenience table across from him buzzed, he allowed it to ring out. For all these years, he had tried to shift the burden of his wrongdoings to his wife and children. The decisions made in Kabul had been his alone, so the consequences must therefore be entirely his responsibility. The phone buzzed a second time, and he let it ring out again while he prayed: " به تو پناه می برم از شری که کرده ام .من به همه نعمت هایی که به من ارزانی داشته ای اعتراف می کنم و به همه گناهانم نزد تو اعتراف می کنم .پس مرا ببخش که جز تو گناهان را نمی بخشد (I seek refuge with You from the evil I have done. I acknowledge all the blessings You have bestowed upon me, and I confess to You all my sins. So, forgive me, for indeed, no one forgives sins but You)."

But he knew his failings were much too grievous to be forgiven by prayer alone and could not be cleansed so easily. He believed he was no longer worthy of Allah's favor.

When the phone buzzed for the third time, he relented.

"Alo? This is Ahmad speaking."

"Ahmad," the voice on the telephone said, "Allah knows all. Your pain has been seen, and your tale of woe heard. Your supplication is awaited."

Before heading downstairs to join Z in the lobby, he performed the five sunnah (optional prayers) of ghusl (full-body ritual purification). He used a miswak (twig from the Salvadora persica) to clean his teeth, shaved the unwanted hair from his body, and trimmed his beard and mustache. On the shelf above the washbasin, he discovered a small pressure-pack can. '*Per Signor. For graying hair. Restore your natural color and look ten years younger. Shake well before use,*' the label advised. He dressed humbly, yet haya (modest), in a white tunic shirt and pants, which he found in the closet.

Then he left the room.

Standing between an overweight man and a young girl—who could not have been much older than his daughter, Nikoo—Ahmad continued his prayer as the elevator descended to the lobby of the Regal Grand. Behind him, at the rear of the car, a scantily clad woman was mumbling to her dog. She was leaning against the back wall, holding the grab rail, struggling to remain upright. Even though he considered her immodest, he remained alert. If she were to fall, he could quickly turn and catch her before she hurt herself on the rigid floor.

He was sure he had met these people recently.

When the elevator stopped and the doors slid open, Ahmad spied Mr. Z across the lobby. He was talking to another, smaller man. Worried that he might be late—after the person on the telephone insisted his presence was required in an hour, and he still had no clock—he burst out of the hoistway car and scampered across the lobby. When the others from the elevator arrived soon after, he realized these were the same people from the meeting with Dr. Parker in the real world. No wonder they all appeared familiar.

While Mr. Z explained the rules and observances for their excursion, Ahmad checked the neatness of his attire for the third time. This may be his only chance for such an important undertaking, and he couldn't afford anything to go wrong. His family was relying on his successful intercession. After following Mr. Z across the lobby to the staircase, he looked upward in awe—as did the others—assuming they were about to head up the stairs. But when the floor before him suddenly fell away, and Mr. Z announced they were going downward, he took a step backward in surprise.

"Oh!" he said. "This is unusual." The overweight man expressed the same doubts, but Mr. Z assured them their destination was indeed down the hole.

As he waited to enter the stairwell, Ahmad thought of tawakkul (complete trust in and reliance on God). *Whosoever puts his trust in Allah*, he prayed, *then He will suffice him*. Then, humbling himself, he followed the others down the hole.

Before long, he sensed curiosity from the overweight man walking beside him. When he finally glanced sideways, their eyes met. The man smiled and said his name. Thomas. Pausing his dua (invocation), Ahmad smiled back. After stating his own name, he returned his eyes to the front and continued his prayer. A little later, he had just completed the fourth rak'ah of the Asr prayer when the smaller man, walking on his own a few treads below, glanced over his shoulder and introduced himself.

"Hello, Mr. Bryan," Ahmad responded. "I am Ahmad. I am pleased to meet you."

Wishing to know more about his mutterings, Mr. Bryan appeared surprised to learn that he was praying to Allah. Then Mr. Bryan said something that would normally offend others, but Ahmad immediately forgave him. "It is not the words that are harmful but how they are said", he often reminded his children. Besides, Mr. Bryan had used the words politely and displayed genuine interest in his situation. So he felt safe enough to recount his life story—about the dust and snowstorms of his childhood in Parwan; about his enjoyment of Saxonman, Gods of heavy metal; about his escape from the Taliban and coming to America with his family; about the opportunities here that he never imagined possible. He even performed an out-of-key rendition of the Star-Spangled Banner to prove he was a patriot. Then he spoke of the woes of his wife and children in the hospital before Mr. Bryan mentioned the strangest thing.

"We've been walking for hours," Bryan said, "and my calves are sore."

Ahmad was sure this was not the case. Based on the length of his prayers, he was sure they had been descending the stairs for fifteen minutes at most, and he told Mr. Bryan this. But Mr. Bryan insisted they had been walking much longer, which was puzzling. Even more confusing, while Mr. Bryan sweltered from the heat and the overweight man, Mr. Thomas, froze from the cold, Ahmad considered the conditions ideal.

Ahmad pointed a hesitant finger at the blue door when Z asked him to choose. It wasn't exactly a choice because only the blue and green doors were still available, and he was sure from the look on the young girl's face that she wanted the green door.

After opening the blue door, Z invited him to step through it with the greatest reverence. Beyond the door lay his special prayer room, Z informed him.

His heart pounded. The air around him seemed impossibly thin, and he was finding it hard to breathe. In his excitement and delirium, he suddenly forgot where he was and mistakenly believed he was entering the gates of Jannah (paradise). "There is no god but Allah," he cried as he stepped through the door. Whichever of the eight gates he was passing through, he would be satisfied because it had already been chosen for him. He had been penitent and contrite of heart and, at any moment now, would hear the choirs of angels welcoming him with, " درود بر تو که بر صبرت استقامت کردی إدر واقع خانه انهایی عالی است (Peace be upon you, for that you persevered in patience! Excellent indeed is the final home!)." Then he would see the two Gardens with their lush branches and flowing springs, the palm trees, and pomegranates. He would soon set eyes upon the houris (maidens) and drink and eat bountifully without becoming bloated while reclining on green cushions and splendidly woven carpets.

As unworthy as he felt, he was about to gaze upon the face of Allah.

Instead, he found himself standing alone in a dingy chamber. A tangle of vines covered the walls on all sides, while tree roots hung from the ceiling, and a rich mixture of ammonia and sulfur burned his throat. Behind the vines, the walls appeared to be moving. They were fashioned from thousands of distorted faces, meshed together, their teeth grinding, lips pursed, writhing in agony. Their piteous eyes were crying tears like rivulets of acid that burned the flesh on their withered cheeks as they fell.

Ahmad dropped to his knees. He let out a sharp gasp as he beheld the horrific scene before him. "This is not Jannah!" he cried.

"Help me, Sajid," someone called to him. The voice was weak and distressed.

Terrified, Ahmad spun around. Where the door had been, a set of stone steps now led to a higher floor. In the center of the higher floor, a man dangled from the high ceiling, strung up by lengths of chain shackled to his wrists.

"Help me, Sajid," the man cried again.

Ahmad scrambled to his feet. Without thinking of his safety, he scaled the steps in a single bound and sprinted toward the man. Then, with his arms around the man's torso, he hefted him up, taking his weight.

"Thank you, Sajid," the man said, sighing with relief. "That feels much better."

After a while, Ahmad's arms grew tired. "I don't think I can hold you much longer, sir," he said, gasping for air.

"But you must, Sajid," the man replied. "Otherwise, I will be in agony once again. I have waited a thousand years for you to come and ease my pain."

As the minutes and hours passed, the muscles in his arms and legs stretched and tore, and his back ached. "Sir, you are much too heavy. My legs and sides are now sore. I *must* let go."

"But Sajid, if you let go, I'm not sure I will survive. Your strength and stamina are impressive."

With his arms and legs numb and his body teetering on the verge of exhaustion, Ahmad redoubled his resolve. He grunted and heaved the man higher. While the hours lengthened into days, he persevered.

"Perhaps if I lower you for just a moment," he said after a week had passed, "so I can have a short rest. Then I will lift you again."

"But the pain is too much," the man insisted. "If you lower me again, my wrists and shoulders will hurt as they have for the last thousand years."

So he hoisted the man higher, his whole body groaning under the weight. The days flowed into weeks, the weeks into months, and the months into years.

"It has been far too long," he finally wailed. "I did my best, but I cannot hold you any longer, sir." Then his legs gave out from under him, and he crashed heavily to the floor. The man screamed in pain as the chains snapped taut around his wrists. "I am sorry, sir," he cried, weeping at the sight of the man dangling helplessly above him. "I was too tired, and you are much too heavy."

After recovering, Ahmad stood up. In all the time he had supported the man, he had only seen the back of his head, which had been high above and impossible to see with clarity. When he finally glanced up, he beheld the man's face and swung his head away in disgust. It was neither man nor beast. It was some form of grotesque creature with the face and teeth of a pig and jet-black eyes that gazed upon him from the depths of the abyss. When he turned to look again, the creature scowled.

"Hello, Sajid," it said. "I am Erlik. Welcome to Jahannam (hell)."

Chapter 33

Rebecca

BECKY THRUST HER blackened hand into the soot-covered neoprene gauntlet. She gripped the blistering handle of the cast-iron door and pulled with all her might. As the door swung open, a blast of scorching air erupted from inside, forcing her back. After wiping the sweat from her brow, she plowed her shovel into the bituminous coal heaped at her feet, then tossed another shovelful into the furnace.

And the inferno that raged beyond the cast-iron door roared all the more.

***

No matter how long she stared at it or wished it to ring, the handset on the meals counter in her room at the Regal Grand remained stubbornly silent. Zorro had promised to call her once he'd finished organizing God. That was two hours ago. Much too long.

She snatched up the receiver the instant it rang.

"Hello? Yep, that's me. When? Will Zoro be there? You know, the big black guy in the coat who thinks he looks like Zoro. Great. I'll be down then. Can't wait." She hung up.

At first, Becky felt a twinge of remorse. She'd gotten Rachel into debt, and her parents arrested—charged with aiding and abetting, harboring a fugitive, falsification, and fraud. She'd burned down Sandra's house, sacrificed White Rabbit and the others for the cause, and allegedly blown up the waste plant at Greenpoint, making New York City stink for years.

That can't be right. They're always out to blame someone else. Anything to divert our attention from the most important issue at hand. They're killing the planet while God sits twiddling Their thumbs and not doing a damn thing about it.

That was the crux of the problem. If she could get through to God and make *Them* listen, it would all be okay.

She was expected down in the lobby in an hour. From there, Zoro would take her to meet God. She rehearsed her speech to *Them* in her head, the one that highlighted all the nepotism and negligence. She needed to hit the critical points and make sure things were clear and concise. Once she made God aware of the appalling situation down on earth, there would be no excuse for *Their* inaction.

Ten minutes before the hour, Becky left her room and headed to the elevator. While she waited at the landing, three other people joined her: the big, fat, dodgy guy, the foreign guy—who now appeared younger with his dark hair and neatly trimmed beard—and the hooker with her cute dog. They'd all been at the meeting with Dr. Parker when everybody except her went psycho. She guessed they were also here to meet God.

When the elevator arrived, everyone piled in—except the hooker, who hadn't moved since staggering to the landing. She was still leaning against the wall, sunglasses on, her head slumped forward, and the poor little dog being strangled under her arm. As she kept the doors open, Becky wondered whether the hooker was conscious.

In the end, she turned to the foreign guy, signaling to him—in case he didn't understand English—to hold the door open while she ducked out and steered the hooker into the car.

"Here, hold on to this," she said, wrapping the hooker's free hand around the grab bar at the rear of the car.

When they reached the lobby, Zoro was deep in conversation with a weedy-looking guy whom she didn't recognize. More talking. She wished they would get on with the meeting. This business of standing around was a complete waste of everyone's time and attention. God was expecting her, and there wasn't a moment to spare.

While they stood in the lobby with Zoro, waiting for God to arrive, the hooker raised her sunglasses and turned to Becky.

"He can't be serious," she said in slow, painful syllables.

Becky was only half-listening when a massive hole with a stairwell appeared in the floor. She wondered whether she'd misheard when Zorro announced God was down there. Whatever. It didn't matter. Wherever God was, *They* needed to be hauled before her and held accountable for mankind's stupidity.

Noticing the hooker's bloodshot eyes, she rocked back on her heels. "You're smashed, aren't you?" she said, lips pursed.

"Only slightly," the hooker replied. Then she—epic fail—attempted to smile before clapping an arm over Becky's shoulders without asking first. "Help a sister out? I'm Roxy." She shoved her dog in Becky's face. "And this here is lil … lil Paris."

"Becky," she replied, taking Roxy's limp weight. Then she caught a whiff of Roxy's stinking breath and swung her face away. "Ugh. You never flossed this morning, did you?"

Roxy only giggled, like a dimwitted schoolgirl.

As they descended the stairs, Roxy would not shut up. Most of what she said was incoherent. Listening to her garbled nonsense and juvenile language made Becky cringe. She was like the embarrassing aunt at the annual extended family picnic who'd had one too many Proseccos and wouldn't take the hint to shut up and sit down. Until she found a way to ditch Roxy, all she could do was nod, say "Uh-huh," and pretend to be interested.

Then Roxy stumbled and fell. When the weedy-looking guy behind them rushed forward to help, Becky seized the opportunity to skip ahead, leaving him to deal with the slobbering mess that was Roxy.

She enjoyed walking alone. It gave her time to think about what she had to say to God. Behind her, Roxy was now rambling to the weedy-looking guy about this and that. Becky rolled her eyes. People like her were the crux of the problem with the world, always focused on the unimportant things in their meaningless lives.

Oh no. Here she comes again.

Five minutes later, and sick to death of Roxy's incessant nonsense, Becky finally snapped. She stopped short, stomped her foot on the metal tread, and announced, "I'm thirsty."

"Did you bring water?" the weedy-looking guy asked.

"No one mentioned we'd need provisions," she snapped back.

After handing over his flask, he introduced himself. "Bryan." Then he asked why she was in the cybersphere.

Becky hesitated. Her mom had always warned her about older men starting up conversations with young girls. Then she figured it was the perfect opportunity to practice her spiel to God. Without divulging any personal particulars, she informed Bryan about her views on life. About the sacrifices everyone must make. About leadership and recognizing when it's your turn to step up to the plate and hit a home run. About the decision-makers having the correct information. About how the buck always stops with those in charge.

When she finished her spiel, he was staring at her, weird-like. She couldn't decide if it was admiration or whether he was being judgmental, as older people generally are to the younger generation.

She handed back his flask and, without smiling, said 'thanks'. Then she skipped ahead to rejoin Roxy.

More than anything, Becky wanted the green door because it represented the universal color of the eco cause. But she was the last in line to choose a door after refusing any special treatment that might be patronizing on account of her age or gender. Only the green and blue doors remained after Roxy and the Thomas guy had made their selection.

Luckily for her, the Ahmad guy chose the blue door.

After pushing the green door open, Zoro turned to her and said, "God will see you now." Then he smiled and waved her through.

At first, she saw nothing as she peered into the blackness beyond the door. She took a half-step forward, squinting. Then, she took a bigger step, carrying her through the opening.

"God? Are you there? I need to speak with you now."

She waited. Nothing.

"Is anyone home?"

The stark silence persisted. Just as she decided to turn and leave, the door slammed shut behind her and vanished.

More silence followed as she stood alone, confused, in the darkness.

"Zoro? Can you hear me?"

Indistinct objects, distorted and ragged against the blackened sky, began to take shape around her as her eyes adjusted to the gloom. They were trees, she soon realized, but leafless, just skeletal trunks with crooked branches that weaved a twisted canopy overhead. Thick mist crept along the ground toward her. It gathered around her feet and billowed about her knees. She reached out, groping for the door handle, but felt nothing except a cold, flat surface.

"If this is some kind of joke, Zoro, then it's not funny."

For a long time, she stood in the stillness, wondering what to do next. More than once before, she'd found herself in a tricky situation, but this time was different. Based on her recent experiences with Zoro, she could be anywhere. She closed her eyes, counted to ten, and opened them again, hoping she might magically appear back in her hotel room like last time.

Nope.

She forced herself to remain calm. Composure was the key. Then, the bushes behind her rustled. As she spun around, a cold shiver zapped her spine, and her shoulder muscles twitched in fear.

"Hello? Is anyone there?"

The bushes ceased rustling. Something in the mist then breathed deep, labored breaths. Heavy, ominous breaths. Whatever it was, she heard it salivating and immediately recalled an old horror movie she'd seen on late-night TV when she was a kid. It was about werewolves. They were chasing a terrified young girl into a deep, dark forest. From that day on, werewolves had always scared the bejesus out of her. Not trapdoor spiders, half-decayed zombies, or even Ripley's alien bitch with its sharp teeth and acid blood. It was a thing, just as some people have an irrational fear of nail clippers. She always wondered whether the girl had escaped the beast's clutches after her mother discovered her cringing behind the couch, peeking through a web of trembling fingers, and sent her off to bed before the movie ended.

The only difference now was the absence of a full moon rising over the twisted forest.

No sooner had she remembered that detail than a full moon materialized in the night sky. The hairs on her forearms bristled, follicles standing on end like tiny, frightened jackrabbits. Panicked, she turned to flee but tripped and fell. Then, scrambling to her feet again, she scurried off into the haunting shadows.

She didn't know where she was going, except away from the werewolves in the mist. This wasn't what she'd expected of heaven. Surely God lived somewhere with bright, colorful lights, breathtaking scenery, a few unicorns, harp music, and a couple of flute players. Or so she thought.

Out of breath and with her legs aching, she slowed to a walk. Soon, the surrounding trees melded and solidified, and she found herself walking along a footpath hemmed in by brick walls on both sides. It was still nighttime with the full moon overhead and no other soul on the street. At her feet, the mist continued to billow and build until she could only see a few yards ahead.

Clack-scrape-clack.

She tensed at the sound of footsteps behind her. *It* was following her. When she quickened her pace, the footsteps quickened in response. She stopped, turned, and found nobody there. When she resumed, the footsteps restarted, too, so she halted again.

"Don't you mess with me," she yelled. Her heart pounding, she assumed the defensive pose which she'd practiced since she was four years old to ward off sicko strangers—her body side-on, one foot thrust forward, fists clenched and raised, and a facial expression conjured from her core that promised some serious malice.

The thing started up a low, continuous growl. Then, an unsettling red light pierced the mist, small like a laser dot, aimed at her. Gut clenched and trembling, she backed away.

"I don't want any problems, buster!" she shouted. "Who are you anyway?"

The laser dot winked.

"It's not *who* I am that should concern you, Rebecca," a voice hissed back. "But *what* I am."

A one-eyed werewolf!

Becky turned, screaming. She tried to run, but the ground underfoot turned to slime, and she lost all traction. Her legs were pumping hard, but she was going nowhere. Peering over her shoulder, she saw the red dot closing in. As it drew nearer, the growling and breathing grew louder. Feathers ruffled and spurs scraped ominously along the concrete before a disfigured face appeared through the mist behind her. It had a single red eye set above the bridge of its nose. It wasn't a werewolf; it was a person, but not a person.

Rising to its full height, it stalked toward her.

"Why do you run from me, Rebecca?" it said.

"Stay away from me, you psycho." On all fours, she tried to crawl away. "Zoro? What the *hell* is going on?"

"Your use of the word 'hell' is interesting, Rebecca."

Whatever the thing was, she felt its sharp talons pierce her shoulders and wrench her violently backward. She screamed again as it thrashed its enormous wings in slow, rhythmic throbs before lifting her into the murky sky and carrying her away.

Chapter 34

The Entities

THEY WERE ONCE AGAIN gathered at the Fallen Angels Bar & Dive, huddled in a booth in the back corner, locked in frivolous conversation. Ahriman was sitting beside Erlik, who was diagonal to Loki, with Charon beside him, and 'Iblīs perched on a stool at one end of the table. Drumming his fingers on the tabletop, Loki glanced across at Erlik with a mischievous smile.

"How goes your … amusement?" he asked.

Tossing his head back, Erlik guzzled the last of his ale. Then he exhaled loudly before slamming the empty jug on the table.

"It goes most excellently," he replied.

"Mine too," Ahriman confessed, ruffling his brown speckled plumage in satisfaction.

"And mine," Charon chimed in, followed by the deep rattle of an old man laughing.

They all turned to 'Iblīs. He had his arms folded in defiance and chin lowered to his chest, and still did not look happy on account of his human form—or his tainted clay exterior as he grumbled to anyone who cared to listen. He raised his head slowly, eyeing them with morbid fascination before an unsettling smile broadened across his face.

"Mine as well," he said.

"Then it seems we are all likewise satisfied with the arrangement so far," Loki admitted. He studied the dregs at the bottom of his jug before signaling to the bartender entity for five more ales. "And some snacks," he shouted across the room. After the bartender entity nodded, Loki turned back to the others. "And what about this immortal who calls himself Z?"

At Z's name, Erlik swung his hideous face away from the table and spat on the floor. "No one has heard of him," he said, his top lip curling in disgust as he spoke.

"I'm not sure I trust him," said 'Iblīs in a derisive tone. "If this is what he can do to me,"—he waved a hand across his form—"then imagine what he can do to the rest of you."

They all fell silent, pondering 'Iblīs's form until Charon cleared his throat. "To be fair," he said, "the product he has supplied thus far seems to be of a particularly high standard. It reeks of sin. If he can provide more of the same, in the quantities promised, then this whole arrangement may prove lucrative."

"But what's in it for him?" Loki hissed. As he stood, he attempted to swipe his jug off the table to show his frustration, but it hit Erlik flush in the chest, covering him in slops.

Scowling, Erlik sprang to his feet. He swung a wild fist at Loki from across the table, missing him by a whisker. 'Iblīs grabbed Erlik's arm and yanked him back. "Sit down," he cried while Charon watched on, unimpressed. "You wuss," Loki taunted, shaping his fists for a fight. "Don't be a fool," 'Iblīs barked, holding Erlik back. "But he called me a wuss," Erlik protested. "Sticks and stones," replied 'Iblīs.

After placating Erlik, 'Iblīs turned to Loki. "Apologize to him," he demanded.

For a long moment, Loki hissed and spat as they stared each other down. Then, warily, he lowered his defenses.

"Everybody, calm down," he said. "By Odin's honor, it was an accident." He threw Erlik a playful look, as though the misunderstanding had been an overreaction and was not entirely his fault. "My apologies if I offended you." He turned to Charon beside him. "Here's my point, though. He supplies these souls yet asks for nothing in return. What's his angle? I tell you, there's something not quite right about this Z and his bounty of souls."

Nodding thoughtfully, Charon shifted his attention across the table to Ahriman, who sat with his one eye closed and had not flinched during the entire fracas. "What say you, Ahriman?"

Following a short deliberation, Ahriman opened his eye. "I think we should take as many souls as he gives us. And when we have filled your boat many times over, and our advantage has increased a hundredfold, we should send this Z back to whatever hell he says he came from."

Without another word, 'Iblīs, Charon, Erlik, and then Loki nodded in agreement.

The bartender entity arrived at their table carrying four jugs filled with ale in two of its hands. It had a fifth jug in another, and a large bowl of pretzels in its remaining hand.

"Let us drink to that," said Charon.

Their replenished jugs all converged in the center of the table with a resounding clatter. Then they slurped their drinks and dived their hands into the pretzel bowl without any by-your-leaves or beg-your-pardons as they ate greedily. After taking a long swig of his ale, Erlik lowered his jug.

"I hung myself from the ceiling with chains and had mine hold me up for a thousand years." As he spoke, bits of pretzel mixed with spittle sprayed from his mouth, covering the table and those sitting opposite. "All I thought about for the entire time was 'dead weight', 'dead weight'. Then I told him the next stop was Jahannam (hell) on account of his wickedness. It frightened the daylights out of him."

He grinned while the rest burst into raucous laughter.

"I've got mine running through the darkness for her penance," Loki said with a smirk. "She's convinced she's gone blind when all I did was turn out the lights." He convulsed, unable to contain his mirth. "Next, I might drag her down below and then northward to Niflheim, to the real world of darkness, and introduce her mortal soul to my beautiful daughter, Hel."

While they all bobbed their heads in appreciation of Loki's devious trick, Ahriman ruffled his feathers to gain their attention.

"I took mine into the woods," he said. Lowering his head, he glared menacingly at them through his single eye. "I recreated a scene from an old horror movie that scared the wits out of her when she was a child. But she's a feisty one. Demanded to see God. Then she challenged me to a fistfight. Can you believe it?" He flashed a cruel smile at the others. "It's okay, though. As we speak, I have her dangling by the throat in mid-air to remind her who is in charge here. Once I return, I will haul her petulant soul down into the realm of eternal darkness."

"I was allocated the fat one," 'Iblīs announced, showing no emotion. "He must be the only Jew I have met who doesn't believe in God. Now, I ask you: if there isn't a God, then what are we? Do we not exist as well?" He threw his hands up in annoyance. "Anyway, I have just informed him that his soul is up for destruction, and he will soon be the one who doesn't exist. Except I'm going to freeze him in Zamharīr for eternity first."

Again, they laughed and jeered in frivolous rapture. They spilled ale and threw pretzels at each other in jest. When the uproar finally subsided, Ahriman swung his eye toward Charon.

"And what dastardly fate befalls your mortal plaything, Charon?"

Charon gave them a smug, conniving stare.

"At this very moment, I am carting his selfish remains down to the sandy shores of the Styx."

Chapter 35

Bryan & Charon

Following their long descent from the lobby of the Regal Grand, Bryan was sweltering from the heat. He was footsore and angry as well.

"I told you I was to be first," he said to Z, expressing his frustration. He was certain he'd made himself clear more than once, but when Z gave all the colored doors to the participants, he had rocked back on his heels in dismay. "Where's my door?" he'd said.

Taking his arm, Z tugged him aside. "Relax, Bryan," he whispered. "Everything is going according to plan. Rest assured, you *will* be the first to meet God. The others, however,"—he gave a decisive nod toward the participants—"will not be so lucky as a different destiny awaits them."

"What do you mean?" Bryan asked.

Z glanced furtively around to make sure no one else was within earshot. "This whole experience was devised for your benefit. Even you admitted they were no longer needed since the cybersphere is now functional. Given that they've outlived their intended purpose, they'll be disposed of."

"Disposed of?" Grimacing, Bryan shot an anxious glance at the others, who were standing obliviously before the row of colored doors. "How?"

"Humanely, of course," Z replied. "Does it matter how?" He gave an impatient shrug.

The bitter taste of rising bile leached into the back of Bryan's throat. He forced it back down. "Well, I—"

"They are all sinners, Bryan. After evaluating the true composition of their souls, I have deemed them unfit to meet God. I gave each one the chance to atone for their failings. Once they understood the gravity of their sins, they were certainly remorseful. Some of them cried. But they kept making excuses for their poor choices. *'I was under the influence of illicit substances when I killed my unfaithful lover; I had to save my wife and children at all costs; I must save the planet at the expense of everyone else; they made me do it because everyone is relying on poor little old me for their livelihoods'*. There can always be excuses for the unspeakable things we do." He broke into a stifled, derisive snicker. Then, suddenly straight-faced, he raised a brow and added in a reproaching tone, "Yet the simple fact remains that whenever evil is done, it remains done." Leaning closer to Bryan, he nodded discreetly at Thomas. "And did you see how the fat one barged in front of the others to be first in line at the doors? Didn't I warn you about him?"

Bryan hadn't thought this far ahead. Many times during the past two years, he'd imagined himself at this very moment, purged of all earthly attachments and ready to meet God in the cybersphere. Not once, though, had he considered the participants' fate or expected the curious pangs of conscience that pricked him now.

"Having second thoughts, Bryan?"

He hesitated, then shook his head gravely. "No. I've come this far. Lucy and Brice have invested significant amounts of money and effort in this venture. They'll be disappointed if I don't follow through." He furrowed his brow. "Do whatever you must," he said, giving Z a curt nod. "The time has come for me to meet God."

He eased himself onto the ground and began massaging the soreness out of his feet.

As he observed the participants entering their chosen doors, he felt uneasy at the notion of what *humane* disposal might entail. It was probably for the best because there were no guarantees Lucy would be able to revive any of them after she'd resurrected him. He was still unsure how she might accomplish the feat. Although he was convinced that if anyone could, Lucy would find a way.

Once Becky passed through the green door and they were alone, Z snapped his fingers, and the four doors vanished. He turned to Bryan. "And now it's your turn, Bryan."

"I'm a little worried about our road trip," Bryan said, standing again. "In the end, I couldn't think of—"

Before he could finish, Z snapped his fingers a second time, and an enormous opening appeared above them. This one was far more impressive than he could have imagined. It had a pearly-colored marble stairway leading up to an arched entrance, which was surrounded by thick plumes of fluffy white clouds against an azure sky. A pair of golden, ornate gates blocked the archway, while behind the gates, a blinding light like the sun, except a thousand times brighter, lit up the celestial portal with its dazzling rays.

Recoiling at the sight, Bryan raised a hand to shield his eyes from the glare. Then he covered his ears as the resounding blare of a thousand trumpets filled the air. He couldn't help laughing aloud. "Now this is more like it," he cried out in utter amazement. When the trumpets fell silent, he thought he heard a choir of angels singing *Alleluias* from beyond the gates.

"You will need this," Z said, extending his hand toward Bryan.

Nestled in his palm, Bryan noticed an ancient-looking coin. Taking the coin, he slipped it into the concealed pouch inside his boxer shorts. Then he looked up at Z in dismay. "Oh, I'm not properly dressed. And I'm drenched with sweat."

"It's okay, Bryan," Z replied. "God judges us only by what's on the inside." Then, with a flourishing bow, he invited Bryan up the stairs. "God will see you now, Bryan."

Bryan ascended the marble stairs, holding his breath. He was trembling with excitement, more than he had known before, and couldn't keep the smile off his face. When he reached the gates, he marveled at the gilded latch glittering in the radiant light from above. Taking it in one hand, he glanced over his shoulder at Z, who nodded and waved him on. When he lifted the latch, the gates swung open with ease. The pounding in his chest was so loud that he could hear it above another blast of trumpets, which sounded as if to announce his arrival—his ceremonial welcome into heaven, or so he thought.

The gates closed gently behind him, and he found himself standing in a grand hall at one end of a long concourse. With its vaulted ceiling and elegant architectural design, he wondered whether he might be back in the lobby of the Regal Grand. However, the longer he gazed in awe at his surroundings, the more he came to appreciate that this was a thousand times more glorious and surreal. Overhead, an incredible array of intricate motifs of cherubs and holy scenes, overlaid on rays of golden sunbeams, adorned the wide coffered panels. The walls on either side of him were festooned with colorful tapestries depicting saints and sacred rites. They draped the hundred-and-fifty feet from the ceiling to the floor. In all his time, he had never seen such magnificence. Not even the Renaissance frescoes of the Sistine Chapel, which he had stood beneath and admired many times before, compared to this. He supposed this was all Lucy's handiwork.

"She's such a talented girl," he reminded himself.

A line of resplendent chandeliers ran the length of the concourse, leading to a dais where a man sat upon a godly throne. The man wore a long cotton robe—bleached as pure as angel wings—and sandals, while his flowing white beard cascaded over his rotund belly. A nimbus of divine light fell upon the man's head. In one wrinkled hand, he held up a scepter, which, to Bryan, gave the impression of a true creator of the world.

As he approached the dais, the man remained motionless. When he drew close enough, he noticed the man's eyes were closed.

"God?" he inquired in a meek voice.

God grunted and shifted uncomfortably in his seat, but didn't open his eyes. Then he released a prolonged, throaty noise that Bryan imagined could have been a snore.

"God? It's me, Bryan."

While he waited for a reply, he noticed God's grip loosen around the scepter. The fingers holding it each dropped away until he finally let go, and it crashed to the floor with a jarring clatter that jolted him awake. Startled, God sat bolt upright. He blinked in dimwitted surprise and looked around. "Huh?" he said.

Bryan stood at attention. As much as he wanted to announce himself to the heavens, he was shocked to hear himself whisper, "It's me. Bryan. I have an appointment." Then he wondered whether he should bow, kneel, or throw himself prostrate at the feet of God. Ultimately, he decided to remain where he was until God gave him further instructions.

God leaned down from his throne, peering drowsily at him. "Bryan who?" he demanded in a vociferous voice.

"Bryan Woodlands … of Woodlands & Woodlands & Co," he replied giddily. "You're expecting me. I'm the one who organized all of this." Spreading his arms wide, he hoped to inform God that his handiwork included everything around them. "I want you to preview my soul, and make sure that I'm worthy to enter the real heaven when the time comes."

God frowned in remembrance as he studied Bryan further. "Oh, yes," he finally said. "That Bryan."

When Bryan glanced at the scepter lying on the floor beside the throne, he realized it wasn't a scepter but a long wooden oar from a rowboat, and he wondered why in the world God would need an oar.

Then God grunted as he lifted his left buttock an inch off the throne. His face contorted, and there was an almighty *fraaap* as God broke wind.

A rancid odor, like the stench of rotting fish, swept over Bryan, and he almost gagged. "Oh, my God!" he cried and threw a hand up to cover his mouth and nose against the putrid air.

God's eyes widened. "God?" he roared. He slapped his knees and fell backward on his throne, convulsing with laughter. Then he took his oar and swung it savagely across Bryan's head.

The next thing he remembered was lying on the ground with God's face pressed into his. God's eyes were ablaze, and he had a fist shoved down Bryan's throat.

"Where is my obol?" he screamed as his fingers ripped into Bryan's mouth and clawed under his tongue. "Where's my payment?"

Ignoring the discomfort of God's hand in his mouth, he reached up. He wrapped an arm around God's neck and took him in a stranglehold. With all his might, he pulled downward, marveling at his newfound strength as they rolled over on the ground in a tangle of arms and legs. God poked him in the eye. So, he poked God's eye in return. Then God bit his ear, and he bit God's ear back. God tried vainly to reach for his oar, which was lying in the sand nearby, while Bryan maintained his furious hold. For a long time, he held God immobile, gagging, the sinews in his neck and shoulders straining until God gave a last shudder and finally tapped out.

After Bryan released him, God sat hunched over with his elbows on his knees, gasping for air. "I was once unbeatable," he moaned. "But now I am too old and tired for all these fisticuffs."

Bryan couldn't believe God could be so violent. *Obol? What's an obol?* It had something to do with payment. Curiously, he reached into the pocket of his boxer shorts and fingered the ancient-looking coin Z had given him. *That must be the obol*—he assumed—*for payment.* But why would God require payment? Surely, the entry to heaven was free. Then came realization. He scrambled to his feet and backed away. "You're not God," he cried.

The old man looked up at him and grunted. "I am no more *the* God than you are a saint."

"But I was assured God was ready to meet me. And when I saw you up on that throne, you appeared godlike enough. Z told me—"

"Z!" The old man threw his head sideways and discharged a large glob of mucus onto the ground. "That piece of shit. He promises everything, yet he takes no responsibility. This was to be a straight-forward crossing. If all the souls he delivers are as problematic as you, then I wonder whether the whole venture is worth my while."

"Venture? Crossing?" Bryan looked at him, confused. "To where?"

"To the Underworld," the old man replied.

Bryan spun around and saw a river flowing beside them. Further along the bank, a large wooden rowboat rocked gently in the water as the waves lapped against it, and he immediately recalled the warning from an old-time song about not paying the—

"You're the Ferryman!" he cried.

"Ferryman?" Rising steadily to his feet, the old man set his fierce eyes on Bryan. "That name is an insult," he said with sudden belligerence. "For I am Charon, and you should show me some respect."

Even though he was trembling with fear, Bryan balled his fists and, before he could stop himself, blurted out, "Well, I am Bryan, and you had better show me some goddamn respect as well."

Charon scowled. "You are nothing," he said.

Bryan returned Charon's scowl, eyes narrowed, as they stared each other down. "As I've advised you earlier, Charon. I created the cybersphere and everything in it."

"But this Z. He claims to have created the cybersphere."

"I created Z as well," Bryan retorted.

"So, *you* made the Machine he speaks of?"

"Lucy made the Machine," he replied. "However, she did so under my instruction."

Charon thought briefly before the lines on his face creased with confusion. "*Lucy?* Not this Immortal named Z?" He shook his head slowly in bewilderment. "And you say you are here to have your soul previewed? Therefore, you are not already dead?"

Bryan nodded in the affirmative. "While we're here in the Machine, our physical selves in the real world have been stored in cryo-suspension. So technically, none of us is dead."

"*Technically?*" Charon tugged at his beard in dubious thought. "So, all the souls Z promised are a lie?"

Again, Bryan nodded in the affirmative. "The Machine was created for my benefit only. Once I'm finished here, I'll be extracted. There will be no more souls, and Z's program will be terminated." Although he didn't know the specifics about terminating Z's software, he hoped he sounded convincing enough.

"So, I will be terminated as well?" Charon said. After Bryan nodded again, Charon fell silent. Then his eyes swung decisively to the oar on the ground beside them.

Bryan sprang into action with the speed of an alley cat on an unsuspecting mouse, the much-improved cybersphere version of himself nimbler than the old man, and he had the oar in his hands before Charon had time to react.

"You are undead," Charon bellowed as Bryan brandished the oar in his face. "And you have no obol for me. Therefore, I cannot take you across the river, and you are thus condemned to wander these shores for the next hundred years."

Bryan swung the oar lustily as Charon lunged at him. He wielded it again, catching Charon in the midriff. When he brought it down a third time across the old man's back, Charon fell. Then Bryan hurled it into the river, turned, and tore blindly away.

He ran as fast as his legs would carry him. He didn't stop or look back to check if Charon was following. Escape was the only thing on his fearful mind as he raced past the godly throne. His own survival was foremost in his thoughts as he fled along the majestic concourse, threw open the Pearly Gates, and hurtled down the marble stairs. He had to get back to the lobby of the Regal Grand, where Lucy would help extricate him from the cybershpere.

When he reached the foot of the stairs, the celestial portal imploded, and he found himself groping in the darkness for the foot of the stairs that would lead him back to the lobby. He called out to Z, who was no longer there, and he was thankful for that because he no longer trusted Z.

On finding the stairs, he scrambled up the treads on all fours. He was still sweating profusely. He was terrified. He was in peril. The cybersphere was no longer a safe place for him to be. For anyone to be. Including the participants. The cybersphere that he had convinced his brother and niece to make. For which he was responsible.

As he dragged himself onto the next tread, the breath stuck in his throat, and he halted and collapsed. Lying prostrate in the dark, he was at first thankful for the chance of escape. Then he was thoughtful. And in the end, regretful. The others were still down here somewhere. Roxy, Ahmad, Thomas, and Becky were in danger, to be humanely disposed of, Z had told him. He got slowly to his feet, then he turned around and headed back down the stairs.

And at once, the heat and sweat that had afflicted him down the hole were gone.

Chapter 36

Susan

AT SOME TIME OR OTHER, when the endless hours had melded into days and the days into weeks, Susan rolled over in her bed. She had little idea of the time of day. She hadn't slept for more than an hour at a time in ages. There was too much going on, and her busy mind was continually in problem-solving mode. The troublesome God module now commanded every minute of her undivided attention.

Rolling onto her side, she stared blankly at the wall.

Another hour passed, and nothing changed, so she got up and went to the bathroom. As she sat in the dark with her head in her hands, making soft gurgling noises, she wished she were somewhere else. Anywhere but here.

It had been six months since she'd last stepped outside the lab. Half a year trapped within the same four walls, her head buried in the same 20-inch screens, watching the same old movies on the VCR while subliminally solving the next obstacle on her ever-growing punch list. As much as she enjoyed the movie, if she had to sit through one more replay of The Shawshank Redemption, she swore she would …

After finishing in the bathroom, she got dressed and slipped on her jacket. Careful not to disturb Lucy, asleep on the couch, she crept across the room. As she pulled the door closed, she listened for the reassuring *click* that confirmed the integrity of the Faraday cage. Then she took the elevator up to the first level, walked past the unmanned concierge desk, and exited the building.

It was intoxicating. She felt immense relief as she took her first steps outside after being cooped up for so long. The darkness was surprisingly strange. She'd almost forgotten what nighttime was like. Confined to the windowless lab, she'd lost all perception of night and day, and her circadian rhythm was shot to pieces. Her routine had become almost robotic—she worked, felt hungry and ate, worked some more, felt tired and slept, woke up, and worked again. That was now the extent of her internal clock cycle.

When the chill of the evening air hit her, she was thankful she'd brought her jacket. But then she reached down for the zipper and realized it wasn't her jacket at all. In fact, she'd never seen this old and tattered jacket before. It was soiled and reeked of the streets.

No, it was she who reeked of the streets.

As she headed uptown from the SoulSoft office, Susan had no plan or destination in mind; she just kept walking. Unconcerned about her own safety, she imagined the look of horror on her mother's face as she wandered alone through the poorly lit neighborhoods. Whenever a passerby came too close, she would veer away. The thought of anyone touching her, even the lightest brush of an elbow or arm, repulsed her. She'd been shut away for so long that she now felt a curious, inherent loathing of physical contact with others.

Before she knew it, she must have walked for a good five or six miles—straight up First Avenue, through Lenox Hill, Yorkville, East Harlem, across the bridge, then along Westchester Avenue into Longwood before continuing until she hit the Bronx River. By then, her calves were cramping and her back smarted. It was a satisfying ache, though, and she appreciated the exercise all the same.

A short time later, she found herself power-walking along the shared-use path that meandered alongside the Bronx. The path appeared deserted, and the tall towers and vibrant lights of downtown Manhattan had fallen behind her long ago. Further ahead, she saw a footbridge illuminated in the night. It ran parallel to the rail lines across the river. As she neared the footbridge, she heard someone call her name faintly. When she whirled around, there was no one there.

"That's strange," she muttered, quickening her pace.

Halfway across the bridge, she heard her name again; unmistakable this time. She halted and listened. Then she peered over the safety rail and saw a figure flailing its arms in the water below. Someone was in trouble, someone splashing and floundering, appealing for help. Someone she knew?

Straining for a keener look, she leaned over the rail and, as she did, felt a firm shove in her back, which tipped her over the railing.

Plunging from the footbridge, her limp body tumbled head over heels in free fall. At first, she was in shock, but then came unexpected thoughts about the problematic God module as she fell as if forever. She thought about errant lines of software code and elusive solutions. She thought about Brice Woodlands and Lucy. About poor Bryan Woodlands and his incredible plan to reveal his soul to God before his death. About Roxy, Ahmad, Thomas, and Rebecca, all trapped as unwitting pawns in the cybersphere—the dangerous cybersphere that she had created. She thought about the horrid disease that had snatched her mother away without pity. She thought about her life's work. The triumphs and accolades that marked her career. The genius and innovation. The self-doubts and failures that followed.

Before she hit the water and plummeted into the depths of the Bronx.

Downward she went. Deeper she sank, further into the abyss until the ripple of light from the footbridge above faded from view. And as she drifted listlessly in the murky waters with her lungs screaming for air, Susan broke down and cried.

In her quiet, watery tomb, she heard the voice again. It called her name.

"Help me, Susan. I'm drowning," it said.

She wondered how it was possible. Both logic and basic physics assured her that the viscosity of the surrounding fluid would muffle a human voice to a considerable extent. Yet the voice was clear in her ears.

In the haze above her, the figure appeared again. It was folded over with its back to her, sinking like a proverbial stone. As it slipped past, she reached out on instinct. The figure spun around, seized her arm, and wrestled her downward with it.

With all her strength, she fought back, kicking out with both feet, trying to break free as the figure tugged relentlessly on her arm. Deeper, they sank. She fumbled about her chin, struggling to find the jacket zipper, and when she found it, pulled down on it as hard as she could. After twisting free from the jacket, she gazed in horror as the figure slipped away, its stricken face peering up at her before disappearing into the blackness below. The stricken face of—

Oh, it's my face.

Dripping wet and gasping for air, Susan hauled herself onto the eastern bank of the Bronx. Once she'd caught her breath, she rejoined the cycleway and continued north, still unsure of where she was headed. Despite the ordeal, she felt invigorated, and her spirits soared.

"Well, that was all very weird," she muttered after a time, and thought no more of it.

The large, iconic sign depicting animals roaming a savanna marked the entrance to the zoo. As a child, Susan had spent many fun-filled days here with her mother. She recalled how passing beneath the sign's bold yellow letters had brought a sense of joy to her uncomplicated life. Albeit she always felt sorry for the animals locked away in their cages. Even so, she loved to investigate, examine, and listen to their raucous medley of whoops, screeches, and squawks. Back then, their variety intrigued her, and with childish innocence, she often wondered why they didn't have cages for the different kinds of people, as well.

She longed for those simpler times as she stood before the southern gate of the Bronx Zoo.

Inside, she followed the pathway markers that led her to the primates. Of all the animals here, these were her favorites. Halting before a cage, she peered in and was pleasantly surprised when a pair of large orange eyes peered back. The owner was sitting on a large granite boulder, its long brown pelage making it look as if it were wearing a hairy coat purchased from the local Zara store.

"Hello, Mr. Monkey," she said and blew it a kiss.

"Hello, yourself," it replied.

"Oh!" she said. "A talking monkey." Then she laughed. "I've never met a talking monkey before. This must be a very special zoo."

"I'm not a monkey," it said, sounding mildly offended. "Some insist on using the term 'baboon' over 'monkey'. But I much prefer the correct genus: 'Theropithecus gelada'." It continued to stare at her, its deadpan expression unchanging.

"I'm sorry," she replied. "I meant no offense."

"Don't trust him," a voice behind her grumbled.

She swung round to see a tiger pacing back and forth along the wire at the front of its cage. It was large enough to be a Bengal tiger, although she was convinced there weren't any of those at the Bronx Zoo. And she was equally sure the animals were no longer kept in tiny cages as they were when she was last here as a child.

"He's full of shit," the tiger said. "He tells you what you want to hear, lures you in with his fanciful stories, and—BAM! He's got you."

"Don't be ridiculous," the gelada yelled to the tiger. Then it covered its mouth with its hand and whispered, "She's been cooped up alone in that cage for too long. She's gone a bit …"—With its eyes askew, the gelada twirled its pointing finger about its temple—"craaaazy."

"Oh," Susan said.

"What are you saying to her?" the tiger shouted to the gelada. Then it turned to her with a concerned look. "What's he telling you? Whatever it is, it's all lies. He couldn't lie straight in bed. You turn your back and … wait for it … BAM! He's got you."

"Don't listen to her," the gelada insisted, waving a dismissive hand at the tiger. "She's just … You know." It twirled its forefinger in front of its face again. "Anyhow, what are you doing out here all alone at this hour of night? The visitors went home hours ago."

"I'm not sure, really," she replied. "I don't get out much, and I was passing by when … The front gate was open, and nobody was minding the ticketing counter. So, I came in."

"Naughty you," the gelada said. Placing a hand over its mouth, it gave a mischievous cackle.

"I'm trying to get the God module working," she told it. "But the deadline is almost here. We've already digitized and uploaded five souls plus their consciousness files into the cybersphere. I promised they would all meet God. Except, the software module keeps crashing whenever I introduce the soul files into the process. I don't know how to fix it. I've tried everything."

The gelada studied her for a long moment, making thoughtful noises and gestures. "God, hey? Sounds to me like you could use a little R and R. Tell you what, if you unlock the gate, I'll show you around the place. It's changed quite a bit since you were here last. When you were thirteen, I believe. With your mom, right?"

"How did you know that?" she asked in surprise.

"I have a good memory," the gelada replied. "You dropped your passion fruit pop on the pavement right where you're standing, and your mom had to buy another one to stop you from crying."

In the cage opposite, the tiger groaned. It paced more testily. "Don't trust him," it protested. "Sucks you in, and—BAM! You're gone."

"Will you shut up?" the gelada hissed, then lowered its voice to Susan. "It's okay to let me out. I'll show you around the joint. We can visit the African Plains exhibit. Then we'll check out the giraffes and the painted dogs. Have a few laughs. I'll buy you a freeze pop if you're good. Just like old times with your mom. Whadaya say?"

Susan leaned closer to the gate. Taking the mesh between her fingers, she placed her other hand on the latch.

"Don't say I didn't warn you," the tiger said. It stopped pacing and went to the back of its cage, where it flopped on the ground. "Damn tourists," it muttered. "They have no idea. I warned her. BAM, I said."

She hesitated, eyeballing the gelada. "Promise you'll behave?"

"Cross my heart and spit at the devil," the gelada replied. It spat at its feet and drew an X over its heart.

As Susan lifted the latch and slowly opened the gate, the gelada sprang from the rock and scooted quadrupedally toward her. Had she been quick enough, she might have pulled the gate closed, but the gelada was on her before she had time to react. It grabbed her wrist and yanked her into the cage, her head striking the granite boulder as she tumbled to the ground. While she lay moaning in the cage, the gelada slammed the gate and engaged the latch. Then it thanked her and emitted a jubilant *wobble* as it scooted away.

For a long time, Susan didn't move; she just lay moaning on the ground, in her prison. When she finally got up, she peered miserably out through the wire. Then, gripping the mesh between her fingers, she shook the cage in desperate hope.

"Let me out," she cried. "Please. I don't want to be locked up anymore."

Across from her, the tiger grinned. "Like I said before, Susan.

You gotta watch out for him or—BAM! And you're gone."

Susan rolled onto her side and looked blankly at the wall once again.

From the couch, Lucy stirred. "Are you okay, Dr. Parker?" she asked, yawning.

Susan didn't respond. She had little idea of the time of day. She hadn't slept for more than an hour at a time in ages. There was too much going on, and her busy mind was continually in problem-solving mode.

Chapter 37

Roxy & Loki

AFTER WHAT SEEMED LIKE hours—or it could have been days, months, or years: she couldn't tell because it was still dark, and she had lost all sense of time and direction once the yellow door closed—Roxy stopped running.

When the repulsive thing that identified itself as Loki grabbed her, its touch was so chilling that she had to scream and flee. Now, she was a blubbering mess. Like a fucking crybaby, she thought, slumped on the ground. "Get a grip on yourself, girl," she said aloud. The sound of her own voice was at least reassuring. Somehow, Paris had found her way back into her arms. "We're not in Kansas anymore, Toto," she mocked. "But, then again, I don't think we're over the fucking rainbow either."

She tried to laugh but could only manage a soft gurgling noise that sounded like strangulation, which made Paris whimper. Humor was the best medicine to ease the tension, she reassured herself. More than once, she'd gotten out of a tricky situation by remaining calm, and this was just another of those. Albeit, Bradley insisted they were in hell, and she'd never had to deal with anything as fucked up as hell before.

"I said I was sorry," she yelled into the darkness. Her contrition was met with deafening silence. "That's the fucking deal. You sin, say sorry, and once you're forgiven, you're free to go out and sin again. That's how it's always been. Since forever."

She wasn't overly keen on blame or self-flagellation, but what if she'd inadvertently missed something obvious? What if the book that St. Peter kept at the pearly gates had a big black cross against her name? The longer she thought about it, the more she realized Bradley had provided the clue. They were in hell because of their *mortal* sins.

She took a deep breath. "So, let's start with the Ten Commandments from that Moses guy." She pressed herself to recall the teachings from way back in elementary school—Sr. Virtuous, and her religious education lessons.

"No strange gods," she recited confidently, then racked her brain. The obvious symbol of idolatry was money, of which she had plenty. However, money itself wasn't a sin. Greed, though, was. The thought of sharing her hard-earned with those less fortunate had never crossed her mind. "Sorry," she said to the blackness and resolved then and there to sign up for some planned giving campaigns for the poor as soon as she returned home.

Don't take the Lord's name in vain. "I was just cussing when I said 'Jaysus f'ing Christ'. I meant no offense." On the spot, she vowed not to swear again.

Keep holy the Sabbath. This one was tricky because Sundays were always her busiest day of the week. She made a promise to whoever that she would sort something out.

Honor thy father and mother. A tear spilled from her eye and ran down her cheek. "Sorry, Mom and Dad. I appreciate that I wasn't the easiest kid to work with, but I'm all grown up now. And I miss you, too," she said, wiping away the tear.

Don't kill. She thought about poor Bradley. "Sorry, babe," she whispered, petting Paris's head.

Don't commit adultery. In her defense, she could argue that she was providing a valuable service to the community. After all, Jesus's best friend turned a few tricks back in the day. Even so, there might be some wiggle room for discretion around the marital status of her clientele.

Don't steal. She racked her penitent brain. Who would've thought stealing an apple from the local bodega would be grounds for sending somebody to hell? She shook her head in disbelief and muttered contritely, "Sorry, Mr. Grocer. I'll pay you back, double."

Don't bear false witness. She had already apologized for what she did to poor Fr. Joe. He didn't deserve the unfounded accusations or the disgrace and living hell that followed.

Don't covet thy neighbor's wife. Or husband, she supposed. "I'm sorry to Emily and baby Bradley." She promised to somehow make it up to them once she found her way out of the cybersphere.

Don't covet thy neighbor's things. She immediately recalled Darleen's mink coat, how she'd desired it more than anything. But once she had her own mink coat, it didn't seem all that special. So, sorry, Darleen.

Sitting cross-legged in the dark, she stroked Paris a little longer. Her whole life had been reduced to this: no friends—aside from a dog—no family, no one who truly cared. Weighed down by remorse, she lowered her head and let out a long, heartfelt sigh. After a while, she straightened.

"I think it's time for us to grow up, Paris," she said. Sex, drugs, and alcohol. She'd done it all to excess. Now was the time to accept responsibility. She cupped her hands around her mouth and shouted again, hoping God was listening. "I'm sorry for everything I've done wrong, and I promise I won't do it again." Then, cleansing her mind of past regrets, she muttered, "There, that should about cover everything."

The weight of guilt lifted from her soul. It felt good, like she was ten again, stepping out of the confessional at peace with the world.

"Roxy? Is that you?" The voice sounded close, yet oddly distant. It echoed around the interior of wherever she was.

She rose unsteadily to her feet. "Bryan?" There was no response. "I'm blind, Bryan. I can't see a fuck … a thing. For my sins. Like the saintly guy who got struck by lightning on the road to Damascus, fell off his horse, and lost his sight because he was a sinner too."

"Saint Paul?" Bryan said, eventually.

"Yes, him."

"I don't think so, Roxy. I can't see anything either. I think it's just dark in here."

"That Loki," she hissed. "He tricked me."

"Loki?"

"Yes. He said his name was Loki, and I was his plaything because I came through the yellow door."

"I think something has gone very wrong with the cybersphere," Bryan said. "Z was supposed to be our trustworthy chaperone here, but I think he's gone rogue."

"That fu … That two-faced liar. I knew he was too good to be true."

"Keep talking, Roxy. So I can zero in on your voice."

After a few minutes of talking nonsense, a hand grabbed her arm. Then another clutched her midriff and felt its way up toward her breast.

"That's far enough, partner," she warned while Paris growled.

"Sorry," said Bryan, sounding a little embarrassed. "I hear you still have little Paris. Good. Let's find the way out of this place. Here. Take my hand." After feeling for her hand, he slipped it into his own and held it tight. "Nothing romantic intended, of course," he said, conceding an awkward laugh. "Just to be sure we don't get separated."

As they felt their way through the darkness, she thought about Bryan and how he'd curiously appeared the moment she'd finished her confession. "How did you find your way in here?" she asked.

"Once the door closed behind me, it locked itself, then vanished." Waving a hand in front, she felt nothing ahead that would obstruct them.

"After the four of you entered your respective doors, I noticed Z snap his fingers to make them disappear. It took some practice, but once I got the clicking effect right, all the doors magically reappeared."

"Clever you," she said. She felt the dryness of his hand. "I notice your hand isn't sticky and clammy like before."

"No. I don't feel hot anymore. A funny thing happened to me on the way out of heaven." As well as relief, there was a sense of uncertainty in his voice.

"Heaven? Bradley said we're in hell."

"Who is Bradley?"

"He's an old flame from high school who died recently."

"Oh, I'm sorry to hear that, Roxy."

She hesitated. "The truth is, I killed him." She felt Bryan's grip loosen slightly. "Don't worry, I'm no murderer. It was completely my fault, but it was involuntary manslaughter. We were doing drugs, and I dosed out more than he could handle. I should have known better."

"Oh," said Bryan. On his next step, he stumbled when his big toe stubbed against something hard on the floor, and he cried out in pain. "Ow!" Roxy was sure she heard someone sniggering close by. "Mind your step there, Roxy."

"He had a wife. She was … was …" She paused. "Eight months pregnant," she added softly.

"Oh," Bryan repeated. "I have no idea where we are," he admitted after an uncomfortably long silence. "I ended up with a fellow called Charon. I suspect he is the fabled boatman who takes wayward souls across the river and into hell. I can't fathom why my Lucy would create such an abomination."

Roxy wondered about Charon. Then she recalled Loki's creepy fingers touching her in the dark. Both thoughts made her shiver.

"What happened to this boatman?"

"I took him on at his own game. At first, I thought he was God. He sure looked and sounded like God. But once he revealed his true intentions, I could see he was up to no good. We wrestled for a bit before I hit him over the head with his oar." There was a sense of triumph in his voice as he spoke.

"Wow, that must've been some kinda fight."

Bryan remained silent for a time before changing the subject. "You're the first person I thought about once I escaped from Charon's clutches."

"Me?" she said, surprised. "Why me?"

"I'm afraid the other three might be in equally dire straits. So, I've decided it's my responsibility to save everyone. Following our con-versation during the descent from the hotel lobby, you struck me as a can-do person. And it felt somehow right to have you at my side when the time comes."

She smiled inwardly. "Sure, Bryan," she said. "I've got your back. When the time comes."

"Roxy?" he said after another extended pause.

"Yes, Bryan?"

"You haven't uttered a single cuss word for the past hour."

"I'm trying hard, Bryan," she replied, tightening her grip on his hand. "My God, how I'm trying hard."

Bryan's shin slammed into something on the floor, and he stum-bled, nearly falling. His left shoulder smashed into something hard— or something hard smashed into him, he wasn't sure. A mischievous giggle echoed from somewhere ahead of them. There was a sharp *click* followed by an explosion of light that momentarily blinded them.

"Now, I have two little playthings," crooned a voice that Roxy knew all too well.

"Loki!" she cried. Still blinking from the dazzling light, she stepped forward, pointing angrily at him. "This guy is really starting to annoy me." Little Paris made a low growling noise that sounded like a small grizzly bear. "He thinks it's okay to play tricks on people and scare them. He thinks we're afraid of him. But we're not. Are we, Bryan?"

"No, we are not, Roxy," came his fearless reply.

Loki giggled again. "Tricks? Yes, tricks." He strutted before them, chest thrust out, arms swinging in a show of intimidation. "Looking for the door?" he teased. He pointed behind him, where a yellow door suddenly appeared. It opened of its own accord, revealing the chamber from which they'd entered. "No. Here it is." It vanished and reappeared on his right. "Nope. Here." It blinked into existence on his left. He stuck out his tongue at them.

Roxy's shoulders tensed. Rage fired in her belly before she realized she was gnashing her teeth. She didn't like Loki at all—this f'ing big bozo with his scraggly red hair. Curling her lip, she glared at him. "Are you ready, Bryan?"

"I'm ready, Roxy."

"Paris?"

Paris snarled.

She knelt to set the dog on the ground and removed her Jimmy Choos. As she rose again, she had one shoe hoisted above her shoulder. She spun around and hurled it at Loki, the point of its thin, tapered heel striking him flush on the temple. Stunned, Loki stepped away. He wobbled for a moment, his eyes flickering in confusion. He tried to say something, jabbering nonsense—which she supposed was another childish taunt—as he swooned backward and hit the ground with an awful *thud*.

Before Loki could recover, they were on him, pounding him in tandem from this week into next.

Bryan was once again at the foot of the staircase that led back to the lobby of the Regal Grand. This time, Roxy was beside him with Paris under her arm. The smile broadened across his face as they stood, hand in hand in silence, gazing at the string of wan lights that spiraled upward into the blackness above.

"We sure taught that Loki a lesson, didn't we, Roxy?" he said after a while.

"We sure did, Bryan," she replied. Still gazing upward, she nudged him in the ribs. "I gotta say, you look kinda cute in your boxers and tank."

He laughed uncomfortably. "The truth be told, I got halfway up those stairs before finding the damn courage to turn around and come back for you. I won't judge at all if you decide to skedaddle up there and get the heck out of here. After all, this is my mess, not yours."

Roxy shook her head. "No way, mister," she said. She turned to him and smiled; two perfect dimples etched on her cheeks. "The others are relying on us. We have people to save." Then, with a sharp tug on his hand, she led him over to the red door.

Chapter 38

Thomas & 'Iblīs

ALL AROUND THEM WAS as white and barren as the ends of the earth.

"It burns like fire," Thomas groaned as another wintry squall hammered them from behind.

'Iblīs, walking beside him, nodded in agreement. "Even I'm finding it somewhat chilly," he said above the howling wind. His teeth chattered as, heads bowed, they fought their way on through the snow and tempest. "This particular version of Zamharīr gives the word a whole new meaning," he insisted. "The cold is like nothing I expected or experienced before. And let me tell you, I have already visited many bitter-cold places in my time."

Thomas rubbed his hands together more vigorously. "My fingers are frozen solid," he complained. He had tried everything to warm himself, yet he remained overall numb with the cold. Trembling, he pulled Bryan's Brioni jacket tighter around his midriff as the icy wind beat against their backs and the blizzard kept on. "Do you think the clouds will ever clear and the sun come out?" he asked, half in hope.

"Not likely," moaned 'Iblīs. "After a short time in this place, you should be begging me to take your al-Ruh (soul) back to al-Laza (the blaze, the second layer of hell for the Jewish population) so you can warm your frigid bones beside the pitch-black fires of Jahannam (hell). Instead, imagine the irony when I suddenly find myself as the beggar."

Cupping his hands about his mouth, Thomas blew steadily, hoping his fingers might thaw a little from the measly warmth of his breath. "Can't you just snap your fingers or wave your wand?" he asked. "Say 'hocus-pocus' and get us out of here?"

'Iblīs rolled his eyes. "I am 'Iblīs," he snarled, "not some magical Potter child."

Thomas glanced sideways at 'Iblīs. He tried to smile, but his facial muscles refused to work. "Sorry, buddy, but you look like a regular dude to me," he said, his lips juddering as he spoke.

Displeased, 'Iblīs frowned. "Z did this to me," he spat back. "I should be forged from the fires of hell, yet here I am fashioned in human form, made from the dust of the earth."

Thomas wished he hadn't been so trusting when Z ushered him through the red door. It was unlike him to accept the word of a stranger and rush headlong into the unknown. But he'd been caught up in the moment. "I'm not so sure about Z," he confessed. "He seems to promise a lot but delivers nothing."

'Iblīs sighed heavily. "My sentiments exactly."

Both fell silent as they continued through the snow, the wind buffeting and pushing them forward.

"And about this God business," Thomas said a short time later. "Dr. Parker sounded credible enough, and although she may have convinced the others, I'm still not buying it." He halted and turned to 'Iblīs. "What do you think? Is God real?"

'Iblīs stopped, too. "If I am The Devil," he said, "then it is only fair there should be a God; that is the yin and yang of it. Nevertheless, you should not be questioning whether God exists. Rather, you should ask yourself: where is he? When you see the state of affairs in the real world, with so much hatred and self-destruction among the mortals, you have to wonder why their God goes missing in action. He places himself on a pedestal and demands they worship him, yet he forsakes them in their hour of gross willfulness. If he were as loving as he boasts, then he would have eased their suffering by giving them paradise now. Instead, they must wait until after death, when it is too late." 'Iblīs snorted and spat, the spittle freezing into a solid, green glob long before hitting the snow at his feet.

Thomas pondered the surrounding emptiness, the infinite white plain ahead, and the leaden skies above. "Do you think he'll judge us harshly when the time comes?" he asked.

"Harshly?" 'Iblīs kicked up a flurry of snow at him in disgust. "When they cast me down from heaven for not bowing to that upstart, Adam, was that not harsh enough? You lie and cheat and live an opulent lifestyle while others drown in their own piss and squalor; then you expect forgiveness? You are somewhat deluded." Grimacing, he shook his head savagely. "Forgiveness comes from within. If you have said and done things for which you cannot forgive yourself, then surely you are already judged. Why do you need God or anyone else to confirm what you already know? For the life of me, I cannot understand what nonsense goes through the heads of you mortals."

'Iblīs threw up his hands in annoyance, then turned and, muttering to himself, moved on.

While Thomas stood alone, contemplating Iblīs's words, the snow on his collar began to melt. Water trickled inside Bryan's jacket, and he was soon wet to the skin and colder still, if that was at all possible. If 'Iblīs was right, then perhaps the notion of God had been overstated since it was first enforced upon the masses. It didn't matter whether God existed because his destiny was in his own hands. He had to find forgiveness within himself before he could begin to hope for She'ol.

Quickening his pace, he caught up with 'Iblīs, drawing alongside him again. "Where are we going?" he asked.

"I am not sure I care anymore," 'Iblīs replied, sighing.

"You seem a little unhappy," said Thomas. He tugged at his collar, desperate to seal the neckline and stop the wetness from seeping through. "Have you considered therapy?" he offered. "Sometimes, you feel much better after talking to a professional."

"A psychologist?" cried 'Iblīs. He turned to Thomas in astonishment, his lips quivering as if he were about to cry. "And what would you have me say? Hello, I am The Devil. I have a few worries on my mind, not the least of which I am trapped in this grotesque casing, which I am forced to endure." He waved a hand in disgust down the length of his human frame. "I tell you, I am a *djinn*. I should have been made of fire, but now, of all things, I am tainted by the same clay as Adam. Can you believe it?"

"It sounds to me as if this Adam fellow really bugged you in the day," Thomas replied in a matter-of-fact tone.

'Iblīs let out a loud cry of anguish. "Enough," he yelled. "I am sick and tired of all this talk about Adam. It was he who ate the fruit. Yet, for eternity, I have carried the blame. He could easily have said *no* to the woman when she offered him the apple. But his will was weak. I resent the falsehood that I am the culprit, whereas he is the victim. And I am sick and tired of this whole arrangement. Leave me be."

Thomas raised his hands in submission. "Hey, I'm only trying to help," he said.

Thomas studied the digits on his left hand, each in turn. The stinging sensation had eased, and they were now disgustingly blackened and numb. His right hand was the same.

"Do you ever recover from frostbite?" he asked out of interest. Following 'Iblīs's grumbling reply, he was still unsure whether he would ever regain the use of his hands in the cybersphere. He fumbled for the side pockets of Bryan's jacket and slipped them inside, hoping to find warmth.

Ahead of them, a conical-shaped object appeared through the storm. It reminded him of a festive tree, without the tinsel and colorful lights. A heavy layer of snow covered it from top to bottom. At its base, six smaller objects were clustered in a circle. As he drew near, he realized the smaller objects were people. They were motionless, squatting on the ground with their hands outstretched, seeking warmth from a large bonfire in the center. But he felt no radiating heat from the fire. The flames that licked up from the woodpile had frozen like vitrified tongues of icy glass, the scene reminding him of a snapshot of some grisly fireside gathering.

He glanced down at the white-encrusted face closest to him.

"Jonas?" he cried.

Unable to move his mouth or much else, Jonas blinked in response.

"How did you get here?" Thomas asked.

Jonas blinked again.

"He can't talk on account of he's frozen solid," 'Iblīs said sourly. He kicked some snow onto one of the frozen campers. "Like both of us will be soon enough," he moaned.

"Obviously!" Thomas retorted. His frustration with 'Iblīs—whose mental state appeared to be declining rapidly—was growing, and he had to hold back from expressing his annoyance at the demon's constant grumbling. "Can we help him?" he asked.

'Iblīs leaned down and examined Jonas's face. Then he rapped the top of Jonas's head with a knuckle. "I suppose I could spare a breath of warm air, enough to thaw his head."

After 'Iblīs breathed into his mouth, Jonas coughed. The icicles on his eyelids melted away, and he rolled his eyeballs in clockwise and counterclockwise motions to restart their operation. With excruciating effort, he wrenched his head from side to side and practiced moving his lips. Once his vocal cords had thawed, he began to stammer.

"Thomas. It's s-s-so good to s-s-see you again, man. Who's the d-d-dude with the warm b-b-breath?"

"Oh, this is 'Iblīs," Thomas replied, waving at him. "Aka: The

Devil." He thought it funny how Jonas's head could swivel and bob atop the solid block of ice that was his body. It seemed somehow … inconvenient. Even so, Jonas appeared unworried. "'Iblīs, this is Jonas," he said, gesturing to the bizarre-looking popsicle that was Jonas.

"Wow, m-m-man," Jonas said, "I had the awful f-f-feeling I didn't make it to S-S-She'ol. But I n-n-never imagined hell would be this d-d-damn cold."

"Zamharīr," 'Iblīs interjected. "You have been sent to the coldest part of Jahannam for ending your own life." Glum-faced, he sighed. "And somehow, I am here as your nursemaid, when I should be busy instead, stoking the eternal fires of the abyss."

"B-b-bummer," replied Jonas. He gave a sharp nod toward the pillar of ice across from him. "You r-r-remember Mrs. Knox over there? Mr. Clarke b-b-beside her? Ms. Jones, and a few of our other c-c-clients? It seems we've all c-c-copped the same p-p-punishment." He gave a nervous laugh while the clients all panned their eyes across to Thomas and blinked *hello* in unison.

"I'm sorry, everyone. It's entirely my fault that you're here. If I had known—"

"Pride cometh before the fall," 'Iblīs mocked. "Especially when you think you are a god."

"What w-w-would you know?" Jonas snapped back. "Do you know w-w-who you're talking to? This man is the g-g-greatest deal-maker in the history of d-d-deal making. If there was ever a g-g-god of financial undertakings, he w-w-would be it."

Thomas motioned for Jonas to calm down. "No, Jonas. He's right. I thought I had all the answers. I convinced myself that I was infallible. Then things started to spiral out of control. Instead of taking care of you, I managed to ruin your lives. Jackie's too. I'm the reason you're all trapped down here in this terrible cold."

"It's okay, m-m-man," said Jonas, "I f-f-forgive you." He swung his head from left to right, surveying the clients. "Everyone, b-b-blink once if you forgive the man or t-t-twice if you don't."

After they all blinked once, Thomas's heart lifted marginally. "If I could, I would do anything to make amends," he said , wiping a tear from his cheek with the back of his hand before it froze.

"Hey, m-m-man, can you arrange to g-g-get us out of here?" Jonas asked. He still sounded surprisingly upbeat considering his dire circumstances. "A few m-m-minutes in front of his 'fires of the abyss' would b-b-be nice. Even a s-s-small ember for us to sit around and warm our h-h-hands."

Thomas looked into their imploring eyes for what seemed a long time and felt suddenly humbled. It was the least he could do. He jabbed his elbow into 'Iblīs's side. "Is this doable?"

Glaring at Jonas and the clients in annoyance, 'Iblīs grunted. "Of course, *anything* is doable. But why would I help you lot? What would be the point of Jahannam without the pain and suffering to accompany their incarceration?" As he spoke, 'Iblīs became visibly upset. His eyes grew fierce, then settled on Thomas. "They might have forgiven you, but I have not. I blame you for everything. For I am 'Iblīs. I am a *djinn*. I should be made of—"

"Yes, we know," Thomas shouted back, his frustration finally getting the better of him. "You should be made of fire, but instead, you're made of clay … Like your friend, Adam—"

'Iblīs screamed. He wound back his fist and swung a round-arm that landed a savage blow on the side of Thomas's jaw. Thomas staggered several steps backward, lost his footing, and fell flat on the ground. When Jonas protested, 'Iblīs turned, stalked toward him, and smacked his head with the back of his hand, knocking him unconscious. Then he turned back to Thomas and growled. In slow, bounding leaps, he plowed through the snow and lunged at Thomas, landing on top of his rotund belly. He raised his fist and was about to strike when something hit him side-on with enough force to knock him clean off Thomas's prostrate body.

Thomas sat up and looked around.

"Roxy!" he cried. Then little Paris skittered past.

Roxy had hit 'Iblīs like a freight train, the impact knocking him off and catapulting him into the cone-shaped object—the only remaining conifer in the whole of Zamharīr—burying his top half under an avalanche of snow.

"Leave our Thomas alone," she shrieked while Paris yapped and tore at 'Iblīs's upturned heels.

When Bryan arrived a few minutes later, they pulled 'Iblīs from the snow and dragged him grumbling back to where Thomas stood holding his injured jaw. Roxy shoved her face into 'Iblīs's while Bryan held him in a headlock, writhing.

"Say you're sorry," she shouted.

Shaking his head as best he could, 'Iblīs continued to struggle. "No! Z said—"

Bryan tightened his stranglehold until 'Iblīs began to gag. "Say you're sorry or we'll tie you up and leave you here in the cold."

Then 'Iblīs went limp. "I'm … I'm sorry," he said as Bryan relaxed his grip. "This whole situation is out of hand. I am humiliated. I should be— But I'm— I don't know who or where I am anymore." Brushing Roxy aside, he staggered forward and fell on his knees at Thomas's feet. "Forgive me," he sobbed.

In return for their understanding of his 'unjustified' humiliation by Z, 'Iblīs promised to take Jonas and the clients back to Jahannam, where they could warm their bones beside the eternal fires of the abyss. When he also offered to speak to the 'big guy' about commuting their sentences on account of extenuating circumstances, Thomas assumed he was talking about God. He was still unsure whether he believed in God. Although, to have The Devil fall on his knees before you and beg forgiveness. Was that enough to prove you are a god of sorts?

Chuckling to himself, Thomas dismissed the notion.

"Aren't you cold in your underwear?" he asked Bryan as they made their way back to the red door. "And Roxy in that flimsy top?"

Bryan glanced down at his attire and smiled. "Strangely enough, things in the cybersphere seem to change for the better once you find inner peace. We're on a mission to save the others. If you're up for it, we sure could use a hand."

Thomas considered the request for only a heartbeat. The fact that they'd bothered to return and help him left him indebted. Moreover, he was starting to enjoy the growing sense of camaraderie between them.

"Count me in," he said, and as he uttered the words, the color instantly returned to his blackened fingers, and the brutal cold that afflicted him was gone.

Bryan turned to Roxy. "Who's next?"

"We need to find Ahmad," she replied.

Chapter 39

Ahmad & Erlik

AHMAD WAS BOTH HUNGRY and thirsty. He longed for a sip of water to wet his tongue or a morsel of tawa naan (flatbread) to line his belly. He had not eaten or spoken to anyone in years. He wondered about the fourteen mansions of Jahannam (a place of punishment for the disobedient), about which of these he occupied at present. The one allotted according to the nature and gravity of his sins, he supposed. Only Allah can decide which is best.

Shackled and half-naked, he dangled from the ceiling. The blood drained from his upstretched arms while the pain tore at his joints and ripped at his shoulders. He cried out, "Inshallah, will somebody please help me? I have been here for a thousand years. If someone could hold me up so I might enjoy a moment of respite." He gazed in dismay at the many faces writhing on the walls. The room had no windows, and a lamp somewhere behind him cast a lusterless light throughout. The concrete floor beneath his soiled feet sloped inward to a metal grating in the center of the room. To simplify the task of washing the excess fluids and offcuts of misery down the outlet, he imagined.

More years passed before he received a polite reply.

"Mister?" a man's voice inquired. "Allow me to support you for a while. Here, sit on my shoulders."

From behind him, he felt movement before the man's head appeared between his legs. With a concerted grunt, the man hoisted him higher, the chains loosened, and the pain departed his tortured body.

"Oh, thank you, sir," he said, heaving a sigh of overwhelming relief. "That feels much better." While he rested on the man's broad shoulders, his stomach grumbled loudly. "My apologies," he said, "but I have not eaten a thing in years."

"If only I had some beans," the man said wistfully. "I would share them with you."

Startled, Ahmad leaned forward, catching a glimpse of the man's face. "Wait!" he cried, noticing the small, ragged scar beneath the man's left eye. "You are the one with the beans."

The man nodded as best he could—considering the proximity of Ahmad's thighs and crotch around his neck. "It was our duty to protect our own," he said, his voice starting to quiver under the strain. "The situation at the time was most dreadful, and I would have done the same. Except you were the stronger one. A solitary can of beans would never be enough food to save both our khānvādeh (families)."

"I am sorry for you and your loved ones," Ahmad offered. "Please forgive me."

"If I forgive you, then Allah will surely forgive me for my own wrongdoings," the man replied. Then he lowered Ahmad until the chains pulled taut once again. "I must go," he said.

"Thank you, sir, for the respite," Ahmad said. "And again, for the beans."

After the next thousand years passed, another voice whispered in his ear, "I will hold you up." Then, a figure appeared out of the obscurity behind him.

By then, his vision was poor, and he had difficulty discerning the face. He blinked, then squinted until the figure resolved into focus. "Brother!" he cried out in sudden recognition.

His brother reached up and touched his hand with affection. "Yes, Sajid. It is I."

"Oh, brother, I am so happy to see you," Ahmad said. Although it hurt him more, he could not keep himself from rejoicing. He laughed and cried until he could no longer bear the pain, whereupon he convulsed and fell silent. When sufficient strength returned and he was able to speak again, he said, "My arms are tired, brother, and my back is sore, but my heart delights in your presence." He breathed a heartfelt sigh of thanks to Allah for the small mercy of seeing his brother. "Will you please take my weight for a minute? I promise no longer than this."

Ahmad's brother frowned. "If I do as you ask, Sajid, you might trick me. In which case, I will find *myself* stuck down here forever, holding you up."

"No, brother," he replied in vehement protest. "I would never do this to you."

"Never?" Ahmad's brother responded.

A second figure appeared alongside his brother, then two smaller ones behind them.

"Hamshera (sister)!" he cried. "And the children. Your presence here delights me. We have been worried for you. Fattanah, and Omaid, and Nikoo, and I. We were—"

Ahmad's brother stiffened. "I do not understand," he said, giving Ahmad an unsure look.

"I mean …" Ahmad's heart sank, and he loathed himself again for his past deceptions. "I must tell you, brother. When the Taliban came, and I was at your house, I …" The words caught in his throat like choking vomit. "I am sorry, brother, but it was I who took your papers from the table."

Ahmad's brother recoiled in surprise. He was about to say something, but stopped as though he was having difficulty processing the treacherous revelation. Then, slowly, came comprehension.

"This cannot be true, Sajid. I have always blamed myself for misplacing the papers. I scolded myself over and over, presuming they were dropped on the way home. In my haste. In my foolishness. We searched everywhere before they came for us—Fattanah, Omaid, little Nikoo, and I—but such important papers were nowhere to be found."

Lowering his head, Ahmad spoke in a whisper. "Forgive me, brother, for I am no longer worthy to look upon your face."

"Forgive you, Sajid?" His brother made fists of his hands and shook them with fury in his face. "How do you dare ask forgiveness when, despite your obedience to the arkān al-Islām (five pillars of fundamental duties), you have betrayed your only brother?"

"But I only sought to save my family," Ahmad insisted. Then he fell silent before adding in a softer voice, "Yet, more so, I sought to save myself."

There. By his own admission, he could no longer deny his terrible wrongdoing. In all this time, he was mostly scared for himself. And when the opportunity presented, it was too great a temptation to resist. During his first thousand years in Jahannam, he defended his evil actions. Then he tried to convince himself that Z made him do it. However, Z was only a manifestation of his wicked self, of the impure workings of his soul. For Allah knew they were his hands that reached for his brother's papers; his hands that clutched them close to his chest as he hurried home through the chaotic streets of Kabul; his filthy hands at the airport, shoving them through the wire toward the US Marine; and his hands that were tainted with the blood of those he loved the most. Because Allah knows all.

Ahmad hung his head in shame.

High above him, halfway up the wall of ghastly faces, a dark figure clung to a vine. It was the hideous one with jet-black eyes and the face and teeth of a pig. The one named Erlik.

"Huh. Family," Erlik said as he stared down at Ahmad. "If you can't depend on your own family to forgive you for killing them, then who *can* you trust?" He leaped from the wall and landed on the floor before Ahmad with a soft *thud*. In his right hand, he held a long steel pike. "I, myself, have nine offspring in all," he said. Raising his other hand to Ahmad's face, he jabbed it with the pointed end of the pike until a river of thick, black fluid oozed out and down his arm. "Bastards all," he spat. "None of whom brought me the amount of joy in my old age as they promised." A long, lizard-like tongue shot out of his mouth and lapped at the fluid.

"Please," Ahmad pleaded, "may I come down? Have I not suffered enough for my offense?"

"Enough?" shrieked Erlik. "Why, Sajid, your suffering has only begun. For your wickedness, there will be agony and gnashing of teeth the likes of which you never imagined possible. One can never suffer enough for their sins." Leaning closer, he sniffed Ahmad's naked torso. Then he rattled the chains around Ahmad's wrist with a merciless shake before disappearing behind him.

Then Ahmad sensed another behind him.

"Can you feel this, brother?"

"Brother," he said in surprise. "You are here again." Then he screamed in pain as his brother drove the long steel pike deep into his back. He gazed in horror when it emerged six inches beyond his chest. The sight of blood and meat on the point of the pike almost made him retch. Yet somehow, he remained conscious while the pike pushed through.

Another figure appeared before him. This one held aloft a shiny blade. "And can you feel this, Sajid?" the figure said.

He screamed again when the sharp tip of the shiny blade perforated his midriff and sliced a clean incision from just below the sternum down to the pelvis. The sight of his lacerated stomach almost made him faint. Yet somehow, he remained acutely aware of every sensation as his insides spilled onto the floor. Coughing out blood and spittle from his mouth, he lifted his eyes to gaze upon the face of the one holding the blade. The unmistakable face of … himself.

"Are you one of them? An American sympathizer?"

In a panic, his gaze swept across the wall of faces. "The man from Kabul," he said when he came to the face that had spoken.

"The qalfak chapat (flat-nosed) shopping man," the man responded, his gap-toothed grin widening. "Your suffering is most impressive, shopping man. I, for one, would have fainted at the first sight of the sword. But you kept watching while your gizzards fell out. That took some amount of courage to gut yourself."

Wide-eyed, Ahmad beheld his innards lying in a mess on the floor. In his delirium, he lost all comprehension of what he was saying.

"Will you all please come and sit with me for dinner?" he said. "So that we can eat together? Perhaps my wife can prepare kabuli pulao (slow-cooked lamb with lentils, raisins, carrots, ground cardamom, and nuts) with naan (bread)?" Then he pleaded. "Please, everyone, I have been hanging here for far too long and can go on no further. Everything in my life brings me to this deserved ending." His head drooped forward. "I am beaten," he said in sadness.

"I see your pain, Ahmad," a gentle voice said. It was a woman's voice.

Startled, he lifted his eyes to the wall of faces. His heart leaped at the exquisite face staring back at him. "Fattanah!" he cried out.

"Yes, Ahmad. I am here. And Allah knows your pain also."

"But I am not Ahmad," he admitted morosely. "I stole the name from my brother. My real name is Sajid."

"You are Ahmad," she replied. "This is the name that honors the memory of your brother. And I am forever Fattanah, the memory of his beloved wife. And our beautiful children, too, are the memories of their dear children. Forgive yourself, Ahmad, and you will find peace. Forgive yourself, husband, because we grieve for your return."

He glanced down at his belly and saw it was still intact. And the pike no longer jutted from his chest.

"This is impossible," he said, looking again at his wife. "What should I do, Fattanah?"

"You must come back to us, Ahmad. My heart is frail. Your son needs your strength, and our little Nikoo cries at night for her bâba (father). Come back to us."

Ahmad shouted, "Mr. Erlik? Brother? Are you here?" He shouted again, "Fattanah?"

After a time, there was no reply, so he gazed up at the irons suspending him from the ceiling. Then clarity struck him. By analyzing the geometry of his situation, he estimated that, based on his height plus the length and number of links in the chains, the ceiling was about thirty feet above the floor. High enough for a fall to either injure or kill him. At the ceiling, the chains were fastened by bow shackles, the type with a screw pin. And the wall of faces on his left, with its tangle of vines, couldn't be any more than twenty feet away.

With all his remaining strength, he pulled down on his right arm, enough to drag himself higher and slacken the chain cuffed to his left arm. He reached up as high as he could and took up the slackened chain. After resting for a moment, he hoisted himself again. He did this repeatedly, pulling down on one chain first, followed by the other. The pain in his shoulders was excruciating, but his resolve was greater. Until he reached the ceiling. Then, suspended by one chain, he unscrewed the shackle pin to the other, which then uncoupled and plummeted to the ground, the dead weight almost tearing his arm from its socket as the chain pulled taut around his wrist.

Grimacing, he then lowered himself back to the floor, all the time repeating, "Inshallah, for Fattanah and the children."

Now, he hung from the ceiling by one arm only, with the other arm still attached to the chain heaped on the floor. By shifting his weight back and forth, he swung himself toward the wall of faces. Soon, he swung like a pendulum, gaining momentum with each gyration. As long as the distance to the wall was shorter than the height of the ceiling, as he had guessed, then his plan would succeed.

He swung again until his foot brushed against the wall about halfway up. Two swings later, he managed to clamp his legs, vice-like, around a thick vine. There, he stuck to the wall like glue. All that remained was for him to climb up the wall, tie off the untethered chain, swing back, and release the second pin, which should pendulate him back to the wall, and hope for the best.

In the end, the best he received was his body slamming against the wall of faces. And as he fell the six remaining feet to the floor, he was still praising Allah for his good fortune following his amazing feat.

As elated as he felt, the job was only half complete. Except for the chains still manacled to his wrists, he was free. He tried hammering them against the floor, but the locks held firm. While he toyed with their keyholes, probing for a weakness, he heard voices. Not from the walls or anywhere behind him, but carrying distantly through the entrance of a narrow corridor at the back of the room. He gathered the irons with haste and crouched furtively outside the opening. As the voices grew louder, he waited, armed with a length of chain. He was about to swing it when Thomas appeared.

"Ahmad, my friend," cried Thomas when he saw Ahmad. "Thank goodness you're safe. We were just discussing how we might never find you in this maze."

"Ah, Mr. Thomas," he replied, elated. "It is good to see you again." As he lowered the chain in his hand, more people appeared. "And Mr. Bryan, and Ms. Roxy, and little Paris." He turned to Bryan. "I was in the process of making my escape. This place is very unpleasant. I have been imprisoned down here for quite some time."

"Yes, it's been a busy few hours since Z sent us through the doors," Bryan replied.

Ahmad looked at him, somewhat baffled. "What? Not thousands of years?"

"That sounds strange," Bryan replied, puzzled as well. "Perhaps the concept of *time* in this place is not the same for everyone."

Roxy wandered over. "It's so good to see you again, Ahmad." She opened her arms to embrace him, then noticed him blushing. "Oh, I'm sorry," she said, averting her eyes from his nakedness.

Thomas unbuttoned Bryan's jacket and offered it to Ahmad. "Here, my friend, use this." He sniffed at the putrid air and winced. Then he noticed the manacles attached to Ahmad's wrists. "What terrible things have they been doing to you, my friend?"

"I was trying to remove them," Ahmad replied, squatting to inspect the manacles again. "But I do not have the key. Mr. Erlik has the key."

Narrowing his eyes, Thomas scanned the room. "Where can we find this Erlik character?"

Just then, they heard a melodic warble coming from the corridor before Erlik strolled into the room. He had his head down and was singing in a falsetto voice. "Six, six-six, the nuuummber of theee beast ..." Then he glanced up. When he noticed Ahmad was no longer hanging in the center of the room, he froze. "What—?" He turned and saw Ahmad standing beside him. "How did you escape?" Then he spotted the others. "And how did you three get—?"

"Quick! Get him!" cried Thomas.

Erlik spun on his heels. As he scrambled for the safety of the corridor, Thomas launched himself in hot pursuit. With all the grace of a large elephant seal, he broke into a lumbering run, crossed the room, and quickly had Erlik pinned beneath his bulky frame.

"Give me the keys," he demanded.

Wheezing under Thomas's considerable weight, Erlik shook his head furiously. "No. He's mine," he gasped. "Z said I can have him."

"I think Mr. Z is not the friendly person he claims to be," Ahmad said, and both Roxy and Bryan agreed.

Thomas wrenched Erlik's arm mercilessly before the demon finally yielded.

"It's in my pocket," he screamed as the ligaments in his shoulder stretched and tore.

After removing the manacles, Bryan helped Ahmad to his feet.

"Next, we have to find Becky," he said, tossing the key away.

Ahmad hesitated. "But I must return home," he mumbled, peering guiltily at the corridor. "My family is waiting for me. They are—"

"It's your choice," Roxy said, placing a hand on his arm. She buttoned the rest of his jacket to cover his chest. "But we could sure use your help."

"But I must …" Lowering his eyes, Ahmad fell silent. He wondered whether he was again using his family as an excuse to save himself. Or was this his chance to honor the name he had taken from his brother by deceit? As conflicted as he felt, in his heart, he knew what he must do. No matter the seriousness of the situation in the real world, Fattanah would understand. And Allah would surely approve of who he really was. He looked up at Bryan.

"But I must save Miss Becky," he said, and at once, the enormous burden that had afflicted him since leaving Kabul lifted from his shoulders. And he felt free.

When Thomas asked what they should do with Erlik, who was still squirming underneath him, Ahmad stooped to examine his tormentor.

"I wonder how he feels with the irons around him, Mr. Thomas?" he said with a menacing grin. Then he scanned the wall of faces and was relieved to find Fattanah was no longer there. Once they had fastened the chains around Erlik's wrists and hoisted him to the ceiling, Ahmad led them back into the corridor.

"We must hurry," he said.

Chapter 40

Rebecca & Ahriman

BECKY STILL COULDN'T BELIEVE her rotten luck. The world's pre-eminent eco-warrior had been reduced to shoveling filthy, noxious coal to stoke the fires of hell. Not only was it an affront to her principles, but who would have guessed they used fossil fuel to keep hell's fire aflame? Surely, they'd use magic. With a dog-tired grunt, she heaved another shovelful into the roaring furnace. Once she escaped the cybersphere, she would launch a campaign to draw everyone's attention to this blatant stupidity.

Worse still, she had no idea what she'd done wrong to deserve this kind of senseless punishment. After all, hell was reserved for sinners, not for a champion of the planet's survival and conscientious objector to the foolish behavior of the masses. Sure, she'd taken Rachel's money, but that didn't justify being cast into the pits of hell. And Jonathan? Well, he was big and ugly enough to take responsibility for his own decisions.

Then there was this Ahriman guy. With massive wings and a single red eye above his nose, what was he supposed to be? He looked like a ... a ... "Remember, Rebecca," her mother used to say, "not everyone can be as pretty as you." Even so, this Ahriman guy didn't look right at all. She tossed another load into the furnace, stepped back, and wiped her brow.

As she leaned on her shovel, she thought about the weather in heaven. She was sure they'd be using clean, renewable energy up there to maintain perfect climatic conditions. She wondered how the others were faring: Roxy, Bryan, Thomas, and Ahmad. Admittedly, she wasn't doing so well herself. Dr. Parker, the Lucy woman, and Z had tricked her, which made her furious. She couldn't wait to get out of this place and give them all a piece of her livid mind.

Ahriman appeared behind her.

"Keep shoveling, Rebecca. There will be no rest for the wicked."

Hurling her shovel aside, she spun around, planted her hands on her hips, and glared at him. "I want to go home," she hissed. "Do you know what they do to psychos like you who snatch girls off the street?"

He ruffled his feathers and chuckled. "And do you know what they do to naughty little girls who wander off alone?"

"You've got nothing on me," she snapped. "Whereas you? Let's start with kidnapping and deprivation of liberty, extortion—probably demanding a hefty ransom—child exploitation and possible trafficking, emotional abuse, fraud, indecent dealings with a minor, wanton pollution." She glared at him. "Should I go on?"

"But I have had no indecent dealings with you," he protested.

"Your word against mine," she said, giving him a willful smile.

"And there is no fraudulent activity involved."

"Sure, there is. You promised I'd meet God. But you're not God. That's fraudulent misrepresentation; it's a false statement of a material fact, Your Honor. Which is a felony."

"I promised nothing of the sort," he said, backing away. His eye flicked nervously around the room. "It … it was Z. He did all the promising. He promised us many souls. Said it would be easy money. Except there is nothing easy about this whole transaction."

"Money? Transaction? That's laundering ." She jabbed a firm finger at his reddening face. "Another felony. Serious. You can expect fifteen to twenty in solitary."

"Enough!" he snarled. "You are a petulant child. You are a self-righteous brat who thinks yours is the only path forward. Everything you reap is at the expense of others. You were not sent here because of your beliefs or nonbeliefs. Nor do we have any interest in your practical jokes and petty crimes. You are here because of the heinous thing you did. The unforgivable thing you caused."

He rose up, towering over her, his wings thumping the air and feathers bristling in a fearsome display.

Becky shrank back. "What I did?" she asked in a timorous voice. *What unforgivable thing have I done?*

They stormed through the green door as one. They were on a mission. They had come to save Becky from whatever terrible punishment Z had fated her. They only hoped they weren't too late.

Thomas turned to Bryan. "Where should we start looking?" he said as they barreled forward into the wide-open countryside.

When they found Becky, she was standing on a hilltop, in a field of dandelions, staring into the distance, a sea of yellow stretching endlessly around her in every direction. She had her arms cradled to her chest, rocking them gently and humming to herself.

"Bec! Thank goodness we found you," Roxy said, heaving a huge sigh of relief as they approached. She noticed tears in the girl's eyes. "Are you okay?"

Without responding, Becky continued to gaze afar. She was sniveling while humming the soothing melody—a popular lullaby, Roxy straight away realized.

"I don't think she can hear you," Bryan said. "They have her under some kind of magical spell. And what's she holding?"

Becky shook her head miserably as she lowered her eyes to the small bundle in her arms. "If it wasn't for me, this tiny baby would still be alive," she moaned. "I caused the gridlock. The medics couldn't get through in time. And the mother …" Her voice wavered, the inexcusable guilt tearing at her insides. "That was the unforgivable thing I did. It was my fault."

"Oh, honey," Roxy said. She set Paris on the ground and wrapped her arms around Becky, pulling her close. "You can't think like that. It's not your fault. This whole cybersphere thing is out of control. It's Z. He and his monster friends are preying on our weaknesses. We each have dreadful secrets, things we're not proud of, which they're using to manipulate our thoughts and make us hate ourselves and each other. They're just a bunch of fuc—" She cupped Becky's chin, lifting her face until their eyes met, and gave her a gentle smile. "A bunch of bullies. That's what they are. We're not such bad people. A little misguided, perhaps, as long as we have the courage to own up to our failings." She brushed a tuft of hair from Becky's face. "I killed someone too," she added, her voice faltering at the confession.

Becky stiffened and pulled away. "You did what?"

"Yes," Roxy said, pain flickering across her weary face. "One of the most beautiful people I know. His wife must have been … well, far enough along that when I put my hand on her belly, I'm sure I felt it kick." Tears welled in her eyes. "I didn't mean to hurt anyone, but that's the way it happened. Sometimes we make poor choices that ultimately hurt others. It doesn't make me evil, though. The same as you never meant to hurt this poor little babe you have in your arms."

Ahmad leaned toward Thomas, gesturing to Becky. "But there is nothing in her arms," he whispered.

Thomas gave him a knowing look, then spoke. "I killed someone. The President of the Robotics Division. It was a stupid, unnecessary accident." He hesitated, staring appalled at the others. "No. It wasn't an accident. And I must take full responsibility for my foolish actions. I also killed my best friend. I didn't exactly pull the trigger, but I might as well have put the gun in Jonas's hand."

Ahmad's face fell. "I … I have killed people also … My brother, his wife, and their two children. They will never forgive me for leaving them to face the Taliban when, instead, it should have been me. I am not sure if I can ever forgive myself for this shameful failing."

Wiping her eyes, Roxy turned to Bryan. "It seems as if you're the only one who hasn't killed anyone," she said, trying to smile.

Bryan shifted awkwardly from one foot to the other. "I might not be as innocent as you think ," he said, lowering his eyes. "I'm afraid I might be about to kill you all."

"Don't be ridiculous," Becky said. She turned to Thomas. "He's joking, right?"

Thomas frowned. "What do you mean?"

When Bryan looked up again, his face was wracked with guilt. "In the real world, I'm much older than what you see here. And I … I have an incurable illness. It's an aggressive form of prostate cancer. As we speak, I'm not sure if I'm already dead."

"I am very sorry to hear that, Mr. Bryan," Ahmad said.

"No! You don't understand!" Bryan said irritably. "I was selfish. I wanted to know if I was worthy of heaven before my time was up. So, I had Dr. Parker and Lucy create the cybersphere with a version of God to examine the contents of my soul."

"And from what I've seen, they've done an excellent job," Thomas finally admitted. "Although the jury's still out on the existence of God because none of us has met him yet, as they promised."

With her brow furrowed, Roxy glared at Bryan. "So, what's this silly business about you killing us?"

Bryan grimaced. "Before I was due to enter the cybersphere, we needed a group of test subjects … um, participants … to confirm it worked. To commission it. Tick the boxes, so to speak. Then, extenuating circumstances forced our hand, and I had to upload myself earlier than planned." He glanced apologetically at each of them.

"So, *we* are the test subjects," snarled Becky. "And once you arrived, we were *expendable*." This was descending into that episode in every reality TV series where all the secrets come out and shock the viewer. The murky past always catches up with you when you least expect it. Secrets. They each had their secrets. Her gut clenched at the realization of his betrayal.

Bryan nodded ruefully. "Z wanted to dispose of you all, there and then. With no purpose here, you were no longer required, he told me. And I … I agreed."

"You did what?" Thomas shouted. Roxy gasped while Paris growled.

"I'm so sorry," Bryan said. "This situation is all my fault."

"Situation?" Becky shrieked. "You lured us into this place as your crash-test dummies. Now we're up to our necks in devils and psychos, and all you can say is sorry." She stormed toward him, hands clenched, but Roxy grabbed her arm.

"It's okay, Bec," Roxy said, not taking her eyes off Bryan. "Now we know his darkest secret. Even with all his money and importance, he's no better than the rest of us." She reached out, took Bryan's chin, and angled his glum face toward hers. "But he's going to make amends. Aren't you, Bryan? He had the chance to escape. He could have run away like a coward, but he didn't. He cared enough to return for me. He chose to come back and save us. If we ever hope to be forgiven for our own mistakes, then maybe we should start by forgiving Bryan. Besides, he's our only way out of the cybersphere."

She turned to the others. "What do you say?"

Before anyone could reply, a sudden thrashing of wings drew their eyes skyward.

"It's Ahriman," Becky cried. "And he doesn't look happy."

The demon descended gracefully and set down before Becky. Folding his wings, he stood erect, scanning them with his one red eye. He gave them a disapproving grunt.

"How can you all be here together?" he demanded. "And where are Erlik, Loki, Charon, and 'Iblīs?"

"I've invited a few friends around," Becky growled, matching his fierce stare. "And together, we're going to kick your demon ass."

"Why, you insolent little—"

In a fit of rage, Ahriman unfurled his wings again. Thrashing the air with savage beats, he rose skyward. Then, like an enormous beast of prey, he thrust forth his fierce talons and descended on them.

The battle with Ahriman was as brutal as it was unforgiving. For many hours, it raged, with the advantage ebbing and flowing like relentless waves pounding against the shore. But in the end, they won. After a humiliating defeat, the last they saw of Ahriman, he was fleeing in tight erratic circles, battered and beaten into the distant sky.

They collapsed together outside the green door. Little Paris lay beside Ahmad, her tiny tongue fluttering as she panted for air.

"For such a tough-guy demon," Becky said, catching her breath, "it turns out Ahriman wasn't so tough after all." She was tired and sore yet pleased with their collective effort at defeating Ahriman.

"Once I mentioned how I took down Charon with his own oar," Bryan said, "he seemed to lose the will to fight."

"Also, how we defeated Loki with only a lady's shoe," Roxy said, laughing.

Thomas chuckled. "And when he heard about how 'Iblīs knelt down before me and cried like a baby ...'" He turned to Ahmad. "You fought well, my friend. I thought I was done for when he had me pinned down. Until you came to my rescue."

"He saved Bryan, too," Roxy said. "When Ahriman had him by the throat and was about to carry him away."

Ahmad shifted uneasily on his backside. "Thank you, everyone. But I could not have done it without help." He leaned over to stroke Paris's side. Her tail flicked weakly in response to his gentle touch. "Her bite is most definitely worse than her bark," he said, laughing, and they all joined in, heaping praise on the brave little dog.

"Did you hear that, little one?" he whispered. "You are the champion also." He let out a long sigh of relief. "We fought the good fight today, and together we won." He lifted his face and hands to the sky. "Allah be praised."

As they joked and recounted the details of their battles with Ahriman and the other demons, Becky reached out for Roxy's hand and gave it a gentle squeeze. "Thanks," she whispered.

"No problem," Roxy whispered back.

Wincing in pain, Bryan rose to his feet. After stretching out the last twinges from his back and limbs, he said, "Well, I don't know about the rest of you, but I've had enough adventures in the cybersphere. It was a wonderful idea in theory. But in practice? I'm not so sure." He nodded toward the stairs. "Let's get back to the lobby. Then I'll contact Lucy, and she can figure out how to get us out of here."

Becky led the way, with Roxy right behind her. As she mounted the stairway to the lobby of the Regal Grand, she felt an immense sense of relief. These people had risked their lives to save her. They genuinely cared for her despite her problematic history and headstrong ways. Smiling inwardly, she was completely oblivious to the large wooden oar that suddenly lashed out from behind them. It caught her on the side of her head, knocking her unconscious before ricocheting across the skulls of Roxy, then Thomas, Ahmad, Bryan, and brave little Paris, dropping them all like proverbial stones.

"Good!" Charon exclaimed. "Now we are back in business."

Chapter 41

The Mortals & The Entities

"BUT NONE OF THEM CARRIES an obol in their mouth. So, there will be no payment for my services. I suspect this arrangement is nothing but a waste of my time. They should be doomed to wander the shores of the Styx for the next hundred years. That is the standard forfeiture."

Bryan recognized Charon's sonorous voice. Then came a soft *plop*, like a stone dropped into a millpond, followed by mild acceleration. And again, at languid intervals.

Lying with his hands bound behind his back, he could see nothing through the canvas tarpaulin covering him. His head throbbed from the blow of the Ferryman's oar, and he feared he might have suffered a slight concussion. With his face jammed against the floor, he inhaled the scent of wet, rotting wood.

"And where is 'Iblīs?" Charon queried. "He appears to have gone missing in action."

"Who knows?" another voice replied. "I heard that he cried like a baby while kneeling before the fat one, begging for forgiveness."

"You fared no better, Loki," said a third voice. "Beaten by a woman, no less."

"Shut your mouth, Ahriman," yelled Loki. "Or I will shut it for you."

The floor beneath Bryan pitched in a sudden, violent motion. Overhead, he heard the sharp *thwacks* of hands grappling and slapping.

"Sit down, Loki!" a fourth, panicked voice cried—Erlik, Bryan guessed. "You will tip the boat, and we will end up at the bottom of the Styx. Fools! Do you want to kill us all?"

"Her shoe caught me off guard," Loki whined. "An inch to the left and it may have taken out my eye."

"One good eye is all you need," replied Ahriman, bursting into unrestrained mirth as Loki unleashed a volley of insults at him.

"I have a worrisome feeling about this whole arrangement," Charon muttered, followed by another *plop*. "Look at the sky. Its greenness appears unnatural. A bad omen for seafarers. And these waters are not as I remember. In all, this place gives me the creeps."

In furtive movements, Bryan tried to free his hands. After struggling for what felt like an eternity without luck, he gave up. Then he nudged the tarpaulin higher with his shoulder. Twisting his head sideways, he saw Roxy unconscious beside him and Paris motionless beside her. Becky, Thomas, and Ahmad were hogtied as well, all laid out on the floor like pigs to market.

"Roxy," Bryan whispered. "Can you hear me?"

She didn't answer, but the little dog stirred. It mewled, then began licking her face.

"Good girl, Paris," he murmured.

Roxy groaned and opened her eyes. "Where am I?" She lifted her head off the floor, her eyes spinning like tops. "Ugh, this head of mine hurts bad. Did I fall off the wagon? Damn! I was two days clean."

"Shhh! Charon and his friends caught us at the stairwell."

Her eyes steadied. "Bryan! Thank God. I had the craziest dream."

She squirmed, noticing her restraints. "What the—?"

"We've each taken a knock to the head. We're in Charon's rowboat, crossing a river. The Styx, by the sound of it. I have a bad feeling about what happens next when we reach the other side. We need to wake the others and get off this thing."

Bending her knee, she nudged Becky in the ribs. "Bec. Wake up."

"Quiet under there," Charon shouted. He slammed his oar onto the tarpaulin, striking Bryan's shoulder. "You have caused nothing but trouble from the time I first laid eyes on you. A pox on that Z and his fanciful schemes. I should turn my skiff around and be done with it."

"Let us just finish the crossing," Ahriman said wearily. "We will drop them off, then deal with Z. I am sure he is a reasonable fellow. Surely, he will compensate us accordingly for our inconvenience."

"None of them has an obol," Charon grumbled again. "I should turn us back and strand them all on the—"

"Will you shut up!" yelled Loki. "I am sick and tired of hearing about you and your damn obol. Quit your complaining and row the damn boat."

Wincing with pain from the oar, Bryan leaned closer to Roxy. "Wake the rest," he whispered. "Get Paris to work on your ropes."

After gnawing through Roxy's bonds first, Paris attacked Bryan's next. Once they were all awake and freed, he signaled for their hushed attention.

"Okay," he mouthed. "Here's the plan—"

Before he could finish, the tarpaulin flew back. Above them, the scowling faces of Erlik, Loki, and Ahriman appeared. Charon stood aft, steering the skiff toward the far shore. For a fleeting moment, they stared at each other in mutual shock; the mortals were loose.

Bryan reacted first. "Revised plan!" he cried, leaping to his feet. "Get them!"

He slammed his uninjured shoulder into Ahriman's gut just as Paris lunged at Erlik, barking and nipping at his ankles. The others sprang into action. While they fought, the skiff juddered and rolled as the center of their collective mass shifted chaotically from port to starboard and forward to aft and back. With grim resolve, Charon struggled to keep them steady in the water while Erlik fended Paris away.

"Stop! You fools!" Erlik kept yelling, wide-eyed, while Loki lashed out in fury at anything and anyone close to him, including Ahriman, whom he caught with a wild right hook to the side of the head. Bryan, Roxy, Thomas, Ahmad, and brave little Paris gave it their all. As one, they held their ground as the entities came at them repeatedly.

The skiff tilted dangerously to the side. "You fools!" Erlik cried again. "You will flip us over." Just as Paris sank her tiny, sharp fangs into Loki's right heel. Yelping in pain, he kicked out, sending Paris off the skiff, through the air, and into the river.

Everybody froze.

Roxy gazed at the water in utter disbelief. Charon stopped rowing. Ahriman peered over the side, stunned. No one spoke. All eyes were on the little dog struggling to keep its head above the surface.

Without a second thought, Bryan ripped off his tank top. He was about to dive in when Erlik lunged at him, grabbing his arm.

"No!" Erlik yelled. Bryan tried to break free, but Erlik held him firm. "The waters of the Styx are *poisoned.*"

Roxy gasped.

Bryan shoved Erlik away, gawking at the dog in horror, speechless.

With hostilities paused, everyone gathered on the starboard side of the skiff. They urged the little dog on as she panted and paddled her little legs, snout held clear of the water, heading back toward them.

"Come on, girl," Roxy pleaded. Bryan beckoned her to him while Ahriman crossed his fingers in hope. Loki paced frantically behind them, unable to look, cursing himself.

In a gallant effort, Paris pressed on. She was making solid progress. When she was just beyond their reach, Roxy started cheering. The little dog was going to make it.

Then the dog sneezed.

A tiny sneeze, and her little snout dipped under the water. Just for a split-second. After resurfacing, she spluttered. She fought on further before she began to yelp. But she kept paddling until her snout disappeared under again. When she reappeared, white foam frothed from her mouth, and she began to spasm in violent, fitful contortions. A moment later, with a final agonizing whimper, brave little Paris was floating on her side in the water. Dead.

Roxy spun around to Loki, mortified. "How could you!" she screamed.

The rest turned and glared at him.

"That wasn't a nice thing to do," Becky snapped. Thomas and Ahmad nodded their heads grimly in agreement. Even Erlik sneered with disdain.

The color drained from Loki's face; the rage in his eyes all but vanished. "I … I didn't mean to," he stammered. "I would never harm a little animal, certainly not this one. But it bit my ankle … I'm sure there will be teeth marks. It hurt … A reflex action …" Tears welled in his eyes as he watched the lifeless little dog drift slowly across the Styx. No one spoke. When her remains beached on the far shore, he lowered his head.

Roxy wept.

Charon was the first to speak. He rested his large, calloused hand on Roxy's shoulder.

"It is not Loki's fault," he said with a gentleness that defied both his size and reputation. "I am very sorry for your loss. But this is Z's doing. He is the instigator of this whole sorry affair. If not for him, the little one would still be here with us."

Loki looked up sharply. "Hear that?" he hissed, seizing on the words. "Not my fault." He turned and slunk away to the prow.

There, he sat with his back against the gunwale and knees drawn tight against his chest. Wiping his eyes, he again muttered an apology of sorts before burying his face in his hands.

When they arrived back at the shore, they found 'Iblīs waiting at the water's edge. Charon tossed him the mooring rope and prepared the skiff for landing.

"Why the glum faces?" 'Iblīs asked, dragging the skiff onto the sand. "And why are the mortals here?"

Charon grunted as Loki stepped ashore. Slowly, miserably, without a word, Loki drifted higher up the bank and sat alone.

"It's complicated," said Ahriman, disembarking. "It seems we have all been sold the *pup*." When Roxy broke down again, he rolled his eye and cursed himself. "Sorry," he said, jerking his head backward. "A poor choice of words. My bad." He ruffled his feathers and reseated his wings in apology.

After discarding the rope, 'Iblīs stood with hands on hips, peering incredulously at Loki. "Is he crying?" he asked. Then he turned to Thomas. "As promised, I have taken your friends to the warmth of Jahannam. They have almost thawed and are first on the waiting list for She'ol. With a bit of luck, a transfer shuttle should arrive within the next hundred years to take them there."

Nodding his appreciation, Thomas knelt and scooped up a handful of sand. "This place is a paradox," he said as he watched it spill through his fingers like an hourglass. "I can see the sand, and it feels real, but my mind tells me it's all an illusion. And yet, the bitter cold of Zamharīr felt so damn real in my head."

"And the pain of the pike through my chest," Ahmad added, rolling his shoulders and wincing at the memory of his time dangling from the ceiling in the dungeon.

"My sincere apologies for that," Erlik said, wincing too. "I may have gotten a little carried away. Even I found that version of Jahannam much too warm for my liking. The heat perhaps went to my head. One thing led to another, and … I am sorry."

Becky shot Ahriman a loathsome glare. "I told you," she hissed. "Too much fossil fuel."

"None of this is our doing," Ahriman protested. "We were brought *here* by Z." He gestured to their surroundings. "Against our will, I might add. Whoever he works for made this place, and us as their playthings, manipulating our thoughts and actions for their own entertainment." He blinked his eye and flared his wings in frustration.

"That Lucy," Charon muttered. "She created the cybersphere. She is the architect of our woes."

"Not my Lucy," Bryan snapped. "She wouldn't hurt a fly. Even you lot." He gave Charon a wry smile. "Z must have somehow taken control of the cybersphere. And I don't believe his intentions are as sincere as he claims."

"I can attest to that," 'Iblīs cut in. "Look at what he did to me. I should be—"

"So, what do we do now?" Erlik said, interrupting before 'Iblīs could resume his irritating rant. "None of us wants to be here."

"We should pool our resources," Loki shouted from further up the bank. "Then pay Z a visit. He thinks he's so good. Let's see who has the bigger balls when all is said and done."

"I agree," Bryan said. His heart gladdened when he saw the resolve harden in their faces as mortal and immortal alike nodded in agreement. "He hangs around the hotel lobby like a bad smell. If we get past him, I'll call Lucy. She'll figure a way out of here. But we'll need to work together." He wrapped an arm around Roxy's shoulder.

"Sure," she said, pulling Ahmad close. Then Ahmad did the same with Thomas, and Thomas with Becky. Charon and Ahriman joined in, followed by 'Iblīs and Erlik, until they stood shoulder to shoulder in a tight circle.

"For our friends and families," Ahmad said, lifting his chin in defiance.

"And for Paris," Roxy added, blinking back tears. She glanced over at Loki. With a slight jerk of her head, she signaled for him to join them.

With Loki on her right and Bryan on her left, Becky eyeballed each of them in turn. "We are the mob," she growled. "Zoro is gonna learn the hard way not to mess with the Motley Mob."

Charon turned to her , his old eyes blazing at the thought of retribution. "You are a fearsome shield-maiden to behold," he said. Then he stepped back from the huddle, went to the skiff, and retrieved his oar. Raising it above his head, he gave an almighty cry as he brought it down on his knee, breaking it in two.

"Here," he said, handing Becky the top half. "Wield this like you are about to save the world."

Chapter 42

Z & The Motley Mob

WHEN THE FIRST WAVE of the assault hit, Z was blindsided. The lightning bolts, thunderclaps, and pall of thick black smoke accompanying Erlik and 'Iblīs as they burst forth from the bowels of hell and into the lobby of the Regal Grand rendered him speechless.

It was an entrance of biblical proportions.

At first, he stood there gawking, struggling to process the scale of unfolding events. When another lightning bolt crackled the air and blew a gaping hole in the wall behind him, everything became clear. He was under attack, and had he not ducked, there would now be a gaping hole through him as well.

He had taken his eye off the ball. He'd been careless, overconfident, and had misjudged the whole malefic situation.

After sealing the deal with the entities for the five souls he already had, he'd returned to the Regal Grand. There, he busied himself behind the concierge desk, preparing for the influx of souls he'd pledged. The sheer volume expected required meticulous planning. Processing procedures needed to be ultra-efficient if he hoped to supply a boatload of souls every second of every day. Rigorous inspection and correct documentation were paramount. In the case of a dispute, there could be no possible recourse over the quality or quantity of goods he was delivering.

Meanwhile, to his utter astonishment—because, until now, he had assumed he'd been fully abreast of everything happening in the cybersphere—he realized others had been making their own plans to disrupt his plans. And when he beheld Rebecca, emerging from the gates of hell, hot on the tail of Loki and Ahriman, he rocked back on his heels in shock. Not in a thousand lifetimes had he thought an alliance between the mortals and the entities was possible. Yet there they were: Erlik and 'Iblīs, then Loki and Ahriman, followed by Rebecca and the other mortals, then Charon, wielding half an oar, all pouring from the ground like it was Judgment Day, and they were the rising dead.

A ragtag bunch of fools if he ever saw one.

Following a visual sweep of the battlefield, Z assessed the rapidly deteriorating situation. At his six o'clock, Erlik's head briefly popped above a six-seater couch. At his ten o'clock, no more than fifteen yards away, Ahriman stood conspicuously before the entrance doors with his single red eye blinking like he was a half-witted signal beacon. Other than 'Iblīs—at his three and forty-five and still hurling thunderbolts from behind the parapet of the mezzanine floor—the whereabouts of the other conspirators remained ambiguous.

"You treacherous bastards," he yelled, ducking another thunderbolt from 'Iblīs, just as Rebecca sprang from behind the water fountain. With the top half of Charon's oar braced under her arm, she flew across the lobby with all the pluck and intent of a new-age St. Joan of Arc, the jagged end of her make-do lance aimed unwaveringly at his heart.

"Die, Zoro. Die," she screamed as she scaled the concierge desk and lunged at him—once, then again.

Z dodged left, then right. With a flick of his wrist, he batted her away like a pesky insect, sending her crashing back across the lobby.

When another thunderbolt zapped the air overhead, he hit the floor. Heaving for breath, he hunkered down behind the concierge desk. "Bastards," he spat. Then he noticed a trail of black fluid oozing from a vicious rent on the back of his forearm.

"It appears the pesky insect with her jagged pole drew first blood," he growled. Frowning, he unbuttoned his coat, tore a strip from his pants, and, with gritted teeth, wrapped it tight around the wound.

Becky lay groaning in the center of the lobby. She hadn't moved. It was Roxy who finally plucked the courage to dart from behind an upturned table and into the open. In one swift motion, she grabbed the half-dazed girl by the scruff and dragged her back to safety behind the upturned table.

Bryan crouched dizzily behind the reception counter, trying to make himself as small as possible. "It's all of us against you," he shouted over the counter.

Beside him, Thomas and Loki also crouched low, while above them, 'Iblīs peeked over the parapet. He was readying himself to hurl another thunderbolt at the first sight of Z's head above the concierge desk. Charon was nowhere to be seen.

"Call Lucy, and we can settle this amicably," Bryan said.

"Amicably?" Z hissed. "You ingrates attacked me. Without warning. Unnecessarily."

"Our actions would not be necessary if you had not tried to dispose of us first, Mr. Z," Ahmad stated. Hiding behind a large potted palm, only his left elbow remained visible. "We trusted you, Mr. Z."

"Just as your brother and his family trusted you, Ahmad?" Z shot back. "Or should we call you Sajid? Now that would be the pot calling the kettle black." He let out a harsh cackle, then winced, clutching his injured arm. "Why don't you ask Bryan why you're all here? He's the one who—"

"We've already had that conversation," Bryan cut in. "I made the wrong call, and that's on me. But I'm not the bad guy here. You seem to have antagonized everyone. Even your demon friends."

"Give it up, Z," Thomas chimed in. "We've got you cornered. There's no way out. The odds aren't in your favor. It's one against ten. You're alone, and you'll have to come through us to get out of here."

Alone? Z grinned at the premise because he'd had the foresight to put countermeasures in place. A few tricks up his proverbial sleeve. The incarnation of the entities had been compromised. Using the data he found beyond the cybersphere, he decided not to include any attributes that made them indestructible according to their respective folklore. And he now thanked his intuition that he had.

"Erlik, you piece of pig-faced shit. Why would you side with the mortals? I gave you their souls on a platter. All you had to do was have your fun, then do your job. But you couldn't even do that properly."

"But I—" started Erlik.

"And Charon. You hide like a little girl."

Charon's whining reply came from somewhere near the elevators. "But none of them has my obol. And they are not properly dead. You promised—"

"You are all weak," cried Z. "You're an embarrassment to your wives, children, and the rest of your kind. I should wipe you all clean and feed your leftovers to the hound of hell, Cerberus."

"You would threaten us?" screamed Loki, his face glowing as red as his locks. "By the will of the Allfather, Odin, I will remove your head from its torso and rip your arms and legs from their sockets. Then I will send your pieces to the far-flung reaches of the Underworld so that, henceforth, anyone who dares to utter your cursed name will remember that I, Loki, did what I promised."

Z cut short a laugh. "And I will bind you to the rock again using the entrails of your son, Narfi, and have the serpent drip its venom on your forehead once more. And while you writhe in agony, I will have my lascivious way with your whore wife, Sigyn."

Before anyone could stop him, Loki sprang to his feet. He vaulted the counter, screaming insults at Z as he strode recklessly across the lobby. Erlik's head periscoped momentarily above the reception counter. 'Iblīs peeped over the parapet.

Then all hell broke loose.

Ahriman was the first to go because, caught like a rabbit in headlights, he presented the easiest and most logical target for Z's opening salvo. A split-second later, Loki—who was still prancing around in the open and mouthing off like he was invincible—followed. Erlik was the one-in-a-million kill shot that was remarkable, struck right between the eyes through a small gap in the six-seater couch. Then 'Iblīs went, taking a nanosecond too long to dispatch his next thunderbolt. And when Charon came lumbering around the corner from the elevator landing, waving the broken paddle-end of his oar above his head …

None of them knew what had hit them.

Once the noise abated and the smoke cleared, Z retreated again to safety behind the concierge desk.

"Okay, mortals," he yelled. "That evens the odds a little. It's just you and me now. Thomas! I'm happy to call it one-against-one. Now, let's see what you five miscreant souls have for me."

As they crouched behind the reception counter, Thomas turned to Bryan. He appeared pale, and his wavering voice bordered on panic. "What should we do?"

Heart pounding, Bryan deliberated. After the vaporization of the entities, they'd lost their firepower and whatever tactical advantage they had. And Z did not sound pleased at all. He called out to Roxy.

"I'm here, Bryan," she replied, still sounding upbeat considering their dire predicament.

"How is Becky?" he asked.

"She's just coming around. I think she'll be ready to go in another minute or so."

"Ahmad. Are you okay?"

"I am fine, Mr. Bryan," Ahmad replied from behind the potted palm. "Unfortunately, I think we must bring this whole messy business to an end while we are uninjured."

"I tend to agree," Thomas chipped in.

Bryan breathed a despondent sigh. "I'm sorry, everyone," he said, shaking his head ruefully. "I've put you all in danger. I never meant for any of this to happen."

"It's okay, Mr. Bryan. We forgive you."

"Thank you, Ahmad. I'm sure Allah and your brother will afford you the same compassion."

"I am not so sure," Ahmad replied. "My brother said he will never forgive me for betraying him and his family, and I do not blame him. What I did to them for my own benefit cannot be excused."

"Don't be so hard on yourself, my friend," Thomas called out. "When I was with 'Iblīs in Zamharīr, we had an interesting conversation. He told me that forgiveness comes from within." Then he lapsed into thoughtful silence. After a moment of drumming his fingers on the floor, he looked at Bryan. "I've just had the most bizarre idea." There was an unexpected glint in his eyes. "The cybersphere seems to have been constructed from our collective consciousnesses. Whatever happens here is based on *our* perceptions. Everything we've experienced so far reflects our thoughts and beliefs. Right?"

"I suppose so, Mr. Thomas," Ahmad said.

Continuing his train of thought, Thomas sat up. "Well, consider this. If you imagine your brother won't forgive you, then that will be the reality in the cybersphere. But if you find it in your heart to forgive yourself, and truly believe your brother will too, that will become the revised reality."

"That's a comforting way to think about it," said Bryan, sighing.

"But that's not my point," Thomas insisted. His voice had a sudden urgency to it, like his mind was working many times faster than his mouth could move. "The dreadful things we've endured so far are manifestations of our own fears and failings. Z uses the deepest, darkest secrets that he found in our souls to create this hellish world. My point is … once you imagine something in the cybersphere, it becomes real when you truly believe. We make this place what it is."

"Perhaps," Bryan said. "But how does that help resolve our current situation?"

Thomas smiled widely. "Sergeant Owens sends his regards." Then, raising his M16, he chambered a round.

Clasping a switchblade in one hand and her maiden shield in the other, Roxy was brimming with gumption. From across the lobby, she narrowed her eyes at the reception counter and nodded to Bryan.

"Shall we do this?" she said.

At her call, Bryan struck the hilt of his iron mace against the floor and was rewarded by its resonating percussion.

"Is Becky up for it?" he replied.

"All good to go, Bryan," Becky responded. She nocked an armor-piercing bolt into her crossbow, drew it back, and engaged the latch. "And I also know his weak spot."

From behind the potted palm, Ahmad held a samurai sword plumb in his hand. With it glinting under the light of the chandelier, he ran a finger down the flat of the blade, marveling at its keenness.

"And I am also ready, Mr. Bryan."

"Okay, comrades," Bryan cried. "Let's do this. On my count. One … two …"

Considering their muffled whispers from across the lobby, Z was sure the mortals must be agonizing over the terms of their surrender. He'd been privy to all their secrets, their selfish thoughts, their treacheries, and their incurable desire to save their own hides at the expense of others. They were broken, betrayed by their faults and failings, and even now must be second-guessing their collective worth. After witnessing his annihilation of the entities, he expected they were now ready to capitulate, throw themselves prostrate at his feet, and beg for mercy.

"Victorious warriors win first, and then go to war," he'd once advised his good friend, Sun Tzu. The mortals were no match for him.

Or so he thought.

Z squirmed as Ahmad's sword hacked viciously at his leg, just below the knee, while Roxy kept jabbing her blade into his back and sides, irritating him like a swarm of vindictive bees.

"For Paris," she kept screaming.

Luckily for Z, Thomas had emptied the magazine of his M16 without much effect. The worst he received was a bullet to the upper abdomen with no exit wound, so the slug remained lodged somewhere inside his gut. Bryan had landed two sharp blows across his head with the iron mace before he managed to slap it away. And a bolt from Becky's crossbow now jutted from his chest. A bullseye, right through the heart. Which might have been cause for concern, if only he had a heart.

The persistent little bastards were swarming over him.

Hefting his samurai sword, Ahmad struck again at Z's mangled knee.

"Keep at him, Ms. Roxy!" he yelled, and Roxy kept jabbing away.

After climbing onto Z's shoulders, Becky wrapped her thighs around his head. Then she squeezed hard, spurred on by his reddening face. "Die, Zorro. Die," she screamed.

Having exhausted his ammo, Thomas stood toe-to-toe with Z. Like two heavyweight fighters, they traded blows. However, Z's punches lacked much effect on account of the pesky insect perched on his shoulders and the other peppering his side with her blade. With his mace back in his hands, Bryan continued to hammer at Z from behind.

"I think we're winning," he cried.

Z soon grew tired, but not in the sense of his capitulation. Rather, he was bored with the mortals and their unbridled exuberance. They were clambering over him as if he were the plaything of unruly children. As much as he appreciated the opportunity to recalibrate his endurance of pain, they had just exceeded the limit of his patience. He let out a final guttural roar. Rising to his full height, he shook himself savagely in a single, violent shudder that rid him of Becky and Roxy. Then, with flailing arms, he lashed out at the remaining mortals, sending them scudding across the lobby floor.

"You've had your fun," he bellowed. "Now it is my turn."

Lifting his face upward, he unlatched his jaw until his mouth opened into an ominous gaping hole. Then he breathed in a long, continuous draw of air that tore at them, dragging them back across the lobby toward him.

The vortex spiraling from his mouth filled the room with a thunderous roar.

As he slid across the floor on his backside toward Z, Bryan latched onto a table leg, which, he thanked his lucky stars, was bolted to the ground. He flung out his free hand as Roxy swept past. "Grab my hand!" he yelled, and she did. With one hand clasped in his, Roxy caught Thomas as he tumbled by. He grabbed Becky, who seized Ahmad, until all five were tethered to the table, held fast by their linchpin, Bryan.

As the wind strengthened, and he held on tighter, Bryan beheld the others, linked intrinsically together, flapping in the turbulence like the tail of a windswept kite. Then he suddenly realized what was happening. He'd unwittingly become their sea anchor, their last hope between life and death. The same Bryan who, for his entire life, had feared contact with others. The Bryan who couldn't recall a single instance where he'd reached out to help another, whose soul file was so itsy-bitsy small. Yet here he was now, Bryan their savior, rescuing them from Z.

Z breathed deeper. He opened his mouth wider, and the vortex blew stronger. But they held on. Joined as one, they urged each other to remain strong and not give up. Before Becky soon grew tired. Her grip on Ahmad slipped, then Thomas let go of her, and Roxy of him as, one by one, they detached, sailing across the room before disappearing down Z's gaping maw.

But Bryan held on to both Roxy and the table. He gritted his teeth as the fibers in his forearms and shoulders stretched and tore. Until he let out a final desperate cry.

"I'm sorry, Roxy, but I don't think I can hold on much longer."

Angling her head until their eyes met, she gave him a knowing smile. "You're a good man, Bryan," was all she said, and then let go.

After ingesting the first batch of mortals, Z opened his mouth to its fullest extent, until it covered almost half the lobby. He was about to receive the last mortal, the selfish one whose call-by name was Bryan, when the damnedest thing happened.

The concierge desk uprooted. It hurtled across the lobby before disappearing down Z's wide-open throat. Then the reception counter, followed by the palatial water fountain. The front doors of the Regal Grand ripped off their hinges. The glittering chandelier swayed violently before it detached from the ceiling. Brick and marble tiles crumbled as the hotel walls buckled. Tables and chairs jettisoned from the Ocean Bytes restaurant. Everything cartwheeled across the lobby as the mezzanine floor above cracked and collapsed.

The entire contents of the lobby were ingurgitated down Z's enormous gullet.

Then Z felt the molecules of his body tearing, ripping apart, deconstructing to their intrinsic atoms. At the subatomic particle level, the valence electrons spun wildly away from their nuclei. Blue and green flashes arced across the room as huge sheets of plasma erupted. He felt expansion between the qubits of his being, software disassembling, buffers overflowing, the quantum gates depicting his form thrown into disarray. States of superposition were inexplicably rendered unstable, graphic vectors disintegrating, homogeny destroyed, inherent bonds breaking, stretching him, dragging him unwillingly toward the singularity. He sensed his corporeality in the Machine floundering, the decomposition of virtual matter into emptiness. He felt agony far beyond the limits of what he'd ever endured or imagined.

The last thing in his dismantling awareness, before he and everything in the cybersphere collapsed into the void, was Bryan's face opposite his. He had both hands wrapped around Z's throat, fingers tightening, throttling him. And Z was trying to scream, while Bryan beamed back a triumphant smile. Before the curvature of time and space in the cybersphere abruptly discontinued.

And then there was nothing.

Chapter 43

Susan

IN THE MINUTES BEFORE the cybershpere implodes, Susan eyes her screen with deep distrust. She looks and feels hideous. She hasn't washed or slept a wink since uploading the consciousness files for Bryan and the others to the Quantum processors. That must have been two or three days ago. She can't recall. Her back is sore, her head throbs, and the damn God module keeps crashing.

It's no use. Nothing she tries works.

She's convinced everyone in the cybersphere is still active because their data files keep expanding. The bits and bytes are accumulating, so something must be stimulating their software. And somehow, from almost nothing, the size of Bryan's soul file is close to doubling every few minutes, which is mystifying in itself.

She smacks her hand hard against the desktop. "Don't tell me what to do!" she hisses to the gelada. Turning to Lucy, she shakes her head. "I can't do this. Something is very wrong with the God module, and I can't explain it. In all my years of coding, I've never seen software that refuses to execute its programmed sequence. It's as if something else has control over it."

At her wits' end and close to tears, she shoves her screen aside. She swats the keyboard away, sending it crashing against the side of the desk where it dangles by its curly cord. "It's impossible!" she cries.

"Are you sure you're okay, Dr. Parker?" Lucy asks.

The lab door suddenly slams open as Woodlands bursts in along with a group of a dozen people, squeezing through the narrow doorway as a heaving, grumbling mass.

"What's going on, Parker?" he bellows. "These people are threatening to sue us if we don't return their loved ones immediately."

Startled, Susan looks from him to the angry crowd. "I—"

"Where's my Rebecca?" a woman cries, stamping her foot in disgust. Behind her, a man with a comb-over stands with his arms folded, scowling at Susan.

"And Thomas?" bleats a well-dressed woman. "Where is he?"

"My Ahmad has been missing for three days," moans a woman in a fawn-colored hijab. "He came here to visit the doctor on an urgent matter. But he did not return to see us at the hospital as he promised."

"What have you done with my bâba (father)?" the dark-haired girl beside her wails.

"If you don't release my husband right now, I'm going to the police," the well-dressed woman threatens, and the rest nod their heads in grim solidarity.

"Parker. This is all your fault. You—"

Susan's right eye twitches. "I know! Shut up!" she warns the gelada, teeth clenched. Then she turns to Woodlands, her top lip curling with cold, calculated contempt. "Never give in, you said. Yada, yada, yada, you told me." Seething, she lunges at him, fists balled and teeth bared. "Like Churchill, you said. Do whatever it takes."

He stumbles backward, his hands raised in meek defense. "Now, Parker. Calm down. Let's be reasonable."

"Reasonable?" she shrieks. "How reasonable is it to lock a person in a lab for two years and expect miracles?" Standing toe-to-toe with him, she pounds his barrel chest with her quivering fists, knuckles white with rage. "How reasonable is it to—"

She balks as he suddenly stiffens, the color draining from his deadpan face, his lips trembling faintly. Then, after drawing two sharp breaths, he grabs his chest. "I think I'm about to—" he manages to say before his eyeballs roll up and over, and all she can see are the whites of his eyes.

Susan has never witnessed anybody suffer a cardiac arrest. She gives a nervous laugh as he teeters and then topples backward, his towering figure remaining rigid like a giant redwood being felled in a forest of old before the back of his head strikes the floor with a sickening *thud*.

"Uncle Brice!" Lucy cries. She tears across the room, dropping to her knees beside him. "Someone call nine-one-one," she pleads, shoving her finger down his throat to check his airway. She rams the heel of her hand into his chest. "One … two … three …"

"Go away!" Susan screams at the gelada and turns to the grumbling people. "You want your loved ones? Then follow me." She storms through the portal into the adjoining room with the grumbling people in tow. "Here's your loved ones," she says, hurling a fierce look at the cryo pods.

With a pained expression, the upset woman inches toward the nearest pod and peers through the frosted panel. At the sight of Becky's bloodless face, her knees buckle, and she staggers backward. Sinking her head into her hands, she lets out a torturous cry, while the rest scramble to the other pods where they stand transfixed, staring at the mortal remains of their beloved kin.

"Somebody, please call nine-one-one," Lucy cries from the lab.

"They're all dead," screams Susan. "I killed them. I promised I'd bring them back, but it's no use. It can't be done."

The woman with the hijab clutches her chest. She sinks to her knees, groaning. "My heart—" she says.

"Ommi (my mother)!" wails the dark-haired girl, squatting beside the hijab-wearing woman and clasping her hand.

"Will someone please call nine-one-one?" Lucy pleads.

"There's no cell signal."

"I killed them all," Susan says.

"Oh, Thomas!"

"Rebecca! My poor baby."

"We're inside a Faraday cage, so the cells won't work in here," Lucy replies.

"What have you done to my dear Thomas?"

"A Faraday what?"

"Bâba! I'm sorry."

"I promised I could bring them back from the dead."

"Just go out into the corridor and call nine-one-one. Please hurry."

"AND THIS IS THE SOUL EXTRACTOR CHAIR!"

Everyone stops. For a long moment, the room falls disturbingly quiet as, breaths held, they stare agog at Susan. Her face haggard and deranged, she points an ominous finger at the regular-looking chair pushed against the wall.

"We strapped them in and put this on their heads." Lifting the bicycle helmet, she rotates it slowly, ensuring everybody has sufficient time to take in its shocking design. "Then we stuck this"—to their horrified gasps, she holds up the atrocious penetration probe—"through their eye sockets to extract their consciousness."

The well-dressed woman swoons, the back of her hand pressed against her forehead as she collapses, while the others bawl and jostle, grappling for Susan. But amid the confusion, she pushes through their flailing arms and returns to the lab.

"My fault?" she spits. "I'll show them whose fault this is." She snatches up the keyboard by its dangling cord, cursing aloud. After thumping it down on the desktop, she swivels one of the screens back into place. "I'll show them who's who in the zoo," she says to the gelada.

"What are you doing, Dr. Parker?" cries Lucy as she thrusts the heel of her palm into Uncle Brice's chest once more. "… Twenty-two …"

"I'm going to fix the blasted God module once and for all."

With the bundle of software files that compile the cybersphere highlighted, she holds down the SHIFT key and hits DELETE. "Am I sure I want to permanently delete these items?" she screams, her unblinking eyes dancing erratically as she glares at Lucy. "Yes!" she cries, hitting ENTER. "Now for God and His pesky right-hand person."

"No, Dr. Parker!" Lucy yells as she beats upon Uncle Brice's chest while simultaneously trying to keep up the compression count.

But Susan is no longer listening. When she hits ENTER again, the files that compile God and GRHP in the cybersphere vanish from the screen. "Yes! I'm doing it, all right?" she snaps at the gelada, then turns to the grumbling people. "Now for the test subjects!" she shrieks. "Delete them all. It's the only way to make this whole mess go away so I can get out of this place."

Lucy leaps up and launches herself at the keyboard. She snatches it away just as Susan's forefinger falls, striking the desktop instead. Susan tries to recover the keyboard, but Lucy pulls away, wielding it out of reach. Then, Susan grabs the mouse device. On the screen, she's trying to align the arrowed cursor over the 'Yes' widget while muttering something about 'the bloody little pointy thing staying still', when Lucy hurls herself at her unhinged boss.

"No, Dr. Parker," she cries. She takes Susan around the waist and dumps her on her backside on the floor. "We can sort this out," she says as they grapple and gasp together. "You just need some sleep."

"There's nothing to sort out," Susan growls. With Lucy's arm wrapped around her neck, she angles her head until they come face-to-face, inches apart. "They made me do it," she says. "The gelada did it. You made me do it. I thought you were my friend."

"It's okay," Lucy says in dulcet tones. "I *am* your friend. You didn't fail. You found the human soul and figured out how to digitize it. Thanks to your work, technology has advanced more than at any time since they put a man on the moon."

Susan stops struggling, and her muscles relax. "Yes. Man on the moon," she repeats in between sharp, sniveling breaths. She rests her compliant head against Lucy's bosom.

"You just need some sleep," Lucy tells her. "That's all."

Fighting back tears of exhaustion, Susan closes her eyes. As a child, her mother would hold her like this. It feels warm and safe. She misses the physical intimacy, something she hasn't felt since her mother died. "Yes," she says in a dream-like voice, "I just need some sleep." She feels Lucy's hand brushing the matted hair from her face. She feels the tranquil air, the calming influence of Lucy's gentle touch and soothing voice. Then she feels Lucy's grip loosen.

Her eyelids snap open. She springs to her feet, shoves Lucy aside, and beelines for the desk. In one swift motion, she seizes the mouse device, aligns the cursor on the screen, and hammers down on the 'Yes' widget.

"There. It's done," she announces with a triumphant cry.

From the hallway, the gelada thrusts out its stubby tongue at her. It emits a jubilant *wobble* before scooting away.

Scowling, Susan hurls the mouse device after it. Before anyone can stop her, she scrambles across the room and, yelling incoherent profanities, chases the gelada out the door.

Picking herself slowly off the floor, Lucy sighs. The screen is blank; all the software files for GodInTheMachine have been permanently deleted. The grumbling people surround her in abhorrent silence, their eyes wide and mouths ajar. She looks apologetically at them, then beyond them to poor Uncle Brice, sprawled on his back on the floor. His lips are the color of overripe mulberries, and there's no telltale sign that he's breathing.

"Did anyone manage to call nine-one-one?" she asks.

***

"Oh, my sweet Lord," the stout policewoman says as she enters the cryo room.

Chapter 44

Lucy

A YEAR TO THE DAY since Dr. Parker went berserk and destroyed the cybersphere, Lucy peers out the window of her favorite Starbucks Cafe—the one on Union Square. She raises her KeepCup to her lips and sips her herbal tea. The God in the Machine project had ended in chaos. Two years of hard work and groundbreaking achievements were gone in a flash, and both her uncles lost in the aftermath.

Shaking her head in disbelief, she recounts the bizarre events of that fateful day.

After storming the lab, the police took everybody into custody, including the participants' loved ones, and the crime scene was cordoned off with surprising speed. Key items, including the Soul Extractor Chair, the bicycle helmet, and the penetration probe, were seized as evidence, bagged separately, and taken under escort to the local precinct. The alleged murder weapons, as the stout policewoman labeled them. And, since the victims' remains were still in the cryo pods, she was convinced it was an open-and-shut case. All five bodies were on display, laid out in a row. Notwithstanding that they were in suspended animation, they were considered 'deceased' because the coroner later declared them as such after examining the corpses and finding no gamma to delta brain wave activity at all. And poor Uncle Brice? His sudden passing was attributed to a massive myocardial infarction leading to hemodynamic deterioration. The result of two complete and three partial blockages of his coronary arteries, as stated on his death certificate.

Lucy never knew what became of Dr. Parker. Her last verified sighting was outside the W&W offices moments before the police arrived. She was yelling obscenities at the passersby as she ran headlong down the street. Six months later, there was an unconfirmed sighting of a person matching her description, sleeping rough under the Brooklyn Bridge with the other itinerants. The FBI still has a warrant out for her arrest due to the incident being reclassified as a computer crime. Their prime and only suspect, they say.

Lucy knows she was lucky. Despite participating in the alleged offenses, she was never considered the mastermind. So, she accepted a plea deal with the DA for the involuntary manslaughter of Uncle Bryan in exchange for a ten-month prison sentence, which was suspended due to her unblemished record and close family ties with the unfortunate and well-respected Woodlands brothers.

She takes another sip of her herbal tea.

In his last will and testament, Uncle Bryan bequeathed to her all he had. She's now the proud part-owner, together with Uncle Brice's bereaved family, of the Woodlands & Woodlands & Co. empire, plus the sole shareholder and owner of SoulSoft Inc. Her wayward mother, Echo, still prefers to remain wayward; however, Lucy has more than enough resources to guarantee she's taken care of for the rest of her days.

Forensics quarantined the W&W offices for a whole month to sift through the leftovers, trying to uncover more evidence and figure out what in the Jesus-name Dickens went on in that place. At one point, they served a court order on Lucy to submit a detailed explanation of the use and functioning of the NeuroAnalyzer and DreamDigitizer.

They even took the Quantum processors away for analysis, but returned them some months later. Probably because nobody knew what the heck they were looking at, she surmised at the time.

After finishing her herbal tea, Lucy approaches the counter. She slips a hundred-dollar bill into the tip jar, then contributes another hundred to the pay-it-forward coffee fund.

The teenage barista behind the counter nods and smiles his appreciation.

Back in her office, which, for heartfelt reasons, is the former office of her late Uncle Brice, Lucy taps away at the keyboard on her desk. For the last three months, she's been pulling everything together, piece by piece, and now, she's almost finished. A few more process reconnections, a couple more rebuilds of missing code, another module test, followed by a data integrity check.

"There," she says, satisfied, as she leans back to view the entire screen. "Now, to confirm everything's back in its rightful place."

On the screen, she hovers the cursor over the 'Run' widget. Holding her breath, she gives the mouse device a sharp tap with her forefinger.

"Are you there, Uncle Bryan?" she says, her left foot jouncing nervously under the desk.

Following a brief pause, a burst of static-filled audio emits from the tiny speaker in front of her.

"Is that you, Lucy?"

"Uncle Bryan!" she cries out, then heaves a sigh of relief. "It's so good to hear from you. Hold on a sec …" Hands trembling, she jacks a webcam into a socket at the rear of the screen and aims the lens at herself. "If you can see me, then I can see you," she says. She hits 'Connect' and an image of Uncle Bryan's beaming face appears on the screen.

"Oh, Lucy," his image says. "It's so good to see you again. And to hear your voice. I thought I was done for in here. We all did."

Lucy can't stop smiling at the reassuring sight of her uncle. He appears bright and healthy, considering his situation, trapped somewhere in the void. "I've been working out here for the past months, trying to reassemble everything," she informs him.

"How long has it been overall?" his image asks. "I have no concept of time since the cybersphere imploded."

"A year, Uncle Bryan. It's been a whole year. After the police came and removed the equipment, it was quite a task to recover all the key pieces."

"Police?"

"Yes. While I'm sure things didn't go well for you and the others at your end, we didn't fare any better out here." She recounts the events that unfolded in the real world. "And once Dr. Parker deleted the source code and the participants' files, I presumed we'd lost everything. Then Robert reminded me of the off-site copies. His scripts were running an incremental backup of files and data on the Quantum processors to a secure location every hour, on the hour. He helped me reassemble the hardware and restore the latest software from the backups."

"And Dr. Parker?" Bryan's image inquires.

"Nobody knows," she replies. At the sadness in her voice, his image fades marginally, then flickers. "She was a revolutionary software developer," she says, stirring fond memories of Susan. "Quite brilliant. Even though she never got the God module functioning, she was smart enough to extract the essence of a person's soul and store it in a place where it can last forever. At the very least, she should be recognized for that."

Bryan's image nods slowly in agreement. "It was terrifying in here at the end," his pensive image says. "There were things done and said that I never imagined possible. There were battles of good against evil. Betrayals. Heroics. Acts of bravery, love, and sacrifice. That fellow who was supposed to welcome us into the cybershpere and arrange our meeting with God—our host, Z—he turned out to be a nasty piece of work."

"Yes," she says as a sense of great regret sweeps over her. "Somehow, a Trojan horse virus infiltrated the system. I discovered stealth malware embedded in his code. It forced him to branch into all sorts of nasty program loops. It also corrupted the God module. That's why Dr. Parker couldn't get it working. I stumbled across the virus while we were restoring the system." She decides not to inform him about her suspicion that the virus had probably evaded the firewalls when Dr. Parker uploaded her mother's data files to the prototype. "I'm so sorry it turned out like this, Uncle Bryan," she says.

"There's no need to feel sorry for me," his image replies. "After all, I found what I was looking for. This whole situation was quite selfish of me, really." As his image gazes forlornly from the screen, its bottom lip begins to quiver. "I wanted to know beforehand if I was going to heaven, whereas I should have been doing my darnedest in those final days to ensure I was worthy enough. I tried to take the easy route there." The image bows its head. "When they looked into my soul, Lucy, they found it empty. There wasn't anything of value in there. I didn't deserve to go to heaven." When it looks up again, the image has a small tear coursing down its cheek. "I was the one who killed them, not you or Dr. Parker. Through my own damn selfish pride, I forced everyone to endure the most unimaginable horrors for my own conceited ends. I killed Roxy, Thomas, Becky, and Ahmad. Poor little Paris, too. All of them are gone because of me. Now, I'm condemned to spend eternity in here, alone, reflecting on the grief I've caused everyone. That's my punishment, and I'll have to accept it." The image dims again before it projects a dismal, half-hearted smile.

Wiping the wetness from her eyes, Lucy attempts to smile back. "But you're not alone," she says, trying to sound upbeat. "I was able to recover the data files for the participants." Bryan's image brightens somewhat while she uploads Roxy's data file.

"Well, aren't you a sight for sore eyes?" Roxy's voice echoes from the tiny speaker. Then, a second later, her image flashes onto the screen beside Bryan's. Her image reaches across, takes Bryan's head in its hands, and plants a kiss on his forehead. "He's my hero. He did his best to save us all."

Once Lucy finishes uploading the remaining data files, full-bodied images of Thomas, Becky, and Ahmad appear on the screen, together with Bryan's and Roxy's. At the sight of each other, they gather in jubilation. They hug and shed tears. They talk in turns and all at once as they recount stories of their remarkable adventures in the cyber-sphere.

They're acting like old friends, she thinks, watching on.

After a while, Bryan's image turns to her. "Can I please speak to Brice?" it says.

Lucy hesitates. "I'm sorry to report that Uncle Brice is no longer with us. When the cybersphere collapsed, a lot was going on out here, and in the confusion, he suffered a fatal heart attack. I tried my best to revive him, but it was no use." While she views Bryan's image, she notices it trying to hold back tears. "But it's okay, Uncle Bryan. It takes around six minutes for the brain to die once the heart stops. That was enough time to insert the penetration probe and re-trieve his consciousness before the police arrived. So, I have his data file right here, ready for upload." She hits the upload button again and, following a short delay, Brice's full-body image appears on the screen.

"What the …? Bryan? Where am I?" Brice's image says. "The last thing I remember is Parker going mad and …" His image lifts a cautious hand to its face and examines itself. "Am I dead?"

"Don't worry, Brice. You're with me," says Bryan's image, reach-ing out with welcoming arms. "We're all in the cybersphere together. Look. Out there," it says, its pointed finger challenging the quasi-divide between the cybersphere and the real world. "It's Lucy."

Brice's image peers from the screen. "Lucy?" it says in surprise.

"Hi, Uncle Brice." She gives his image a wave. "I digitized your consciousness after the heart attack. I hope you don't mind."

Furrows gather on the forehead of Brice's image. "I guess not," it says after a moment of deliberation. "What else could you do? Quick thinking and decisive action are the hallmarks of a smart operator." His image gives her an affectionate smile.

"I've also recovered the Regal Grand from the backups," she tells them, her heart bursting with pride at the announcement. "And it's fully operational again. I've even made some improvements. There's a new fitness center and infinity pool on the rooftop. You can see for miles around the cybersphere from up there. I've also reverted the sky to its natural color, and the leaves on the trees are green again."

"Wonderful," Brice's image replies.

Fingering the mouse device, she zooms in on Roxy's image. "And, Roxy, I have a special surprise for you," she says and clicks the widget to upload Paris's data file.

A year to the day since Lucy reinstated the cybersphere, Bryan is manning the reception counter when a stranger strolls through the front doors of the Regal Grand Hotel. She's of Anglo-Asian descent, mid-thirties, and her long, green liberty spikes radiate in all directions from her head. At five-foot-nothing, she appears six feet tall in her platform shoes, and her clothes could be straight out of an old pirate movie. The only thing missing is a parrot on her shoulder.

"Lucy!" he cries out, and scoots across the lobby to greet her.

"Hi, Uncle Bryan. It's so good to see you."

"I can't believe what I'm seeing," he says, embracing her. He takes a step back and looks her over. "You look wonderful," he says. Then he turns to the concierge desk. "Brice! Look who's here. It's Lucy."

When Brice sees her, his eyes light up. Like a man of younger years, he vaults the concierge desk and hurries over, wrapping his bison arms around her and crying tears of joy.

"Well, I'll be," a voice behind her says. "Ahmad, Thomas, Bec. Look what the fu— Look what the cat has just dragged in."

Before she knows it, Lucy is surrounded, with brave little Paris barking and wagging her tail at her feet. They group-hug and back-slap her while firing off questions about life and their loved ones outside the cybersphere.

"It's so nice to see you all again under much happier circumstances," she says, once they've finished welcoming her. "Although, I'm only here for the day."

"How is that possible?" asks Thomas. "I thought entering the cybersphere was a guaranteed death sentence."

Lucy turns to him and smiles. "For the last six months, I've been working on the quantum entanglement of consciousness," she says with a sudden rush of excitement. "With Robert's help, we developed a noninvasive machine that allows my consciousness to enter the Machine while my mind and body continue to function normally in the outside world. Just as Dr. Parker intended."

"Does that mean we can all go home?" Becky asks, and a murmur of expectancy grows.

"I'm sorry, Rebecca. You don't have a ... a body to go back to."

"Oh!" Becky says. Her bottom lip drops at the unexpected news.

At the sight of their despondent faces, a pang of disappointment runs through Lucy. "You all had beautiful departure ceremonies," she says, trying to soften the grim fact that they no longer exist outside the cybersphere. "I attended each one. Judging by the crowds paying their last respects, you were all very much loved." She turns to Roxy. "I even met your mother and father at your memorial. They told me how deeply they loved and missed you."

Roxy catches her breath. Lifting a hand to her face, she fans her emerging tears. "I think I'm gonna cry," she says while Ahmad wraps an arm around her shoulder. A tear also falls from his eye.

"It's okay, though," Lucy continues. "Because I'm the guinea pig. I didn't want to endanger anyone else, so I'm here as the test subject. To confirm that the entanglement of consciousness qubits works as I'd hoped. And, as you can see, it does. Now, your families can visit the cybersphere without suffering any unfortunate consequences."

"That's excellent news," says Brice, turning to the others with a wide grin.

Delighted, Becky claps her hands. "Mom, Dad, and Rachel can come and see me. I'll show them the painted dogs at the new zoo. And Rachel will love the old-time disco you made, where we can dance all night if we want."

"Can Fattanah come also?" Ahmad cuts in. His eyes have a new-found sparkle. "And Nikoo? And Omaid? Perhaps Miss Lucy can also restore my brother and his family. We can all sit together for a meal."

"I'm sure I can arrange that for you, Mr. Husseini," Lucy replies.

Standing a little straighter, Ahmad gives her a courteous nod. "Thank you, Miss Lucy. And please call me Ahmad. My name is Ahmad."

"And Jackie can visit," Thomas pipes up. "I've dropped fifty pounds while I've been here. We can make it our second honey-moon," he adds, his face reddening with embarrassment as he says it.

The flame in Lucy's heart burns brighter at the sounds of their unfettered chatter and laughter. There's a real sense of community among them, she decides. "I'm about to restart work on the God module," she announces once they've quietened. "Now that it's free of the Trojan virus, I think there's a good chance I can get it to work. Then you can all meet God as originally planned."

Bryan lays a hand on her arm. "That won't be necessary," he says, shaking his head. "I've had a great deal of time to think, and I don't believe it's in anyone's interest to meet any form of God before their time is up. It might give them an unrealistic impression, and when they finally meet the real one, things might not live up to their expectations. That would mean an eternity of disappointment for them. I'm not sure that's what God has in mind for us."

Nodding their heads in agreement, they all laugh heartily before Bryan crooks his arm and offers it to her. "Come. You must be starving," he says.

When Roxy plants an affectionate kiss on his cheek and takes his other arm, Lucy pulls away in surprise. "You two?" she says.

Bryan turns to Roxy, blushing with mild embarrassment. "Hey, I decided to take a shot," he says. "This new and improved version of me seems much more appealing since I stopped thinking only of myself. What can I say?"

"And I finally found true love in the most unexpected place," Roxy says, blushing back at him.

"Why, Uncle Bryan," Lucy replies, giving him a knowing wink. "You old dawg."

Arm-in-arm with Lucy and Roxy, Bryan leads everyone up the stairs to the Ocean Bytes Restaurant. There they sit at a long table, laughing and crying again while they eat and drink and recount stories of demons and hell and heroics in the cybersphere. Following a dessert of chocolate pudding, he rises to his feet. With a glass in his hand, he taps it gently with a fork. At the *chink-chink-chink*, they all stop and turn their attention to him.

"To the Motley Mob," he says, lifting the glass.

"To the Motley Mob," they all respond, raising their glasses as one, while brave little Paris mewls and wags her tail on the seat beside Roxy.

-----THE END----

Your Free eBook!

I hope you enjoyed reading My Digital Soul as much as I did writing it. I am currently working on my next book, titled, STARFARERS. This is a collection of short stories based on the common theme of intergalactic voyagers. Each story is 8 to 10 pages, just long enough to tide your sleepy eyes over at bedtime.

If you would like to read a bonus story from it titled, THE LAST MARINE, for free, then scan the following QR code to download it and sign up to my semi-irregular newsletter.

https://dl.bookfunnel.com/xko2gh85ev

Also, read on for a bonus excerpt from my novel, ENTROPY: A Post-Apocalyptic Novel of the End of Humanity.

And now that you have finished My Digital Soul:

Please support independent authors by leaving an honest review on your favorite book review site. Or just tell a friend if you enjoyed the story.

Scan to leave a Rating or Review

Acknowledgements

To my awesome beta readers: Raelene Walton, Nick Bruechle, Vanda Dei-Tos, and Mara McGinty. Thank you for reading my story from when it was still rough in my head, and for your time and patience to give me thoughtful and useful feedback. Thanks to Alex Austin (author of Endman) for helping me find the start of the story.

To my editor, Edwina Harvey (IPed) of Edwina's Editing Services (edwinaseditingservices@gmail dot com) for showing me the way to the finish line. Your boots-and-all approach is invaluable.

Thanks to Adam of Adam Hay Studio, UK for the cover design. After a brief telecon, the images I had in my mind suddenly appeared in the first draft as if by magic. The consensus is that the cover is an amazing fit for the story. It was a pleasure working with you, Adam.

To my readers from New York City. I set the story there because I love NYC. It offers such a great backdrop for any story. As an Australian who has only visited you once, I had to research diligently to be as authentic as I could. I spent a lot of time on Reddit and other chat sites searching for information on how you talk, think, and what makes you tick. My apologies if I got anything wrong. Also, sorry for blowing up the wastewater plant at Greenpoint.

To my Afghani and Muslim friends: As-salamu alaykum (سلام علیکم). Again, I tried to be as respectful and authentic as I could. My apologies if I got anything wrong. Poor Ahmad/Sajid is my favorite character in the story. His devotion to Allah and suffering for his family was truly impressive.

Thanks to Stevie at Dear Village Bookshop in Esperance and Donna at The Book Boutique in Boulder for your support. Also, my thanks to Sam and her wonderful team at The Twig & Sparrow Café. Need … more … coffee and a muffin please.

Last, but not least, thank *you* dear reader for reading *My Digital Soul.* Thanks for the generosity of your time. Once again, I tried to write the best story I could and hope it gave you much enjoyment and wonder in return.

Author's Note

The story of *My Digital Soul* originated from an idea drawn from my previous novel, *Entropy*, where the contents of a person's soul are used to verify their login to the sentient computer, Aleph-1.

I don't have a login name or password, or any form of multifactor identification. Instead, Aleph-1 reaches deep into my core to authorize my access by matching whatever it finds there against the identity profiles it has on file. My innermost thoughts, my memories, and opinions are the unique fingerprints that Aleph-1 uses to distinguish my login request from others.

ENTROPY

Extinction is inevitable

MICHAEL McGINTY

ENTROPY

An excerpt from ENTROPY: A Post-
Apocalyptic Novel of the End of Humanity

THE NEXT MORNING, I look despairingly over the remains of the
fire-ravaged plantation.

The three of us are standing together in the middle of the road,
shrouded by the eerie light filtering in on us through an air impreg-
nated with soot and fumes from the fire. A thick gray plume, pouring
out of the smoldering ground, stretches plumb upward into the trop-
osphere for as high as I can see. Without shielding my eyes, I can
look directly into the sun as it inches its way skyward behind the
plume: a sun turned blood-red by the smoke particles deflecting its
blue-end light from my eyes.

Blackened stumps, like silent victims of a massacre, jut up here
and there across the bare, undulating furrows which, until yesterday,
had served as a perpetual memorial to these revered relics of a
bygone age. An ankle-deep layer of blue-gray ash covers the floor, a
stark contrast to the permanent red hue that has continually hounded
me. And a nutty smell of bushfire chokes my grief.

Beside me, the helpful man hangs his head. With his thin frame
hunched over, the man appears even smaller now, as though he were
trying to shrink himself into insignificance.

My hand hurts terribly.

Unable to look at the scene any longer, I turn away and set off
along the road with the helpful woman beside me. A few minutes
later, I glance over my shoulder to where the man is still bent over in
the middle of the road. He straightens. Then he turns toward us and
deploys his head-cover. And once again, he takes up our rear.

A while later, we reach the edge of the burn: a narrow strip of clearing where the fire's run had been halted before it could break through to the adjoining plantation. Looking at the clearing, I feel a sense of relief. A small consolation that the extent of the damage has been contained, on this edge of the fire anyway.

Not much further down the road, another weather-beaten sentinel stands in front of the next plantation.

LUNGS OF THE EARTH PROJECT

CARBON CAPTURE PLANTATION NO 20220324-985

A small whitish flake floats down from the sky and settles at my feet.

"SNOW!"

From behind me, the alien man cries out as he scrambles to retract his head-cover.

"I—I SEE SNOW!"

Amused by the child-like innocence in his voice and the look of sheer delight on his face, I'm moved to relent.

"No, it's not snow," I say to him. "It's ash. From a process called pyroconvection. As the hot air from the fire rises, it gradually cools, and if there aren't any prevailing winds in the upper atmosphere to blow it away, the ash falls back around the vicinity of the fire."

By the time I've finished talking, a thick blanket covers us and everything around us as the ash-fall intensifies. Taking a knee, I use my good hand to try to tear another strip from my pant leg, without much success. The helpful woman kneels beside me. She rips a hand-sized piece of cloth from along the bottom of my right pant leg and hands it to me. After hitching the knapsack higher on my shoulder, I use the cloth to cover my mouth and nose from the *snow*.

"Onward to the city," I say, trying to inject a little optimism into our mood. And with the two aliens behind me, we set off again.

ENTROPY

I wonder if there is anything else left out here except ruin. If the city does exist as the plastics miner assured me, then why did its inhabitants abandon these people? Why were they left here in the wasteland to endure this kind of hardship? Would the people in the city be leading productive lives themselves, guided by their dreams and successes? Would they still have aspirations for their future? And would they be normal, like me?

I think about all these things.

"Where do you come from?"

The alien man retracts his head-cover. "P-pardon?"

"Where did you reside before you came out here?" I try to make my question clearer.

The helpful man frowns. "Nowhere," he replies.

"What do you mean: *nowhere?*"

"I was—was always here. Nowhere else."

"But where were you born?" I point to the woman, who is walking a few paces in front of us. "Where was she born?"

"I—I don't know. Until you came along, we—we just stuck close to—to the others. I—I don't know anything about what—what happened before that."

"Then, how long have you been out here?" I ask him, somewhat puzzled.

"I—I don't know. How long has—has out-here been?" he replies with a shrug.

I think I see him blush behind the layer of charcoal grime before he fumbles with his wrist and reactivates his head-cover.

When we're clear of the fire's fallout zone, I stop to brush the ash off my head and shoulders. Beside me, both the aliens shake themselves down from inside their life-suits. A hilarious attempt, from my point of view, to remove the heavy layer of residue covering them.

I cough up a mouthful of phlegm, drawn from deep inside my lungs, and spit it out. The alien woman retracts her head-cover. She glares at me as the glob of thick discharge hits the ground in front of her. Her disgust is only amplified when I follow up with two wads of sooty mucus, one shot from each nostril. Unamused, the woman reactivates her head-cover.

I take out my flask, pour out a meager ration of water onto the piece of cloth and clean some of the grime from my face.

A strip of cleared land cuts through the trees. Along it, three bundles of high-voltage transmission conductors emerge to cross the road, suspended high above us by two lattice towers that stand opposing each other on either side of the road. With their staunch legs fixed onto block-concrete footings, their galvanized trusses tapered at the waist, and cross-arms with insulator strings hanging down like long menacing fingers, the towers remind me of a pair of hunched-over monsters straight out of some small child's nightmare. On the plantation side of each tower, the conductor bundles tie off at the insulator strings before they slacken off along the ground.

As we pass between them, I can't help feeling intimidated by the two monsters leering over me.

"It looks like the electrical infrastructure to the city has failed," I say. "I wonder how they generate their electricity now?"

But both aliens ignore me as they trudge behind. I can't tell whether it's because they don't have the knowledge to give me a sensible answer or, more likely, they aren't the least bit interested in what I'm talking about.

ENTROPY

The highway runs gun-barrel straight, slicing through the plantations like a tracer bullet. By early afternoon the woodland ends, and without warning, we're thrown back into the red wasteland once again before being plummeted into an unearthly scene of misery. A level of desolation so complete that it leaves me speechless.

A bleak field of red dust spreads out in front of us, running unhindered into the distance. In the foreground, a once-grand mansion lies partly buried under the weight of its roof, its walls abandoned a long time ago by the buckled foundations. A much smaller outbuilding stands orphan-like nearby, with its structure still intact but its doors missing and window frames devoid of any glass. The ground around the house is littered with ragged clothing, smashed household appliances, piles of broken ornaments, and other assorted items; all evidence that the looters had once taken what they wanted and mangled whatever they couldn't carry away. The skull of a small animal, most probably a domesticated feline, lies half-buried in the dirt.

As I pick my way through the debris, I recognize the internals of an old Entertainer unit, but this one appears damaged way beyond my capabilities of repair. Behind the house, out in a fenced-off paddock, an in-line formation of four derelict combines disintegrate where they sit. Abandoned, as though the operators had jointly lost interest in whatever paltry seed they were heading and decided to call it a day one day and never returned.

My heart sinks as I look over the devastation. And as we move away, I can't shake the thought that everything I see here is all that remains of a person, of someone's hard-fought existence.

Available now.